SILENT BLUE

N
W
E
S
THE SHIP GRAVEYARD AND WRECKLEAF FIELDS
BLACK ROCK
THE ARENA
ALBATROSS
THE HUB
BIO-GEN LAB
BOAT HOUSE
CONCORDIA ON THE BAY
FWG BASE
RESORT ROW
LUXURY SECTOR
MARINA
LITTLE BAY
ZEPPELIN PAD
PLAYA ROSA
ENTRY POINT
LOCAL DISTRICT
THE OVAL
PANACEA
OUR BEACH
GABRIEL'S CAVE

PANACEA

SILENT BLUE

JD STEINER

EBook ISBN: 979-8-88716-027-6

Trade Paperback ISBN: 979-8-88716-025-2

Hardcover ISBN: 979-8-88716-026-9

Cover design and artwork by Justin Scott

Published by Bow's Bookshelf, Inc.

Anna Stileski, Publisher

Join our Bow's Bookshelf Reader's Club for new projects, deals, and giveaways. Sign up at Bowsbookshelf.com.

To those who refuse to quit. What feels like the end is often just the beginning. Follow your own light. It always knows the way.

PREFACE

I had my fantasies about leaving this place—living some kind of normal life. But I should have known I'd never really leave. I belong here. This is home, like it or not—where it all began, and where it will end.

This island and me, these people... we're all the same, we're all one. A terrible Beauty.

CHAPTER 1
WHAT I DESERVE

IT ENDS HERE...

WEDNESDAY, SEPTEMBER 4TH

Three days ago, I woke up with my head in my mother's lap. I thought I was dead—convinced, really. But it wasn't the end, at least not for me. Part of me, a bigger part than I want to acknowledge, wishes it had been the end.

Matriarch Giovanni is dead. And on this perfectly beautiful, sunny afternoon, we are gathered on Albatross Island—at the arena—for her funeral. Our sister maids, Cecelia, Rena, and Cassidy, all perished as well, along with the countless test animals who were sentenced to a life of torture in the laboratories on Black Rock.

The fire that I started in the assembly room after blasting through the warehouse full of bottles and destroying a control panel spread quickly, too quickly. The sea of spilled Aqua Tonic —William Banks' toxic and addicting energy elixir—proved to be quite the conductor of flames. We don't know the details, but I imagine Giovanni tried everything she could to get the others out, even after my mother begged her to come with her and Lillian, out of the building and down to the water.

Anastasia's whereabouts are unknown. But we assume she, too, is dead. By the time my mother and Lillian reached the dock and surveyed the situation, she had disappeared. But Devin still lay where Ana had caused him to drop. I will never, ever, be able to stop replaying that scene in my mind—his final resolution as he let me and Alakier go, then his look of pain and terror as the white-hot beam from the gun Ana fired shot through him and crumpled him to the ground like a fallen soldier.

My mother and Lillian had no choice but to leave him there, to leave without Gio. They had to take the remaining boat and get away from the island as fast as they could, knowing the inevitability of the destruction to come.

The currents stole their boat severely off course, eventually swallowed it. Fortunately for them, the Madoosik had already eaten, and the terrifying hybrid monsters did not make another appearance.

They came upon shore far from the gatehouse, fighting the tail end of the night's ravaging storm as they trudged across the broken landscape. They reached the bottom of the stone stairway leading to the base just as the night lit up with the explosion on Black Rock.

After we witnessed the destruction from the top of the base, and he realized the labs were gone—along with all the Aqua Tonic within—William Banks took my head in his hands and slammed it into a rock. The lingering effects still catch me by surprise, blurring my vision and my thoughts. With the residual pain of my battered body, but mostly because of the pain in my heart, I don't know if I'll ever be the same. How could I be? After everything I've done, after everything I put into motion… I'm not sure I deserve to feel anything but this devastation.

To make things feel even more unstable, it's been eerily quiet the last few days. As planned, the entire breed retreated to the relative safety of Albatross, and we know nothing of what is going on back on Panacea. There has been no word from or about Leyla, Alakier, and Esmerelda. I feel confident they escaped unharmed. It seems as though we collectively silenced William Banks, his scientist-cohorts, and the rest of the greed-driven monsters of the Panacea Island Branch of The First World Government. But there is no way to really know. I offered to do some investigating, but my mother will not let me do anything until I'm completely healed. I begrudgingly agreed to wait, but only because I want to keep my eyes on my best friend.

Kendra is nearly inconsolable. She has moments of clarity and what seem like acceptance and calm. Then she dissolves. Back and forth—an ebb and flow of sorrow and grief for her mother, like the waves spilling onto the rocky shore where we will release our loved ones to the ocean. I try to gently remind her to be strong for her unborn baby. It helps, for the briefest of moments at a time.

Now at ceremony, for the first time in a long time—maybe ever—my mother, Matriarch Tatiana, has very little to say. She is grieving as well, and her grief has trapped her voice inside of her. But it's now that we need her the most, to console us, to guide us. *What will happen next? Are we safe?* But she just can't.

After the shortest of announcements, she forces herself to say the thing we've all been dreading. "Please follow me now for the release." The catch in her throat is an audible reminder of Giovanni's permanent absence.

The arena is silent. We all stand and slowly make our way outside, like the sacrificial herd we have become. There, on a long, gilded stand, four adorned nautilus shells resting on their own beds of grass, driftwood and Wreckleaf represent our departed. My mother stands alongside Kendra, behind the last one in the row, and nods her head. The grieving mothers of Cecelia, Rena, and Cassidy take their places behind the shells representing their daughters.

"Maids, may the lives of our loved ones not be forgotten," my mother begins, her voice shaky. "We release them back to the ocean, of which they are a part of. May they find peace, as we find peace as well."

She stops and clears her throat.

"The lives of our sisters, our daughters, our mother, Matriarch, and best friend"—she's barely holding on—"will not have been in vain." Her jaw clenches. "The crimes of the men responsible will not go unpunished."

"They've been punished, Mother." My voice escapes me without my consent. "They have been... the labs were destroyed. Their plans are ruined. They can no longer grow Wreckleaf... at least, not for a long time. Leyla Banks got off the island with Alakier. She's going to expose all of Officer Banks' corruption and—"

"Stop!" My mother commands.

I'm halted mid-sentence. Fire burns in my cheeks as I realize everyone is gawking at me. My outburst is inappropriately timed. I bow my head and gaze at the ground. But just as I begin to shrink away, a flame lights in my belly as well.

"No. I will not stop. I'm sorry, mother, but I won't stop until everyone knows what happened, what we all did to destroy William Banks. And everyone needs to know that I vow to do whatever I can to ensure—"

"Nerissa!" Kendra shouts. "You've already done enough. You've done too much, again. Now shut up and let us mourn our dead." Her voice bends and halts before the last word comes out.

I am silenced, and stunned, and hurting as though I've just been stung by a poisonous insect. But she's right. This time, as my gaze falls, my heart sinks into the ground with it. I am emptied at once, of breath and hope... of all feeling. I'm instantly numb, and deservingly so. That's right. Shut up, Nerissa.

After my mother places Giovanni's crown atop her nautilus shell, the rest of the ceremony is a blur. I'm vaguely aware of words spoken by each of the mothers and watching as the vessels are released, one by one, into the current at the water's edge. I regain only a small sense of the moment as my mother hands Kendra Giovanni's vessel. There is a muffled mix of sobs and words as Kendra places the nested shell into the water. Unable to watch any longer, I walk away—back toward the protection of the covered arena.

I walk slowly, not by choice but out of necessity; my legs are wobbly and unbalanced. When I reach the arena, I stand with my back to the ongoing ceremony, steadying myself on a rough-hewn wall. I can barely hear them, can barely feel anything. I close my eyes and fight the approaching dizziness.

My ears are suddenly filled with an unfamiliar whooshing sound—I'm sure it's another residual effect of my head injury. The noise grows louder, bigger somehow, and it makes me feel like I might pass out. Great, like anybody is going to want to come to my aid right now. Maybe I'll just pass out and never wake up. That may be preferable.

Someone screams, which confuses me.

A second scream rises, then another. I spin around and

realize at once that the strange sound was not inside my head but came from above. Descending upon the rocky alcove, some kind of hybrid chopper appears out of nowhere. It resembles a dark, iridescent dragonfly, but with four rotating propellers on each 'wing.'

Devin told me they didn't use choppers. I guess some secrets are kept from everyone.

Inside the bizarre craft sit three men—one at the controls and two strapped on the open sides, manned with large weapons. The whooshing morphs back and forth into a buzz as the aircraft effortlessly darts and hovers above.

As the fuzz inside my head keeps its grip on me, nothing seems real. But this is as real as it gets. The two men with weapons aim at the funeral ceremony and open fire. Five maids drop immediately. My feet feel stuck in mud, and all I can do is watch in horror.

"Nerissa John, this is a gift from Officer William Banks." A voice booms from inside the chopper. Everyone scrambles—some jump in the water, others dart behind rocks. But it's useless for many.

More weapon fire. More screaming. Blood. Death... more death.

"Water Dolls," continues the omniscient voice from above, "you can thank your own Nerissa John for this visit. She is responsible for this retaliation."

Another round of fire. I shut my eyes tight and shake my head back and forth, forcing myself to clear the fuzz and regain sharper focus. But when I open my eyes, I wish my efforts had failed. Fifteen yards ahead, clear and undeniable, a foot lies motionless just behind a dark, jagged boulder. I recognize it instantly.

My heart is in my throat.

I will my feet to propel me forward, and they do, without

haste, without thought or concern for my safety. The gunfire just misses me twice as I land behind the boulder next to my mother. There is no sound but the chopper above, and I frantically examine her.

"I'm not dead yet." She grunts.

Hot tears spill over my cheeks into her blood-soaked hair. "Mom... I'm so sorry." I lay my head upon her chest and weep, smelling her familiar scent, which only makes me cry harder. She reaches up with her left hand and strokes my head. "Please don't die," I beg.

"I'm not going anywhere. We've got too much to do." She forces a tiny smile, then winces in pain.

"Nerissa John, you can end this all right now," the voice from the chopper announces. My head bolts upright, and my mother grabs my hand. "Come out, or the consequence will be total elimination."

"No, you're not going anywhere," she pleads.

How did things come to this? How did we get here? Because of me, that's how. I've caused enough pain, enough misery. It ends here.

I rise from my position, turning away from my mother as she fruitlessly grips at me. "I will come out if you stop shooting and let the rest of us go!" I yell as loud as I can.

"That is the deal."

"How do I know you'll keep your word?"

He actually laughs. "You don't."

I look back at my mother, her face wracked in physical and emotional pain. She shakes her head, barely able to move.

"But... Ms. John," the speaker continues in his metallic, robotic voice, "what you can be assured of is this. If you do not come out, every last member of your family will die here today, and you will watch."

My mind twirls. I look around, searching for survivors.

"Kendra?" I yell.

Nothing.

"Kendra!? Are you alive?"

"I'm alive." From some unseen hiding place, her weak voice rises above the chopper's buzz.

"Are you injured?"

"Nothing serious."

"Is the baby okay?"

"Yes."

"Lillian? Are you okay?"

Nothing.

"Lillian! Answer me!"

"Ms. John, your time is running out. Come out now, or we will finish this job."

"Okay! I'm coming out.... You keep your word. No more shooting!" I turn toward my mother, her eyes a mix of fear and sadness.

"Please don't, my baby. Don't go."

"It's your only chance."

"What will I do without you?" She chokes on her sob.

"You will live." I bend over and kiss her lightly on the forehead. "I love you, mom."

"*No*. No, you will not do this...." She fights to get the words out, then closes her eyes, unable to watch me leave toward what is most certainly my death.

I step out into the open, fully expecting to be taken down immediately—surprised when I keep walking forward. "Kendra!" I call. "My mother is alive but injured. Please take care of her." I proceed slowly, waiting for the pain to come. "Kendra... I love you! You are going to be an excellent mother!"

"Nerissa! Don't do this. You don't have to do this!"

I stop just below the hovering dragonfly. Tears pour freely down my face. "I do! I do have to do this!"

It's the only thing I *can* do.

"Ms. John, fall to your knees, and put your hands behind your head!"

I comply and fall, my left knee instantly torn by the sharp, rocky ground. I lift my hands up to lace my fingers behind my head and against my shorn copper hair—suddenly filled with an uncanny, nostalgic love for the unkempt nest that once adorned me. A love so deep, so intense, and so complete—for this crazy, unconventional life of mine, for my family, for my experiences, and for my stubborn refusal to conform. My mistakes, my indiscretions, my flaws. For my compassion, my unyielding love, and my loyalty. All I've ever wanted was for those I love to be happy, to be free, to have a better life, to fulfill their dreams. Maybe now, they can.

A smile so bold, so pure, so unleashed from the shackles of fear and doubt, spreads across my face. I gaze out at the raw and rugged beauty of the ocean in front of me and emblazon its power within my soul. I close my eyes. This will be the last thing I see.

A shadow drops in front of me. I don't look. I won't look. The ocean, the beautiful ocean—my silent blue, my freedom.

Someone grabs my wrist, and a tight band locks around it, then onto the other. A hand moves under my armpit, lifting me to my feet.

"Walk. Now step up."

He never leaves my side as we step onto some platform, which then lifts into the air. When will the pain come? When will I feel the shot rip through my flesh?

Hands at my shoulders guide me to sit. "It'll just be a short flight, Ms. John," he says as he straps me in, which strikes me as ironic.

Against my own damn will, my eyes flutter open. As the chopper bends and turns, I get one last look at what remains of my breed. There doesn't appear to be many survivors; dozens are gone. Just before they're out of sight, I see Kendra run to my mother's side, then look up, searching. Waving goodbye.

CHAPTER 2
AWAKENING
LIFE AS I KNOW IT RUSHES OUT OF ME IN ONE FULL EXHALE.

SATURDAY, SEPTEMBER 7TH

I thought the bastard was dead. At the very least, denounced from his throne. I've never been more wrong in my life. Officer William Banks, my father, is alive and well.

"Miss John, are you comfortable?"

"Go to hell."

"You're still as spiteful and difficult as always."

"A chip off the old block, I guess." I spit at him, and he laughs that nauseating, pretentious laugh of his.

"Well, aren't you a little fighter?"

I'm barely coherent. After the men in the chopper took me from Albatross, they brought me here, to what I believe is the boathouse—the gray steel building marking the gateway between Panacea and Black Rock. But I can't be sure. I could be anywhere. Once in the air, I was blindfolded. We landed only a short while later, as promised. The landing was relatively easy but not perfect, as though we were on level but rocky ground. The short distance from the chopper to where I am now—the tiny space they've locked me away in—proved too difficult for me to walk blindfolded, fighting off grief and a head injury. So someone just picked me up, threw me over their shoulder, and moments later, literally dropped me on the floor in this dank, smelly room. They left the blindfold on and my wrists bound, and I've been sitting here for what feels like forever. Numerous attempts to engage my CNI failed. And as the pain in my index finger made itself known—I could only assume my Crystal Nailbed implant had either been severely damaged or ripped out altogether—the reality sunk in that I was truly alone and that nobody could help me. Only when I threatened to kill myself by bashing my head into the wall were my unanswered screams finally addressed.

"I have to go to the bathroom."

I was taken, still blindfolded and bound, to a toilet. My pants were pulled down, and I was instructed to do my business while my guard stood beside me and watched.

"Untie my hands."

"No."

"How am I supposed to.... Look, buddy, you're going to have to wipe me yourself if you don't untie me for a minute."

That convinced him. As he untied my hands, I considered ripping off the blindfold, but quickly decided against it. I didn't want to see that sick face watching me.

Instead, as I peed what felt like an aquarium's worth, I started humming. Why not? I'd take a shot at enchanting him.

He laughed. "They told me you'd try that."

"What are you talking about?"

"C'mon, Doll. Your game is over. I know who you are.

Everyone does now. Right now, you're just too weak. And frankly, you're not looking too tempting. So don't bother. Just shut up."

He was right. I was too weak. I'd been here for what felt like an eternity. Had it been hours? Days? A week, even? I couldn't sense any light coming into my prison cell. I didn't know if it was day or night. And I had only been given a few small sips of water. My mind filled with images from Albatross, some fuzzy, some as sharp and painful as a knife in my heart.

My breed had been decimated.

"So, Miss John, did you like my chopper? Were you surprised?" William's pompous voice pulls me back to the moment. "It's a beautiful piece of machinery, isn't it?"

"Yeah, I was surprised. I didn't think there were any choppers."

He chuckles. "Is that what Devin told you?"

William sounds amazingly confident for somebody who's just been ruined. He must just still be playing his self-righteous act, though he must know he doesn't have a leg to stand on. I won't take the bait, and I won't answer him.

"I swear, that boy is not the sharpest knife in the drawer. The next time I see him, I'm going to have to remind him that he does not in fact know everything. And neither do you, by the way. You both could use a lesson in humility and a reminder of what the word respect means."

He doesn't know. He has no idea that Devin was shot.

"But... if I had to guess, I'd say that moron step-son of mine is dead. Like I said, he's not the smartest. I sent him to do a job on the Rock before you and your cohorts burned it down. I'd bet he didn't get himself out. Nobody's heard from him. How does it feel to know you probably killed him?" He chuckles again, and I feel like throwing up. "What a night you had, Miss John."

"It sure was. And I'd do it all over again."

"For what? To have your friends and family nearly eliminated? To have your boyfriend killed? To know you caused all of it?"

"No..." I'm grinding my teeth together so hard, it hurts. I will not allow him to see me cry. "I'd do it all again just to watch your stupid face when Walter pinned you down and Officer Klein shot you. My sacrifices weren't for nothing. Your labs are destroyed. You're finished. You and your dirty business, your lies, your deceit. Your precious AQT. It's over."

He lets out a laugh comparable in volume to his scream when the tranquilizer tore through his thigh. It scares the hell out of me, and I find myself shaking and cowering. He leans over to where I sit on the floor and rips the blindfold from my face. The room is dimly lit, but I still have to squint. I turn my head up to look at him. He just keeps laughing, his mouth open and his too-white teeth flashing at me. He wants me to witness his absolute amusement.

"Why are you laughing?" I say it so quietly, I'm not sure I spoke the words out loud.

"What did you say?" He just keeps laughing.

"Why are you laughing?" I force myself to speak a little louder.

He ignores me and wipes his face with his shirtsleeve, finally regaining some composure. The last of his laughter dies off.

"What's so damn funny?" I yell.

He stops in mid-chuckle and locks onto my eyes. Then he bends over, grabs my chin, and squeezes hard. Our faces are inches apart, his eyes tearing into mine with such intensity, tempting me to look away.

"I'll tell you what's so funny. You are."

"What do you mean?" I try to sound tough—unaffected. But my thoughts race with my heart, and I'm starting to get dizzy.

"You did indeed destroy my labs. My entire building, for that matter. But you certainly did not destroy me or my projects." He sucks in a breath, nearly overtaken once again by laughter, but controls himself and continues. "I'll admit, I was a little upset when that explosion went off. Perhaps I overreacted. How's your head, by the way?"

His grip on my chin loosens with his pretend concern. My gaze on him is magnetic. I can't look away, waiting for whatever will come spewing out of his mouth next. It's like I'm watching a magic show—illusion mixed with clever deceit and distraction. I'll figure out the trick. I will.

"My god, Miss John, how vain are you? How naïve? Do you really think you're that powerful?"

I can't help myself. "What are you talking about?" I ask.

"Aqua Tonic is bigger than you. Or me. It's bigger than the building it was housed in. Yes, you did set me back quite a few months. Closer to a year. And I was very angry... at first. But honestly, we needed a rebuild. We needed bigger, better... and that's precisely what we'll get. You seem to have forgotten that I have investors. I have very, very wealthy investors. They know how big this will get, and they helped to remind me to have a bit more patience."

Yeah, I know his main investor. So help me, if I ever see Alexandria Allerton Bigelow again, I will kill her. I can only hope Moriyah is all right.

"So thank you, Miss John. The future of Aqua Tonic, in partnership with Bio-Genesis Wave Technologies and the Panacea Island Branch of the First World Government"—reciting the titles like he's delivering an advertisement—"is bright." He devolves back into his deafening, defiant, bellowing laughter. I want to plug my ears, but my wrists are still bound.

"Everything was destroyed," I try to protest. "All the files, the computer systems, all the AQT. It's all gone."

"Oh, you stupid little hybrid. We gave you beauty, for sure, but the brains don't match." His face lights up with glee. "Who in their right mind wouldn't have a backup? Backup files, backup systems, backup samples. We'll have to recreate it all, but it's all there."

"No." I shake my head. He's lying, like he always does. And then a spark flares in my mind. "Leyla got Alakier off the island. She's going to expose you."

William considers me with disgust, his smile folding into a pinched frown, like he just ate something sour. He clasps his hands behind his back and paces the short length of the small room. I've hit a nerve. He knows I'm right. He knows what her escape means.

He clears his throat, putting two fingers against his lips while his other hand remains behind his back, and finally speaks in what feels like a well-thought-out stream. "My wife had nothing before she met me. I took her and her son in. I gave them a life they could only have dreamed of before. There were conditions, of course, which she fully knew. They were unspoken but not unwritten. She had her role, I had mine, and she agreed in earnest. It is therefore so very unfortunate that she was caught breaking those conditions. And it was equally unfortunate, and devastatingly disappointing, when she felt the need to falsify documents in an attempt to salvage the life-style she and her son had grown accustomed to."

Wait. What is he saying?

"My reputation, my position in the First World Government, has come under attack by a malicious, cheating woman who hasn't anything to fall back on without the life I've provided her. Her accusations are a feeble attempt to discredit my important work on this island and to take what doesn't belong to her in any way."

"Are you crazy?" I demand, as if I expect him to agree with me. "Do you really think anybody's going to believe that Leyla... what? That she cheated on you, and now you want out of the marriage, and she's somehow made up everything she's going to turn in to the authorities?"

"That's precisely what she's done." He actually smiles. "So glad you understand. I've thought about how to say that for some time."

"What about Alakier? He's a Dolhuphemale. He's with her."

"So what? A number of people in the First World Government know we reintegrated your breed back onto Panacea three years ago." He scoffs at me.

"But Alakier is male."

"Again, so what? He's an anomaly."

Livid now, I try to stand up, but with my wrists tied and starvation setting in, I fail. "He is not an anomaly, and you know it. He was created by you! And you were going to clone him."

"Are."

"What?"

"Not *were*. I'm telling you we *are* going to clone him. I hate to admit it has been, as you told us it would be, difficult to recreate the growing conditions for Wreckleaf. We'll keep trying, but we'll also proceed with a new harvesting hybrid."

"How? He's not here. That's not..." I can't pretend to ignore the defeat.

"Stupid hybrid."

"Why didn't you just clone us, *Dad*?" I spit. "Could've saved yourself some time."

"Well, I'll keep that suggestion in mind, dear daughter. But the truth? I despise you and the rest of your hoard of bitches. The sooner I can be done with you, the better. And cloning you would have been too easy. I am a man of high standards."

I choke out a disgusted laugh. "Yeah, I know your kind of standards."

"You know nothing, Miss John."

"Leyla will tell them. I'll tell them—"

He chuckles again. "Tell them what, Beauty? And—ha—who are *they*? They are my kind, not yours."

I hang my head and close my eyes. Life as I know it rushes out of me in one full exhale.

"Now, Miss John, I trust that you fully understand your position. Or lack thereof, at this point. And I imagine you are quite hungry."

I try not to seem interested, but my stomach growls audibly at the suggestion of food.

"I will send someone to get you cleaned up, fed, and properly rested. I will be back tomorrow, and you and I will discuss our new arrangements together."

"What *new arrangements*?" I sneer.

"Well, since you're responsible for destroying my labs and the delay it has caused, you will be working for me. I'll still need Wreckleaf."

"Why do you need Wreckleaf now? You can't do anything with it."

"We have simple but functional facilities at the base. Formulations and experiments must continue, as always. And you are going to help me. Aren't you excited?"

I spit at him again and miss.

"You are going to learn that I am in charge. There will be new, strictly enforced rules. And I will deal with nobody except you. Your life depends on it, as do the lives of the rest of your living relatives. Do not fuck with me, Miss John. Or I will crush you."

I look him dead in the eyes. "You haven't yet. Go to hell, Officer Banks."

He simply gazes at me, smiles, then turns and leaves the room. The door closes behind him, and I hear the lock turn. I am alone—my breath the only sound, fast and ragged.

The tears spill from my eyes, and I don't even have enough energy to try holding back the sobs.

CHAPTER 3

GHOSTS

I DON'T WANT TO WAKE UP...

MONDAY, SEPTEMBER 9TH

I can only remember this happening a few times before, but it's happening now—a lucid dream. I know I'm dreaming, but I'm fine with that. Because this dream is so much better than any reality I've experienced in quite some time. Please, don't let me wake up.

"I miss you, Gabriel. It's so good to see you."

Gabriel stands before me, smiling and bright-eyed. He's skinny, even for him, and dressed in an unfamiliar outfit. But he's here.

"Remember, child, I have never left you." He strokes my cheek with his ancient fingers, then playfully rubs the top of my shorn head and rests his hand on my left shoulder. His touch is just as I remember it—kind, patient, and loving. "Here. You need to eat some of this."

"Wreckleaf. Where did you find this?"

"I have my sources now that you're no longer delivering to me."

"I'm sorry, Gabriel. Everything is messed up."

"You do not need to apologize to Gabriel. I'm the one who's sorry."

"No. You were murdered."

"Yes. I was unfairly taken from you. But I was unable to fight. They told me they would kill you, too, if I did."

I start to cry, and he softly wipes my face. I quickly realize it's because I can't do so myself. My wrists are still locked together but now above my head, not by ties but by some kind of metal contraption. My whole body seems bound to an upright board. "Here, child. Eat, now. It should pull you out of this."

I do as he tells me, the slippery fronds filling my mouth with delectable flavor. I feel the Wreckleaf's energizing effects almost immediately.

"Gabriel, where are we?" I look around the dimly lit room. It's small but much more spacious than the cold, concrete-floored cell in which I fell asleep. Another reason I don't want to wake up. This room is warm and furnished... like a mini house. It's comfortable, and it even smells nice.

"I guess this is home for a while, child."

"I'll stay here with you forever. I don't ever want to wake up."

"Gabriel cannot stay, but I'll be back. I must go now."

"No, please don't leave, Gabriel. I don't want to wake up. Please...." I beg.

He doesn't answer me. He doesn't speak another word. He just turns, walks to a door at the edge of my vision, and disappears, like he's stepped into a black hole. He's gone—again.

I open my mouth and scream a silent scream. I thrash against my restraints, feeling my feet are bound as well. My mother's voice rings in my ears, a painful, lingering memory....

"Gabriel is dead... we suspect a drug overdose. Gabriel is dead.

Gabriel is dead. Gabriel is...."

"No! Stop it. Shut up!" I scream back at her disembodied voice. The room spins and darkens. Now I want to wake up. Wake up. Wake up, Nerissa!

I force my eyes open and gain focus just as a door slams against the wall.

"What are you yelling about?" someone shouts.

I fight my way back to full consciousness and concentrate on the figure standing in the doorway, a still-blurry silhouette against the bright sun streaming through the open door. Where am I? Not in my dark, cold cell anymore.

"Who's there?" I ask, squinting against the glare. The unknown person walks in and closes the door. My stomach drops when Officer Emanuel MacNamire turns to face me, his twisted smile a reminder that my perfect dream is over.

"Hello, Doll. So what are you yelling about?"

I don't answer him. I feel dizzy, disoriented. Maybe I'm still dreaming.

He walks toward me, eyeballing me up and down, licking his lips. "You look nice." He lifts his chin and raises his eyebrows. "Pretty dress."

I look down at myself in utter confusion. I'm wearing a soft pink dress with spaghetti straps and a slit up the thigh. It hugs my body. My feet are bare. And just like in my dream, both my wrists and ankles are bound—attached to some kind of upright table. Now I pray I'm still dreaming.

"So, Beauty." Manny walks up to me. He's so close I can feel the heat rising off him, and can smell his body odor. "Who were you talking to just now? I heard you all the way next door." He wraps his fingers around my throat. "Answer me. Now."

"I was having a bad dream."

"Aww... that's too bad." He loosens his grip but leaves his

hand there. "You've had a rough couple days. Poor baby." His other hand comes to my hip, and he sucks in a deep breath, seeming to absorb a piece of me; his eyes flutter and close.

"Get your filthy hands off me."

His eyes snap open, and he smiles. "You're not in any position to be giving orders now, are you?" He buries his face in my neck and takes a long sniff.

"Get off me, you pig." I thrash against the table, whipping my head from side to side. He strengthens his grip around my neck, then I feel his lips and tongue at my ear. "Stop."

He squeezes hard, and I can barely breathe. His other hand lifts up my dress while he slides his tongue from my lower jaw all the way up to my temple.

Against the growing pressure at my neck, I start to hum and feel the vibration against his hand. He freezes instantly, then releases me, pulls his face away, and lets go of my dress. Regarding me with utter contempt, he raises an open hand and brings it down hard across my cheek. My vision sparkles for a brief moment.

"Go ahead. Sing me a song. Try to enchant me, you little slut."

I know before he does it that he's going to hit me again. I can see it on his face. I'm right. This time, he strikes even harder, and I taste blood. When I open my eyes and straighten my head, his hands are at his belt. He's already unlatched the buckle, pulling it from his pant loops. Whatever he plans on doing, it's not going to be good.

"Kiss me, Manny." I force the words.

"Nice try." He wraps the belt around his hand and snaps it on my open thigh. The pain is a hard shock, and I can't help but yell out in agony. He does it again.

And again.

And again.

From behind tear-flooded eyes, I watch Manny's hands move again to his pants. He unzips himself, and I think about Kendra. I can't imagine the fear, the horrific anticipation she felt. And for her, there were two of them.

The door crashes open behind Manny, and he fumbles to contain his exposed parts before he pulls up his pants.

"What the hell is going on in here?" Officer William Banks asks. The irony of this particular man coming to my rescue doesn't escape me. "Answer me, MacNamire. What are you doing?"

Manny completes his wardrobe adjustment and turns to face his superior. "Sir, I was approached with misconduct, and I thought I ought to remind this hybrid who's in charge."

"And who exactly *is* in charge?" William snips.

"Oh. You are, of course, Officer Banks."

"That is correct. Do not make me remind you again. Now get yourself together and move aside."

William walks toward me, surveying the battering his subordinate just delivered. "Hmm... I did like that dress. MacNamire!"

"Yes, Sir?"

"Get Hani in here to clean her up."

"Yes, Sir. Right away."

"And MacNamire," William barks. "Remember, she is mine. Not yours."

"Of course, sir." Manny turns to leave, but looks back at me one last time and, from behind his boss's back, winks.

"That's one class-act friend you've got there, Dad." I have to push past the pain to get the words out.

"That idiot isn't my friend. He works for me. And he's the best damn plant guy you could ever meet."

"Creepy plant guy," I mumble.

"What?"

I ignore him. He pretends not to care.

"So... I trust you had a good, long rest? Do you like your new housing?"

I have no memory of anything since a woman brought me a plate of mediocre food and a glass of water in my last prison room. I want answers, and I want them now.

"Where am I? How did I get here, and how long have I been here? And what is with this dress? And why am I tied up?"

"Woah... slow it down."

"No. Just answer me."

"Miss John, must I remind you—"

"Yeah," I say, "that you're in charge. I know, but I can't remember how I got here, and I'd like an explanation. Please."

He produces that gross, fake, pompous chuckle. And he seems to puff up his chest in satisfaction over my plea. But before he answers, if he was going to at all, there's a soft knock on the door. He turns to open it.

"Ah, Hani. Perfect timing. Please see that Miss John is cleaned up and taken care of." William is almost jovial.

The slightly rotund, dark-haired woman at the door nods and looks at me. I recognize her instantly. She gazes at me only with a sense of duty and no hint of recollection. She wouldn't. She succumbed to my kiss, just as she should have that night at Black Rock in the tank room—with no memory of it. She was there the night I discovered Ana and Alakier, and now she's been given orders. I am a job. Nothing more.

"Miss John, this is Hani. She doesn't speak much, but she takes orders well, and she will attend to your needs."

She spoke the night I first saw her. In fact, she was singing. Maybe she just doesn't like to speak to *him*.

"You mean she'll clean up the blood your man spilled? She'll change me out of the dress you had me put into just to satisfy your twisted mind? Will I get a new one?"

"That is correct. I bid you a good evening, Miss John. I will be back tomorrow to go over the Cooperative." He steps toward the open door.

"What Cooperative? What are you talking about? The Cooperative is over."

He stops and regards me like an intellectually challenged child. "The *new* Cooperative. Remember? Our new arrangements?"

"No. No way. I'm not agreeing to any *new Cooperative*. No chance in hell."

"You will, and you'll do so with a smile on your face." He steps through the door, and leaving me fighting to catch my breath again.

"Wait!" I yell. "Wait. Come back. Please?"

I suppose for dramatic effect, he lets a few seconds tick by before reappearing at the door. "Yes, Miss John?"

I clear my throat and try to calm myself. "How long have I been here?"

He seems to consider whether or not to answer, but his twisted expression suggests he's eager to deliver his unsettling response. "Since Saturday."

"What day is it?" I ask.

"Monday."

"Why can't I remember anything?"

He smiles. "You were given an antidote to help you relax and transition."

"An antidote? You mean you drugged me. In the food?" I'm shaking with anger.

"Don't you feel rested? And your head injury seems to be all cleared up. Isn't that nice?"

"You drugged me," I say plainly.

"Yes. You'll get used to it. Good evening, Miss John."

CHAPTER 4
THE NEW COOPERATIVE
NO EXCEPTIONS WILL APPLY.

Dolhuphemale member: Nerissa, daughter of Matriarch Tatiana

Assigned name: Nerissa John

Age at transition: 17

Address: First World Government, Panacea Island Branch Base One

Employment: Ambassador and Harvester of C. Periculosis Abscondita/Dolhuphemale-Government Consultant and Liaison/Voluntary Test Subject

Duties will include but are not limited to: regular harvesting and sole delivery of Caulerpa Periculosis Abscondita/Wreckleaf to FWG Officer William Banks; sole correspondent with remaining Dolhuphemale breed in strict compliance with direct orders only; willing participant in sharing all knowledge in regards to breed and acquired Wreckleaf intelligence; willing participant in Aqua Tonic trials and other experimental formulations.

All outside communications will cease, effective immediately.

A daily schedule will be predetermined to include harvesting, information-sharing/collaboration, injection(s), and any other work/duties deemed necessary and appropriate.

In strict compliance, Dolhuphemale member Nerissa John will be allowed to live, as will remaining Dolhuphemale breed, with the understanding that breed will stay contained to Albatross Island. Entry onto Panacea Island by any Dolhuphemale other than Nerissa John will be considered trespassing and any/all subjects will be deemed criminal and will be treated as open targets. Breach of any part of Cooperative on the part of Nerissa John will result in breed elimination. No exceptions will apply.

CHAPTER 5
BEDTIME STORIES
I WAS SICK OF KEEPING YOUR SECRETS...

TUESDAY, SEPTEMBER 10TH

"I will *not*. You're crazy. You can shove that piece of paper up your—"

"You will sign this or suffer the consequences. I am one hundred percent serious, Miss John. Now, I am going to unlock your wrists, and you will do what needs to be done. Do you understand?"

I robotically mimic his tone. "Yes, I understand... I will do what needs to be done."

He leans in close and uses a key to unlock the shackles containing my wrists. The relief is more than welcome; my fingers started tingling hours ago. "You know, I could really use a stretch. How about you unlock my ankles, too?"

"Not just yet. One thing at a time. I will give you your freedoms, eventually, but you must earn them."

Lowering my hands and rubbing my wrists, I try to appear calm and compliant. Carefully, I raise my eyes and look around the room, noting a small window above the sink and the door he's left ajar.

"I like my little house. Where exactly are we?"

"Oh, I think you've figured that out."

"The top of the base? One of the red-roofed cottages," I surmise.

"Very good. Now, let's take care of business."

He holds the paper in front of me; it dangles between his two fingers like an invitation to rampage. I snatch it right out from under his stupid face, rip it up violently, and throw the pieces to the floor. He just stands there, observing, with no expression. I scream and yell and grunt as I flail my body back and forth, reaching down to my ankles to free myself.

He calmly puts his hand on my chest and forces me to rise back to a standing position. I look him in the eyes and take a swing at his face. I miss the first time but hit him with my other fist just above the eye. He lets out a quick moan, then steps back.

I'm breathless, rigid, and ready to fight. "Hey, Daddy, how about a kiss?" I hiss at him.

"Hey, that's a great idea." He steps forward, leans into me, and I'm ready to take his face in my hands. Instead, he strikes me in retaliation, and the wound Emmanuel MacNamire gifted me with at the bottom of my left lip reopens.

I sincerely wasn't expecting it. I don't think William was expecting to do it, either. He steps back again and takes a deep breath, pulling gently on the edges of his shirt sleeves and tilting his head from side to side in a feeble stretching motion. We just stare at each other. Then he turns and opens a small cabinet drawer of what serves as a kitchenette here. But this looks less like a place to cook dinner and more like a doctor's office.

He produces a needle, then reaches down into a small

refrigerator and brings out a chunky vial of cloudy white liquid. He flips the plastic top off the needle with a quick flick of his thumb, inserts the syringe into the vial, and draws out a carefully measured dose. He's obviously done this before. Then he replaces the vial and turns toward me.

"I suppose that's for me," I growl.

"As I have tried to make clear, Miss John, I am in charge, and you will comply."

"Cheap tactics. You should play fair."

"As the old saying goes, 'All is fair in love and war,' Miss John."

I smile as the tears escape my eyes. I don't feel afraid; I feel out of control and defeated. And angry as hell. "So which is this? Love or war? And please, call me Nerissa."

"I like your name, Miss John. I named you myself."

"Why didn't you just name me Nerissa Banks?"

He laughs. "We both know I couldn't do that. Some things need to remain between friends."

"Friends? I'm not your friend."

"Of course not. I mean your mother."

I hardly have the chance to say another word—how dare he talk about my mother?—before William lunges at me and injects the white fluid quickly into my shoulder. It burns, and then it doesn't. I don't feel anything at all.

"All is fair in love and war, Miss John."

When I wake up who knows how many hours later, Hani—the dark-haired woman from the labs—hovers over me, blotting my lip with a damp cloth and humming a soft, beautiful melody. It takes me a few minutes to regain awareness as my eyes flutter open and I adjust to a light above my head. A quick survey of the room tells me it must be nighttime; both the window above the sink and the seams around the door are dark.

I try to lift my head, and Hani softly places her hand on me to ease me back. I'm horizontal—lying down.

"Try to relax," Hani says, her voice like a warm blanket. "I'll lift you up." She leans over, and a soft click sends my 'bed' into a slow, mechanical, vertical adjustment, my feet supported by a small ledge. "There you go. Are you thirsty?"

"Yes, please." My voice is gravelly, and my mouth feels like cotton.

She holds a glass of water with a straw in front of me. I'm about to drink, then halt abruptly. "This is just plain, clean water. I promise."

I have no reason to trust her, but I take a long, deep drink and drain the glass in seconds. There's a quick knock at the door, and it swings open before Hani answers it.

"Ah, good. You're awake. We have unfinished business to attend to." William is not dressed in his usual formal attire but has donned casual gray workout pants and a perfect t-shirt in the exact color, the entire ensemble matching his hair. His eye is bruised and swollen. "Thank you, Hani. You may leave."

Without saying a word, Hani nods, turns obediently to gather a small bag, and walks to the door.

"Wait, I have to use the bathroom," I say, not really needing to go.

"Hold on, Hani. Please take her. You know the protocol. Next time, try to get her to the bathroom before she's fully awake."

Hani nods again, then goes to the kitchenette and proceeds to fill another needle just as William did before.

"This is actually a good idea," he says. "Perhaps she'll be a bit more agreeable. But don't give her a full dose. I need her to sign some paperwork."

Hani walks toward me.

"No, Hani," I mutter. "Don't do this, please. He can't make you—"

I hear William laugh from behind her as he watches his slave do his dirty work. Hani looks me in the eyes, then glances down and uses a technique opposite William's—she gently inserts the needle under my skin at my shoulder and presses lightly on the plunger.

The rush is almost instant, but instead of everything going black, it all just goes fuzzy and soft. All the edges blur. And my head swims over my body. A warm sensation spreads through me, then that too distorts and numbs. With no control over myself, I let out a huge sigh, then start to laugh.

I'm faintly aware of Hani turning to look at my father before retrieving a small key from a hook above the sink. She unlocks my wrists first, and my arms drop to my sides, which makes me laugh again. Then she unlocks my ankles, and I have to balance myself against her as she helps me place one foot then the next onto the floor. The room doesn't exactly spin; it pulsates. And I'm like a wide-eyed child, moving in what feels like ultra-slow motion, noticing every tick, every minute movement, but as one fluid, continuous action.

I look over at my father. He's smiling at me. And for *one second*, I feel something other than pure hatred for him. But even in this forced, euphoric oblivion, I shake away that hint of acceptance or empathy or whatever it was.

Hani brings me to the bathroom and closes the door. She lifts up my dress, which only now do I realize has been replaced. This version is much less "cheap prostitute" and more "mythical goddess."

"Oh, Hani… look at my dress… It's so beautiful."

"Sit down."

I plop down on the toilet and try to pee, but nothing comes out. "You know, I don't think I have to go."

"I figured not. I just brought you a little while ago."

"You did?"

She doesn't answer me but reaches into her pocket and produces something that makes me blink and try to shake myself back into full awareness. "I had to take this off you. Your hand was swelling up, no doubt from the shiner you gave the Officer," she whispers. "It would have cut off your circulation."

"My ring." I hold my right hand up in front of me and observe it as though it isn't mine. "Well, that is something." My knuckles are black and blue, my middle and ring fingers swollen like two sausages. Between that and the mangled CNI on my index finger, I hardly recognize this appendage as a part of me.

"Let's put it on the other hand," Hani instructs. She grabs my left hand and attempts to put the ring on my middle finger, but I pull away from her.

"No."

"Come on. We've got to finish up in here. Put it on."

"No."

"What's taking so long in there?" William shouts from behind the door, and Hani jumps, visibly shaken by the voice of her oppressor. She shoves the ring back in her pocket, helps me get up, and washes my hands.

"Nerissa, do as he asks. He *will* punish you if you don't," Hani softly advises, then opens the door.

I turn to look at her and cup her cheek in my hand as we stumble through the bathroom doorway to rejoin my father. "Emancipation ignites power and fuels responsibility..." I slur, then blow a skeptical puff of air through my loose lips.

"What did you say?" William demands.

"Nothin'." I wave a hand at him.

He glares at me. "Contain her, Hani."

Hani returns me to my metal bed and locks my ankles inside the cuffs. Out of nowhere, William produces another copy of the new Cooperative and holds it up in front of me, this time not so close that I can grab it. The room is reduced to that single white piece of paper, my heartbeat, and the shiny silver pen William holds between his fingertips.

He will punish you...

"All right, Miss John, it is time to sign this document. Hani, stay. You can actually be our witness."

"Like you really need a witness..." I mumble.

"Just making things official. Now sign it," William orders.

"I don't want to." Even I realize I sound like a spoiled toddler.

"Well, I am confident at this point you understand the consequences of *not* signing it."

"Yep. You're gonna kill me. Got it."

"Well, yes, that is true. But not before we will kill every last one of your surviving family members. While you watch. Then we'll kill you. Eventually."

I swallow hard and try to concentrate on the almost-pleasant buzz of my most recent injection. "I think you're bluffing. You need us."

"Miss John, I assure you, if you choose not to comply, I am done with our games. Remember, we have collected the male Dolhuphemale's genetic material. We will produce a suitable Harvester. Or I'll just take your suggestion and clone you. Then I'll erase your pathetic lot."

"I don't believe you."

William grits his teeth and exhales through his nose. He

holds his index finger to his mouth. "MacNamire, bring me the Water Dolls."

I snap to attention. What is he doing? He's trying to scare me. The room changes energy from a pleasant pulse to a fast throb, my heart keeping time with it. I look at Hani, pleading silently with her. She looks down.

Seconds later, there's a hard knock at the door. William opens it, and my breath catches in my throat. *No.* But my voice is paralyzed.

William grabs Lillian's hair at the back of her head and pulls her from Emmanuel's clutches and into the room. I almost can't tell it's her. Her mouth is covered in thick, silver tape, a blindfold over her eyes. Her hands are tied behind her back. But it's her.

Against my drug-induced stupor, I pull myself up and away from the table, trying to stretch as far forward as my locked ankles will allow me to reach her. "Lillian! No, let her go. She hasn't done anything... please..." I reach and stretch and flail against my confines.

I would expect William to laugh, but when I look in his eyes, search his face... there's nothing. He is as dark and emotionless as death itself.

"Miss John, this will serve as a reminder that I am not taking our situation lightly, and neither should you." He tightens his grip on Lillian's hair. "Fall to your knees," he commands her. He pushes her down, and she crumples under his force. Then he pulls the blindfold from her face, and our eyes lock instantly. Her terror is unbearable to witness.

"I'll sign it. I'll sign it right now. Give me the pen. Give it to me."

William looks at Emmanuel, and the Officer jumps to attention—retrieving the document and pen. He's barely given it to me before I'm fumbling, trying to sign legibly against the palm of my other hand.

"Wait," William says.

I look up, confused.

"I want to read it first, out loud, to you, so that you understand perfectly."

"I do", I say. "I understand. I'll sign it now." But he looks again at MacNamire, and that's all it takes for the Officer to rip the pen out of my hands and give it back to William. He proceeds to read it, slowly, methodically, over-annunciating every last word. When he looks up, I nod in agreement and reach my hands out so I can sign it and we can finish this.

"You read it now, out loud, back to me," he insists.

"I... that's not necessary. I'll sign it. I'm not sure I can see well enough..."

But he makes it clear with his continued grip on Lillian that this is a non-negotiable order. I do as he says and strain to read it aloud, quickly but clearly. As I reread my new duties and the new laws I will be governed by, fear and defeat sink into my heart.

When I look up, he nods at me, and I finally sign the document. I shove the crumpled paper back at MacNamire. "There. There it is... it's signed. I agree to everything. Now just let her go. She'll go back to Albatross and won't ever come back. Right, Lillian?"

Lillian nods frantically, the tears pouring down her face and snot flying out of her nose as she tries to calm her breath.

MacNamire gives William the paper, who grabs it in his free hand to examine the signature. Then he places the paper on the counter, takes the pen, and signs his own name as well. He never loses his grip on Lillian's hair, pulling her at an awkward and uncomfortable angle as he leans over and signs.

When he rights himself, he hands MacNamire the document and pen.

"It's official. Welcome to our partnership, Miss John. MacNamire, the other, but keep her outside."

Emmanuel disappears out the door for just a moment and returns with an unknown guard who holds in his ruthless grip another of our sister maids, Sarah. At eighteen, she's just come of age. She's also bound at the wrists, blindfolded, and her mouth taped. My mind refuses to believe what I'm seeing, challenging my reality as a drug-induced hallucination.

"These two were caught last night just as they were trying to leave Panacea. Lucky for me, I suppose." And there's William's signature chuckle. "They wouldn't explain what they were doing here. Looking for you, perhaps."

"They were just scouting, I'm sure..." I say quickly, trying to ease his tension.

"The Season is over. And there will be no more of that. I told you, all Dolls are fair game now."

"But they didn't know that. Let them go," I plead. "It's not their fault."

"Well, they should have known. After what you all did to my labs, to my building... you must have known there would be consequences." He pulls Lillian's hair, shaking her back and forth in anger. She lets out a muffled cry from behind the tape.

"No... not this."

William looks at the unnamed man and nods. The tall, muscled guard pulls off Sarah's blindfold, pushes her down to her knees on the manicured path just outside the door to this cottage, retrieves the knife strapped to his waist, and slits her throat in one seamless motion.

Blood spills freely from Sarah's neck as her eyes meet mine then quickly roll back. Her body falls limp, the guard lets her go, and she slumps sideways to the ground.

"No!" I scream and squeeze my eyes tight. "Sarah... No, no..." I grab the edges of my bed as the room spins and I start to fall forward. Hani catches me and eases me back, then I gag and throw up what little is in my stomach. I open my eyes and catch Lillian's gaze just before she closes her eyes and waits for the knife to end her as well.

"I signed your paper," I scream, sobbing now. "I signed it!"

"Yes, just in time. Let this unfortunate but necessary exercise be a reminder to you of the seriousness of our situation. Remember, these two were caught easily on their own. We know how to deal with your kind now, Miss John. And don't forget, I have a chopper." He smiles. "Albatross is easy to access now."

I'm hyperventilating, and I can't stop.

William turns to the others. "Get this one out of here." He shakes Lillian's head, and MacNamire, his obedient puppy, snaps into action, relieving William of his grip on her and forcing her to rise. The two turn, and as Lillian faces Sarah's fate, her muffled moans and wails rise past the tape over her mouth. They step over Sarah's body, carrying and spreading her blood on their shoes, tiny splatters landing in front of them with every step. Lillian has been spared—for now.

I'm watching a movie. This isn't real.

"Clean that up," William snaps at the guard. The man bends over, grabs Sarah once again by her beautiful, cinnamon-red hair, and drags her away with no effort or emotion. A smeared pool of her blood is the only thing left of her.

"Hani, see that Miss John is made comfortable. I'll be back in one hour." He turns toward me. "We'll have dinner together. It will be nice."

I'm falling through a frozen lake. Dying.

Hani and I are alone again. She makes fast work of cleaning me up. She wipes my face with a damp towel, erasing the tears and spit and vomit. I am limp, silent, in shock. She removes my dress and retrieves yet another from a small closet in the corner of the room. This one is yellow with lace and says, "modern flower child." When she's satisfied with my appearance, she goes to the refrigerator and takes out another vial. This finally gets me speaking.

"What are you doing? Please don't give me anymore of that."

"This one is different," she says quietly. "And I'm sorry. I have to. It's my job."

"I thought you cleaned the labs."

"Well, I did, but they're gone and... how did you know I did that?"

"I saw you." It just comes out. Why not? What do I have to lose now? "I saw you cleaning in the tank room. I snuck up on you and kissed you."

"What? You *kissed* me?"

"I enchanted you. You won't remember. I was trying to help Anastasia and Alakier."

Her face lights up at the mention of them. "Ana and Alakier? Is he okay?"

"I think so. William's wife Leyla got him off the island. They're going to expose his work and..." Then I remember Leyla has been made out to be nothing more than a lying, cheating wife whom nobody will take seriously.

"I'm glad to hear you think he's all right. I cared for that boy. And his mother."

"Like you're caring for me?"

"Yes, I suppose something like that."

"Hani, the Officer said you don't talk much. That's not true, is it?"

"I don't talk much in front of him. He thinks I'm slow, or challenged, and he doesn't like my voice."

I contemplate that statement, struck by the absolute insanity of it. William Banks doesn't like your voice, so you shall be silent.

"I swear I'm going to kill him one day," I say.

"Don't worry, dear. That man is going to kill himself. He'll be his own ruin. He doesn't understand how life truly works."

Her words stun me—her own proclamation. And they ease my ravaged spirit the tiniest, tiniest bit.

"Now, William will be back shortly. Allow me to do my job. It won't hurt." She goes about filling the needle, returns the vial to the refrigerator, then walks toward me. There's nothing I can do—no fight left in me. She gently inserts the needle into my upper shoulder and pushes down lightly. It's not even halfway empty when she jerks it out, turns, and squeezes the rest into the sink.

She looks concerned, her mouth pressed tightly as she sighs hard.

The buzz still comes easily—the last one not yet worn away—enough to make my eyes flutter closed and to not know when Hani leaves and when William arrives. I welcome the buzz this time. It's not strong, but it dulls the sharpness of the things I've just witnessed, makes them feel even more like they happened in a movie. Or to someone else.

"Miss John, are you resting comfortably?" he asks with what sounds like genuine concern—surely a hallucinatory side-effect of the unknown drug they're pumping into me.

"As a matter of fact, Dad... I am." I open my eyes and giggle against my own will.

"Wonderful. Let's celebrate our newfound partnership with a fabulous dinner and drinks." He spreads out his fingers and waves a hand over a golden wheeled cart packed with covered dishes, bottles, and glasses.

"I'm not very hungry." The drugs have left me with zero appetite. Surely, he must have known they'd do that.

"Well, suit yourself. Don't mind if I do." He pulls up a chair and sits down directly at the cart. He pours himself a tall, fluted glass of sparkly pink wine and drinks it down. Then another.

"Actually, may I have a glass of that? Please?" I know by the decorative bottle and the color of the liquid this is the same wine Esmerelda served me at the Banks' house, when Leyla, she, and I joined forces and vowed to take down William Banks. It seems like a lifetime ago. And I'd do anything to be back on that twinkling patio, with those two women, in that moment, now.

William stands and retrieves the key. He unlocks first my wrists, then my ankles, and assists me in sitting at our makeshift dining table. Regarding me, the dress I'm in, and the compliancy he knows he has enforced in me forevermore, he's pleased. Then he pours himself another glass of wine and one for me.

"To the new Cooperative." He raises his glass, waiting for me to do the same.

With great effort, I lift my glass and touch it gently against his.

The wine goes down too easy, and I lose count of how many glasses I consume as William opens another bottle, then another still. He can definitely outdrink me, finishing two or three to each of my own. He seems unconcerned about me mixing alcohol with whatever concoction I've had injected into me, so I try not to worry and to just enjoy the wine. But soon, my head spins, followed by the room, and everything blurs and distorts again.

William is clearly drunk now, laughing and carrying on. I've never heard him sound so loose and out of control. I'm not even sure what he's saying; I don't even care. Then Gabriel's voice rings unannounced in my head.

You are always free, because you always have the choice.

He's right. Right now, I am free. I'm free from my shackles, so that's something. And I'm free from feeling pain, however temporary. I'll allow myself to enjoy that. And I'm free from ever worrying about needing to enchant someone to get pregnant—my previous sole purpose on this planet. I'm free from the rollercoaster of romance. I am free from ever having to give a crap about someone knowing who I really am. Isn't that what my ultimate goal was? To be who I really am? For the world to know?

Well, I got my wish, didn't I?

"You know, I think I need to lay down." I stand on shaky legs, knocking over a glass and a half-full bottle on the cart. All William can do is laugh and watch me.

I stumble over to my table-bed, which is still in an upright position, and fumble for the button Hani pushed to change it from vertical to horizontal. I eventually find it, and before the bed is fully flat, I ungracefully maneuver my way onto it and succumb to its hard, metallic lack of comfort. I don't care. I'm free, remember? My eyes fall closed, and I'm vaguely aware of William chuckling behind me.

"You are an impetuous child, Nerissa," he slurs. "But you remind me of myself in some ways."

Impossible. We are nothing alike. I feel myself dozing off.

"I'm going to tell you a story," William continues. "A bedtime story, just like my dad used to tell me." He snorts. "When I was a child, I had a dog. His name was Charlie. I loved that dog... more than anything."

He loved something? Doubtful.

"You know, my dad killed that dog right in front of me."

I think I actually hear a small sound of emotion, a tiny halt or stutter in his voice.

"Miss John? Are you awake? Nerissa?"

I don't make a sound, but I hold on to consciousness, just to see what he does.

Satisfied I'm either asleep or passed out, he continues, preaching his reverie to what he assumes is only himself and an incoherent hybrid. "I liked to write... a long time ago. Not unlike Devin—your Devin, believe it or not. I kept a diary, like that damn journal of his. It was mine. My secret. Nobody knew."

His story pulls me into a weird visual mix of him and Devin, writing in journals as they sit side by side under the junipers.

"My dad came looking for me one day. He pulled me right out of school and brought me home. He wouldn't say what was wrong. Wouldn't let me see my mother. He brought me to my room and locked the door. The man was scary, no doubt about it. Then he pulled my diary out from under his shirt and waved it at me. The dirty bastard..."

As close as I am to falling off the edge of consciousness, William's story keeps one foot rooted in time.

"He didn't yell. Didn't seem angry in the least. So odd. He spoke like it was a normal, everyday conversation. 'You know better than to write about our secret.'"

William coughs and snorts, then knocks over a bottle. I hear another being opened and the sound of wine pouring into his glass, then sloppy gulping.

"He said I put the future at risk if anyone found that diary. Like they would. He must have torn my room apart just to find it himself."

I'm in a pre-dream of young William in his room, in his

childhood body with his adult face, talking to his father. I'm not sure he'll continue, as he seems to have dozed off himself. But he finally does speak again, loosely connecting his thoughts and sentences, slurring his words.

"That exposing our secret would mean the end to his life's work, blah, blah, blah..." William laughs violently. "Everything he cared about would come to an end."

Now in my early dream, William is standing in a green forest, examining plants, then at the ocean's edge, taking samples and observing something in the distance...

Their secret.

"Bastard had it all planned before he let Charlie out of my closet. I know it. The dog barely got a chance to lick my face before he snatched him away from me." William lets out a soft, audible cry, morphing further into my twilight sleep—Charlie the dog jumping in the ocean to meet someone or something. "Kindness makes immediate cruelty that much worse. My dad pet Charlie's head, looked right at me, and snapped that poor dog's neck. Right there. Just like that. I couldn't even mourn the dead body lying on the floor. 'Take a good, long look,' he said. 'Because that is what it feels like to lose everything you love.'"

Glass crashes to the floor and shakes me awake. But I don't move. William's shadow dances on the wall in front of me. He's standing, pacing, stumbling. He picks up a glass and fills it. Then he takes a long drink and drops it to the floor, where it breaks and joins whatever came before it. He grabs the open bottle, and his shadow brings it to his lips; he drinks and drinks and drinks. When he pulls the bottle away, he lets out a long, deep belch, then falls back into his chair. He laughs and sucks in a sloppy breath, then finally exhales and moans a painful, tortured sound.

"You stupid old man..." It's almost impossible to understand him. "I was sick of keeping your secrets. Like they were all that ever mattered to you. Letting nature take its course. Why didn't *I* matter? To prove some theory? Man made them... they were ours... and they had what we wanted."

My eyes pop open.

"You dirty old bastard. Got what was coming to you... Shoulda done it a long time ago. You killed my dog..."

CHAPTER 6
BACK IN TIME
WHY AM I ALIVE?

"Why did Neptune die, Mommy?"

"All living things must die, Nerissa. It's the very nature of life."

I don't like that answer. It makes me feel scared. I bend over and pick a small yellow flower from the ground and place it in the crook of dead Neptune-the-cat's neck, inside the nest my mother crafted for him. The nest lays atop a ledge on a gray rock wall under the canopy of ancient trees.

"Do we have to bury him? Why can't we put him in the water, like we always do when someone dies?"

"Cats don't come from the water," my mother says. "They're land animals. We should bury him. The earth is his home."

"Where did Neptune come from?"

"You know we don't know that. He just appeared one day."

"Like us?"

She stops fussing about with a grass weaving she's been working on for days and turns toward me. "What do you mean, like us?"

"How did we get here?" I blink at her.

She pauses and seems to consider her response carefully. "We are creations of the Universe, just like Neptune."

"Where is his mom?"

"I don't know. I think Neptune was very old. His mother is probably long gone as well."

"What about his dad?"

"So many questions..." She turns back to her project.

I stroke the still, soft white fur on Neptune's cheek. Squeezing my eyes shut, I wish really, really hard for Neptune not to be dead. I silently promise to do anything, imagining his different-colored eyes staring up at me, but when I open my own, his are still closed—fixed in their final position.

"Do you think Neptune's dad didn't love him? Like my dad? And that's why he was here all alone, like we are? Or maybe he got in trouble and he had to come here. Maybe he was in danger, too."

My mother stops what she's doing again. "Nerissa, what is going on inside your head?"

I suddenly feel terrified, unsure of who I am, of everything I know—or think I know. "Why am I here, Mommy? Why am I alive? Why do I have to die? Why do *you* have to die?"

She exhales and walks toward where I stand in front of Neptune. "You are here because you are loved, just like Neptune was." She joins me in petting the top of his head. "Neptune was not in trouble or in danger, and he most definitely was not alone. Just like you. You are loved, and you are safe. Nobody is coming for you... and you are going to live for a long, long time. That I can assure you."

"How do you know?"

"The folly of rich men is cruel and runs deep. But they will leave us all alone. He told me so." She quickly crosses her arms and sighs.

"Who told you?"

She doesn't seem to want to answer my question. Inhaling, her eyes dart from the ground to the sky, making invisible trails as she contemplates her response. Finally, looking directly at me, she holds my gaze in an impossibly long, uncomfortable silence. "Your dad. He told me they'll leave us alone. Probably forever. You never have to worry. Now forget about all this. I know you're sad and confused because Neptune died, and that stirred up all kinds of questions. But Neptune loved you, and so do I. And I know he'd agree that all the things you're thinking about right now aren't things for children to concern themselves with." She ruffles my hair and smiles at me. "Now, why don't you go find Kendra and play? We'll say goodbye to Neptune this evening at the ceremony. You'll have another chance to see him. Run along, now." She returns to her weaving. Conversation over.

I reach back into Neptune's nest and stroke my friend's fur from the top of his head to the tip of his skinny tail. Tears form in my eyes, and I wipe them quickly away. Then I reach back to Neptune's perfect face, pinch together his whiskers on one side of his mouth, and pull them out in one quick yank. I have to flatten his lip back into position, and a small pang of guilt rises in me. I shove the whiskers in my pocket.

"I have a delivery for you, Matriarch Tatiana."

I turn back toward my mother, and she's standing before me, having magically changed into a flowing white dress. Where once there were trees behind her, now a glossy, golden light dances. A dog with a broken neck sits at her side.

"Thank you, Gabriel," my mother says as he hands her a small envelope.

"Gabriel? What are you doing here?" I ask, my eyes wide and unblinking.

He turns to me. "Look at you, dear one. So innocent. Gabriel is everywhere. Here." He hands me a thick frond of Wreckleaf.

I devour it. "But... Gabriel—"

"It's time to wake up now."

"I don't want to."

"C'mon, you're no longer a child," he urges. "Wake up."

"But I want to stay with Neptune. And my mother."

"You have a piece of each of them. Of all of us. Now... you got what you came here for, child. Wake up."

CHAPTER 7

THE POWER OF SURRENDER

YOU MUST DEFINE YOUR LIFE'S PURPOSE AND RECONCILE WITH IT.

WEDNESDAY, SEPTEMBER 11TH

Darkness will not release its grip. I'm in a hole, buried in black earth. The sounds of life beyond just barely come through. There is shuffling, doors and drawers opening and closing, the scrape of something being dragged across a floor. But I'm mummified, plastered in place, my bones like petrified wood; my skin ancient, hardened parchment. My mouth is open, dry as baked stone; my lips and face stick to the metal coffin inside which I must be resting. The light behind my eyes brightens painfully. I try to move my head, to open my eyes. Both attempts fail, but I produce a nearly inaudible moan.

"I am almost done, here. You'll need to get up and get going." The voice is excruciatingly loud.

I try again to move, to open my eyes, as the commotion carries on behind me, around me, inside of me.

A soft click sounds directly behind me, and now I'm moving. My entire world vibrates, and I'm lifted from lying to

53

drifting upright. My body slides a little, and that finally opens my eyes.

"What are you..." I can't finish my own sentence, feeling urgently nauseous. All I can manage after that is a groan.

"Put your feet on the ledge. Hold yourself up." Like a prophet, this master of my universe produces a large blue bucket as I finish my ascent and promptly throw up. Twice. She holds the bucket still, waiting patiently. When we're both satisfied that I'm done, she walks away. I close my eyes again and hear the toilet flush, then the sink turns on. The bucket bounces off the edges too loudly.

I can barely hold myself upright, my head swimming painfully, my limbs weak, and my arms dangling. "Can you please put me back down?" I grumble.

"Nope, sorry. You need to wake up and get going."

"Going?" She doesn't answer me, just continues on with whatever it is she's doing.

After a few more minutes, I finally force open my eyes, straining for vision against my hangover and the bright sun streaming in over the sink. Hani moves like a busy bee, darting from one spot to another—arranging things, organizing, tidying up.

"What's going on, Hani?" I ask weakly.

She doesn't look at me. "I brought you breakfast and an energy elixir that should help. There's a change of clothes, some toiletries in the bathroom, two large collection satchels. Let's see... have I forgotten anything?" Seemingly satisfied with herself as she looks around the room, she adds, "Nope, that's it. Everything's here. I've been instructed to tell you that you must read the note I've left here. It's imperative."

"Yeah, okay... I'll read it." That is, if I can ever see properly again.

Hani goes to the sink, lifts the key from its hook, and

approaches me. First she unlocks my ankles, and as she leans over to unlock my wrists, she whispers, "This is a big day for you. Please don't make him angry." And my wrists are suddenly free.

I carefully step to the floor with her help and steady myself against a chair.

"They're going to be so happy to see you," she says quietly.

"Who?"

"Your breed. You're going to Albatross today to harvest. Now, get yourself going. Eat. You need it. And be careful. I'll see you later." She looks at me, concern in her eyes over what must be my pathetic appearance. "It's a big day." Then turns and exits the cottage, leaving the door open just a bit.

If it looks like a trap and feels like a trap... it must be a trap. I'm standing alone in my prison-house with the door open and nobody to stop me. Wait, I know. I'll make a run for it, and as soon as I walk through the door, William Banks will be waiting for me, laughing, having his next form of torturous punishment ready and waiting for me.

I gingerly step up to the counter where Hani laid out a breakfast of assorted fruits, muffins, and a big slice of some kind of smoked meat. Next to it is a tall glass with a bright green smoothie of sorts, and next to that I see a bottle of Aqua Tonic. Guess he had reserves.

I seethe. All I want to do is knock everything to the floor with one fell swoop of my arm. But even as William's token of cruelty and sarcasm eats away at my patience, I realize I'm absolutely starving, despite being sick moments ago—maybe because of being sick moments ago. I honestly can't remember the last time I ate, and my instinct takes over as I gobble down the fruit and devour both the large muffins, barely taking a breath. I swig down some of the green drink. It tastes like an imposter Wreckleaf smoothie—sharp and tinny in my mouth.

The meat is next. I don't know what it is, but I know it's not fish, so I don't care.

As I breathlessly finish every last bite, nearly unaware of anything else, my still-blurry eyes settle on the bottle of AQT. My focus sharpens dangerously as I read the label: The Elixir of Life. Then I grab the bottle and smash it into the sink to my left. Blue-green glass and liquid shatters and sprays everywhere. I stop abruptly, forcing myself to take deep breaths as I regain my composure and survey the mess.

Nobody comes to the door. Nobody apprehends me. Nothing.

I wipe my face with the back of my hand, step carefully away from the sink, and tiptoe over the glass strewn about the cool, gray tile floor. Sitting on a small side table are two large, neoprene bags with a note addressed to Miss John propped atop them. I'd recognize the envelope and the handwriting anywhere.

I snatch up the note and rip it open. I'm a wild boar in an English garden, ready to tear this place to shreds.

Dear Miss John,

Thank you for your company during our lovely celebration dinner last night. Regrettably, I fear you may not remember much. We must do it again soon.

As you will see, you have been left provisions, as well as everything necessary to carry out a substantial harvest today. You are to go to Albatross and inform your breed of the laws of the new Cooperative. I've left a waterproof copy for you to deliver to the remaining Matriarch.

I do not think I need to remind you, after what you witnessed last night, but please be advised you are once again under strict contract. If it is broken, I will kill the remaining captive Dolhuphemale, and then we will eliminate the remainder of your breed in its entirety. And as you know, you will witness every death before your inevitable own.

Carry out an acceptable harvest and return by sundown. No one will stop you unless I give them explicit orders to do so. But do keep in mind all other Dolhuphemales are open targets.

You will be given particular freedoms if you earn them, Miss John. Only if you earn them. However, this first trip to Albatross will be the only of its kind. After today, all others will be strictly controlled. So do enjoy it.

Have a most pleasant day,
William Banks

I crumple up his disgusting, condescending, and confusing note as my head floods with foggy memories of our *"lovely celebration dinner last night."*

Regrettably for you, William Banks, I remember enough.

Twenty minutes later, after a cool shower and the effects of sustenance—the green smoothie and food seem to have done their job—I'm feeling somewhat better. It also helped to take off that ridiculous dress and put on almost normal clothes. I was left swim shorts, a modest bikini top, and a blue cotton t-shirt, along with a thick green rain poncho, which I have no need for today. I'll turn the t-shirt inside out so the logo doesn't show. No need to advertise Aqua Tonic, even if nobody sees me. But there are no water shoes, just gym shoes. Guess it doesn't matter anymore.

I grab the two collection bags and note their size; William's expecting a large delivery. I shove his waterproof copy of the new Cooperative into one of them, strap both to my waist, and turn to leave. My hand finds the doorknob.

I'm suddenly paralyzed. This door is a ticking time bomb. When I open it, everything will explode. But if I don't....

I turn the knob and pull open the door. A rush of fresh air hits me so powerfully, it pulls my breath away, and my eyes flutter. The sun hits my face from the right; it's almost unreal, instantly warming me, promising of its life-giving selflessness. Directly in front of me, about fifteen yards, a tall stand of thick evergreen trees sway in the breeze and release their fragrance. I take an involuntary inhale through my nose. Just beyond the trees, I can barely make out blue. Then I realize this is the edge of the base, and just on the other side of these fragrant beauties, the cliff ends and drops into the wild ocean.

I will myself to step forward out of the doorway. On the manicured gravel path, my shoes crunch softly. I look down and have to jump back, slamming my hand over my mouth to hold back my cries. There was no way to completely clean the puddle of Sarah's blood from the path. New gravel must have been laid in the night, but it couldn't cover everything. How could it have?

Just step over it. Do it.

I stretch my leg, pointing my foot toward where I want it to land over the remnants of the horrific murder scene, then leap out of the doorway and past the blood stains. I shut my eyes and try to focus my breath. Breathe in... breathe out... again.

I open my eyes and look around. Another cottage stands to the right and one to the left, spaced evenly from mine. The path winds between all three, disappearing behind my cottage.

I turn right. Once between the tiny houses, I gain my bearings. Walter's enclosure is down the path now to my left. The main path should lie straight ahead, through a few more twisting walkways. Once there, I'll turn right, walk for a short way, and I should find the front gate on my left at the beginning of the path. Are they just going to let me walk out? Or is someone going to be there? Again, this feels like a cruel trick. But what choice do I have? Return to my cottage and wait? For what? More injections? Another visit from my father? Death?

No.

I proceed forward up the path, the calm and peaceful surroundings pushing hard against my inner turmoil. My senses are on hyper-drive. The soft breeze rustling the leaves above is too loud, the dappled sun is blinding, the smells of the trees and the ocean beyond—the freshly mown grass and the last of the summer flowers—suddenly assaulting me.

I pass a cottage on my right, where a man sits at a desk in the window and watches me walk by. He's like a gargoyle guarding his temple, a stony, stoic smile twisting his face, attempting to distract me from his ugliness. I hold his gaze until my head can no longer stretch that far, and I almost fall when my foot catches a flagstone at the edge of the path.

I regain my balance and look up. Just ahead is the main path, the very one I first walked with Devin, then with my mother, Gio, Kendra, Leyla, and Lillian. And ultimately with Alakier draped over my arms just before William Banks slammed my head into a boulder—that one, just over there— as we witnessed the explosion on Black Rock that I naively assumed would be his demise. I'll never assume anything ever again. Now, being here again, especially in this capacity... what a mind-job. I plod forward.

Once on the main path, I start to think I'll actually be able to leave. But as I walk up the slight incline to the front gate, hope and anticipation spill out of me. An armed guard waits for me at the gate. Will I be apprehended or shot as William watches and laughs?

I approach the guard, his mask of duty and diligence making his face look like carved marble. He doesn't flinch, his grip on his weapon unwavering. I stand directly in front of him and look up as he looks down. He's a full foot taller than me, and his absolute stillness almost convinces me he's a statue until he finally breaks his position, turns his back to me, and addresses the keypad.

A quick moment later, a familiar click and hum opens the front gate. The guard turns back around and just stares at me.

"Can I leave?" I finally ask.

"You are free to go." He sounds like a robot. Maybe he's not even real or at least not even human—a manufactured slave of William's.

I am free to go.

He doesn't have to tell me twice, and even though I'm still not convinced this isn't part of some big, cruel joke, I don't hesitate. But robot-man has a few final words.

"Be back by sundown. Do not be late."

I don't answer Mr. Charming. I just meet his gaze and nod so he knows I've heard him. The gate closes behind me, and the air rushes out of my lungs.

I'm ready to take off running, then I see I've been left a board. I've never been happier to have one, and after a few hitches as I get it going, I'm up and flying down the road. Somehow, it knows my voice and responds appropriately.

As I pick up speed and the distance between me and the front gate widens, my eyes flood with tears. I let go. The gravity of my situation overwhelms me—guilt, fear, anger, and sadness. What will I find when I'm finally back on Albatross? I don't know if I should even go. Will my mother be alive? If she is, will she be happy to see me? How will I tell them about Sarah? About Lillian? How many of my breed are left? Do I even want to know? And what does our future hold?

I'm barely paying attention to where I am, then something catches the corner of my eye as I pass it. I slow down and turn around, hovering for a moment to catch my wild breath and wipe my tears. Then I ride back down the dark, hidden path into the forest, where my mother, Gio, Kendra, Lillian, Leyla, and I held hands for the last time before we took the base.

At the small clearing in the trees, I hop off the board and shut it down. The sudden and absolute silence is unnerving. I am utterly alone.

Both my old board and Gio's are still here, ghostly remnants of our past lives. But hers, unlike mine—which is propped upright against a tree—lies flat upon the forest floor, already collecting leaves and debris from the changing seasons. My body crumbles, melts on top of itself, and I fall to the ground to lay myself across her weathered board.

The pain in my chest is unbearable, unlike anything I've ever felt, threatening to rip me in two. Devin appears in my mind's eye, then Kendra, then my mother lying injured in the rocky cove on Albatross, crying.

I suck in a deep breath. "I'm so sorry..."

Who have I become? How did I get here, and will I ever be able to undo all that I've done?

I lie on the forest floor, half-sprawled across Gio's board, and cry for an indiscriminate amount of time. It could be minutes; it could be an hour.

Be back by sundown. Don't be late.

My head snaps upright as I still my mind and concentrate on those words. But I can't fathom getting up and taking any kind of action. I have no more fight left in me. What if I just choose to stay here? To never show my face again to anyone.

What if I just leave? I could swim out to Our Beach, hide in the caves, and live alone for the rest of my days.

But he'll kill them all—whoever's left. He'll kill Kendra and her unborn baby. And my mother... but he may choose to that anyway. I roll over and look up at the canopy, filling my body with the fresh, green air.

"Help me, Universe. What do I do?"

Nerissa, you must define your life's purpose and reconcile with it.

Gabriel's wisdom floods my mind in an unexpected rush.

No one can tell you your purpose except yourself.

A warm wave of clarity washes over me; Gabriel's voice comes to me as though he were standing by my side. Word for word, deeply ingrained in memory, I recall his message of the power of surrender...

Know, dear one, with every fiber of your being, that you are exactly who you are supposed to be in exactly the right time and place. Know that if you are unclear of it now, your life's purpose will reveal itself to you when it is time. And above all else, know that you are already free, because you always have that choice.

That's it. I close my eyes one last time, take a deep breath, and hold it in for a moment, along with my newfound absolution. When I open my eyes and exhale, the forest is a little brighter, the edges a little sharper. My swirling thoughts have settled, softened with calm and certainty. I'm no longer trembling, no longer crying. I'm still afraid. But somehow, that fear now fuels me. I rise up off the ground.

I know who I am. I know my life's purpose. I am a catalyst of change. I've always known that, and somehow, it seems clearer now than ever, even if I don't directly create the change myself or see it to its completion. I am what has set things in motion. That change cannot be undone. And the change yet to come *will* set us free. I will do *whatever* I must—whatever it takes. Freedom comes in many forms.

I brush the leaves and dirt off me, walk to my original board, and bring it to life. It's like reuniting with an old friend. I leave the secrecy of the forest while still holding the hand of fear and ride out onto the road.

It's time to go to Albatross.

CHAPTER 8
REUNION
THERE IS NO LIGHT. THERE IS NOTHING.
JUST ME.

WEDNESDAY, SEPTEMBER 11TH

It may not be my best idea, but time's not on my side, and I need to shave off a few extra minutes from my journey to Albatross. So instead of continuing down the main road toward Playa Rosa, I turn left just past the luxury sector onto resort row. The shops and cafes lining the right side of the street are all buttoned up for the Season. This is a tourist's playground, and they're all gone. These establishments will remain closed until a few weeks before the start of the next tourist Season next year in mid-May. I've only come down here once before during off-season with Kendra. We were just curious, but there's honestly not much to see, and it's kind of creepy.

As I keep to the left and pull into Concordia on the Bay's property, I regret my decision. All the resorts employ off-season custodians to oversee the grounds and accommodations. And since I'll essentially have to break the law to gain access to the beach, I'm really taking a chance trying to enter the water from here. I should have just continued to Playa Rosa and done things the normal way. But I'm here now, and honestly, I feel the need to see it—empty, quiet, and mine alone—disarmed of its power.

I drive around to the side of the main building and park my board against the wall next to the employee entrance. I'm either going to have to break in or climb this mile-high fence— two unfavorable options.

The fence is out of the question. It's got to be ten feet tall— a thick, tightly woven, black-metal link. There's no way to grab a foothold or even a toehold. Even if I somehow managed to climb it, I'd be met at the top with a backward-curving, slick-metal security shield. Check this off my short list of options.

I focus on the door. There's the standard crystal swipe above an ordinary doorknob with a regular-looking lock built into it. My CNI is out of commission, so the swipe is useless. Even if my crystal was still intact, I'm fairly certain it would have somehow been deactivated. I've only got one choice left, and if it works, it may set off an alarm or something. Although alarms aren't typical on Panacea. There's no crime here. Ironic. But I've got to try, and I also need to be ready to hop back on my board and head to Rosa should things get crazy.

I scan the ground around me. At the edge of the sidewalk, I find a rock that fits my grip well. I come down hard on the swipe. Then again. A quick flash of green lights up, followed by yellow. I try the knob—still locked. I smash the rock into the swipe again, and the light goes out, then quickly changes to red. No. I wiggle the knob back and forth to no avail. I disarmed the swipe, but it didn't click open the lock.

I look around, not sure what I'm searching for. I can't smash my way through this door. I can't even muscle past this knob. The only thing left to try is to pick it open, but it's not like I carry around a set of lockpicks with me. I need something like a paper clip or a hairpin, something I can bend and insert into the lock. Who am I kidding? I don't even know if I can do that.

I close my eyes and turn my face up to the sky, patting myself down, searching for something to magically appear. I'm about to give up and race to Playa Rosa when my hand lands on one of the neoprene collection bags William left for me. Opening my eyes, I look down. How does it close?

With a buckle. I unhook the bag from my waist and study the closure. It's an ultra-thin, coated, yellow metal contraption, like a super-skinny belt buckle sewn into the neoprene fabric. I can bend it. I try to rip it from its setting, but it's too tightly sewn. I bring it to my teeth and tear at it like a rabid animal. I slice the seam with my front teeth, then rip the rest open with my fingers. Yes. I've got it.

I stretch and bend the square of yellow back and forth until it breaks, then open the entire thing into one long piece. I insert it into the lock on the doorknob with no idea what I'm doing. I wiggle it back and forth. It catches on something but just for a fraction of a second. I try again and again.

Think.

I bend the end of the metal into a tiny U-shape, then take a chance and break it into two pieces. Squatting down, I insert the longer of the two pieces back into the lock and feel around, listening carefully. When I feel that slight catch again, when I hear it, I insert the other piece, and with a moment of pure luck, I somehow seem to find the right angle for another little click.

I freeze, afraid any little movement will undo my actions or set off an alarm. Neither happens. I leave the metal pieces as they are and stand up slowly. When my hand falls on the knob, it turns and opens as smooth as glass.

Not aware I'd been holding my breath, I exhale hard as the

door peeks open. I grab the torn collection bag and shove it into the good one still attached to my waist.

A quick glance around confirms I'm still alone, undetected, and ready to make my way through the employee area and out onto the beach pavilion. I remove my metal "keys," step into the building, and close the door quietly behind me. It's as quiet as the blackest sleep. And nearly as dark. Except for the faintest emergency lights dotting the walls in widely spaced increments, the locker room and hallways of Concordia are thickly shrouded in the darkness and hush of the off-Season.

Winding through the barely navigable employee wing, I finally find myself at the last hallway before the doorway to the beach pavilion, and an unexpected light halfway up the wall illuminates my final steps. I didn't think I'd see it, but of course, I should have expected to. The slashed portrait of Alexandria Allerton Bigelow, victim to my frenzied attack with a metal tail comb, has been replaced by a new tribute to *Concordia's fairest Beauty.* There she stands, a full-body rendering, her hand on her hip, her head tilted to the opposite side, that stupid, doggish grin on her face. That vain, plastic, *I-fail-to-see-how-this-information-is-any-of-my-concern* bitch. Of course their *Champion* would have a new portrait hung and lit, even when there's nobody around to admire it or bow down in front of it. How could they not honor the woman who *brought Concordia to life,* the woman who ignored our pleas for help, who ignored the corruption of William Banks? The supposedly moral woman who turned the other cheek in the face of lies and deceit and murder. The woman who I'm sure will fund the rebuild of my father's labs and the new Bio-Gen building—maven of the new and improved Aqua Tonic.

I stare at the portrait. "Alexandria, I'd like to make you a promise, fair Beauty. If I ever have the nauseating displeasure of seeing you again, I will kill you."

Thankfully, while reeling in my disgust and despair as I exit the building, I remember to leave the door propped open for my return. I slide a heavy, emptied flowerpot into place and turn to face the beach. The pavilion is empty, no chairs, no umbrellas, no stocked towel stand or drink carts waiting to serve the masses. The sand is unraked, leaves and twigs littering its usually pristine appearance. It's beautiful, more perfect this way than any other way I've ever seen it. But for just a second, I imagine it full—the sights and sounds. The smells of the busiest part of the Season. I imagine Gabriel walking toward me, his wide, toothy grin lighting up my heart. Then I imagine Devin, and I squint to peer down the beach all the way under the Junipers. There are no loungers, no people, no Devin.

A cool breeze off the water grabs my attention and reminds me why I'm here. I take off my shoes and t-shirt. It's time to go.

The ocean is cold and refreshing, and even though I've thought this a million times before, it's never felt better than it does today. Today, it's like a tonic, a liquid salve against every inch of my body. It's medicine for my soul—for my battered, broken heart—and I soak it in. I'll never take this feeling for granted ever again. It may very well be my last time. I have no way of knowing. I guess I never did. Then again, no one ever does.

Just beyond the swimming barriers, the current grabs me. It's only September, and the changes are already noticeable. The water churns a little deeper, a little darker, commanding just a little more respect than it normally does. In a few more months, harvest becomes a dangerous challenge, even for the strongest of us. But as always, it remains a necessary practice —an essential, life-giving practice.

Against the currents and my weakened state, I make my way to Albatross as quickly as I can. I feel like a bird who's been let out of her cage, free to fly through my liquid paradise. As I approach the northeast side of the island, I slow down almost involuntarily. The flutter in my gut and the heaviness in my chest remind me of what I'm about to do—what I'm about to face. The things I'll need to say.

I swallow hard, resolve to be brave, and dive under. I enter the in-tube, and as usual, the current works against me. But I push on, winding my way through the underwater caves, and finally come up at the Hub for a much-needed breath. This is it. I turn toward the far-right lead, which will deposit me on the northernmost point of Albatross, within a sandy cove protected on each side by rocky outcroppings. This is where my breed—what's left of my breed—should be. The tube will let me out right at the mouth of a wide, protective cavern on the edge of the beach. If they're there, they'll see me immediately. If they're out on the beach, I'll have to walk about thirty yards.

When I approach the opening, I slow down. I break the surface without a sound and quickly scan the area. No one's here. I peer down the sand and spot someone sitting at the edge of the water. The sun glints off the surf, and it's difficult to tell, but I think... I rise out of the tube. It looks like blonde hair, maybe. Both my feet are on the sand, and I walk forward slowly, my heart in my throat.

"Kendra..." The whisper barely escapes me. I pull in as much air as my lungs will allow. "*Kendra!*"

She looks up from whatever she's doing and swings her head side to side, searching for the source of her name.

"Kendra!" I jog toward her. She turns and sees me, recognition spreading across her face. She jumps up, mouth open, wild-eyed, and moves in my direction. I break into a full-on sprint to meet her.

I can't move fast enough, sure that if I don't catch her in my embrace, she'll dissolve before me, a figment of my desperate imagination. A Fata Morgana of the cruelest variety.

Her face twists in a still silent cry. As I reach her, I slam my body against hers, wrapping my arms around her as I try to get closer—to melt into her. She latches onto me, her cries finally uncontained.

"Are you real?" she asks through her gasping sobs.

"Yes. I'm here."

"I thought you were dead."

"I'm here," I assure her. "Kendra, I'm here."

We rock back and forth in each other's arms, crying, never loosening our grips on one another. When I'm convinced she won't disappear, I put my hands on her shoulders and pull back far enough to look at her.

"You're so beautiful. Are you okay?"

She just nods, taking me in. Convincing herself, I suppose, that I'm really here—really real.

I hesitate but finally ask, "Is the baby all right?"

"The baby's fine. How are you?"

"Where's everyone else?" I don't want to talk about myself at all.

"Gathering food and harvesting. Nerissa..." She holds my gaze. "How did you get away? Are you okay? You look... you don't look like yourself."

I inhale sharply, trying to prepare myself to answer her, to be honest.

"*Nerissa?*" I'd recognize her voice anywhere, even through the cloud of emotion. I turn around, overwhelmed by relief, hardly able to stay on my feet as I walk toward her.

"Mom..." My voice breaks. "I'm here. I'm alive."

We wrap each other in an equally passionate embrace and cry with abandon. She's still the Matriarch, still my mother— steadfast, fixed, and absolute. Yet there's a tenderness now—

such a welcome, all-encompassing acceptance. I didn't realize how much I missed her.

She looks at me, smoothing back nonexistent hair from my face, and wipes my tears. She's different in her familiarity.

"Mom..." It's all I can get out. I close my eyes and melt back into her arms. She holds me and gently strokes my back.

"My baby. You're here. I've got you now."

"I wasn't sure if you were... I mean, when I left, you were injured, and I thought..." I can't finish my sentence, the emotion taking complete control.

"No, baby. I did get hit. Knocked down and hurt my head a little. But the wounds were mostly superficial, and I'm almost healed."

I take in a deep breath, inhaling her, so relieved to be in her arms.

Kendra now stands behind me, her head resting against my back as her arms wrap around both my mother and me. I just need to stay here. I need to absorb this love into every cell. I push the thoughts of all the things I have to tell them out of my head.

I slowly become aware of other voices approaching, then Kendra releases us and turns. I hear her talking quietly. I finally lift my head from my mother's shoulder and look around.

Kendra's speaking to seven of our sister maids—Bryn, Meredith, Maris, Kai, the elder Darya, Rain, and Marlow. Sedna and Amelia also come up from the inlet at the mouth of the cavern.

"Oh, good. Everyone is here," my mother says. "Well, almost."

I release myself from her embrace and look around, confused. I spin in a full circle, scanning the beach and the water and the rocks and forest behind us.

"This is everyone?" I push out. "Mom?"

She takes my wrist and pulls me back toward her. Her other hand rests at the top of my chest, above my heart, where she just leaves it, letting her energy and her silence somehow answer my question.

"But there's only..." I do a fast headcount. "Eleven. There's only eleven... twelve, including me. Mom? Is that right?" I can't trust the words that have just come out of my own mouth.

"Yes. At least, that's who's here."

"What do you mean?"

"Lillian and Sarah went to Panacea two nights ago. I didn't want them to, but they insisted. Lillian said she couldn't stand not knowing anything. And that the truth was better than not knowing."

"So they came for me?" My voice shakes.

"To find out what happened to you, if they could. They brought Wreckleaf in case they found you. Which, Amelia, please..." She gestures to young Amelia and the full collection satchel at her waist. Amelia opens it, and the sight of the freshly harvested Wreckleaf makes my mouth water. I devour what's offered, and my mother encourages me to continue until I feel satisfied. Many mouthfuls later, I feel worlds better.

"What's that bag around your waist?" my mother asks.

The time has come.

I reach into the intact collection bag, retrieve William Banks' waterproofed copy of the new Cooperative, and hand it over to my mother. "I have a lot to tell you."

Almost an hour later, the remaining twelve of us have caught up. I've told them everything that happened to me since I was taken off Albatross in the chopper—everything I can remember. Here on the sand, on our beloved Albatross, with the breeze against my face and the sun ascending across the western sky, the news of Sarah's death and what seems like Lillian's eventual fate is of course devastating. From a large, robust extended family of dozens and dozens, we've been reduced to a group of twelve. Thirteen, including Kendra's unborn baby.

"Of course, it doesn't need to be said." My mother addresses the two youngest survivors, thirteen-year-old Bryn and fourteen-year-old Maris. "But just so we're clear, there's no need to wait until you are of age to acquire."

"But no... no one can come to Panacea," I protest. "They'll kill you or take you."

My mother looks at me, about to speak, but then she stops and seems to ponder how to best deliver her next words. "If we don't acquire, our species will not survive. It's always been this way."

"I know, but we're not a secret anymore. We're not even a novelty. We... we're prey."

"I understand, but—"

"No, I don't think you do, Mom. We're outed. We're fair game to anyone and in any way."

"The locals won't hurt us. They're a gentler, kinder group."

"Don't be so sure. William Banks has probably offered a reward for turning one of us in. A bounty. And now, with no tourists to blend in with... Can you at least wait until the next Season starts to try more acquisitions? Just like always?"

"Times are not like always, Nerissa."

"Mom, look what happened to Lillian and Sarah."

She lowers her head and takes a long, deep breath. "I will carefully consider everything, and we'll continue this conversation in a day or two."

"I don't know when he'll let me come back." My own words bring a shiver rolling over me.

"Well, if he needs you to be the only source of Wreckleaf," Kendra says, "and he's using it for God knows what, he'll probably let you return every few days. Or at least once a week."

I frown, feeling a little foolish for not having thought that through already. "Yeah, I guess."

"And we'll have a large harvest waiting for you each time. Just let us know you're coming and we'll..." My mother seems to realize what she's just said; she knows my CNI is completely worthless. I smile weakly in an attempt to ease her mind.

"Our CNIs aren't working right now, either," Kendra says.

"What do you mean?"

"They've been altered somehow. Blocked or something. We're only able to get very weak, broken connections."

"Yes," my mother adds. "The only correspondence with Leyla so far has been very sketchy, and it was difficult to understand—"

"You've spoken to Leyla?" I shout. "Why didn't you tell me that?" I try to calm myself; I just can't let anything get any uglier than it already is. I don't know when or if William will *ever* let me return, no matter what he's said or will say. And I won't let things end here on a heated note.

"I'm sorry," she replied. "It slipped my mind. We've talked about so many things.... Yes, she contacted us a few days ago."

"What did she say?" I lean in, relieved to know Leyla's alive and hopefully well and desperate to know what's happening on her end.

"It was very hard to understand her. The transmission was garbled and fuzzy." My mother shakes her head. "But she sounded well, and she mentioned Alakier 'adjusting,' so I think we can assume he's okay, too."

I sigh in relief, thinking how great it would be to hear her voice. "Can we try now? To contact her? Please? I know she'll want to hear that I'm alive." Saying those words sounds so obscure, so unreal, and so ridiculous. *She'll want to hear that I'm alive.* Really? Is this my real life?

"All right." My mother nods. "Display." But her dark, smoky quartz doesn't obey, doesn't yield to her command. Instead, a twisted, broken, impossible-to-decipher holographic image appears before her.

"Try this," Kendra suggests and speaks into her sparkling citrine CNI. "Contact Leyla Banks."

There's the softest crackling sound, then the short, melodic tone signaling a ping is being transmitted on the other end. It keeps going, three times, four, seven...

"Hello? Kendra?" Leyla's voice is so faint, I figure I'm imagining it—wanting it so badly, my mind has created it for me in a mere whisper.

"Yes. Hi. It's Kendra and Tatianna. And Leyla, Nerissa's here."

Silence.

"Leyla, can you hear us?" my mother shouts. "Leyla? Are you there?"

Nothing.

"I think we've lost her," Kendra says.

"I'm here... here... can you... me now? I'm here... Nerissa? Did you say... is..."

"Leyla! I'm here!" I shout.

"Nerissa... hear... voice and... you're alive." Leyla's transmission gets worse and worse, but I figure out what she's trying to say. It's so good to hear her voice.

"How's Alakier?" I shout.

"Good. He..."

We lose her for almost thirty seconds.

"Nerissa, he's alive." Leyla's voice comes through loud and clear.

"I know," I say. "I know Alakier's alive. How's he doing?"

"Alakier is... good... adjusting to... but I don't... not Alakier."

"She's not talking about Alakier," Kendra says.

The magic and joy are suddenly sucked out of the moment. She's talking about her husband, my father, William Banks. The last time she saw him was at the top of the base as he backed me into the rock wall. My memories are still fuzzy, and I don't know exactly when she got up and left us, but of course, someone must have told her of her husband's fate. That he's alive and well. In fact, I wouldn't be surprised if the pompous ass messaged her himself, just to let her know that even though she escaped his wrath, at least for now, he's not done. Not by a longshot.

"Don't know how... stop him. He's... angry and..."

"I know, Leyla. We know."

"You have to stop him, Nerissa... he'll never listen to me..." For a moment, her voice is crystal-clear. She has no way of knowing about the New Cooperative or what I'm up against. I don't know if anyone's told her how many of us are gone, or if she knows about Devin, and I'm sure as hell not going to be the one to tell her now. But I also don't think she realizes, that anyone realizes, what I'm willing to do to set things right, what I'm willing to sacrifice, or how far I'll go this time.

"I'll do whatever it takes to stop him. At the very least whatever it takes to ensure my family's safe. That you and Alakier and Esmerelda are safe."

"Esmer—she... don't know... she is." The transmission warps and goes fuzzy, then silent. We wait and try to get her back, but that's it. She's gone.

"That was the best we've had so far," Kendra says. "Nothing else has been that long or clear."

"Really?"

"Really."

"She said she doesn't know where Esmerelda is. Do any of you know?"

"No," my mother says plainly.

"Oh, my God... Esmerelda." My mind briefly wanders, imagining the dark horrors poor, sweet Esmerelda may have faced. But I won't allow myself to stay there. "Does Leyla know about..." I pause, not wanting to upset Kendra.

"About my mom? About Matriarch Giovanni?" Kendra finishes my question. "Yes. At least, I think so. I mean, we tried to tell her as much as possible. We have no way to know if it came through."

"Does she know about Devin?" I can barely speak his name.

"We're not sure about that, either," my mom answers. "We thought she said his name once, but we had a bad connection and couldn't really make it out. We honestly just couldn't tell her he'd been shot down. I just... from one mother to another, I... I couldn't deliver that kind of news."

The two neoprene collection satchels given to me by William Banks are stuffed with fresh Wreckleaf. Matriarch Tatiana made sure I didn't have to strain myself, because she too pointed out my appearance as not being the healthiest-looking and instructed my sister maids Kai and Meredith to carry out another harvest for me. William should be pleased, I think. One just never knows the mood or temperament of that man. I could hand him a bag of gold and the only reward I'd get is a slap in the face.

The second bag, the one I partially destroyed to make the *keys* for picking the lock at Concordia, is tied securely at my waist.

Now at the cool mouth of the cavern, it's time to leave. Just as I anticipated, the goodbyes are difficult, to say the least. My mother can barely speak. She just looks at me while she nervously grooms my lack of hair, then rubs my arms, shoulders, and back, like she's petting a cat. Finally, she gathers me up in her embrace and pulls me in tight.

"Nerissa, my baby..." She sighs the words, and they mix with her muffled cry.

"I'll be fine, Mom." It feels like a lie, but I have to say it. And I have to make sure it remains true.

"Promise me. Promise me you won't do anything to make him angry."

"I promise." I shrug. "I promise I'll try."

"And promise me you'll eat and try to sleep. Just... take care of yourself."

"I'll do my best. I promise." But making these vows feels dirty—cheap. I can't possibly guarantee any of these things. And I'm sure my mother knows it, but in this moment, we both need to play along. I can't leave her in any more despair than she's already endured.

When she finally releases me, I turn around to Kendra. Tears streak her face, and we just stare at each other, both of us beyond the need for words. I place my right hand on her belly, and she smiles, nodding.

"What a lucky baby." I look down at my hand. "Be good to your momma. I love you, and I'll talk to you soon."

Kendra puts one hand atop mine, the other behind my neck, and our foreheads meet for a few seconds. "I can't do this without you, Nerissa," she whispers.

My tears fall onto her belly between us. "Yes you can. But I'll be back. Don't worry."

"I can't help it. Don't do anything stupid."

No truer words could have come out of her mouth, and her simple but spot-on instruction makes me laugh, cutting the intense moment so the last thing we share before I leave are smiles.

I finally turn to face the last surviving members of my breed as a whole.

"We will not be destroyed. We are meant to be here." I dip my head and take in one last, deep breath. "We're here for a reason. All of us." I look up at them. "I will not let you down again."

Before we drag out any more painful goodbyes, I turn and step back into the entrance of the underwater caves, into the water, and submerge myself. As I push off the shallow wall and dive into the depths of the cave, I catch the echo of my mother's voice.

"I love you, Nerissa!

I love you, too, Mom. I always have.

Just after I enter the ocean on the northeast side of Albatross, the rain starts. Then the young male dolphin—who escorted Alakier and me the rest of the torturous way to Panacea after witnessing the rest of his pod perish beneath the stinging tentacles of the Madoosik—greets me with a familiar chortle. He's alone, which pains me to no end, and the deep, emotional loss I see in his eyes can't be imaginary.

"Hi. I'm so glad to see you," I say as my hand grazes his side. He's injured, numerous large scratches along his flank. Existing in these waters alone is dangerous, especially for an animal used to depending on a group.

"I need to go, friend. Please try to find another pod... maybe a group passing through the area?" I know this is highly unlikely along the coasts of these cursed islands. These dolphins seemed to have formed an unusual assembly of different ages and genders, like they were all lost or cast out or off-course and had come together by default. But they all came from somewhere, so it's not impossible that others might come.

I take a deep breath and dive under. My friend follows me the entire swim back. The waves and currents are even more formidable now as the storm that's started grows in intensity. I'm grateful for his company. Not until I glide under the ropes at Concordia does he slow, turn around, and disappear.

I don't know what time it is exactly, but just before I left my mother, Kendra, and the other remaining nine, the sun—although cloaked by the incoming clouds—still seemed relatively high. I should have plenty of time until I'm expected back at the base and under William Banks' watchful eye. I scan the pavilion for signs of life before rising out of the water. I'm alone.

A quick run up the beach, and I'm back at the employee entrance where I left the door propped open beside my gym shoes, which are now soaked, and my t-shirt, which must have blown away. I brush the wet sand from my feet, put on my shoes, slide the flowerpot away, and step through the door, closing it securely behind me.

Leaving puddles on the floors as I go, I slog back through the halls of Concordia, choosing not to look again at Alexandria Allerton Bigelow but certainly remembering my promise to her.

"You could have saved us all, Alexandria. You could have saved countless others from your pal William and his disgusting energy elixir," I say as I walk past her portrait. "You have no idea what you've done, either because you don't believe us or because you don't care."

Unfortunately, I know it's the latter. There are people so insidious, so full of themselves and what they believe to be their all-encompassing power, they steamroll their way through the world. Even worse than my father who, in light of Alexandria's role, seems almost like a novice at the game of power and control.

"You'll get what's coming to you." I step into the dark locker room.

When I move past a full-length mirror at the end of a row of lockers, the image of my reflection makes me pause. I laugh, imagining Marcus' reaction to the way I look right now. Marcus. Who would have ever thought I'd actually have a soft spot for that man? But I do, and I know one hand would be at his heart, the other fanning his face in complete exasperation at the sight of me. My hair, which is only starting to grow out, is still somehow plastered to my head. Contrasting against my extra-pale, dull skin, it looks like I smudged mascara under my eyes, though I don't have on a lick of makeup. I'm certainly not the vision of perfection Marcus or Concordia came to expect—far from it. I realize this is part of what caused the concern in my mother and Kendra. I look ill. So does my body. I'm skinny, my muscles soft and weak-looking. Even under my shorts, I can see my hipbones poking through....

Wait. Oh, no.

My hands find my waistline, patting myself down as I spin before the mirror, frantically inspecting my reflection for the second neoprene collection bag full of Wreckleaf.

It's gone. Only one remains securely fastened at my waist. No.

It must have come off in the water without its buckle. He's going to be angry. But it wasn't my fault... the ocean was so rough, it came undone and there was nothing I could do....

Who am I kidding? William won't care what my excuse is. And it is my fault. It didn't have a buckle. No, I used that to craft makeshift lock picks to use on Concordia's employee entrance. Maybe I'll get an A for ingenuity and resourcefulness.

He's going to punish me. Okay.

I take a deep breath and settle my thoughts. *No one can take your power from you unless you allow them.* Damn, I wish I felt more conviction in that.

Back on the road, wet and cold, I now realize why Hani left me a poncho this morning. If I ever get the opportunity to leave the base again, I'll know there's a reason for everything they leave me. For now, I'll drive as fast as possible to get myself out of this storm and hopefully not catch pneumonia.

Along the deserted streets I wind, passing through the luxury sector once again. I didn't even think about it as I was making my way out to Albatross earlier, too distracted by the hopeful promise of reuniting with my breed, but I passed right by the Banks' property, just as I'm about to do again.

I slow in front of their driveway, unsure of why or of what may be behind the gate at the other end. Then I stop.

What am I doing? This is my past life. There's nothing here for me now. Not ever again.

But despite my reasoning intellect, my irrational emotion propels me forward, down the winding driveway, all the way to the black gate. It hangs open, the property an abandoned fortress, already pushing up weeds between the pavers. Beyond the gate, the house's front entrance is still lit. As I push forward through the now driving wind and rain, I can't justify doing it at all. My only conceivable excuse now is to get out of the torturous weather.

When I reach the front door, I'm alarmed to find it wide open, dirt and leaves and the damaging effects of salt-infused island winds littering the pristine entrance to the Banks' showplace of a home. From the looks of it, it's been this way for quite some time, maybe even since the night we destroyed the labs.

I step inside, and a shiver runs through me. This is not the welcoming, warm home I remember. The house is a mess, as though someone went on a rampage—knocking things over, shattering pottery, and ripping artwork from the walls. Dark liquid has been splattered up the stairway and sprayed all over the ironwork railings. The once beautiful, gray velvet curtains hanging in the entryway are torn from their rods, lying in sad, mangled puddles. What looks like couch stuffing clumps in dirty white puffs, strewn across a once immaculate, antique wool rug. Surveying the endless destruction, I feel a cold breeze coming from the kitchen, making me think more than just the front door has been left open. I don't want to look in there, afraid of what I might find. It's a battlefield in here. But I guess it always was.

I quickly talk myself into going up to Devin's room. Yes, that's why I'm here. I just want to… what? Lie in his bed? Smell him one last time? If I'm being honest with myself, then yes. That's exactly why I'm here. I haven't allowed myself to really think about Devin since the chopper took me from Albatross. I want—no, I *need* to feel his energy one final time. To say good-bye. And then I'll close the door. I'll let him go and move on. I promise.

I step over and around the mess in the entryway and halfway cover my eyes as I ascend the formal staircase. I don't want to go up the back stairs; I'd have to walk through the kitchen to do that, then past those pictures of Devin and his *family* in the stairwell. I don't want to see him pretending to be happy. Especially now.

At the top of the stairs is the rich, wood-floored corridor

that eventually meets the back hallway—the one that looks over the garden room. Devin's bedroom is at the corner of that intersection, and I can see part of *her* from here—the woman in the painting by his door. When I move closer, she comes into full view, and I'm relieved to see the magnificent work has somehow been spared. There she stands, in her power and her freedom. I skim the detailed texture, softly tracing the lines of her dress all the way down to the bottom of...

She hasn't escaped what I can assume is William's wrath—not entirely. The inscription. Carefully cut out in a perfect rectangle, the words that came to mean so much to me —*Emancipation Ignites Power and Fuels Responsibility*—are gone. Why was he so careful here? Why did he leave her intact? I don't know that I will ever come to understand this man, who I still can't believe is my father.

I turn left and face the heavy wooden door separating me from Devin's room. One deep breath in, one deep breath out, and I open the door and step inside. No.

Devin's room is destroyed too. Once a luxurious master-piece, the bed is ripped apart, sheets torn, pillows and blankets thrown around the room. The four-poster frame is now three-and-a-half, the closest post cracked off in the middle, the jagged and pointed end as sharp and wicked as a spear. The mattress has been, for lack of a better word, stabbed, like someone jammed a knife into it and dragged it, over and over, its stuffing spilling out like from a gutted animal. And there's blood—just a little, but definitely blood. William must have cut himself in his fury. If someone was lying there when he did this, it would have been a nightmare.

The giant vase I made fun of got knocked over, split now into three uneven pieces. It lies forever ruined on the tomato-and-white chevron rug. I bend down to pick up a pillow beside it, and as tears pour from my disbelieving eyes, I gather the pillow close to my chest, bury my face in it, and sob.

There he is—Devin, his scent. And with my eyes closed, I can *see* him standing right in front of me the last time we were here together, when I asked him not to refer to me by my last name and all he wanted to do was kiss me. My emotions overpower me, and now I can't catch my breath. I cry into the pillow—really, really cry. I allow myself to finally feel the loss of him.

On shaking legs, I right the overturned desk chair and flop down on it in front of Devin's desk, which has taken its own beating. Nearly all the drawers were ripped from their slides and either thrown across the room or smashed to pieces on the desktop. Blank papers are scattered everywhere.

I wonder when William did this and if he ever learned of Devin's fate. I guess it doesn't matter, and I doubt I'll ever find out. Not that I'd want to, anyway.

My tortured sobs and heaving chest have settled a little, and then I see it. Across the desk, wedged between the remaining two sides of a battered drawer and propped against the broken window looking out over the backyard, is a pencil. One nearly perfect, new pencil—the only kind Devin ever used for writing. I wipe my face in the pillow I'm still holding, take one last, long breath through my nose, and stand. My fingertips stretch out as I reach over the desk and try to pluck the pencil from its resting spot. But it's stuck. I toss the pillow onto the bed, lean over the desk again, and yank. This time I get it out—one small victory. I hold the pencil in front of my face like it's a diamond, turning it every which way, admiring its simplicity and beauty, and I'm surprised by the tiny smile lifting the corners of my mouth.

This is how I have to remember him. Playful and flirty and genuine. That first day he showed me around the house, then brought me to meet the horses. My eyes dart from my new treasure to the window and beyond. I stretch my whole body farther over the desk, gazing out at the expansive lawn. My face is as close as I can get it to the window, and I look down. I can see the patio, where Devin and I shared meals, and where Leyla, Esmerelda, and I drank wine and planned our takeover.

My eyes follow the lawn to the edge of the wooded path leading to both Leyla's studio and the stables. Just like the house, the yard and grounds are not how I remember them— not so much destroyed by a raging monster but neglected and overgrown, the edges *blurred* and sloppy-looking. Nobody has come to button up the house and the grounds for the season like the rest of the homes in the luxury sector. The once turquoise pool is littered with leaves, and a faint green veil rests along its sides. The wind has carried various random items from the patio out onto the lawn—a cushion from a chair, somebody's shirt, or maybe it's a dress. And something is lying right at the edge of the path, half-covered by the trees. It looks like some kind of tool—a rake or a shovel. The stormy wind kicks up, and the trees above sway enough to reveal what lies below. It's a full-sized shovel, for sure, but the wind couldn't have carried it there. Someone dropped it, and it sure wasn't a landscaper. Nothing's been done to this yard in weeks.

The horses. Oh, my god. How have I not checked on the horses? He couldn't have... could he?

I shove the pencil in the collection bag, run out of Devin's room, and go straight down the hallway toward the back stairs so I can run out the sliding doors at the end of the kitchen. I move as fast as I can, and as I pass its stand, I notice the bronze statue of Leyla's horse Delia is missing. I do a quick spin, looking for it on the floor, but quickly realize William must have picked it up and launched it over the railing into the garden room. Just before I run down the back stairs, I twist my body and peer into the garden room below for a glimpse of what he's done. One hand slams over my mouth, and my other reaches out to steady myself on the railing.

A moan bursts out of me. I lurch and spin, looking for a way directly down to the room below. I consider jumping over the railing but instead turn and fly down the back stairway into the great room.

How do I get into the garden room from here? Where's the door, where do I turn, which way?

I stampede through the great room into a hallway, opening all the doors—a powder room, a closet, and then a glass double-door that has been smashed and now lies open.

I run to her and crouch down. She's lying at an unnatural angle, her left leg partially draped over the bronze dolphin. Her head rests in a pool of mostly dried, coagulated blood, one eye still open, the other swollen shut. Her body's bloated and most of her exposed skin is bruised.

"Esmerelda..." I sweep the hair from her forehead with trembling fingers. But she's as cold as my rational side expects her to be. "Esmerelda. You were supposed to hide. Or run... no. No..." My tears fall into her hair. I wipe it, dab at it, and my memory brings me back to the night she spilled food on William's shirt. The fear on her face, in her voice—she was terrified of him. She had good reason.

I look around, trying to figure out how she came to rest partially atop the dolphin statue. Then I look up and realize that bastard threw her over the railing. The slight tilt of the bannister above confirms it. But what was she doing up there when she was supposed to be hiding—when she was supposed to meet Leyla at the zeppelin?

Sitting back on the ground, I pull my knees up toward my chest and try to sort out my thoughts.

"I got you into this," I tell her softly. "I'm sorry. I'm so, so, sorry."

I lean over and place my hands on her arm. Her lifeless skin is unnerving, but I don't pull away. I won't pull away. "Esmerelda, I promise you..." I wrap my fingers around her right hand, desperately wanting to feel her return the gesture. "I promise you he will pay for this." I slide my fingers inside her rigidly balled fist. She's stiff, but I want to hold her hand, just for a moment. "He will not go unpunished for all he's done... if it's the last thing I do. I..."

My fingers catch against something rough and scratchy inside her hand. Is it just her skin, changing with death? I push my fingers in a little more, but they stop. There's definitely something in her hand. I concentrate on her fingers and slowly, carefully uncurl the first one. It feels like it's locked in place and if I push harder, it will break off. But there's something there. I force open the second finger, then look at her face. I don't know what I'm expecting—that she may feel the pain of my force and her expression will have somehow changed. But there she lies, exactly the same. Dead.

I push past my own guilt and force open the rest of her fingers. Inside, I find some kind of rolled then folded cloth. It's not big, but it's thick enough that she must have had to squeeze hard to keep it in her grip. Was she trying to hide this from William?

Now, like an archeologist who's just discovered ancient and important artifacts—and with the softest, most deliberate touch—I exhume the folded cloth from her hand. And as I unroll it, my heart drops into my stomach, and my ears fill with the sound of my racing heart. I open it fully and turn it over to read it, which I force myself to do out loud.

"Emancipation Ignites Power and Fuels Responsibility."

She cut it out, not him. That's why it was done with such

precision. Why did she cut this out? She was supposed to have left the island.

"Please tell me you didn't do this for me." I stand, fold the canvas, and shove it into the collection bag at my waist beside Devin's pencil.

"I'll be back. I just have to go check something." I leave Esmerelda, not allowing my shock and guilt to take control—not yet—and head toward the kitchen, out the glass doors, then across the patio and the lawn. Heading to the stables, picking up the shovel as I pass. The storm has grown in intensity, the wind howling, cold, and relentless.

The forested path is dark, and by the looks of it, I don't have long before I'm officially late. I don't care anymore. What are they going to do? Punish me? There's nothing anyone can do to me now that would trump the pain I already feel.

Before I'm even halfway to the stables, the wind carries my suspicions and confirms what I already know. When I get there, I find Delia first. She lies in the enclosure, drained of life, her body nearly unrecognizable after the sun and the elements have claimed her. Her neck was roughly cut open or stabbed by some large instrument. The shovel I drop beside her fits the bill.

I enter the enclosure, the gate left wide open, and search for the others. I walk the length of the fence, then look inside and around the outside of the barn, but there's nothing. The rain beats down on me, and I shiver uncontrollably.

"Neptune! Goliath!" I yell above the storm. The light's nearly gone as I squint down the enclosure toward the opening and into the fields beyond. I wait.

Nothing.

I run, yelling their names over and over. When I reach the opening, I stop. I don't know if I'm ready to face what I may find.

"Goliath? Neptune?" I yell again, then whisper, "Where are you?"

I pass through the space at the back of the enclosure to stand at the edge of the field. I'm alone. Utterly alone. There are no horses, no more flowers, no light at all. There is nothing. Just me.

Please, God. Please. Let them be okay. I close my eyes and just stand there.

A massive lightning bolt streaks across the sky, and I jump. I scan the endless field one last time, but I see nothing. Darkness has arrived. And I'm late.

I turn and leave the field, making my way back through the enclosure, and stand at Delia's side for a moment. "I'm sorry, Delia. You were very loved." There's nothing more I can do for her, but Esmerelda....

I leave the stables and return to the now dark house as quickly as I can. Once inside, I flip on a few lights and dig through the kitchen and dining room for as many candles as I can find. I bring them all back to the garden room, surround Esmerelda, and light them. Then I carefully lower her leg from the statue, place both her hands across her chest, and close her open eye.

"I love you, and I'm sorry," I whisper.

There are four candles left. In the great room, I light two—placing one under what remains of a sheer curtain and another directly under a cloth-covered chair. In the foyer, I light the remaining two candles and ignite the velvet curtains pooled on the floor. I leave the lit candles against a large wooden frame lying broken on its side against the wall from which it once hung. The torn, shredded canvas lights almost immediately.

I walk out the front door, leaving it open as it was, mount my board, and ride back toward the base through the pouring rain, my tears and cries now one with the storm.

The man at the front gate has been replaced by an equally enormous, cyborg-like individual who, I swear, is ready to shoot me like some random trespasser who won't take no for an answer.

"Go get your boss, you idiot!" I scream at the unflinching, inhuman guard. "Let me in. Ask him!"

He turns his back to me for a few minutes. It's pitch dark now, and I'm frozen to the core. If I'm forced to stay out here much longer, I may curl up and die of hypothermia.

Just as I'm sure I won't be admitted back onto the base—which would be just fine with me—I hear the click and hum of the swipe and the gate, and it swings open to let me inside. Before the entrance is fully clear, I push my way in and flip my middle finger at the charming man who I'm sure could kill me with one hand. I run the rest of the way to my cottage.

Although I didn't close the door when I left this morning, it's been closed, and for a second, I worry it's locked. But when I turn the handle, it opens freely. I jump inside and close the door, then lean back against it. My breath is raspy and uneven; my chest hurts with every inhale. The cottage is dimly lit, but I see the meal that's been left for me under a silver dome on the same cart William and I sat at last night. Last night. It feels like a lifetime ago.

There's a soft knock at the door just behind my head. I jump forward, not ready to face my father and whatever evil he'll bring with him tonight. But the door doesn't fly open in typical intrusive William Banks fashion. Another soft knock.

"Nerissa? It's Hani. Can I come in?"

I lean forward and open the door. "Why ask now, Hani?" Her eyes are wide, not expecting my knee-jerk reaction. "Why the manners now? The polite knock on the door. You usually just come and go as you please."

She stares at me for a second, then steps inside the cottage without my invitation. "I was just trying to be respectful."

"*Really*?" She's actually made me laugh, which at this point is like a magic trick. "You were trying to be respectful. That's a good one."

She ignores me and flips on the lights. "Give me the harvest."

I pace the room, not hearing her fully or responding to her at all. She tries to stop me by putting her hand in front of me as I walk.

"Nerissa..."

I keep pacing back and forth. As I turn to face the meal cart, I stop and pull open the silver dome. The smell of roasted duck wafts up at me, and Hani slams the top back down on the plate.

"Not yet."

"I'm starving, and I'm going to eat. Now."

"No, you're not." She steps between me and the cart and puts her hands on my shoulders. "Oh, my. You are so cold."

Hearing her say it suddenly makes it real and makes me fully aware of just how incredibly—maybe dangerously—uncomfortable I really am.

"Come." Hani gently but assertively turns me toward the bathroom. "You're going to get out of those wet things, take a hot shower, and get into some warm, dry clothes."

"But I'm hungry."

"You can eat when you're done. I'll warm everything up. Let's go."

She steers me into the bathroom and handles me like a child. I let her take control; I have nothing left inside me now and no strength to fight. I'm spent in every way. And if left to my own devices, who knows what I may do?

"Where's the other bag?" she asks, an urgency in her voice.

"What?"

"The collection bag. You were given two and expected to bring back two. Full."

"Oh, yeah... I lost it."

"How?" Her eyes dart anxiously to the bathroom door, like someone is just on the other side, listening.

I try to remember the overwhelming day I've had and the order in which everything happened. It all feels jumbled together, images from different moments colliding and combining. "Umm... the water was really rough in the storm. It just came off."

She frowns at me but doesn't say anything else.

"But look at how full that one is," I add. "It's stuffed. He has to be pleased with that."

Hani starts the shower, then flitters about doing whatever it is she does.

"Get in and stay in. Warm up, wash your hair... I'll be right back."

She guides me into the shower, and I realize how unstable I am—how completely physically and emotionally drained I am. She closes the glass shower door, picks up the Wreckleaf harvest, and leaves the bathroom. She's gone to deliver it to Lord William. Fine. He can kiss my ass.

An hour later, I'm clean, warm, hydrated, and fed. I don't even care that Hani's dressed me in some ridiculous black fleece caftan. It's warm and comfortable.

"Come on, you need to sleep." She gestures to my oh-so-cozy, institutional table-bed of metal.

"How about you order me up something a little more comfortable to sleep on?"

"I'll work on that. Just get on."

The door crashes open. In my exhausted state, I don't even flinch. "Oh, look who it is... my dear old dad."

"Miss John. Good evening."

"Is it? Is it really such a good evening? You bastard," I hiss at him.

"Oh..." He forms an exaggerated frown. "Why so huffy this evening?"

I clench my mouth tight and refuse to indulge him in his little game.

"I think these belong to you, Miss John." He places his hand into his pocket and pulls out the pencil I took from Devin's room and the folded emancipation canvas Esmerelda cut from the painting, holding them both up in front of us with his stupid, condescending smile contaminating these two precious mementos. I already know he'll never give them back to me. And I already know he's going to punish me, not just for losing one of the bags of Wreckleaf or for being late but also for going to his house.

I charge at him.

He doesn't have to try hard. He ducks out of the way to avoid my first attack, then he simply grabs me by my throat when I lunge at him again. I swing my fists, then try to scratch at his arms. My last choice is to try kicking between his legs, which he apparently anticipates and avoids. He's cutting off my air, starting to lift up as he pushes me back against the door. The smile never leaves his face.

"If you choose to fight, you will lose. And so will the rest of your breed."

I go slack and stop fighting. He makes sure I'm really done before he loosens his grip. When he finally lets go, I suck in a pained breath and crumple to the floor. He turns his back to me. Hani doesn't come to my side. She stands in the corner, her eyes down, waiting to do whatever William wants her to do.

"Why?" I ask.

My voice is so quiet, he spins around, bends over, and pretends he didn't hear me. "What's that?"

"Esmerelda… why?" I can't stop the tears. I never want to cry in front of him, but I think I'm finally broken.

He snaps upright and laces his fingers behind his back. "Ah, yes. Esmerelda." He nods, speaking as though he's delivering some narrative lesson in a school room, or like he's being interviewed by his fans. "Esmerelda was an interesting one. She really threw me a curveball."

"You killed her."

"Well, technically, yes I did. But if we really dissect the situation, Esmerelda killed herself." He chuckles.

"What are you talking about? She didn't throw herself over that railing."

"No, of course not. I did that. Funny where she landed, don't you think? A little ironic?" He's giddy, and I feel like I'm about to be sick. "But I didn't know she was still there. I was in Devin's room, just, you know, taking a little break after doing some reorganizing. I saw a shadow from under the door, moving in the hallway. I stepped out, and there she was. You should have seen the look on her face. 'Oh, Mr. William, I'm so glad to see you. Did you catch the thieves?'"

"Please stop," I beg.

"I didn't know what she was doing. I do now, of course." He lifts the canvas again. "I didn't care. I grabbed that bitch by the throat. Oh, I guess that's my thing." He laughs again. "And I just… dragged her down the hall a little and hoisted her over the railing. The sound her melon made when it hit the floor and popped open."

"*Stop!*" I yell and slam my hands over my ears.

He bends down, grabs my wrist, and lifts me up off the floor. "Now, why would you deny your father the opportunity to tell you a bedtime story? Hani!"

Hani jumps into action, stepping immediately to his side before she guides me back toward the bed.

"Wait just a moment, Hani." She stops at his command and waits. "Miss John, turn around and look at me."

I reluctantly do as I'm instructed.

"I told you not to be late. You were." He pulls back his arm and launches his fist with full-force directly at my face. The strike throws me backward and sparkles burst behind my eyes. I stumble and crash against the bed, landing in a heap on the floor. The pain is mind-numbing, I'm dizzy, and even my ears are ringing.

"Get her up."

Hani helps me to my feet. She turns me to face him again, the blood pouring from above my quickly swelling eye and blurring my vision.

"You were to fill two collection bags, and you only delivered one." His second strike comes from the other side. Not as strong with his left hand, but enough to spin me around, split my lip, and possibly loosen a tooth. But I don't fall again.

I spit blood on the floor and turn back around to face him. "One more, right, Daddy?" I say through my fat lip and excruciating pain.

"You were not invited to my home today, Miss John. Don't *ever* set foot on my property again!" His uppercut to my jaw lifts me off my feet. My back slams onto the metal bed, my legs still propped on the floor, and I don't move. I can't move, fighting for consciousness, and I've bitten my tongue pretty badly. Blood floods my mouth and sinuses, and he may have broken my jaw. I can't tell; the pain is too much to think with any more clarity.

Hani lifts my legs and slides me onto the bed. I guess the beating's over. For now.

She moves to the counter and retrieves a vial and needle before filling it. When she puts the vial back into the refrigerator, she pulls out a second one and fills another needle. I close my eyes and hold out my arm. Yes, please. I'll take two. Hell, I'll take three, or better yet, all she's got. Take me away. From this place, from this horror, from this life. Take me away from him.

The first needle slides into my arm, and the cloud spreads inside me. I barely feel the second needle, but whatever it is, I no longer feel any pain. Just like that, in an instant, my mind blurs, shutting down and going dark and still. All I want to do is sleep—maybe never wake up. But I have one thing left to say.

"I promise to never set foot on your property again... only because there won't be anything left. Fuck you, Officer Banks."

CHAPTER 9
SURVIVAL
LIKE FATHER, LIKE DAUGHTER, I GUESS.

OCTOBER

I've lost track of what day it is. William likes it that way. And I've become more than just his source of Wreckleaf. I've become his pet, which he also likes—very much. Not the kind of pet that is treated like a part of the family, unconditionally loved and cared for, our affections mutual and mutually expressed. No, I'm more the kind of pet to an owner who does just that—*owns* their *companion*. I'm expected to heel at his side for long stretches of time as he parades me around like a trophy animal he just subdued.

William is a monster, more so than I realized. He disguises all his atrocities behind his prep-boy formality, the perfect annunciation of his carefully chosen vocabulary, the tastes he's grown accustomed to, and the high standards he expects from everything and everyone around him. But that's only his meticulously crafted façade. He's a beast, capable of things I didn't realize anyone could fathom. And the problem is, I never know which side of him I'll get.

I've been hit in the face more times than I can count. He seems determined to take my beauty away forever. I've been wined and dined equally as much—each time with an injection or two and paired with jumbled, blurry stories of William's past. I'm like his confessional, perfectly riding the line between awareness and drug-induced amnesia. But when Hani injects me, unless William is watching, I don't get a full dose. Sometimes, I wish Hani would give me the whole thing. I don't want to remember the things he tells me. Not now—not anymore.

The injections are closer together now, as I've become William's personal test subject. Some are even given in the middle of the night. Those I don't remember clearly, sometimes not at all. Who knows? I may be imagining them or dreaming them. The lines of what's real and what's not are blurrier by the day.

I don't know what they give me; he'd never tell me but there's a kind of pattern.

When I wake up, I'm now greeted by a man who calls himself my day nurse and who gives me something very stimulating. My heart speeds up immediately, making me wide-eyed and almost manic. The day nurse, who has the warmth and personality of a bag of rocks and whose name I still don't know, takes my vitals. Every couple of days, he draws my blood. If I had to guess, I'd say this morning dose is the Wreck-leaf-infused drug simulating the condensed effects of Aqua Tonic—the same thing they gave to some of the lab animals. But I'm a Dolhuphemale. I'm used to C. Periculosis Abscondita coursing through my bloodstream, even though it's not the processed version I'm getting now. If he's giving those creatures anywhere near the amount he's giving me, they're living short and tortured lives.

That fast and furious buzz always ends with a massive crash. Not long after dosing, I can barely hold myself up or keep my eyes open. Next comes what I've affectionately termed the *Long-Dark-Haul*. This one is also an upper, but it's different. I get this intense pressure in my head for a few minutes, then a burst of laser-sharp focus and clarity, followed by hours and hours of near OCD. I'm compelled to achieve—to perform tasks to perfect completion. I feel no physical weakness or discomfort, no hesitation, no emotional attachment to anything or anyone, and no remorse. These are the slots of time William has me work in the test labs. He often watches, the corners of his mouth turned up in evil subtlety as I administer drugs to the innocent lab animals, even as they cry out in pain or fear. Or I clean up after them or remove their dead bodies. This is also the drug he gives me before he sends me to Albatross for harvest. This is what he meant when he told me my first visit there would be the only of its kind. It's the only time I've been back while not under the numbing and emotionless effects of the *Long-Dark-Haul*. I imagine this routine will continue through the fall and winter, with the extreme danger of the ocean and the fear it would naturally invoke.

As a sort of consolation, William's told me the Madoosik tend to go into a kind of semi-hibernation in the colder months and that they'll leave me alone. But I don't care—not when I'm on that drug. I don't care about anything.

Every time I arrive at Albatross, my mother and the rest of the breed are shocked and concerned by my state. And it doesn't affect me. I don't respond, I don't return their attempts at affection. I can't help it. I can't even explain it to them, and in the moment, I don't want to. But after every visit, back on the base and once the *Long-Dark-Haul* has worn off, I cry. I ache to return my mother's love, Kendra's love, the care and concern from the rest of our breed.

In response to my tears and the emotions upon returning to the cottage—which I'm starting to learn how to control—it's then time for Hani to inject me with a sedative. Although, I'm sure I'd be given it anyway, even if I didn't cry or get upset. It's just the order of things. I don't mind this one, because it takes the emotional pain away—or at least numbs it a bit. And it soothes the battering my body takes from the water, the elements, and from William. This is usually just before dinner, and if I'm graced with my father's company, I'm dosed with another drug just before or upon his arrival.

That one always kills my appetite, no matter how hungry I was right before. When no one's watching, Hani only gives me partial doses. We don't talk about it; she just gives me some, then squirts the rest in the sink. She has to give me at least a little, so I "act" right in front of William. At these twisted daddy-daughter dinner dates, he always offers wine, which I always accept.

I've been given other *freedoms*, as William promised. But they're not so much freedoms as just other ways to submit to him. There's no consistency to their timing and no way to plan for them. He allows me short jaunts off the base, drug-free—though I'm sure there's no such thing for my body at this point; I'm toxic from the constant barrage. I usually get forty-five minutes, sometimes up to an hour. He knows this isn't enough time to visit Albatross. And if I'm not back promptly at the time he sets for me, I am punished. After I came back late from that first solo venture to Albatross, anyone would have thought I'd never make that mistake again. But I did, one more time. It was the last time.

My punishment for being late again was a punch in the stomach that knocked the wind out of me. In typical William fashion, he showed condescending remorse for his deplorable action and promised me a nice surprise—a visit to see Lillian. I reacted as he expected, maybe even exactly as he wanted, but I will never be able to un-see what he showed me that day.

William and I walk down the gravel path toward the farthest corner of the base. I have to hold my bruised stomach as we walk, in terrible pain, but my eagerness to see Lillian helps me keep up with William's ridiculous pace. We pass Walter's enclosure, but it appears empty. I don't ask where Walter the security animal is. I don't want to know.

We round a final bend in the path, and there stands a lone cottage, much bigger than the rest but otherwise outwardly identical. Just beyond and to the right of the cottage, built into the rock with an open area in front, sits a large, hydraulic lift manned by a helmeted operator. It carries supplies and materials down the cliff to the rocky shore and the boathouse.

William opens the door and steps aside. "After you, Miss John."

The inside of this cottage is entirely different than anything else. The sleek, reflective, sterile environment reminds me of one place and one place only—a mini version of the old Bio-Gen building and the labs on Black Rock. Three closed doors dot the single hallway, all with the same small, vertical windows.

"Last room, please." William gestured with an extended arm.

I stop in front of the last door and peer inside. The sight makes my head swim in dizzy circles. I don't wait for his invitation to open the door before I step inside the blazing-white room.

Lillian has become a prisoner now, contained in an enclosure similar to the clear boxes in which Rena and Cecelia were caged. But this entrapment is even more cruelly violating. Completely naked, she's suspended at a forty-five degree angle in some kind of clear, gelatinous liquid; her position appears to allow access to every part of her body. Some kind of breathing apparatus, not unlike a diving regulator but smaller, covers her mouth and nose. Her eyes are taped shut, but she's cocks her head in wary anticipation at the sound of my footsteps—she can obviously hear. As soon as William speaks, her entire body jolts in fear.

"Isn't this a masterpiece of scientific advancement, Miss John?"

I can't speak at first, but when I see Lillian turn her head at my name, as if waiting to hear my voice, I answer him. "It's the farthest thing from advancement. It's barbaric. You're torturing her. Lillian... I'm here. It's Nerissa."

"She's not in any pain, I assure you."

"Yeah, right." I know he'll quickly grow impatient with me not agreeing with him, but I just can't be okay with this. "What are you doing to her?"

He only stares at Lillian and her constraints with total admiration.

"I asked you what you're doing to her. Tell me!"

William snaps his head in my direction. "Miss John, you will mind your tone with me."

I lower my gaze and take a deep breath, my sore stomach reminding me to either comply or pay the price—again. "Yes. I'm sorry, of course. I'm just curious. Would you explain what you're doing here? Please?"

He turns his head back and lifts his eyes slightly, apparently pleased with my compliant answer. "Miss Charles is helping us with some hybrid technology." He smiles and sighs through his nose.

Before I lose it again, I bite my lip.

"We'd like to see what happens when certain species are combined," he continues. "Miss Charles showed up at just the right time. We have a live host. Isn't that lucky?"

"But... I thought it was—"

"What, impossible? You know it's not... look at yourself."

"No," I say, "I thought it was illegal."

"You also know that's not true. We sell hybrids all across the island during the Season."

"I don't mean the little harmless souvenirs. I mean the full-sized ones, like me... I thought that was illegal. That *I* was illegal."

"Well," he scoffs, "not entirely. Depends on who you are and who you know."

Just as the words leave his lips, two men dressed in lab coats enter the room. The first is a short man carrying a foot-long cylinder along with some other tools on a silver tray, including a large needle and a vial. The other is a well-groomed, handsome younger man, holding some kind of electronic device.

"Oh! What perfect timing. Miss John, we are most fortunate today." William sounds positively giddy. Lillian thrashes in slow motion, the gelatin preventing normal movement.

"Why... why are we so... fortunate?" Tears form in my eyes, because I already know the answer. And there's no coincidence in the timing of this.

"We are here just in time for implantation." He turns and looks right at me. But I don't return his stare. I'm locked on to the scene unfolding in front of me.

"Good afternoon, Officer Banks," the short man says.

"Indeed it is. Same to you, Dr. Picker."

"This is my apprentice, Dr. Bigelow."

"Ah, yes. The newest addition to our team. Congratulations on your advancement and welcome to Panacea. I think this was a wonderful idea, and I'm sure you'll be quite happy here." William offers the young doctor a hearty handshake.

"Thank you, sir. It is a pleasure to make your acquaintance. I hope to do Bio-Gen proud, sir."

"Well, you come from pristine lineage and with sparkling reviews, young man." William beams with pride.

The young doctor can only respond with a faint blush and suddenly shy eyes.

I must be hallucinating all of this—another drug-induced fantasy. This can't be real.

"All right, gentlemen... and lady." Dr. Picker flashes me a quick glance. "Shall we begin?"

"Yes, please. Tell me, Dr. Picker, what's the next specimen for trial today?" William asks.

The next?

"We're going to give the Harvester another round," Dr. Picker explains. "We cleaned up the host's internal organs a little and discovered she'd had a previous miscarriage. That probably contributed to the loss of the first trial. She should hold it this time."

My head fills with a steady buzzing and images of baby Charlotte's funeral. The room begins to spin and I feel a cold sweat pass over me.

William notices me swaying next to him and grabs me roughly. "Oh, no. You're going to want to see this. It's simply fascinating." He squeezes my arm hard, drawing me back to full attention.

"Dr. Bigelow, the anesthesia," Dr. Picker instructs.

"Yes, of course—"

"Excuse me, doctors," William interrupts.

"Yes, Officer Banks?" Dr. Picker turns toward him.

"Let's skip the anesthesia, shall we?"

"That is not advised, sir," Dr. Bigelow replies, a slight pause in his delivery. "This procedure will cause significant pain."

"Yes, I'm sure it will. Nevertheless, we don't want to take the chance of any drug interfering with implantation. We don't want to lose another opportunity. And rest assured, this breed is very hearty. Very strong. Isn't that right, Miss John?" He squeezes my arm.

I can't speak.

He squeezes me again even harder and shakes me into focus. "Isn't that right?"

"Yeah... um, right." My eyes fall to the floor, and I lower my head again.

"Officer Banks, this is highly unusual, and I don't recommend—"

"Do as I say," William interrupts. "Now, let's begin."

The room stalls in an awkward silence. There's a shuffling and the sounds of tools sliding off the tray—a click and a twist. Then a rubber fabric is snapped and smoothed out. I start to cry, moving side to side with tiny, dreading steps.

William grabs my chin and forces it up. "You will watch."

I struggle against his grip and squeeze my eyes shut.

"Open your eyes."

I shake my head again.

"Open your eyes now, or things will be ever so much worse. I promise you." He squeezes my chin so hard it feels like he could dislodge my teeth from the outside. He brings his mouth down to my ear. "Open your damn eyes right now," he spits through clenched teeth, "or you will have to watch much worse than this."

I force open my eyes. The dammed-up tears flood down my face. When my vision clears, I stare straight ahead but cross my eyes just enough to blur my focus. Even with that, I can still see too much.

Dr. Picker has opened something at the bottom of Lillian's enclosure, where some of the items on the tray have already been inserted. And he's slid his arms into two built-in *gloves*, extending into the gelatinous world in which Lillian is trapped. Without moving my head, I flick my gaze toward the apprentice, Dr. Bigelow. He's watching William, then briefly meets my eyes, turns, and types something into his device. He returns his attention to the impending procedure, then types more. Back and forth he goes—watching, then typing. I try to focus on his notetaking. Just a new doctor taking notes, learning, observing —I can do that. That seems normal.

Lillian's muffled screams rise through the liquid and the glass, overtaking my world. All except for his voice in my ear.

"Don't ever be late again, Miss John."

NOVEMBER

Someone is in my cottage. I don't know who—I don't really care. I hear them slide something across the counter. I think. It's completely dark, and I can't see anything. It must be the middle of the night. My head is swimming in the wine I had just a few hours ago.

"Hani?" I ask weakly.

"Just relax. I'll be finished in a moment."

I stop trying to see and let my eyes flutter closed again. The needle slides into my arm with a tiny pinch, and a cool wave washes through me, forcing me to inhale sharply. Then everything relaxes. Everything feels better.

"That's it. There you go. Now sleep, child."

THE NEXT NIGHT

William dances with my mother on the pier at Wave nightclub. They're comfortably up against each other, William's hand on the small of her back, the other holding hers, raised by their sides as they dance and spin to some unheard melody. They're smiling and laughing. They can't see me. In fact, I can't even see myself. But I'm here, and I'm aware.

Devin steps up to them. "Just like old times, huh? I have a note for you, Dad. Here you go." He hands William an envelope that looks just like the kind his father uses, and William stops dancing with Tatiana to open it.

"What does it say?" my mother asks.

"It's from Gabriel." As he reads, William's mouth twists up in exaggerated happiness, and his eyes follow. He tilts his head back and laughs.

"What does it say? Read it to me," my mother says.

"Oh, yeah, yeah... this is good." He takes a deep breath and wipes the tears from the corners of his eyes. "Get this... 'Dear Master Banks, I am so pleased that you helped me to finally understand how things really are. I'm done being used, and I am entirely at your disposal. Gabriel.'" He throws his head back in laughter once again. My mother joins him, producing a shrill, ear-splitting cackle. My disembodied head vibrates, and Devin suddenly appears inches in front of my face.

"You hybrid slut."

My eyes open, and I jolt upright. Only my ankles are bound. The room is dark and silent. I'm alone.

SOME OTHER DAY

I've only got fifteen minutes before I'm late. He gave me one hour and I decided to go down to the river. It's different there in the fall and winter months—not lush, no full canopy. Not barren, by any means, just starker, colder. But the water stays quite calm, and even though I wanted—needed—the river to bring me some peace of mind, some sense of belonging or hope, some little scrap of joy, it didn't. It couldn't. I am a shell. Nothing more.

I'm just about back to the front gate, and I'm on time. I hope William is pleased. I hope he's proud of me.

LATER THAT DAY

I remove the dead creature from its cage. The soft fur only covers part of its body now, the rest having fallen out from stress, or toxicity, or something else. It doesn't matter.

Some guy in a lab coat is talking to me. William isn't here, for a change.

"When you're done cleaning out that cage, prep it for a new subject. And don't forget to switch out the dosing chart. We need to start over."

I don't answer him, don't need to engage in idle chit-chat. I just follow his drone of endless instructions. Hours go by. By the time my duties are all fulfilled, the *Long-Dark-Haul* is wearing off, and it's time to leave. I don't say goodbye.

As I step out the door of the makeshift lab, I briefly consider turning left to check on Lillian, if she's still there—or still alive. Instead, the door to her prison opens and William steps out, looking over a clipboard as he closes the door behind him.

"Ah, Miss John. I've been informed of your efforts today. Good work."

"Thank you."

"I'm headed back toward your cottage. Walk with me."

He passes me and waits at the main entrance. My head feels strangely detached from my body as my thoughts readjust to actually caring about anything. But the tail end of the *Long-Dark-Haul* is slow and sporadic, my emotions and reactions ranging from complete apathy to being overwhelmed with sadness or rage. This is not the time I want to be with anyone, let alone walk with William. But I have no choice.

He holds the door open for me as I approach him, a small smile softening his features. "After you, Miss John."

I step out onto the path. The air is crisp and cool as the sun descends behind us. A small shiver rolls through me, and I cross my arms over my chest.

We walk in silence side by side for most of the way. But when we come to the place we'd turn at if we were headed to Walter's electrified enclosure, I can't help myself.

"What happened to Walter?"

William briefly slows his pace. "I wondered when you would ask. If you would ask."

"Is he dead?"

"I honestly don't know."

He sounds sincere, and for some reason, I believe him. "Why don't you know?"

"Well, the last time I saw that creature was when he held me to the ground just before Klein shot me in the leg. That's the last time I saw Klein, too."

"Oh."

"I woke up in Walter's enclosure something like twelve

hours later. I was completely alone. Everyone was gone. At first I thought I was dead."

He should have been. They should have finished it.

"I guess it wasn't your time," I say.

William stops and turns to look at me. "Yes, that's right, Miss John. I have much left to do. So much life left to live and work to be done." He puts his hand on my shoulder. Part of me wants to step back, not sure what to expect, but I don't. "You know, you can be a part of that."

I just stare back at him, my mind a web of chaos and contradiction. William breaks my trance by removing his hand and gesturing down the path for us to continue toward my cottage.

When we're at the entrance, a strange sense of comfort comes over me. William reaches past me and opens the door, stepping back to allow me to enter. But before I step in, I can't help but ask, "How is she?"

He tilts his head slightly and raises his eyebrows. "I'm sorry?"

"Lillian. How is she?"

His head straightens, and he nods the tiniest nod. "Miss Charles is doing quite well. It finally stuck."

"Stuck?"

"The implantation. It took another round, but the last one finally stuck. Miss Charles is pregnant and things are going along smoothly."

Things.

"When is she due?" I ask, with no emotion.

"The metabolic rate of the trial fetus is quite fast. The gestation should be less than half the normal rate. It could even be a third of a regular pregnancy, but we're not sure of the exact time. But after it's born, it will grow and mature quickly."

"What is it? The fetus?"

William smiles at me. "It's a Harvester."

My face freezes in a twisted grimace. Of course it's a Harvester. I wonder when he would have told me if I hadn't asked. I force my face to unscrew as I take a deep breath and step into my cottage. William watches me in silence.

"Is Hani coming?" I ask.

"As always. And I'll be back in an hour or so. Let's continue our lovely conversation with dinner and wine, shall we?"

I close my eyes, and I know by the darkness seeping into me—by the heaviness in my chest and the aching pit in my stomach—the *Long-Dark-Haul* has worn off.

Without turning around, I force myself to answer him with a steady voice. "Yes. That sounds nice."

"Wonderful." William shuts the door, and I'm alone. My strength runs out of me, and I wilt to the floor, expecting the usual torrent of emotion. But the tears don't flow this time. The shaking and crying don't come. Just the cloak of darkness —the veil of nothingness.

Hani comes and goes, leaving me clothed in a lace lavender dress, dosed with less than half the usual pre-dinner cocktail of drugs, and sitting at the overly elegant food cart, waiting for my dinner guest.

I decide not to wait for William to pour myself a glass of wine. Even after I asked Hani to give me the full doses, she refused. I said if she didn't, I'd tell my father what she'd been doing—cutting all my doses in half or more, trying to spare me from the oblivion they produced at full strength. But she knew I was only saying that, only wanting to escape what's to come and what has already been—the things swirling around in my thoughts, behind my eyes, and in my heart any time I can actually feel. Hani knows I'd never do or say anything to hurt her, or get her in trouble. She's kind to me. My only true friend, it seems.

So, wine it is. My drug of choice to pick up the slack, to numb away the gap left from the incomplete dosing.

My choice to start without him may land me in trouble. But I don't care. I put the glass to my lips and take a sip. The cold, bubbly liquid slides down my throat, coating my insides with deceptive promise. A compromise, at the very least. Take care of me now, and I'll pay the price later—the price I've convinced myself is worth it. I gulp down the whole glass and promptly pour another.

William knocks on the door and opens it as I'm putting down the bottle.

"Well," he chuckles, "someone was thirsty."

I reach under the cart and retrieve a second glass from the next rung of shelves and place the perfect, sparkling crystal flute next to mine. My arm is heavy—or maybe it's the bottle—but it's hard to aim, and I miss the glass twice, pouring a little wine on the cart before I'm able to fill William's glass. He watches me, seemingly amused by my attempts, one knuckle over his broad smile.

I lift the glass and hand it to him. He takes it with gentle fingers. "Thank you, Miss John."

I don't answer but look him directly in the eyes.

"Thank you, Nerissa," he says and tilts his flute toward mine. "Cheers."

I slowly lift my glass and clink it on his. "Cheers."

The intoxication comes on slowly; I must be developing a tolerance. But I try to make it seem like I'm incoherent even before dinner is over. I slouch low in my chair and close my eyes while William cuts his food into perfect, bite-sized morsels, scraping his knife and fork against the plate in an inescapable and jarring rhythm.

"Oh, Miss John." He clears his throat. "Nerissa... you are a cheap date." He chuckles. "But I do love our dinner chats. And I think you'd actually like my stories if you could pay attention. Your mother always said you had a fascination with such things. For uncovering the truth."

A lot of good it's done me.

"Like father, like daughter, I guess." He's beginning to slur. Even with my eyes closed, I can tell he's drinking down another glass of wine, the slurping and swallowing exaggerated as he gets drunker and drunker. "You know, I knew you'd... you'd challenge me one day. I just knew it. Even when you were a small child, I could tell... and she told me. I just thought you might be older. But that night you came ashore with Anastasia... it was... just... perfect..."

My eyes snap open. He doesn't notice, his own focus untrained on anything in particular.

"My father did not like my ideas..." he continues. "Oh! You're awake."

"What are you talking about?" I stare at him without moving.

"I know. It must be confusing." He stands up, fighting for balance, and walks toward me. "Let's get you to bed." He stumbles into me and awkwardly tries to help me up from my chair. I hesitate, then rise and allow him to guide me.

"You were talking about when I was a small child. What were you going to say?" I ask as he gently directs me to my bed.

"Time for you to sleep now." He pushes lightly down on my shoulder, and when I sit down on the bed, he leans over and grabs both my feet in one sloppy movement to swing them onto the bed as well. Nearly falling over, he retrieves the blanket bunched up on the floor and, without smoothing it out, throws it on top of me. "Lie down."

I follow his order.

"We'll talk again soon... I'll explain everything. I promise." He turns away and walks to the door. He doesn't lock me in my restraints. "Goodnight... Nerissa." Then he turns out the light and exits the cottage.

CHAPTER 10
THE VOID
SURVIVAL.

TIME UNKNOWN

Darkness.
Fog.
Endless cold water.
Faces.
Voices.
Dreams.
Icy fingers.
Blurred images.
Hallucination.
Needles.
Apathy.
Emptiness.
Hate.
Confusion.
Death.
Discomfort.
Wine.

Stories.
Lies.
Delays.
Excuses.
Denial.
Pain.
Futility.
Empathy.
Connection.
Survival.

CHAPTER II

BIO-GENESIS

ALL I CAN DO IS AGREE.

THURSDAY, FEBRUARY 27TH

"Come on. I've got a big surprise for you." Everything is dark and blurry, and William's voice comes at me like we're in a tunnel. A sharp slap of freezing water hits my face and forces my focus into a sharp return. William is wearing a thick blue poncho and boots, walking backward in front of me and coaxing me down a slick wooden pier as he shields himself from the cold wind and sea spray. I'm standing, observing myself, not yet able to connect my head and my thoughts to the rest of my body. I'm also in a blue poncho, and sensation quickly returns as the wind against my damp skin rolls a violent shiver through me.

"Where am I?" I ask, unsure if I'm even awake.

"Look around!" he yells over the sound of the turbulent water surrounding us.

I do as he says, and just like the feeling returning to my body, attaching all the parts together, recognition dawns. "Why are we here?"

119

"I told you. Because I've got a surprise for you."

"What is it?" I ask, even though I'm not remotely curious. The last time William had a surprise for me, I had to watch Lillian being violated by a piece of man-operated machinery that implanted some kind of beast in her womb. No thanks. No more surprises. I'll take a pass. The only thing I want to know is how I got here. William notices my detachment.

"Oh... come on, now. You're going to like it, I promise."

"How did we get here?" I ask.

"Is that a rhetorical question?" He laughs at his own lame joke.

"No."

I'm forgetting big chunks of time—the things I've done or said. And I don't remember how I got here, how I happen to suddenly be standing in this wretched place. I don't even know what day it is. Months have gone by in this fog. I hate myself for checking out. I hate myself for the surrender, for my submission to him and to my new reality. Eventually, I even gave up trying to understand that night after dinner, when he thought I was asleep or passed out. I stopped trying to coax an explanation out of him. I just finally couldn't take the brutality and the uncertainty of it any longer. It's easier now, even without my full memory. Nothing has been as vivid since that last particular evening. Perhaps he's designed it that way. That's fine.

The punishments and extreme cruelty have stopped. At least, I think they have. He's softer now—not kind, as he still knows exactly how to bite with his words and his presence. He's just a bit more human. But he's still just as intimidating and I'm sure as unstable, and I know not to test him. I know he could flip that switch at any moment, so I just go along with want he says and what he wants. I play along, and sometimes he can actually be nice, charming—or at least it seems that way as long as I not only comply but engage him, indulge him, and *appear* happy. And he allows me more *freedoms,* as he calls it. But my only real consolation is knowing I'm keeping the last of my breed alive.

I can't even recall their faces lately—how they've acted or responded to me when I come to Albatross. I only have bits and pieces, flashes of moments now. It's like I'm living in a stop-frame movie. Or a choppy dream world. The drugs I'm bombarded with daily have caught up, even with Hani still only giving me partial doses. They blur the lines between reality and the dream world. Sometimes, my waking hours are so clouded, I'm sure they're dreams. And other times, my dreams are so clear, so feeling, I'm convinced they're real. I wish many of them were. The dreams of *him*—of us.

What I do know is Kendra will give birth soon. Her belly is big, and she seems more and more uncomfortable. But she's in good hands.

Another flash, a small, fuzzy blip in my memory, is the door at Concordia—the lock I picked and the swipe I smashed. The swipe was finally replaced after being left the way I rendered it for a long time, it seems. But its light was green, and before I chose to smash it again, I put my hand on the knob and turned it. It opened. Someone forgot to reset it. Before I found out who, or why, I turned around, left the property, and went to Playa Rosa to do things the old-fashioned way. I was almost late getting back to the base. Almost.

"Come on. It's freezing out here." William steals back my attention. "Let's walk and talk." He waits for a second, watching me, and when I take my first few steps toward him, he turns around to face the cliff and walks toward the staircase. I follow.

As I soak in my surroundings—the dark island drenched in winter's numbing rains, a fine cloud of misty fog shrouding the unyielding gloom—my mind is bombarded with images, memories of my last night here on Black Rock. These are the things I'll never be able to forget, even if I wanted to.

I walk over the spot where Devin last stood. Even though I'm quite certain this is a new dock, this is the spot where he collapsed under Ana's weapon fire—the place that ripped out and stole a piece of my heart forevermore. I shake the images from my head.

William is at the staircase, also a new version of what once was here. He waits for me. We ascend the stairs in silence, and once we're at the top and out of breath, he finally speaks.

"Whew... that is a lot of stairs."

I don't reply.

"We gave you a very strong sedative for the trip out here. It was a rough ride. But don't worry, I've also given you something to counteract that effect. I want you to be fully present for this."

"You gave me a strong sedative? Why? You realize I'm the only one that would have survived if we capsized?"

He nods his head. "Yes, that's why we gave it to you."

"Ha! What? You think I would have tried to capsize the boat?" I ask.

"Maybe. Or maybe you'd push the crew and me overboard."

"Well, I wasn't planning on it, but I'll keep that in mind." I force a smile.

William actually chuckles, then proceeds down the same maze of walkways carving the approach to the old, long-gone labs. We meander through the rock, and I have to force my mind to block the onslaught of old memories.

He stops suddenly, clears his throat, steps aside, and extends his arm to showcase the *surprise* we've come to see. "I present to you... the new and improved Bio-Genesis Wave Technologies Laboratories and Research Center."

I realize why I didn't immediately see the building, aside from the vicious replay in my head, as we rounded the final turn. For as bright, white, stark, and sterile as the previous building was—in sharp contrast to its surroundings—the new Bio-Gen is as black and impenetrable as the landscape. But it's slick and shiny, the only thing discerning it from the surrounding volcanic rock. The black glass and steel remind me of the Madoosik—shrewd and camouflaged against its environment, its presence commanding and undeniable, ready to snatch up unsuspecting prey with one swift, invisible move. And it's big—much bigger, it seems, than its predecessor. I take it in as it takes my breath away.

"Impressive, isn't it?"

I don't know what to say. Then I notice the one thing that's missing. "You didn't put the name on it this time."

"What?"

"Nothing. Why did you bring me here?"

"Because this is your new home, of course," he says, his chest puffed out, his hands on his hips as he looks at his new *baby*.

"My new home?"

"Yes. It's not completely finished, not entirely operational, but much of what we needed to concentrate on is, and the rest will be complete in time for the opening of the new Season, thanks to my investors. And this will be where you will live from now on."

I feel like a child being told they're moving away from home—the one they've grown accustomed to, to knowing, to feeling ties to, and I'm not having it. "But... what about the cottage?"

"Well, that was always temporary," he says. "Surely you must remember me telling you that."

"But this is going to make everything so much more… difficult. Every time I need to harvest, I'll have to cross the channel. You know I can't just swim to Albatross from here. It's too dangerous. This will take so much longer, and—"

"Yes, it will. But that's okay."

"Are you going to sedate me every time I need to cross the channel?"

"No. I'm going to make sure you know how to handle a boat on your own."

"I'd rather swim. You said the Madoosik are in hibernation."

William laughs. "No, you will take a boat. You *just* said it's too dangerous. I agree. And I said the Madoosik are in a kind of *semi*-hibernation."

Is this William caring about my safety?

"You need to save yourself for the swim to Albatross," he adds.

I guess not.

"Besides, I'm happy to tell you that you'll soon be relieved of your harvesting duties, so you won't even need to worry about any of this." His smile is plastered to his face, unflinching, and he stares at me with a certain eagerness, like he's waiting for me to take some kind of bait.

I wait nearly ten seconds, just holding his gaze, breathing heavily through my nostrils. He never moves, and then I bite. "How am I going to be *relieved*… of my harvesting duties?" I ask softly and slowly.

His face finally unfreezes. "I'm so glad you asked, Nerissa. The answer is two-fold. And I think I should show you instead of telling you. Come with me." He turns on his heels and walks toward the foreboding structure. I briefly consider running in the opposite direction but decide against it.

"More surprises?"

"Indeed."

Walking through the new building makes me feel like I've been given some kind of mind-altering, hallucinatory drug. Who knows? Maybe I have. It's like I'm looking at an inside-out, reverse image of what was here before—like after staring at an object long enough, then looking away to still see its outline. Only all the colors are reversed. The antiseptic, barren white hallways are gone, replaced with sleek, dark, polished granite and deep, coal-colored wood. It's everywhere—on the floors, the walls, the desks and countertops. Only the ceiling varies from this theme, bright white and trimmed in brushed steel. Tiny flecks of gold and silver in the stone catch the light and reflect back onto itself, the space looking more like a temple or luxury hotel. But Panacea has never seen anything like this before.

The new, two-story lobby houses a massive water feature. It's not yet full or operating.

"Isn't this special? I wish I could say this was all my idea, but it wasn't. Let me show you a rendering of what it'll look like when it's complete." William darts behind a desk, giddy and almost flamboyant, retrieves a folder, returns to my side, and opens it. "We're standing here." He points to a spot on the image and taps it with his finger. "Right in front of us," he adds, gesturing toward the large rectangular pool in front of us, "is the Koi pond and fountain. And just there, at the end of the pool, the bust will be erected."

"The bust?" I try not to sound too sarcastic.

"Yes. Let's see. There's an image of it here somewhere…"

As he flips through the papers in the folder, I'm sure he's about to show me some atrocious tribute to himself. Maybe the same artist who gifted him with his bronze dolphin and rider after his implementation of the original Cooperative will be commissioned to create this as well.

"Here, here it is."

I follow his finger to a white marble bust the size of a massive boulder, depicting the one person I would be more than happy to remove from this earth. I can't help but burst out laughing. "I should have guessed! Did she design that herself?"

"Yes, Alexandria designed this whole lobby. Most of the building, as a matter of fact."

"Well, you've got yourself a larger-than-life *fairest Beauty* of them all." I scoff. "I sure hope my room is far away from this." It all just comes out, almost involuntarily, and when I look up at William, I see the disappointment in his eyes. "But the pond is going to be great."

William snaps the folder shut and returns it to its place.

"Miss John, Ms. Bigelow has made it possible to see this project come to life, and it is very important to me. I have much to thank her for." William lowers his head, places his hand on his chest, and takes a long, thoughtful breath. Then he looks up and right at me—right into me. "I would actually like to thank you, Miss… Nerissa. I'd like to thank you."

"Why?" I can hardly breathe.

"I know I mentioned this to you before, when you first joined us, but perhaps it didn't sound as genuine as I felt. But I assure you… I am sincere. I have come to realize that without your interventions last Season, I would not be where I am today, standing here, now. I was impatient, and that would have inevitably caused me to make some irreversible mistakes. But now…"

He steps out from behind the desk and raises his arms wide and high.

"This. This is all a reality because of you, Nerissa." He swings around in a full circle, then stops, facing me with a big, exaggerated smile distorting his features. "It is incredible how the Universe always conspires in our favor, for our best and highest good, whether we realize it at the time or not."

"I guess that's one way of looking at it." I try to sound agreeable. But let's not forget the facts—his marriage is over; his sons are gone—probably dead; he's a murderer and a liar; and the only *friends* he has are those he can pay or push into submission. I think William is certifiable, perfectly happy living in his little dream world.

"It's the only way of looking at it." His hands drift into his pockets. "I have been afforded the best of the best in this new facility. And…" Smirking now, he swings his foot along the floor. "My main investor is, thankfully, my number one fan. She is completely dedicated to the skincare products we create, and she was basically devastated, panicked, when she learned the old labs and production rooms were destroyed."

"That explains a lot," I say without thinking.

William squints at me for just a second, seemingly unsure of my comment. "Yes, it does explain a lot. It explains every-thing. She was going to make damn sure she had her summer supply of product. She is a very smart businesswoman and extremely dedicated."

"You mean addicted."

"Oh, no." He laughs. "Ms. Bigelow never acquired a taste for Aqua Tonic, if that's what you mean."

"You're right," I sneer. "Smart woman."

"Perhaps. But she understands its potential and of course wishes to capitalize on its inevitable success."

"So she understands it's addicting? Highly addicting and dangerously toxic when consumed in large amounts?" I ask.

"She understands perfectly."

"I'm sorry, I don't want to upset you, but aren't you worried it won't get approved? And even if it does, don't you think it'll get pulled off the market when people figure out how toxic it is?"

He doesn't answer me right away; he just stands there, smiling, like he's waiting for me to answer my own question. But I don't.

"Ms. Bigelow is very well-connected. *Very* well-connected. And let me teach you something, Nerissa. With a product such as AQT and with its enormous potential, there are ways around such details."

I nod. "So she built you your very own dream lab. Or production palace, or research center, or whatever you're calling it."

"Yes." He smiles. "She and a very elite collection of others. Fellow investors who know something good when they see it. We have made more advances in this new building in the short time it's been here than we did in... well, years, honestly. Like I said, the best of the best. And I have you to thank. Funny, isn't it?"

"Yeah." A real knee-slapper. "You're welcome." My sarcasm goes undetected. "Well, no offense, but this looks like a resort, not a research facility."

"Yes, well... she had her own ideas about the look. Honestly, that doesn't matter to me."

"Is this what my new *home* looks like?" I ask.

It's like my question pulls William from some kind of infatuated trance of admiring his surroundings, like he's been gazing at his lover with blatant lust and someone's just caught him.

He clears his throat. "Your quarters are... even better. I know you'll be pleased. I was going to take you that way next." He points behind us toward the direction of the old labs and tank room. "But I'd be happy to show you your new accommodations first, if you prefer. As a matter of fact, I have one more surprise for you. I think it's a great place to start."

"Besides my new *accommodations*, you mean?" I dread his answer, but I need to prepare myself, if I can.

His face lights up with a smile I've only seen once before—the first night I had dinner at the Banks' house and William sat across from me. He knew I knew who he was, and he knew I was taunting him. But he also sat in quiet satisfaction and lust for power, knowing he was in control, no matter how comfortable and sure of myself I seemed. And he knew I realized it.

That's what his smile says right now. And it seems like he's remembering the same moment.

"Yeah, sure," I offer. It's the only thing I can do.

"Excellent. Right this way."

CHAPTER 12
SURPRISES

IT'S TIME FOR YOU TO SHUT UP.

THURSDAY, FEBRUARY 27TH

The new building is huge and includes sections that did not exist in the old facility. We've gone up an elevator, and now William leads me down one dark, stretching hallway after another. The corridors are all lined in the same black granite and wood as the lobby, lit by soft wall sconces every ten feet. It has the uncanny aura of a resort or some kind of guest accommodations, a new numbered door coinciding with every other sconce.

"Who else will be living here?" I can't help but ask.

William slows and turns halfway to look at me. "Well, I am, for one." He smiles and turns around again. "Considering I no longer have a house."

Lucky me. And lucky for me, he doesn't seem to care much that I burned his home to the ground last year. I covered up his crimes, perhaps. Another thing for which I'm sure he's *genuinely grateful.*

"And," he continues without looking back, "I suppose it

would make sense for Officer MacNamire to join us as well." I stop. It takes a few seconds for him to realize it, but then he turns back toward me in confusion.

"I don't like him."

"Oh, I know," he says. "Never mind. He'll stay on the base."

"Really?"

"Yes, really. Do I need to remind you? That dimwit isn't my friend. He's just the best—"

"The best damn plant guy you could ever meet."

William smiles. "Precisely. But that does not make him my friend. And I don't need to have him as my neighbor, either. He'll stay on the base. Okay?"

I reluctantly answer, "Okay... thank you."

"You're welcome. It's the least I can do."

William actually sounds nice, kind—I feel like I'm having some sort of out-of-body experience. But instead of rushing past it or pushing it away, I instantly decide to try capitalizing on his strange, sudden generosity and what sounds like concern for my feelings.

"Can I ask you a favor?"

He cocks his head and squishes up his brow the tiniest bit. I regret it immediately. I look down at the dark wood floor, unable to hold his penetrating stare.

"What it is?" he asks, his voice deep and unnerving.

"Uh... I—never mind."

William walks toward me slowly, and it frightens me so much, I don't look up. He steps directly in front of me—close enough that I detect the faint scent of aftershave. He's an impenetrable wall looming over me, and I'm at his mercy in this dark, isolated hall.

"Look at me," he commands.

My eyes dart from side to side in some futile search for relief—or escape. But I don't dare move—don't dare step back.

I squeeze my eyes shut for one second of resolution, then quickly lift my head and meet the intensity of his eyes. My eyes.

"What is it you'd like to ask of me?" His tone is slow and steady.

I can't speak, and the pressure builds inside my head, behind my face and eyes. "I..." Nothing else comes out.

William takes hold of my chin, and I brace myself without losing eye contact. But he doesn't squeeze me, doesn't shake me, his expression and his grip neutral and calm. "Nerissa, you can trust me, you know."

Fireworks explode inside my head, and my body somehow relaxes and tenses at the same time. I want to laugh in his face. Of course, I don't.

"It would mean so much to me for you to realize that," he continues. "We had a rocky start, but like I said, I realize how indebted I am to you. What favor do you want to ask me? Please, tell me."

A rocky start. I have no feeling left in my body. I'm vaguely aware tears have spilled down my cheeks. William looks at me, inches from my face, with what I interpret as a mix of pity, disgust, and something else altogether. I swallow hard and jump off this cliff he's led me to before he can push me over the edge himself.

"Can I please have one day, alone, with no... injections, no drugs... to just... be or go wherever I want? I need to... visit my family. And be able to feel." I close my eyes and squeeze out even more tears. "Please?"

"Open your eyes."

I do as he says, refocusing on him, his face so close to mine.

"Yes. You've earned that freedom," he says. "Yes, you may."

A long, amplified, stunned pause follows. "Really?" I ask. William just keeps a hold on my chin, and for a second, I'm sure he's just playing another cruel joke and I'll be slapped and laughed at. Or worse, he'll lean over and kiss me—reminding me that I belong to him.

He lets go of my chin.

I inhale sharply and search his eyes, holding my breath and waiting for the catch.

"Yes, really. I promise."

"Oh, thank you." Smiling, I release my breath. I clasp my fingers together and step side to side, unsure of what to do with myself and my sudden newfound promise of freedom, even if just for a day.

"You're welcome. But it can't be today."

"Okay, no problem. Tomorrow, then?"

He presses his lips together. "Maybe. Let me see what needs attending to here. You will have many new responsibilities."

"Of course. Yes. I understand." I'll agree to whatever he throws at me now. I get the sense he slightly regrets this one concession, and although he wouldn't say so, he starts to sound like it. Or maybe I'm just being paranoid.

"I'll let you know which day you can have."

"Sounds good. Thank you. Really."

"Like I said, Nerissa, you may not believe it yet, but you *can* trust me."

I take a long, cleansing breath. "I believe you."

"Good."

We stand in a slightly awkward silence, and he stares at me like he wants to reach out and touch me—or hug me.

"How about you show me my room?" I say to break the moment.

"Yes. You're going to be happy with it. It's far more than just a room."

"Right. You said it was a surprise."

"Yes, but the surprise isn't just your room." He smiles.

"I'm excited." I bend the truth. I won't say or do anything that might make him take back what he just promised me.

We stand at a pair of double-doors. The plaque under the sconce declares this is room G23. My new home, I suppose.

"Is this it? My room?" I ask.

"Yes." William beams. "Go ahead. Have a look inside."

I place one hand on each handle and push the doors inward. As I step into the massive space, William speaks into his CNI. "We're here."

The room, as he said, is far more than a room. It's like a luxury hotel suite, fully appointed and equipped, overwhelming in its beauty. I quickly take it in, and my attention is pulled to what lies directly across from me.

I walk in to stand in the middle of what could only be called a living room. A sleek but comfortable-looking beige leather couch sits at the center. Two charcoal velvet chairs rest directly across a gold-trimmed glass table between them. At the far left end of the space is a full, modern kitchen decked out with sparkling appliances and gray wood cabinets. Between the living room and kitchen, a round, marble-topped table and four dining chairs sit beneath an extravagant but tasteful crystal chandelier. I imagine this is where William and I will now share our one-sided dinner chats and wine. It's a big step up from the dining cart in my tiny cottage.

On the other side of the room, a half-wall separates a cozy nook with a beautiful queen-sized bed dripping with expensive-looking cream linens and piled high with satin-covered pillows. Next to it, and what has truly had my attention since stepping inside, a wall of floor-to-ceiling windows runs the entire length of the massive room.

I step forward, as though pulled by an invisible force, toward the windows. This new part of the building is perched high at the edge of the northeast-facing cliffs. The expansive view is breathtaking and includes not only a wide perspective of Panacea's north shore but also a perfect, complete view of the west side of Albatross resting just beyond the western ship graveyard—the invisible world beneath the waves. I can even see a tiny, tiny speck of the north beach, and I would imagine a high-powered pair of binoculars may even afford a sighting of my family if they were in just the right spot.

I raise my fingertips to the crystal-clear glass, like I'm touching Albatross—so close and yet so far away. Resting my forehead against it, I sigh—fogging up the pristine window. Why did he put me in this room? With this view?

Like he's just read my mind, William breaks my fixation on my one true home and the family I desperately long to rejoin. "I wanted to make sure you don't forget why you're here," he says.

I readjust my focus to gaze at him in the window's reflection. "I think I would have preferred a sunset exposure."

He laughs. "Yes, I'm sure. But don't worry. The new observation deck is quite spectacular."

"Why didn't you put the... guest accommodations on the other side? I imagine a room like this facing west would be second to none."

He laughs again. "I do appreciate the consideration. But I assure you, we had our reasons. More importantly..." His voice deepens. "Do not confuse yourself as a guest. You work here. And let that view remind you why."

With my head still against the cool glass, I close my eyes. I can't look at even his blurry reflection anymore.

"So, do you like your new home?" William asks.

I don't open my eyes or give an immediate answer.

"Nerissa?"

"Yes. It's great. Thank you. Thank you for the amazing surprise."

"You're welcome, but this isn't the entire surprise," he reminds me, and I can *hear* his smile.

I don't indulge him.

Silence.

Still leaning against the tall window, I hear my heart beating softly in my ear as I now rest my head against the back of my outstretched arm. I focus on it and imagine sending vibrations of love across the dark, frenetic water, all the way to my mother, and Kendra, and her unborn baby. I wonder if by perfect coincidence they happen to be thinking of me at this exact moment. Can they see this new section of the building from Albatross? Probably not now, but maybe at night, when the lights illuminate it against the black background. Perhaps after I get my day of freedom, to visit, we can talk about it and—

"Hello, child."

My wandering thoughts abruptly halt. And my soft, steady heartbeat quickens. I swear I just heard—

"Nerissa, this is the surprise I was talking about..." Williams says. "Well, one of them."

I don't move. I can't move. Slowly, I open my eyes. At first, I keep them fixed on the glass in front of me and the ocean beyond. William's reflection is still there, in that mirrored, unfocused place just outside my own. But he has morphed into two. Or someone else has joined him.

I force myself to focus on the new reflection in the glass.

What I see can't possibly be real. My heart starts pounding in my head. Pushing myself slowly away from the window, I wipe the tears away with the back of my hand, and close my eyes.

Open your eyes on three. Yes.

One.

Two.

Be brave and don't be disappointed when you open them. This can't be real.

Three.

"Gabriel?"

"Yes, child—"

I don't wait for him to finish. Running to him, I slam against his chest and wrap my arms around him. "Oh, my god. You're alive." I sob into his neck, clutching at him. "How... I thought you were..." I can only cling to him, shaking in disbelief.

Gabriel is here. He's alive. How is this real? I try to make sense of the impossible, all the while rocking him in my desperate hold.

But he doesn't return my embrace.

He does not share in my joy.

He just stands there, stiff, his arms at his sides.

I pull myself away and look him up and down. "Gabriel?" I'm still not sure I'm operating in reality. Perhaps I've finally derailed into full psychosis. I turn toward William and search his face. His wide, brazen smile only confuses me more. "Is he real? Is this real?" I yell.

William doesn't answer me, his face motionless.

"Did you give me something? Am I hallucinating?"

Silence.

"Please! Please answer me! Please..." I sob.

"You are not imagining anything, child," Gabriel says. "I am real. I am here."

My hands dart to either side of his face, staring into his

eyes. "What did he do to you?"

He gently shakes his head. My hands fall to my sides. Then I take both of his in mine. "How are you here? I missed you so much, I—" My cry interrupts the sentence, and I squeeze Gabriel's hands, waiting for him to return my affection, my desperation. My love.

But he just stands there, staring at me with vacant eyes.

I drop his hands and rush at William until my face rises up just beneath his. "What did you do?" I grit my teeth and ball up my fists, doing everything in my power not to hit him, or scratch his eyes out, or spit in his face.

William calmly places his hand on my chest and gently, but with direct intention, pushes me away from him. He looks over my shoulder and nods. Gabriel's hand comes down on my shoulder, and he guides me away from William. Just feeling his touch spins me back around into another maniacal embrace. I bundle myself up against him, taking his hands and placing them around me in an attempt to feel his love. They promptly go slack. I cry, and moan, and suddenly wish this wasn't real. Because worse than facing Gabriel's death is facing a world in which he feels nothing for me.

"What's happening?" I scream as loud as I can. Gabriel doesn't flinch, but William covers his ears, wearing that familiar mix of pity and disgust.

"When you're done behaving like a spoiled child, your questions will be answered," William says.

"A spoiled child?" I ask, completely indignant.

"Yes, and a crazy one at that."

Crazy. I'm crazy? *This* is crazy—unexplainable, without excuse, and just fucking impossible.

I step away, turn my back, and try to calm myself. I pace the room twice, at first breathing fire and ready to explode. Taking deep breaths as I walk, I attempt to talk myself down. I experience what I imagine the last moments of life must be like —a thousand distinct images and thoughts flashing through my mind, some pleasant, some disturbing, but all an intricate piece of the fabric of life. My particular life. And with every educated guess, with every experienced guess, I can only explain this impossible scenario in one way. William has broken Gabriel. He abducted him—told us he was dead—and then he broke him, brainwashed him. Not unlike the way he's beginning to break me but ten times worse. Gabriel's no doubt under the control of some wretched drug, probably something like the *Long-Dark-Haul.* Yes, that's it. Maybe it's even worse than that. It's the only explanation.

I stop and turn to face them. "I understand now."

"Do you?" William asks. "Then please, explain it to us."

Us, not *me.* He wants me to explain it to both of them, like they're of the same mind, like they're together. I walk up to Gabriel, stand directly in front of him, and pretend William isn't even there.

"The *Long-Dark-Haul* is a tough one. But I know how you're feeling right now. I know you can't express emotion. I understand, and it's okay. I know you love me. I love you too, and—"

"What are you talking about?" William interrupts me. "What is the *Long-Dark-Haul?*"

"The drug you gave him," I say, still looking directly at Gabriel. "The one you give me. I know exactly how it feels. Exactly what it does."

William chuckles. My head snaps in his direction. "Would you like to explain it to her, or shall I?" he asks Gabriel. I turn back toward the man I thought was dead, wide-eyed and unblinking, waiting for his response.

"I am not under the influence of any drugs, child," Gabriel says, slow and steady.

"It's okay. I know you have to say that."

"I'm not just saying that. I am of completely sound mind and body," Gabriel insists.

I shake my head.

"Yes."

"No. No!"

Gabriel swiftly takes me by the shoulders and shoves me backward. I stumble slightly, running into one of the gray chairs. Righting myself, I sit down—never breaking eye contact with him. He stares at me, unwavering, his face a maze of hardened lines, causing me to crumble into a wave of my own tears again.

William walks to my side and puts his hand on my shoulder. To my shameful surprise, his touch is somehow comforting. "If it makes you feel any better, Gabriel didn't want to come last summer, and he fought hard to protect you." I look up at William, and even through blurred vision, I see his condescension. "At first."

"You kidnapped him."

"Not really," William gleefully corrects. "He was strongly encouraged to turn himself over to us."

"And you told us he was dead."

"Yes. We had to. We'd made permanent new arrangements."

"And then you brainwashed him."

"*No*. We did no such thing."

"Then why is he acting like this?" I look at Gabriel again.

"Tell her," William urges.

I stare at him, my mouth wide and twisted in disbelief as I wait for his explanation.

"Gabriel is no longer a slave to useless and unappreciated endeavors," Gabriel says.

That's it? I wait for more. Nothing.

"What does that mean?" I ask.

"Master Banks showed me what it means to be a part of truly valuable work."

"Master Banks?"

Am I really hearing this?

"Yes, and I have been given a life unlike any I have ever known," Gabriel says. "The best of the best."

"So... you're a sellout? And a traitor. And a liar..." I can hardly talk or even breathe. "What do you mean by *unappreciated endeavors?*"

"You used me." Gabriel stares at me. "You and the rest of your kind."

"Used you?"

"Yes, and I will never be used again."

I can't help but laugh, as ingenuine as it is. "Gabriel, you were working for Wreckleaf. Copious amounts. You were paid well and treated well. And we always appreciated you, and I... love you. I don't understand."

"How could you? You're not a human being."

His words cut deep, slicing my heart before leaving it there to die. Hanging my head, I whimper as another river of tears pours from my puffy eyes. "What about the Wreckleaf?" I choke out.

"What about it?"

"Don't you still want it?"

"I have all the Wreckleaf I could ever want now."

"I don't mean the fake stuff, or the injections, or the drink. It's not the same."

William laughs softly from some far-off place. I almost forgot he was here.

"Gabriel is not talking about the rendered version. I'm speaking of the real deal. The one and only."

"There is only one source for the real deal," I say. "Out

there!" I point to the ocean on the other side of the wall of windows.

"Not anymore!" William yells with a grin, doing a ridiculous little shimmy with jazz hands.

I close my eyes and sigh through my nose. "Let me guess. This is another one of your surprises."

"Bingo!"

"I can't... I just can't do this... anymore," I whisper, sinking deeper into the velvet chair.

"Don't worry," William says. "You won't have to."

I lift my gaze and just stare straight ahead.

"Gabriel, give it to her," William instructs.

I don't need to ask. I know I'm about to be injected with something. I just never imagined, not in a million lifetimes, that Gabriel would be the one to do it.

Gabriel walks to the kitchen, and I hear a sequence of noises as he prepares a vialful of whatever William has ordered up. The time of day suggests it'll be the *Long-Dark-Haul,* which in all honesty would be fine with me. But it hasn't exactly been a normal day, so who knows what's on the menu.

Gabriel reappears at my side. Looking up, I hold his gaze as he injects a full vial of cool liquid into my flesh. The pressure in my head comes instantly, and I already know but ask anyway.

"Whatcha serving, Gabriel?" He doesn't meet my gaze.

"What you've termed the *Long-Dark-Haul,*" William says. "We can't have you all emotional for our next surprises. I like the nickname, by the way."

"Why make him do it? Why don't you just give it to me yourself?" I ask through the pressure and pain.

He smiles. "Well, I couldn't just deny the man his repeated request. He was starting to annoy me." He laughs. "Once Gabriel came around, he said he wanted to make sure I understood how loyal he is, and he asked to be personally responsible for your injections. I wasn't sure about it at first, but just like you've earned your freedoms, so has Gabriel. And this is one of his. What did you say, Gabriel? That you'd never allow yourself to be used again, and that you wanted to make sure that little... what was it?"

Gabriel looks directly into my eyes. "That little manipulative, hybrid slut was under control."

I stare back at him, unblinking, unfeeling. The *Long-Dark-Haul* is here.

The three of us travel back through a network of hallways, down an elevator, through the overly opulent lobby, and into the heart of the Bio-Gen building. We start on the main level and pass through a series of secured doors, each enormous in size and mass. I know by the change in temperature and color that we're approaching the one place that, under any other circumstance, I would dread. But I don't care right now. I feel no emotion, no concern, no attachment, even though I'm strangely aware of my own disconnect.

William opens the last door with a swipe of his CNI and a code punched into a slick, black keypad, and my exaggerated attention takes in the space at lightning speed. The new tank room is massive. Unlike the tank room in William's last lab, this one is dedicated solely to the growing of Wreckleaf. Six enormous tanks spread out across the room, each one at least triple the size of the original I destroyed. They are filled with what appears to be perfect, healthy Caulerpa Periculosis Abscondita—Wreckleaf, identical to what grows in the ship graveyard, dancing feverishly in immaculately simulated conditions. Impossible. Or so it was believed.

"Isn't it beautiful?" William squeals with joy.

Neither Gabriel nor I answer him.

William doesn't seem to even notice and walks along the length of the tank in front of us, stopping at the far end and smiling at me. "You see, Nerissa? This is what we saved this side for." He points behind himself to a wall no less than two full stories, made entirely of glass facing west. Then he points to the ceiling pitched at a sharp diagonal angle and home to rows of huge, south-facing skylights. "Perfectly controlled amounts of sunlight."

That sounds like an oxymoron to me.

He walks back toward us, skimming the tank with his fingertips and smiling.

"You have achieved the impossible, Master Banks," Gabriel says.

"Yes. Indeed, I have. But not without your help, Gabriel. I am indebted to you. And you as well, Nerissa." He laughs— more like a giggle than anything else. "One big, happy family."

I'm vaguely aware that if I were not under the influence of the *Long-Dark-Haul,* I may have vomited. But I do still wonder, in the far recesses of my mind, why he's indebted to Gabriel. What did Gabriel do to help? And why do I care?

William searches my face for a reaction we both know he won't find in my current state, then he jumps a little in recognition. "Ah, yes. We have a few more stops on the tour, my friends, before our final destination. Please. Follow me." William prances past us like some sort of overpaid, over-exuberant cruise ship director. We follow obediently behind.

At the far end of the Bio-Gen building, opposite from my new quarters, are the labs. I know I'll eventually feel grateful for the fact that they're so far away from where I'll lay down to sleep each night, but as we approach, I'm neither interested nor disturbed. I simply follow William as he directs.

Just like before, there are rooms dedicated to testing new products, and god knows what else, filled with unfortunate subjects living out their tortured days. The demand for the newest biotechnology, along with cutting-edge beauty products—the formulations that hold the promise of youth in a bottle or a tube—justify the sacrifice. The rooms are all larger and more meticulously equipped, Though like before, they are white and sterile. A lab thing, I guess. William shows us every last room, every last dedicated space, narrating the details as we go.

We leave the final room and take an elevator down. Never before do I remember an elevator going to a below ground level. The door slides open, and I hear it, I feel it, and even through the veil of my injection, the sound gets under my skin. It gets inside me.

When I look at William, he's enraptured, happily locked inside his own personal bubble of indulgence—a fool's paradise. I've actually never seen him look so happy—so grateful and complete. It strikes a morbid curiosity in me, even though I already know exactly where we are.

William steps out of the elevator, and Gabriel and I follow. I feel no connection to Gabriel, and I'm distantly thankful for it. He shadows William like a dog heeling at his side. In some other world, at some other time, I'd be mortified. And devastated.

Directly in front of us, a large window showcases William's pride and joy. He puts his hands on the glass, just like Devin did deep in the throes of his addiction. But William isn't addicted to the condensed, manufactured, and toxic components of Aqua Tonic that had Devin in their grip. No. William's high comes from the power of that addiction to what he created and to what he controls—the power he wields over *whom* he controls. And to the fortune it will render him. His greed is almost palpable as he gazes into an assembly room twice the size of the one I destroyed, the AQT bottles churned out by the boatload.

"Has your product been approved?" I ask.

He doesn't turn to look at me. "It will be. And I will be prepared."

"Excellent job, Master Banks," Gabriel says.

"I assume the other assembly rooms are down here as well," I say.

"Yes, just down the corridor. We've added several them."

"Of course you have," I reply.

William stares at his beloved poison for a few moments longer, then breaks his own trance with a spin back toward the elevator. "Come on. I want to show you the new observation deck."

We once again follow him like mindless sheep being led into the unknown. Except my senses are on high, my mind and focus as sharp as a blade.

After walking down a long, stark hall, we take another elevator to the top floor, and the door slides open. The cold ocean air hits us hard, filling my lungs and nose with its familiar scent. A strong pang of days long gone fills me unexpectedly. No. It's too soon to feel.

William fights against the wind and walks out onto the new observation deck. It's strikingly similar to the old one, just slightly larger and fresher. My eyes wander to the wall, devoid only of the mass of tangled orange vines that used to climb everywhere but otherwise nearly identical to where Devin and I first kissed—as the sun went down and we peered onto the edge of the world, when I knew my life would never be the same.

"Come here," William yells over the thundering surf below and the unforgiving wind hitting us from every direction as he walks toward the wall. "Have a look. It's beautiful!"

Gabriel follows.

"It's not safe out there," I say and stay put, even though I shouldn't care about my safety. Not yet.

William looks at me, seemingly puzzled by my comment. He edges closer to the wall and fights for balance against the formidable gusts. Then he teeters and pulls his collar close against his neck. "It's cold. And I have to agree with you. Standing at this wall is not the safest thing in this weather. One strong wind or wrong move could end it all." He laughs, using his brilliant observation as a concession, and turns back toward where I wait beside the elevator.

"You can't even see anything, sir," Gabriel offers. "Let's return when the conditions are more agreeable. For a proper sunset."

"Yes. A splendid idea," William agrees. "Come, I've saved the best surprise for last."

The three of us re-enter the elevator and exit one floor below.

In all my life, I've never taken the time to consider the clarity that comes with surrender. Not even the kind of surrender the *Long-Dark-Haul* provides me—that complete and total lack of concern or emotion or pain, both physical or mental. It's the true surrender that comes with knowing I've already lived my best moments. Nothing I will ever do or feel for the rest of my existence will stand out from the rest of it.

All I have now are my memories. And honestly, if he ever grants me another *favor,* I may ask my father to keep me pumped full of this drug. I'm quite certain that staying in this place of apathy and complacency while remaining wired and hyper-attentive will serve me very well for the rest of my days. What difference would it make? None at all—that's perfectly clear. I don't want to feel anymore. Even in the short-lived shadow of my request to go to Albatross drug-free, perhaps I've made a mistake.

The peak of my life is behind me. I'll live out the remainder of my days like the lab animals—held against my will but done fighting—powerless, and tortured. A sacrifice demanded by the needs of the people. By the needs of William Banks.

As we step out of the elevator, I'm struck by the return to the resort-like feel on this floor. Granite and wood and soft lighting mimic the corridors of the wing across the lobby. But there's something in the air here. I can't put my finger on it—a feeling, or a sound, maybe. I can't be sure, and it doesn't matter anyway.

William leads us down another hallway, past a number of doors, into what looks like a recreational space or a gathering room. It's circular and filled with comfortable seating and game tables and a kitchenette at the far end.

A woman sits on the floor at the far end of the room with her back to us. Huddled against her lap, partially blocked from view, a small child reluctantly accepts her affection, seeming more agitated than anything else. I can't quite see, her dark, ruby hair covering so much of both their faces.

I walk toward her, unconcerned whether William wants me to or not.

Time seems to stand still—or to morph into something else entirely. My heart speeds up. It shouldn't be speeding up.

"Hello?" I say as I clear the last chairs and nothing stands between me and these two strangers.

The woman hears me and turns. I stop.

"Surprise!" William shouts from behind me, startling the child enough to make him look up.

"Alakier?" I whisper. "Anastasia? What..."

She just stares up at me, and a faint smile spreads across her features.

"Hello, Nerissa."

My clarity, my focus, tells me not to react with any emotion. This is not a shining moment. It's a trick, not real, and I won't respond. Even if it somehow is real, it isn't. Just like Gabriel. Here, tangible, but not. And I don't care. I don't want to care.

William stands behind me now. "Isn't the resemblance spectacular?"

"Resemblance?"

William laughs softly. "Well, if you're not sure what I'm referring to, I guess it's even better than I thought."

I turn to face him. "This is not Anastasia. Is that it? She died in the explosion."

More laughter bursts out of him.

I don't wait for his explanation and swing back to study Ana's face. She seems distant, singularly focused on soothing Alakier, whose face is buried in her lap. It *is* her. I know it is. But how did *he* get here?

"Harvester!" William nearly shouts.

Alakier snaps to attention and looks up at William. His eyes are black, all pupil and nothing else, his skin tinged a waxy-gray and with an almost transparent quality.

"Stand."

Alakier follows the command immediately.

"Leave him alone." Ana tries to corral the child, gripping

his wrists and lightly pulling him toward her to return him to her lap. But he just stands there, resisting her like a statue. "He's just a little boy."

He's a soldier waiting for commands.

William puts his hand on my back. "That is no little boy. Far from it."

I don't turn toward him. I can't pull my eyes away. "This is the second part of my surprise," I say.

He pats my back in praise. "Yes. Indeed, it is."

"My replacement. Alakier's clone."

"It was an enormous endeavor. Especially after the destruction last year. But like I said, I have been afforded the best of the best, and you did not destroy everything. Obviously. And you have to agree... the specimen is strikingly similar to my son."

His son. I almost forgot he fathered Alakier.

Anastasia reaches toward the boy and smooths the blond hair from his forehead. She moves with tenderness, but her hand shakes. He doesn't respond at all, his dark eyes locked onto William, his master. His creator.

"Does he speak?" I ask.

"He's shy, but he'll come around," Anastasia answers quickly, obviously thinking I'd asked her.

I hadn't. I look at William.

"He is crafted not to speak unless I or a select few others ask him a direct question or give him an order requiring an answer." William's smile widens. "Anastasia, you would do well to remember his example."

"So he'll be my replacement? My entire breed's replacement?"

"Precisely."

"How will one Harvester do the work of almost a dozen of us?"

William turns to face me, places his hands on both my shoulders, and speaks slowly. "Now, why would you think there'll only be one Harvester?"

As if on cue, or programmed to do so, Anastasia stands and faces us. Her belly is round, swollen with what can only be the next specimen in William's horde. She places both hands on her pregnant belly and gently caresses it, looking at me with a small, determined smile softening her aged and hardened features.

"Will this one look the same?"

William gifts us with his signature chuckle. "Yes, it will. As will all the rest."

"So Ana's just going to keep churning them out?"

"This one is not Ana's," William says, referring to the still-frozen Alakier look-a-like, seemingly unfazed by his surroundings. "This is Lillian's first successful completion."

"Oh." I'm beginning to detect the need to buffer my emotions. But it's way too soon to be feeling anything more than very vague curiosity, if that. Maybe I'm growing a tolerance to the *Long-Dark-Haul*. Great.

"This Doll, this little Beauty, was..." he looks toward Ana and drops his head ever-so-slightly. "Forgive me. She was a royal pain in the ass." He snickers. "We couldn't get her to hold onto anything. But in all fairness, it may have been a glitch on our end, not hers. Like before. Once Lillian's first implantation took, we tried again with Ana. And voila!" He waves a hand at Ana's belly.

"This is Lillian's child." I clear my throat, pointing to the Harvester.

"Yes. And I'm happy to tell you she has been successfully implanted once again."

"Where is she?"

"Well... unfortunately, because of the speed and voracity of the gestation, the first few weeks are very difficult. Lillian is resting comfortably."

"When are you due?" I ask Ana.

She looks at William, as though asking for permission to answer. "Very soon."

"You're assembling an army of Harvesters," I say flatly.

William steps toward Alakier's clone and puts his hand on its head. The replica never moves, just idling there in wait for its next prompt.

"This specimen may look like a child, but rest assured, it is not. HC1 will grow *very* fast. He will hit maturity by mid-June. Then he will live fast and die fast. I will never amass an army, which thankfully, I do not need. But I will require more hosts."

Of course, this is what he's ultimately trying to say.

"You want me to be a host." I blink at him.

William steps toward me again and looks into my eyes. "Honestly, Nerissa... nothing would make me happier. But I'd like you to *want* to be a host. A part of the bigger picture. The greater good."

"My new responsibilities."

He smiles. "Yes."

"One big, happy family."

I swear, he looks like he might cry.

"What do you need Harvesters for? You have Wreckleaf growing in the tanks."

"Good question. The long and short of it is... for backup. As perfect as the simulated environments may seem right now, they're still quite unstable. We're going to need a lot of C. Periculosis Abscondita to keep up with the demands of the upcoming Season. And that's just on the island. I'll need large supplies for mainland distribution."

"If you get approval," I say.

He frowns. "I *will* get approval. It's very close."

"Excuse me, sir?" Gabriel interrupts. I forgot he was here. But he's not really here, is he? Not my Gabriel. We both turn toward him. He stands at the far end of the room by the door, his hands clasped together, waiting patiently.

"Yes, what is it?" William asks.

"Someone needs to speak with you."

"Not now."

"Gabriel apologizes, sir, but Officer MacNamire says it's very important."

William blows out a big breath and a growl. "That little weasel's dick better be falling off. I do not tolerate interruptions."

"I shall inform him such a condition will be required to take you from your business in the future. However, I believe this is an issue in the tank room, not with the Officer's unit, sir."

"*Oh*. Gabriel... you crack me up. Thank you. I almost lost my temper. Ladies." He turns toward us and nods once. "Excuse me for a moment."

William walks back toward Gabriel, past him, and down the hall at a brisk pace, disappearing from sight. Gabriel resumes his relaxed position. He looks directly at me. I hold his gaze.

A big part of me wants to stand in front of him and scream—demanding answers, demanding renewed loyalty.

Instead, I turn back to Ana and the manufactured version of her child. "Are you okay?" I ask quietly, so Gabriel can't hear us. "Are you being treated well?"

"I'm fine."

"You don't look fine," I say. "You're not acting fine."

"Have you looked in a mirror lately, Nerissa?"

Her statement catches me by surprise, and I laugh. "Good

point. Are you in any pain?" I lightly touch her protruding belly.

"Not much. He's keeping me comfortable. I imagine he's doing the same for you."

"Well, I wouldn't exactly call it comfortable." I shift my gaze to the clone, still standing rock-still, waiting for William's next order. "How are you doing with this?"

"Believe it or not, it brings me some comfort. Nerissa... where is he? What happened?"

"Alakier?"

She closes her eyes and nods, seeming to shield herself from any response I may give.

"He's fine," I say plainly.

Her eyes pop open, searching mine frantically. "What?"

"He's fine. He's alive. Really. He made it off the island." Her strength seems to drain out of her. Buckling forward, I catch her and ease her into a chair.

"He told me he was dead," she says, whimpering. "That he didn't survive the Madoosik."

"He lied, Ana. He always lies. Alakier is with Leyla on the mainland."

She grabs my shirt and buries her face in my stomach, sobbing. "I knew it. I could still... *feel* him. Feel his energy. Oh, my god. My boy is alive." She rocks forward and back, still gripping me. "Why did he lie to me? Why? It wouldn't have made any difference. I'd still have to do what he wants."

"Because he wants to break you. He wants you to *want* to," I say, remembering his words to me. "He wants to feel like he's assembled some team of willing and eager participants. His ego demands it." I turn to look at Gabriel, to make sure he still can't hear us. "And we need to act as though we are."

"Why? What difference does it make? William Banks is going to do what he wants to do. No matter how we act."

"Because my mother is alive, and so is Kendra. She's pregnant and close to giving birth. There's less than a dozen of us left. If I can't save them, Ana, if I can't do whatever it takes to keep them alive... then I've lived for nothing." I sit down in the chair next to her. "Then I've lived for nothing. That's why."

She looks down and places her hand on her swollen belly. "I've tried to pretend this is Alakier. It's the only way I've been able to keep myself sane." She laughs. "Yeah, I'll stay sane by pretending the manufactured, implanted hybrid creature growing inside me is actually my real son, who until a minute ago, I thought was dead. Yeah, that's sane."

The irony settles in the silence.

"Well," I finally say, "at least this time it's not really William's child. At least you didn't have to go through that again."

"Alakier isn't William's child."

My head pops up, and I quickly look at Gabriel, who merely watches us. I pull my chair directly in front of hers, my back to Gabriel, our faces hidden and our knees touching. "What did you just say?"

"Alakier is not William's child."

Even though it's way, way too soon, I know the *Long-Dark-Haul* is wearing off. My heart starts pounding and my mouth goes dry as I wait for Ana to explain. I shouldn't care, but I do. "Who's his father, then?"

"Jaxson. His dad is Jaxson," she says.

"Who's that? And how do you... know? What—"

"Because William Banks is sterile."

My head is about to explode. "That's not possible."

"Nerissa, that man is incapable of reproduction. Believe me. After dozens of attempts, he could not get me pregnant. And every time the test came back negative, he punished *me*. Like it was my fault."

"But you said there were girls... two... and you weren't allowed to have them. You must have been—"

"I wasn't. I had a helper. Someone who helped me trick him."

The air grows thick around me, the room closing in. "Jaxson?" I ask, trying to put together the pieces of this disorienting puzzle.

"Yes. Jaxson worked as a lab tech at the old Bio-Gen building. He was so... kind. He saw the way William treated me, all of us, and he... he hated him. So he helped me fake the pregnancy tests, took them into the lab, and used a fetal specimen. William was never interested in being there for any of that. No, William thought he'd gotten me pregnant and left the *business* of it to the lab and staff. He eased off me when he thought I was pregnant. Like night and day. And really, I couldn't take it anymore... not so much the punishments, but the rape."

I can't breathe.

"The first time," she continues, "when I got to a certain point, William ordered a gender identity test. I didn't have any obvious signs of being pregnant, so we were about to fake a miscarriage."

"Oh, my god, Anastasia..." My hands fall to her legs, and I squeeze her lightly.

"But when we reported the sex was female, as usual, William ordered an abortion. So we faked that instead. Jaxson and I... we... fell in love, Nerissa." She looks at me with tears in her eyes.

"So you enchanted him, instead?" I ask.

"No. I couldn't. I mean, I didn't want to, but even if I did... I couldn't. We could kiss for hours. And we did, sometimes." She smiles, and a faint blush spreads over her cheeks.

A light clicks on in my head. "Did he drink Aqua Tonic?"

"No, it wasn't created yet."

I stand up and pace in a small circle, thinking it all through. Then I return to her, once again blocking our conversation from view and hopefully earshot. I sit back down.

"What else was he drinking... all the time? There had to be a prototype." I search her eyes.

"He used to drink something he called Sparkling C, which —" She giggles softly. "I always thought was Sparkling Sea, but..."

"Where'd he get it?"

"Why?"

"Just answer me!" I have to quickly lower my voice again. "I'm sorry, just... do you know where he got the drink from?"

"He got it from the cafeteria. He said there was always a big pitcher of it on the counter, and all the employees loved it."

"He started his trials on his own employees," I say.

"What?"

"So, how did you actually get pregnant, Ana?"

"Well... the old-fashioned way. With Jaxson."

"Are you sure it was him?"

"Positive. Because as soon as we... I was pregnant before William even made his next attempt."

"And you had a boy. You had Alakier," I say softly. I pace, my mind twirling in a thousand different directions as every emotion bombards me. Overcome and without thought, I rush toward Gabriel, my face inches from his. He doesn't move, doesn't change his placid expression. I stand there like a bull, ready to gore my opponent, breathing fire through my nostrils.

"What is it I can do for you, child?" he asks calmly.

"There is nothing you can do for me," I scream in his face. "You can't even deliver an injection properly, can you? I'm not supposed to feel anything. *Anything*! For hours. You're a failure of a friend. A failure of a slave!" I laugh like a crazy person. "You're a traitor. And I hate you!" I stomp back toward Ana and the still statuesque child-clone. "Learn how to deliver a proper injection, you incompetent back-stabber!"

"Nerissa... calm down," Anastasia says softly, pleading with me.

I place my hands on the arms of her chair and lean toward her. "Are you absolutely sure Jaxson is Alakier's father?" I whisper urgently. "Are you sure... that William's sterile? Maybe he wasn't always. Maybe it's just recent..."

"I'm sure, Nerissa. Jaxson is Alakier's father."

"Where is he? Maybe we can do a paternity test," I say.

"He died in the explosion."

My head drops in front of her, and I collapse to my knees, resting my face in her lap, my breathing shallow and fast. Her fingers run over the short hair that once again covers my head. She's gentle. "I'm sorry," I cry. "You didn't want to leave the building—it was for him. You loved him... I'm so sorry..."

"Nerissa, why is it so important for you to know whether William's sterile?"

I have to slow my breathing, to take in the implications, the possibilities of this newfound truth. "Because..." Ana tenses and tries to shield me, her pregnant belly bumping into my head. I try to look up. Gabriel comes toward us quickly, aggressively, and he jabs a needle into my arm.

The effect is immediate. The room grows fuzzy—either that or the inside of my head does. I slide off Ana's lap and puddle into an inelegant blob on the floor at her feet. At the far end of the room, I can just make out two men approaching. The last thing I see before I slip into what is now a welcome oblivion, is Gabriel standing over me, looking somber, the empty syringe in his fingers.

"Gabriel knows exactly how to deliver a proper injection," he says, "and it's time for you to shut up."

BROKEN PROMISES

I'M DELUSIONAL. OF COURSE I AM.

THURSDAY, MARCH 6TH

A full week has passed, and William has not kept his promise. I have not been allowed to go to Albatross drug-free. He keeps saying things like, "Not yet. This isn't a good day." I'm trying to be patient, but it's hard. Especially after my conversation with Anastasia, who once again, to no one's knowledge but mine, is alive. And *well*. I need to talk to my mother. I need to tell her everything I've seen, everything I know. And I need to check on Kendra.

Gabriel has become my new day nurse, or attendant, as he prefers. We don't speak much. I only had one meltdown alone in my room with him. He stayed completely calm. He just met my eyes and allowed my rant. I screamed and cried while I explained all that has happened since we thought he was murdered. All the loss and destruction and pain. His total lack of emotion made it easy for me to decide not to bother ever again. I'm not sure if Gabriel also gets some kind of compliancy drugs. I asked him that as well, but he didn't answer. I almost wish he *was* drugged. It would at least explain things a bit. Just a little bit.

I haven't been allowed to Albatross at all, not even under the influence of the *Long-Dark-Haul*. William says he's all stocked up with Wreckleaf at the moment. I remind him of what he told me about being overly prepared for the opening of the Season and the delicate, unstable nature of the Wreckleaf tanks. I also remind him of his promise to me. He brushes me off and gives me consolation *freedoms* instead. Today, I'm at the river. Alone. I just got here, but I was only given an hour in total.

As always, the water is like an old, familiar friend. It's still a little cold, but the first hints of spring have arrived. Tiny green buds dot the treetops, soon to thicken up the sparser winter foliage. The birdsong is louder and fuller than the last time I was here. Even the smell is different—the full sun warming up the forest floor, beckoning life to emerge.

The island isn't out of the winter woods just yet. Early-spring storms flare up out of nowhere—dangerous and unpredictable. But for now, in this moment and for the next half hour, I'll float in this sanctuary and soak in the sunshine and peace.

I swim to the large bend in the river near the small wooden docks. I'll never be able to come here without thinking about Devin—rising up in the water in front of me after running through the forest, covered in mud and flinging himself into the river without me seeing it. I smile, then sigh. At first, I try to hold back the tears blurring my vision. But I quickly concede, allowing them to fall and mix with the brackish water. It feels good to cry. It feels normal.

I lie back and float, my arms out to my sides. Both my heartbeat and my breathing are slow and steady in my ears. I close my eyes and concentrate on the rhythm. Soon, I'm traveling back in time—the previous weeks and months, the pendulum William Banks has become: one moment, he's ready to punish and torture me, and the next, he's convinced himself he's my loving and nurturing father, grateful and appreciative of my role in his life and ready to reward me for my valiant actions last Season and my cooperative behavior as of late. And with the flip of a switch, he's as cruel as always, and I am dubbed his newest slave, forcefully exposed to his latest methods for rendering me and my breed obsolete. My only purpose now will be as a host to his hybrid monsters. I pray my mind will survive it.

William has not come to my room for dinner chats since I've taken up residency at the new Bio-Gen building. I have to admit, I miss those nights. Not so much for the company and conversations, which are twisted and confusing and for which he still owes me an explanation—another promise he has not kept—but for the wine. The wine seems to be the only reliable thing these days. Not even the drugs injected into me daily are predictable. At least, not since Gabriel took over. He is, as I told him, a failure even as an *attendant*.

Thankfully, Hani still comes in the evenings, always before bedtime and even sometimes before dinner. She is always kind, always gentle, and on the days I can't seem to even remember my own name, she guides me. She helps me. Sometimes, I beg her for full doses of my sedative and whatever else I get. She'll agree to a slightly larger dose but never a full one.

"Withdrawals are difficult, Nerissa. We've made good progress. I'm not going to put you back at square one," she always says.

I want to trust her. I want to surrender my well-being to her. But I don't know if I'll ever be able to trust anyone ever again.

Floating with my eyes closed and the world shut out, an almost photographic memory pops into my mind. My heartbeat and breathing morph into the rhythm and lull of the river and these memorized words.

She floated on a secret breeze,
The air inside and all around forever changed.
Her silken flame became the fire that lights the way. That which
without, I am lost; a nomad in a barren desert.
Every grain of sand I will count.
The rise and fall of the sun for an eternity I will watch.
To voice my admission, to taste her scent, and to breathe the air that
only she is,
My last breath I will save.
Please, without you, I am not living,
Devin

Without opening my eyes, I feel the tears slide down the sides of my face into the river cradling me.

I am not living without you.

A branch snaps on the riverbank, and my eyes snap open. Past the small docks at the edge of the forest come another snap and rustle. I follow the sound with my gaze, concentrating. A head peers out from behind a tree trunk.

"Devin?" I ask aloud and immediately feel foolish.

The man darts back behind the tree—if there even was a man. I'm dreaming or imagining things. My eyes and my mind are playing a cruel trick on me, Devin's poem coupled with my exhaustion careening me into a fantasy state.

But I'm sure I saw someone. Another branch snaps.

I dive under and speed to the riverbank, where I launch myself onto the slick, grassy shore. It takes me three tries to catch my footing. I run with all my might to the trees, retracing the exact path Devin took that day, only in reverse. I skid to a halt, gripping the chunky bark. No one's here. Of course no one's here.

I'm delusional. Of course I am.

Dropping my gaze, I observe my feet covered in mud and scratches. I walk slowly back to the water's edge and look out at the perfect river, undisturbed, unconditional, waiting for me to re-emerge without judgement or concern. I wish I could be so kind to myself. But I'm a fool.

"Gotcha!" A thick rope drops from above my head and wraps around my waist. I spin around to find myself face to face with a tall man, maybe in his late twenties or early thirties, with blond-tipped curls and brown skin. Behind him, a slightly older woman shuffles from side to side, holding herself in an anxious embrace as her acquaintance tries to apprehend me.

"What the hell do you think you're doing?" I struggle against the restraint.

"We know who you are. You're not supposed to be here on the island," he says, his nervousness apparent in his choppy words and quick breath.

"*No.* That's not for me. I *am* supposed to be here. You're thinking of the others. My family. Really, you can ask Officer Banks."

"They said you'd try to trick us," the woman yells from behind. "Remember, Toby? They said that."

"Yeah, you're not going to trick us, Doll," Toby says.

These two are obviously ill-informed and are not going to believe a word I say. So I go slack and relax myself against the rope. "Fine. You're right. Turn me in. I think you'll even get a reward."

The two light up at that suggestion, clearly local and not of the same means as the tourists. "Okay! Let's go, little Beauty," Toby instructs.

"Yes, sir, Toby," I say.

He turns me toward the narrow forest path, and once again, Devin pops into my head. I can't bear to walk down this footpath and imagine him running to me after he took his board as far as he could. I don't want to see his face behind my eyes, desperate to reach me before I walked out of his life for good—like I would have ever been able to do that. I just can't; it hurts too much.

I start to hum.

The nameless woman leading our small party stops abruptly and turns around. "No... don't do that." She points directly at me. "No singing."

I don't stop.

She looks at Toby, whose face I cannot see, then back at me and makes the instant decision to lunge. Her hand shoots out, as if she's trying to cover my mouth. But before she can, I slip my arm out of the rope, and my fist meets her face. She drops like a stone, out cold. Toby gawks down at her for a second, then turns around to face me with wide eyes.

I grab his face and press my lips to his. I count to four and pull away. Toby is drunk with my saliva, his eyes heavy and beginning to close. But he manages a tiny smile, like he's high and wants more.

"We just came to fish..." he slurs, and I cover his mouth with mine again and finish the job.

I'm not sure I've spared Toby's life. I think I stopped in time. But if not, his girlfriend, or wife, or whoever she is to him, will have a very unpleasant surprise when she wakes up.

I will have to have a word with William. My time—my *free* time, especially there—cannot be jeopardized like that. And I got lucky with those two. Things could have turned out so much worse with someone else.

I arrive at the gate with three minutes to spare.

Without you, I am not living.

CHAPTER 14
FUTURE VISION

IT'S NOT TIME YET...

MONDAY, MARCH 10TH,

"I'm sure I can trust you to be cordial and cooperative," William says. "These people are the key to our approval. The gatekeepers, if you will."

I stare straight ahead at the lobby's ridiculous new water feature.

"Miss John? Nerissa... did you hear me?"

"Yes."

"And?"

"Yes, you have my word. I'll be nothing but agreeable." I don't really have a choice, do I? "When did the bust arrive?" I nod toward the massive tribute to Alexandria Allerton Bigelow.

But William is distracted by his own thoughts. "Oh, a couple days ago."

"Why isn't it running? It's supposed to shoot water out of its mouth or something, right?"

He seems to be rehearsing something in his head, his lips moving as he silently recites his lines. He looks at me, then at

169

the stone bust. "Oh, yes. It'll be running soon. Definitely in time for Ms. Bigelow's visit."

"She's coming?"

Now I seem to have his attention. "Of course she is. She's my number-one investor. And she needs to approve all the designs. I mean, this is practically her building."

"I'm sure Bio-Gen's fairest Beauty will be pleased with her larger-than-life replica." My sarcasm catches me off guard.

William snaps his head in my direction and promptly marches toward me. He stands only inches away, staring down, then smooths the collar of my military-inspired, uniform-like gray dress. "Nerissa, this will be the first of many visits from the FWG, as well as from my investors. Today, we will have a combination of the two, and I need everything to be perfect. Do you understand?"

"Why am I even here?" I ask.

He rests both his hands on my shoulders. "Because I consider you an invaluable part of my team. A part of my family. And I'd like my colleagues to see that."

"I'd like to go to Albatross tomorrow. No drugs."

He sighs, then lightly brushes my cheek with the backs of his fingers. I don't move, holding my breath—waiting for his answer.

"Okay," he finally says.

"Really?"

"Yes, really."

I let out a sigh of relief and gratitude, then smile up at him. "Thank you."

He holds his paternal stare, a softness in his gray-green eyes. "You're welcome. Remember, I always keep my promises."

Better late than never.

"But you have to keep yours," he adds.

"I don't remember making any—"

"Excuse me, Master Banks," Gabriel interrupts from the front end of the lobby.

William breaks his unyielding gaze and turns to face him. "Yes, what is it?"

"Your guests have arrived." Gabriel steps to the side and extends his arm toward the entrance. From behind him, two suited men and two uniformed FWG officers—one man, one woman—enter the lobby with Emmanuel MacNamire beside them.

"Ah! Greetings. Please do come in." William bounds toward the group with exaggerated exuberance.

"Sir, this is Officer Stephan Mueller and Officer Julia Nowak," Emmanuel says, introducing the two uniformed guests.

William juts out his right hand to Officer Mueller first, then to Officer Nowak for an overly enthusiastic handshake. "Welcome. It's so good to have you. Welcome."

"And sir, this is Mr. Behnam Abbasi and Mr. Elliot Jensen, two of your investors," Emmanuel adds.

William turns to the two well-dressed gentlemen and extends his hand in greeting once again. "Mr. Abbasi, welcome to Bio-Gen. Mr. Jensen, welcome. It's so nice to make your acquaintances. To finally put faces to your names. Thank you for coming so far. I hope your travels were pleasant. Thank you."

William acts like a star-struck teen, wide-eyed and unable to close his mouth completely. I can see his shortness of breath with the fast-paced rise and fall of his shoulders.

"Alexandria has told us so much about you and your project here," says Mr. Abbasi. "We look forward to seeing your progress."

"Yes, yes of course. I'm thrilled to show you around and explain anything you'd like to know," William says.

"We have a lot to go over, Officer Banks," Officer Mueller adds.

"Yes, indeed we do. Shall we begin with a tour?" William steps aside and fans out his arm toward the opulent lobby.

"Well, Alexandria has certainly made her presence known here." Mr. Jensen smiles and looks around the massive space.

The two investors share a quiet laugh, which seems to please William to no end as he clasps his hands in front of himself and joins in their chuckle.

"Well, she must be quite a visionary... and with very specific standards," Officer Nowak adds. "I wish she were here with us today. I really look forward to meeting her."

"Ms. Bigelow expects to visit soon," William says. "Her schedule is simply unpredictable at the moment. But she'll pop up." He seems to imply that he's one step closer to Alexandria, knowing the ins and outs of her personal life, just a bit more than the rest of them.

"Well, here. Look," I blurt and point to the stone bust of Alexandria at the center of the lobby. "That's her. Can't miss her. So at least you know what she looks like now." The *Long-Dark-Haul* does not infuse manners or decorum. Quite the contrary. I just don't care what I sound like, even though I'm surprised by my need to embarrass William. The world seems to halt as everyone turns to stare at me in silence.

William looks like he's seen a ghost as his eyes bore into mine. He only allows himself a half-second of seeming upset, then bounces toward me with a smile. He wraps his arm around my shoulder and jostles me closer to him. "Everyone, this is my intern, Nerissa John."

The looks on their faces suggest they picked up on the candid roughness with which William drew me near. Between that and what I can only imagine is an expression worn exclusively by the walking dead on my own face, one could understand their apparent confusion.

"Who is this girl, Officer Banks?" Officer Mueller asks.

"This is Nerissa John, my intern," William replies.

"Yes, you said that, but—"

"Nerissa is a year-round resident of Panacea. Island-born. I've known her mother for a long time, and she thought a position with the FWG would be a great compliment to her studies during the year." William's lies come out as easily as ever. "She's been a great intern. A real fast learner."

"Well, that's wonderful, Officer Banks," Mr. Abbasi says. "I think it's a broad and open individual who can see the importance of nurturing our youth and supporting the local community."

"Yes, I truly love giving back to the community. That's another reason this project is so valuable." William places his free hand over his heart.

"You mean the new Bio-Gen building?" Mr. Elliot asks.

"Well, that, yes... but particularly the Aqua Tonic project."

"In what way?"

"Well, take Gabriel, for example." William points to Gabriel, who stands obediently in silence in his gray slacks and collared shirt. "Gabriel, come here, please."

Gabriel walks toward the gathering. William pulls him close, wrapping his arm around him as he did with me but with much less aggression. Gabriel's expression never changes.

"Gabriel is also a local. And you know, you would think..." William pauses, a smirk lifting his mouth as he shakes his head. "You'd think living on an island like Panacea would be amazing. You know, everyone's dream of paradise, right?"

They all look intrigued, listening closely as William weaves his tale of total bullshit.

"But just because it looks like paradise doesn't mean it always is. Gabriel fell onto some difficult financial times a while back." He takes a moment to look down at Gabriel for effect. "So when he came to me for a job, I was more than happy to help. Gabriel started out as a traveling drink server. I agreed to let him freelance with the other big six. After all, if he could get into a better personal situation, I was all for it."

I look at Gabriel as he simply stands there, without reaction to William's lies. Emotionless.

"He's stayed very busy," William continues. "Very popular. But only during the Season. Only for three months a year. Now... with the rebuild and the imminent launch of AQT, I've needed his help here. And he's got an amazing work ethic. So that's year-round reward for this island-born original."

A small snort involuntarily escapes me. Everyone turns. "I'm sorry. Just a little... sneeze."

"Yes, and like I said, with the launch of AQT..." William quickly re-gathers everyone's attention with his loud and commanding tone. "Gabriel will have to work exclusively for me. As a matter of fact, he'll most likely need to hire more servers. More local people are my first choice, as always, and he will be their manager." William slaps Gabriel on the back. Gabriel's wince is nearly undetectable—to everyone but me.

"Thank you, sir, for the generous opportunities," Gabriel spouts, completely monotone. "It's been a true pleasure working for you."

"You're quite welcome, Gabriel. It's also been my pleasure. So," William addresses his guests, "the launch of Aqua Tonic will not only create jobs, it will complement the islanders' and tourists' healthy lifestyles. A win-win."

"Well, Officer Banks, that is quite uplifting," says Officer Nowak.

William stands in silence, once again lifting his hand to his heart and meeting all their eyes with amazingly believable gratitude and humility. Imposter. "Shall we begin the tour?" he finally says.

In unanimous agreement, the tour commences. I fall back and walk alongside Gabriel. From the corner of my eye, I see him looking at me. I slowly turn and half look at him. Our eyes meet, and for one second, he's just Gabriel. My heart sinks into my stomach, and then I immediately feel angry. Not because of the loss of him, but because I'm feeling at all. Period. I'm not supposed to be feeling anything for a long time.

I drop my head. "Gabriel..." I whisper.

He follows my lead and bows his head, holding my gaze as we walk, waiting, I presume, for my next words.

"Why isn't the *Long-Dark-Haul* working?" I ask.

He looks up slowly to make sure nobody has heard me. But we're far enough behind, and everyone else is listening intently to William's glamorized descriptions.

"It's working exactly as it should, child," Gabriel whispers.

"Well, either I'm growing a tolerance to it, or, like I said before, you just suck at giving injections." My whisper has grown louder, and Gabriel's eyes widen in a stern seriousness.

"You need to lower your voice." He looks up at our present company. "And I assure you, I know exactly what I'm doing, like *I* said before."

"Ha! You have no idea what you're doing!" I yell, and Gabriel stops. So does everyone else in front of us. They all turn around, and as I look up, William marches toward me once again, his jaw tight, a bead of sweat rolling down his forehead. He grabs my arm and squeezes so hard I try to pull away.

"Ms. John, what seems to be the problem?" he asks quickly, trying to turn me away from everyone's eyes, blocking me from view with his body. "I mean, are you feeling all right? Do you need Gabriel to take you to sit down or get a drink?"

I get as close to his face as possible. "I'm fine. I'm very sorry for my interruption." I beg with my eyes for him to pardon my outburst. "It won't happen again. I promise," I add in a tiny whisper.

He squeezes my arm again. I close my eyes and bite my lip to keep from crying out. His face morphs from a hardened scowl to a clownish smile. He lets go, and he turns around. "Okay, folks, she's fine. We can continue."

"Are you sure? Are you all right?" Mr. Abbasi seems to be asking me directly, but William still stands between us. He steps aside, and all eyes are on me, filled with concern and definitely some irritation. "Nerissa? Are you all right?" Mr. Abbasi repeats.

"Yeah, I'm fine."

"All right, everyone..." William attempts to regain their focus. "Let's continue." He walks back to the front of the group, and as he weaves past them, he adds, "I guess it would have been worth mentioning that my intern has some... intellectual challenges, shall we say?" He waves his hand above his head. "But I like to give all kinds equal opportunities."

For the shortest, strangest moment, I can only interpret the general sameness of all their expressions as a collective realization, followed by an ultra-fast succession of pity, compassion, then admiration. For who? Me? Or William? Or both.

He's trying to pass off my awkward outburst as a side effect of a mentally impaired individual—to explain away my sudden step beyond the loyal and subservient role into which he's so easily placed on me. Okay, William. Have fun explaining this.

"I am most certainly not *intellectually challenged*," I say, throwing in air quotes for good measure. "I am—"

Gabriel's hand is on my arm. "You need to settle down. Now," he whispers sideways through tight lips.

I spin around, putting my back to the officers and investors, and face Gabriel. "They need to know who I really am. I'm so tired, Gabriel. I'm going to tell them exactly who..." I turn back around to face the tour group. The look on William's face may actually have the power to turn someone to stone. "I'm not just a local... I mean, I am local, but I am a proud member of the Dol—"

From behind, Gabriel slams his hand over my mouth. I grab him and try to rip it away. But his strength is immovable, his grip merciless. I cannot break free, no matter how I struggle. This is a side of Gabriel I've never seen.

"Settle down," he whispers urgently from behind me. "Settle down, now."

"We cannot have these interruptions," William yells a little too maniacally. "Get her out of here!"

Without a second thought, Gabriel grabs my wrist and twists it behind my back until the pain makes anything but submission impossible. He corrals me away, down the hall and out of sight and earshot. He moves so quickly, with such stealth and efficiency, I'm sure when he releases me, I'll look up to see he's been replaced by one of William's gargantuan, not-quite-human guards.

We walk for a long time in silence. The only sound comes from the shuffle of my feet and my inconsistent whimpers. The pain he's caused has been enough to make me cry. But I will not beg him for my comfort. I will not let him win.

Up an elevator and down a long hallway, then another. We arrive at G23, and Gabriel finally releases me. My fingers are tingling, and my arm at the elbow throbs. He pushes open the double doors. "Get inside."

I step slowly into the living area but don't turn around. "Well, Gabriel... you have really become someone... something... else." I can't face him—can't look at him. "I have no idea who you are. I guess I never did."

"I am exactly who I'm supposed to be in exactly the right time and place," he says calmly from the doorway.

"Hmm..." Tears fall from my eyes. "A leader by example. Right? Isn't that what you once told me you were?"

"Indeed."

A soft, sad little laugh rolls out of my throat. "Indeed."

"Get some rest. You're probably going to need it."

I don't ask him what that means. I don't want to know. There's only one thing I do want to know. "You hurt me, Gabriel, but you knew that. Why? And why didn't you just let me speak the truth to those people? I know at your core you must care. You must..." I dissolve into my own sobs again.

He doesn't say a word. I spin around and let him see me, let him hopefully feel what he's done, the pain he's caused—not just physical. "Why?" I yell at him. "Why didn't you just let me speak my truth? What difference does it make anymore? What do you care? You don't! Why, Gabriel?"

"Because it's not time yet."

CHAPTER 15

LIGHTNING STRIKES

I HAVE SOMETHING TO SHOW YOU.

MONDAY, MARCH 10TH

My eyes pop open as the double doors slam against the walls. It's just after 10:00 p.m., and my room and quarters are dark. After the hours passed and nobody came to punish me for my disruption of the tour, I finally lay down and closed my eyes. Sleep came easily. It was the first time in a long time, actually—I can't remember how long—that I fell asleep without first being drugged with some kind of sedative. It was peaceful. Natural.

But my reprieve is over. The entire space fills with blinding white light. I squint to adjust to the sharp contrast.

"Wake up!" William's loud voice is filled with anger and impatience. Hani and Gabriel follow him into my room.

I sit up and swing my legs over the bed. A shiver of fear and anticipation for what awaits me rolls up my spine and over my scalp. William is visibly angry, his jaw clenched tight. He can't stand still and seems to contemplate what he wants to say next

—or do next. Gabriel and Hani just stand quietly, waiting. Hani holds a small, black, zippered bag.

"You have a lot of nerve!" William finally says.

"I'm sorry, I don't understand what you mean," I say, deciding to play dumb.

"You almost ruined my tour. After I told you how important it was."

"How did I almost ruin your tour?"

William stops pacing and plants his feet, staring at me. "Come here."

At first, I can't move, like I'm glued tight to my bed. I look at Gabriel, who's expressionless, then at Hani. Her brow crinkles the tiniest bit, and she nods gently. Prying myself from the bed, I force my legs to take me toward him. I know he's going to punish me—I just don't know in what way or to what extent. I have to convince him it was all just a misunderstanding.

As I step up directly in front of him, I lower my eyes and brace myself for more pain. It doesn't come.

"I thought you were happy here, Nerissa," William says with, to my utter surprise, a soft tenderness in his voice.

Clearing my throat, I think quickly. "I, uh... I am. Happier now. I mean happy. Now."

"Then what was that all about? Why did you challenge me and try to reveal who you are?"

"I'm sorry. I didn't think I was challenging you. It's just that Gabriel was being rude, and then I reacted to being called *intellectually challenged*. Because I'm not... I'm actually very intelligent. Guess it's a sore spot."

Gabriel remains as cold and still as a statue. He doesn't acknowledge me.

"Well, Gabriel is here to assist me. To help keep you... happy."

"Ha. You mean quiet." I clamp my hand over my mouth. "I'm sorry."

"Gabriel assures me he knows you very well. That he can anticipate your moods. And your needs."

Now I really laugh. "Well, at one time, I would have agreed completely. And I used to think I really knew him, too. He fooled me. He's *not* the man I thought he was. So I'd be careful trusting his word."

In what parallel universe did I just warn William Banks not to trust Gabriel? My Gabriel?

"I'll keep that in mind—"

"You know, never mind," I insist. "Look, whatever you think I did or said earlier, I promise, you have the wrong idea. I was about to say I'm a proud new member of the Bio-Gen family and how happy I am to work here on this incredible project. Next thing I know, Gabriel's got me in a vice grip, dragging me down the hall."

"Is that what you were going to say? Really?"

"Yes."

"Because to me, it sounded like you were about to say you were a member of the Dolhuphemale breed."

I scoff and vehemently shake my head. "Why would I say that?"

"Because you are impetuous. And rebellious. You always have been, and no matter how far we've come, I don't think I can ever strip that away from you."

I try to redirect the conversation. "How did the tour go, then?"

William takes in a long breath and seems just as eager to change the subject. "It went well, actually." His entire posture grows straighter and taller. "They were all very impressed, especially after meeting Dr. Picker and Dr. Bigelow. Their expertise endorsements sealed the deal. I'm sure of it."

"So everyone knows about the Harvesters and the way they're created?" I ask, mortified that anyone could be okay with that.

William chuckles. "Don't be daft."

"I'm sorry?"

"Nerissa, some things must always remain private. The officers and investors were here to learn about the progress with Aqua Tonic and to gain reassurance of its potential in the marketplace."

"And its safety," I add.

"Yes, and its safety, of course. My precise records and the doctors' confirmations made it clear to everyone that this is a project ready for approval."

"Unbelievable," I mutter under my breath.

"What did you say?" William sounds angry again.

"Nothing."

He turns abruptly away from me. "Hani, please." He extends his hand, and Hani gives him the small black bag she's been holding. William turns back to face me. "I've had enough of your behavior. So now I have to remind you not to test me."

I don't bother reacting. Not anymore. William's extreme mood swings have simply grown boring and almost predictable in their unpredictability. On this end of his pendulum, there's nothing I can do or say to change his mind or his thought process. William will always need to feel in control, and even if he isn't entirely convinced or committed to his own thoughts, as it somehow seems right now, nothing in my power can alter his decisions once he's made them—as though no matter what, he must prove himself strong enough to command the situation. I don't know what he's got in that little black bag, but I know that whatever it is, it's not going to be pleasant.

William places the bag on the table, opens it, and retrieves

—as I should have expected—a small vial and a syringe. He fills the syringe to capacity with the yellowish liquid and returns his attention to me. Now he really does look insane. His eyes seem to have glazed over, as if the act of filling that needle instantly transformed him into the worst version of himself.

"Sit down," he instructs, and I do as he says. "This is going to hurt."

"Let me do it," Gabriel pipes in, which surprises me.

William doesn't acknowledge him but just turns toward me slowly, holding my eyes with his, our polar-opposite energies swirling around in some sick, twisted dance.

"I'm used to the needles," I say—not to make him feel better, but to let him know I am unafraid and unaffected by his warning.

He smiles. And now I feel afraid. "I don't mean the actual injection will hurt."

Gabriel steps up behind him. "Please, sir. Allow me to do the honors." He puts a hand on William's arm to stop him, and that grabs the man's attention. William looks at Gabriel. "It would be my pleasure to assist you, sir."

William seems to briefly snap out of his trance. "Oh, Gabriel, I've got this one." He turns back to me. "But thank you. Maybe next time."

I scan Gabriel's face, detecting a masked concern behind his eyes. I know it. He briefly meets my gaze, sighs deeply, then looks down.

"This is one of my newest creations," William says. "It was designed to train the Harvesters. It's been quite successful."

When he takes hold of my arm, I don't fight; I don't cower. He jabs the needle into me without a care. I don't flinch. He will not get the best of me. But as whatever poison William Banks has concocted to mold his hybrids into submission enters my body, I'm more and more afraid he will indeed get the best of me.

"Remember…" he says slowly, his gaze grazing over my face in lustful anticipation of my reaction to his power. "I will not tolerate anything less than grateful cooperation from you. And if I need to, I will use this… training tool again."

I open my mouth to respond, not sure of what I'll say, but I can't speak. My face is stuck in a frozen, silent scream as I try to process what's happening to me—what I'm feeling.

He laughs softly. "I look forward to hearing your nickname for this one."

A river of lava has entered my body, lighting me on fire and burning all of me from the inside out. I leap out of my chair and shake my arms, trying to get rid of the heat. I'm hopping, then jumping around the room as the inferno inside me travels down my legs.

The burning spreads to every corner of my existence, and I vomit a hot stew of waste. The lava splatters everywhere, searing the back of my throat. Even my brain feels like it's melting. My fingernails and toenails must be curling back, my hair must be singeing and falling out, my skin turning black and peeling off. I hear myself screaming now, but I'm somehow detached from it. Far way. My voice is surely only coming out as black smoke.

Somehow, I'm still aware that William, Gabriel, and Hani are still here in my room, watching me from some far-off place. A place to which I so desperately want to return.

Without warning, the fire flares into lightning strikes.

My body jerks violently with every bolt through my torso, my limbs, my neck, my face, up and down my spine, and over my scalp. Finally, I can't stand anymore, and I fall to the floor, convulsing in agony, unable to escape myself.

Gabriel kneels at my side. "Try to breathe, child," he says, so quietly, I'm not sure if I've imagined it.

William steps up behind him, blurry and disjointed like a ghostly apparition. "Gabriel, please take over now. See that she doesn't injure herself." I thrash uncontrollably under Gabriel's firm hand and watch William walk to the door. He turns around and surveys his mess one last time, and from that faraway place, I swear I hear him say, "I'm sorry, Nerissa."

"Hani, please get a cold, damp towel," Gabriel says as soon as William is gone. "Hurry."

The sporadic surges of lightning morph into a less random, more consistent shaking. But just as it feels like things may be settling down, my trembling turns into a full-blown seizure. I'm vibrating, electric, buzzing. Even my teeth chatter painfully.

A cool cloth presses against my head, another at my neck. Someone is firmly holding my hand. "This part is almost over. Hang on." Gabriel's voice feels far away—from another time entirely. But like the way he used to be.

After what must be a lifetime, the convulsions subside, replaced by a thick, heavy darkness. It feels like someone's sitting on me, pushing down, making their presence known. But the fire and the lightning and the pain are almost gone. Let it be over, please. I'll do anything.

"Let's get her into bed," Hani says. "She needs to sleep this off."

"Yes. She should be able to walk now," Gabriel agrees. "Come now, child. Stand up."

I don't know how, but with their help, I'm on my feet, one arm around each of their shoulders. I can barely keep my eyes open. "Gabriel..."

"I'm here, child. It's over. You can rest now."

They lay me down on my rich bed and get me comfortable. I'm fighting for consciousness.

"I'm going to clean things up," Hani says softly. "And I'll get more towels." She walks away from us.

My eyes are trying to close, but Gabriel's dry hand returns to my forehead, and I force myself to stay awake.

"It hurt so much, Gabriel. How could it hurt that bad?"

"Because William Banks is a monster," he says quietly. "And he designs things that hurt."

"But... I thought..." My eyes flutter as I desperately hold on to this version of Gabriel. "I thought you liked him now... that you work for... that you hate me..." Darkness courts me.

Gabriel tenderly strokes back my messy hair. "Dear one, you have no idea what you're saying."

"But... you keep making me shut up. You keep trying to silence me, and I don't understand—"

"What you don't understand is that it's not yet time."

"Yet? For what?"

He pauses, and his silence paves the way for the sensation of spiraling slowly backward down a long, narrow tube. I close my eyes and slip away, but I don't want to leave. I want to understand. I force the words out. "Gabriel, what do you mean 'yet'? Tell me."

"Oh, child. Gabriel has so much to tell you," he whispers.

"But, I..." I can't finish the thought.

"Open your eyes, child. I have something to show you." From far, far away, Gabriel's voice holds onto me like a lifeline. I hear a shuffling, something crinkling open. I'm being jostled, nudged gently at the shoulder. But I just want to drift off into the darkness. "Open your eyes. Look here."

"I can't..." I mumble.

"Just for one second. Just look for one second, and then you can sleep."

I push the heaviness from my eyelids and force them open. Gabriel holds something up in front of my face, shielding it carefully so only I can see, but it's out of focus.

"What..." I blink heavily, trying to readjust my vision. It takes several tries before the image and my understanding align.

Held before me, in Gabriel's shaking hand, is a creased and torn photograph. Now I'm speeding back up the dark, narrow tube I'd fallen into as comprehension returns and I grasp what's in front of me. In the picture, three horses stand at a fence, a tall, beautiful boy with wavy, blond-tipped hair standing on the left; his arm is wrapped under the last white horse's face in a loving, happy embrace.

I don't exactly sit up, but he's got my attention, and I lift my head. I'm suddenly sure Gabriel's returned to the robotic, unfeeling slave William seems to have turned him into, and he's just showing me this to be cruel.

"Why do you have this photo?" I choke out, doing everything I can to hold back the tears. "Why are you showing me..."

"I found it."

"Gabriel, what are you doing?" Hani's behind him with fresh towels draped over her arm, her voice thick with concern—anger, even. Gabriel quickly folds the photo and shoves it into his pocket.

"Where?" I ask. But instead of answering me, he addresses Hani.

"This does not concern you," he tells her.

"It all concerns me, Gabriel. I don't know what you think you're doing..."

I let my head fall back and my eyes close again as their words grow thick and distant. Tension fills both their voices, which now have morphed into a song. *The* song. *Let go now, precious one. It's time to rest. Your work is done.* But ... wait ...

where? Where did you find it, Gabriel? Where did you find the photo? I don't know if the words are inside my head or if I mumble them out loud.

My head grows heavier and heavier, matching the pressure I still feel all over my body, filled with the jumbled lyrics to my lullaby and the voices arguing from oceans away. I settle back down into the darkness, falling back, succumbing. The pain is gone. Falling back, falling away...

"In the cave, child. I found the photo in my cave," he whispers in my ear. "It's not mine."

CHAPTER 16
OPHELIA

IT'S YOUR TURN NEXT.

I wake from a black, dreamless sleep. The first rays of sunlight splatter over Panacea Island and slice softly through my window—the only light I see. I rise from my bed to stand at the window, the rest of the world outside still dark and quiet. Even the ocean is sleeping—uncharacteristically calm, like soft-spun glass. The sleepy sunlight bounces off the surface onto my body. I realize I'm totally naked, and I don't remember undressing or being undressed.

There's a soft knock at my door. I turn slowly, trying to grasp what a knock at my door could mean, but I don't hesitate in walking toward whomever or whatever lies on the other side.

As I step past the couch, I notice two neoprene collection satchels. Next to them sits a large plastic tube with a syringe-like tip. Curious.

At the double doors, I pause and take a deep breath, then I

turn the handle on the right and open it slowly. I'm met with two familiar but not quite normal faces.

"Good morning, Nerissa," Anastasia says.

"Come with us." Lillian smiles and holds out her hand.

I take her hand and step into the hall. The once dimly lit corridor is filled with a pulsating, deep blue. And it's cold, which reminds me I'm not wearing any clothes. But I don't stop.

We walk to the end of the hall and face the last doorway. But instead of a door, the opening is covered by a wall of gently swirling turquois water. I poke my finger into it. Nothing happens. I face Ana and Lillian, and they both just grin. They each take one of my hands, and we walk in a chain through the water-filled doorway.

We're somehow swimming through a tube-like coral reef alive with myriad creatures, some familiar, some I've never seen—never even imagined. I put my hand out to graze the wall, to meander over the bizarre lifeforms. But inside my head, I hear both Lillian and Ana say, "Don't touch that. This isn't a pleasure trip."

I retract my hand and continue beside them.

We soon come to what looks like another doorway, with us on the inside of whatever strange room this is, and Ana and Lillian slow. The three of us float silently in front of the softly churning opening. Lillian and Ana look at each other, then at me, then gently put just their faces through the doorway. I do the same.

I take a moment to gather my equilibrium. Because the vertical door has suddenly become the ceiling of a large, white room, and we are looking down. Only our faces protrude into the space.

Below us in the sterile white lab, Dr. Picker and Dr. Bigelow pick up the freshly dead corpses of what appear to be human babies and throw them by their limbs to a third person. In the corner of the room, Devin catches the babies, does some kind of quick survey of each, and tosses them aside. That's where Walter the security animal devours them. Inserted into Devin's arm is a long, clear, plastic tube.

"This will hurt," Dr. Bigelow tells Devin.

"It's okay." Devin shrugs. "I like pain." And Walter growls as a putrid-looking blue-green liquid pours through the tube and into Devin's vein. His eyes flutter, and he smiles.

We remain silent as the baby pile is reduced to almost nothing, but then Dr. Picker spots us. He stands and abruptly plucks Lillian from the watery ceiling, pulling her down into the room, and proceeds to slice open her stomach. Alakier clones pour from her womb.

Ana screams, "My boy!"

She's pulled down into the room next, sliced open the same way. More Alakier clones spill from Ana's insides, mixed with blood and guts.

Devin laughs. "Will the real Alakier please raise your hand?"

All the clones stand at attention and raise their hands simultaneously. Devin is hysterically amused, bouncing in place, wild-eyed and giggling. Then he grabs one of the clones and tosses him into the air above Walter. The clone promptly morphs into a raw chicken and is gobbled up completely in an instant. Devin does the same with the rest of them, one by one.

"No! Please don't hurt my boy! Please... my son...." Ana pleads as the rest of her blood and insides spill onto the floor in front of her.

"Take them all." Lillian counters. "Please. I want to be done."

"*No.*" Did I say that out loud?

Everyone in the room looks up at me, tilts their heads, and

just observes me for one way-too-long moment. I want to leave this place.

I pull back and try to return to the water above me—or is it behind me? But I can't move. And now I can't breathe. I'm drowning—in the air, not the water.

Dr. Picker and Dr. Bigelow say together, "It's your turn next."

I'm trapped. Nothing will set me free. The doctors both reach for me.

"No!" I squeeze my eyes shut. Their hands are all over me, trying to pull me down.

"Open your eyes, Nerissa," they say again in unison.

No. I don't want to. My tears squeeze out from under my tightly shut lids.

"Nerissa, open your eyes."

My lids flutter open, and a river of tears now spills from them. I'm no longer looking down, but up at the ceiling. Hani sits next to me on the edge of my bed.

"Hani?"

"It's okay. You were dreaming."

I breathe. I can breathe again. I'm not trapped anymore. "What?"

"You're fine. You were just having a dream. A bad one, I guess."

She's right. I'm in my room, safe. It's light outside—early morning, by the looks of it. Everything is okay. I'm okay.

But that wasn't *just* a dream.

CHAPTER 17

THE LIES SHE TELLS

I HAVE A VOICE.

TUESDAY, MARCH 11TH

"How are you feeling?" Hani asks as my mind and eyes adjust to the light, then to the room—to my actual surroundings compared to the wicked, twisted dream from which I was just trying to escape. I have to think about it, as I'm not sure myself.

"Umm… I feel all right. Surprisingly."

"You had one heck of a night last night, didn't you?"

She's right. And as I recall the horror of William's *Wildfire*, my anger grows.

"Yeah, one hell of a night."

"Here, this is for you." Hani hands me one of William's signature envelopes, not giving me the chance to say or even think more about what I went through last night. I'm still lying down, not even out of bed. Great. Just the way I want to start my day.

I sit up and cross my legs under me. Let's just get this over with. Hani walks into the kitchen, and I rip open the envelope.

Dear Nerissa,

Good morning. Hope you slept well. You have the day to go to Albatross without intervention. However, you are expected to return with a harvest. Be back on base at sundown. Enjoy your time with your family.

I always keep my promises. Remember, I will expect you to keep yours as well. Soon.

Fondly,
William

William Banks is nothing less than psychotic. Or he has some kind of split personality disorder, like he's two different people, sometimes in the same sentence. I wasn't expecting to still be allowed to go to Albatross drug-free. Not after the punishment I received last night. But who knows? Maybe I really did hear him say he was sorry; maybe he felt guilty. And in his ego-driven mind, by honoring the wish he granted me, he's absolved himself of that guilt.

Whatever the case, I'm free for the day, and that sudden flood of realization launches me out of bed. I get ready, dressing in a slick, black wetsuit of sorts, then I eat the food Hani put on the table.

"Try to fill yourself up, Nerissa. The ocean will still be cold, and you'll feel it today."

"Good. I want to feel it," I snap, then pull myself back together. "Thank you for the delicious breakfast, Hani."

"You're welcome. Now, let's get these collection bags on

you." She wraps the straps, one by one, around my waist and clips them tight. Then she tugs at each, making sure they're secure. "Don't lose them. I couldn't stand watching you go through what you went through last night again."

Her kindness and concern make me stop mid-chew—a soft, spongy muffin filling my mouth with warmth and flavor. I look at Hani, who looks down at the table, now fussing about with the plates so she doesn't have to meet my gaze.

I finish my bite and ask, "Hani, what were you and Gabriel arguing about last night?" I won't tell her what Gabriel whispered in my ear. I think he whispered that for a reason, and until I hear what Hani has to say, that'll stay between me and him. She doesn't seem to want to answer me and only keeps herself busy.

"Hani?"

She looks up. "It's nothing to concern yourself with, dear."

"But I'm confused," I say. "Gabriel suddenly seemed so nice, like he was his old self again."

"Well, you were under the influence of a pretty powerful drug."

"So you're saying I imagined that?" The hope I felt about Gabriel, about him only pretending to be William's loyal servant, is quickly dissolving.

"I'm saying I don't want you to worry about that right now. You need to finish eating and get going. You've got this one day, the whole day, to share with your loved ones, and I want you to go enjoy it."

"So you think this will be the only day he'll let me do this?"

She doesn't answer right away as she gathers up my dirty dishes. "I don't know what Officer Banks will allow you in the future. He's an unpredictable man." She sighs.

"You can say that again." It's clear she's avoiding

answering any of my questions directly, but I have one more to ask. "Where is Gabriel this morning?"

"He was also given the day to do as he pleases. He left the base hours ago."

I'm suddenly arranging my day in my head, figuring out where to go first and where the most likely place will be to find Gabriel.

"Okay, Hani. I'm outta here. Thank you for the food and your help. I'll see you later."

"Please be careful, Nerissa."

"I will. Thanks." I smile at her and walk out the door.

The weather in March on Panacea is fickle. I'm not even to the bend at the old bridge, and I've already been blasted with cold sea spray and violent gusts of wind as well as had the moisture heating and rising off the road, wrapping itself up my legs as I ride in the early-spring sun.

As I approach the bridge, I have a choice to make—turn left toward resort row and go through Concordia, as I've been doing to make better time to Albatross, or go straight and enter the water from Playa Rosa. I've decided I need to go to Albatross before I look for Gabriel. My family has to be my priority. Besides, it may be hard to find him, even though I'm pretty sure I know where to look. Heading toward Playa Rosa may prove too tempting. I imagine myself passing the beach and riding up the hill, past the Oval, all the way to the end of the road—unable to stop myself from trekking down the cliff to Gabriel's cave. If I go there first, who knows how long I'll be.

I turn left toward resort row. Soon, I find myself at Concordia's employee entrance. Just like last time, the door has been left unlocked, and I step inside without any difficulty.

My head fills with my own dialogue and questions, hope and trepidation. I can't wait to embrace my mother, Kendra, and the rest of the breed, this time with feeling. I can't wait to tell them everything I know or suspect. But to my disappointment, even though I'm drug-free, I still feel numb—or at least distracted—and my current surroundings blur around me.

Out on the beach pavilion, it's as though time stands still, with the exception of the early-spring buds dotting the shrubs and trees. The beach remains untouched, pristine in its natural state, and I walk across it.

As I enter the water, Hani's words return to me. Yes, the ocean is still cold—colder than I imagined it would be. I'm grateful to be wearing more than swim shorts and a bikini top. In another month or so, that'll be comfortable again. Only two and a half months until the Season opens.

The swim to Albatross is quick, even with big waves and erratic currents. As I approach the east side, I'm suddenly overcome with emotion. Finally. Just like the very first time I visited after I was taken, before the *Long-Dark-Haul* existed. I can't wait to hug my mom and tell her all I know.

Once I enter the in-tube, I try to determine where my breed will be. I try the beach first. But after an exhaustive search, my heart racing with anticipation, they aren't there.

I look in the arena and the open area next to it. Both are empty and silent. It feels sad and lonely here, and a lump forms in my throat. The last time I stood on this ground was the day my world changed forever. The men in the chopper fired into our gathering and destroyed the majority of my family, then took me. The memories—the gunfire, the screams, death, fear —all come flooding back to me. I hated myself that day, hated what I had caused. I'd quickly come to accept that the only way to stop the pain—for everyone—was to willingly sacrifice myself. William demanded such justice. An eye for an eye.

But the pain hasn't really stopped, has it? Not for anyone. And now, as I stand here, I'm not so sure being drug-free is any kind of salvation. I feel sick, nauseous and dizzy, a sweat breaking on my forehead and upper lip, even though a strong breeze rolls in off the water.

I force myself to unfreeze, to shake the horrible memories out of my head and go find my family.

Back in the Hub, another passageway leads to a shallow, tree-surrounded cavern where we sleep and live when the elements are not ideal. The place where Neptune the cat's shrine was erected.

But I don't expect to find them here. Most likely, they're gathering food and harvesting. But to my surprise, as soon as I'm out of the water, I hear them—quiet voices just a short distance away. They sound happy—delighted, really.

"Hello?" I say so as not to scare them with my approach.

There's a short, silent pause.

"Hello? Nerissa, is that you?" my mother asks. I hear the elation in her question, to which she seems to already know the answer.

I step around a rocky outcropping and out of the shadow of the trees. "Mom, it's me... oh!"

There, in an intimate circle, my family sits on the ground. In the middle, Kendra holds the smallest, most perfect, fuzzy, red-haired baby I've ever seen.

My mother jumps up and gathers me in her arms, squeezing so tight, I have to wriggle free. Taking my arm, she walks me toward the circle. One by one, they all hug me. I kneel beside Kendra and her baby. Her joy radiates like a palpable warmth. She holds her blanketed bundle to her chest, the baby's head nestled just under her mother's chin. Kendra looks at me and smiles.

"She's beautiful," I say. "What's her name?"

"Ruari."

"That's so pretty. I've never heard it before."

"It means red-headed king." She smiles and inhales the scent of the baby's hair.

I tilt my head and search her big, beautiful eyes. "King?" My heart's racing now.

Kendra just returns the meaningful glance and nods.

"Because Ruari's a boy?"

Her impossibly wide smile is all the answer I need. The rest of the maids around us laugh softly, cooing and sighing.

"Oh, my gosh. Kendra... this is so... wonderful. Congratulations. Do you—" Now I can't bring myself to ask how this happened, because I already know the answer. And it's something I'll have to explain to everyone, along with everything else I now know.

"You seem better," my mother says, interrupting my uncomfortable thoughts. "You seem... here. Awake."

I turn to her. "Yeah. He agreed to let me come drug-free. I can actually *feel*." The words catch in my throat, and I have to fight back the urge to cry. "But honestly, I don't feel very good."

"When's the last time they gave you anything?" Kai asks, which I find an interesting question.

"Last night. Something new. Other than that, early yesterday... but it didn't feel as strong as usual."

All at once, I'm thinking about Gabriel and Hani again.

"You may be withdrawing," Kai says. "I understand that can be very uncomfortable."

"Yeah, that's what I was just thinking."

"How did you get William to let you do this?" my mother asks with a concerned frown.

I'm not sure how to answer, because whatever I say is going to upset her. "I had to earn it." It's all I can come up with. But it's the truth.

She closes her eyes for a second and looks as though she's thinking hard, trying to buffer her own response, breathing slow and deep. "Well, I'm so glad you're here," she says, "as yourself. Especially for this." Her reply—and her restraint—impress me.

"Me too. Hey, have you heard from Leyla?"

"No. There's been no communication for a long time. None of our CNIs seem to be functioning."

That's disappointing, but not surprising. I turn my attention back to Kendra and the baby. "When was she—sorry. When was *he* born?"

"March fifth," Kendra says with a swooning sigh. "He's six days old."

"How did it go?" I ask, curious about the process and the pain, morbidly anticipating what William has assigned to me. Soon. My so-called promise to him. One I never made.

"Well, I'd be lying if I said it was easy. But my little guy wanted out, and I'm told it was relatively fast. So, I'm thankful for that."

"It must be a boy thing," my mother adds and laughs. They all laugh.

A boy thing.

"So... how? I mean, why do you think you had a boy?" It's time to tell them what I know, and it's time to ask my mother what's been burning in my heart for almost two weeks.

Kendra looks back up at me with an intensity that makes me think she somehow knows I'm about to ruin things—like I'm about to bring the magical moment to a screeching halt. "We don't know why Ruari is a boy. But we think it has something to do with the Contributor."

I scoff, and a small, sarcastic laugh escapes me.

"What?" Kendra asks. "What is it you need to say?"

"Well, I have a lot to say. To all of you. But... really, Kendra? Contributor? Must I remind you that you were—"

"No. No, you don't need to remind me that I was raped. I'm reminded of that every single day. Without your help. But like I said to you at Gabriel's funeral—"

"Oh... yeah," I say. "Gabriel's funeral. We need to talk about that too. But go on. We'll get to that."

She glares at me, exhaling through her nose like a bull. "I need to feel as normal as possible, Nerissa. And this baby and me? Ruari and I... we're in this together. So if I need to consider his father a Contributor, just let me have that, okay? Is that so much to ask?"

I want to be kind. I want to take her in my arms and coddle her, to tell her that yes, everything is normal, everything is fine, and her baby being born a boy is just simply some coincidence. I can't. "Well," I finally say, "you're right. Your baby is a boy because of your... because of his father. That's correct. And I know why. I know the truth."

They all stare at me, waiting. And I hold them in their anticipation.

"What is it?" my mother demands.

"It's the AQT," I say.

"What are you talking about?" Kendra asks, indignant and impatient.

"The father of your child, of your Ruari, is Tommy Alvarez. One of your rapists."

There's a collective, audible gasp.

"How do you know that?" Kendra's voice trembles.

"Because I do. Because last Season, one thing lead to the next, and the truth unraveled in front of me. And now I understand why. Tommy was an AQT junky. And I killed him."

Two hours later, I've retold the story of discovering who attacked Kendra, how Emily was wearing her necklace—a gift from her brother Tommy—how she unknowingly led me to the marina, where I found Tommy and Bradford, and what I did to them. My mother doesn't seem surprised; I knew she suspected something last Season when she saw the scratches and bruises all over me the morning after I came home drunk. The morning after I murdered two men. I tell them Gio knew.

I tell them all the horrors of the new Bio-Gen building and labs. About the implantations, Ana and Lillian, the Harvester clones, the massive and seemingly productive Wreckleaf tanks, and the imminent reopening and re-launching of AQT. I tell them of Alexandria Allerton Bigelow's part, that her nephew is one of the new doctors working at the labs, how she's basically responsible for the rebirth of William's project, and how, if given the chance, I'll kill her as well.

When I tell them about Gabriel, they have a hard time believing me. It seems they think the constant barrage of drugs has led me to some kind of delusional breakdown. As though I somehow cope with the reality of his absence, of his death, by hallucinating Gabriel and assigning him his evil role of turned traitor—loyal servant to the worst enemy we have ever collectively known. But somewhere, deep inside each of them, I know they believe me. They must.

Finally, I tell them all why I believe—no, why I *know*—the reason Ruari was born a boy.

"So, your theory is that the concentrated chemical compounds of Wreckleaf in Aqua Tonic are responsible for finally creating a male offspring in a Dolhuphemale. Do I have that right?" my mother asks, sounding irritated and somewhat confused.

"Yes. That's correct."

"Do you know why or how?"

"AQT was—or is, I should probably say—making the humans immune to our toxins. Remember?"

"Yes," she says. "That's what you told us."

"Well, for some reason I can't explain completely, that chemical concentration not only makes them immune to our enchantment, it also somehow overrides *our* genetic programming to create female-only offspring. Kind of ironic, if you ask me. A *tool* used to control us, broken by another *tool* used to control us."

"So you're saying the very thing that keeps us alive is suddenly a danger to us?" My mother stares at me with wide, mortified eyes.

"Not at low or even moderate levels. And certainly not in its original form. Not our fresh, alive Wreckleaf. Because most people can't consume it like we do. I mean, it's possible, but most people wouldn't have the patience to build up a tolerance. But the problem is, Aqua Tonic hasn't been designed for moderate consumption. It's an intentionally addictive substance. Almost from the first taste. And that addiction creates the AQT junky. The human man we can't enchant anymore. But now he's the only one who can father male Dolhuphemales."

"This is a lot to take in." My mother blinks and gazes almost everywhere else but at me. "I think we need a break. You need to bring back a fresh harvest, don't you?"

"How'd you know?" I ask.

She points at my waist. "The collection bags."

"Oh. Yeah."

"All right. Meredith, Kai, please take these. They need to be stuffed full."

I unlatch the bags at my waist and hand them to my sister maids. They don't hesitate before quickly disappearing for an impromptu harvest. "The rest of you, please, give me some time alone with my daughter."

The other maids follow my mother's instruction, filtering slowly away from us. Kendra starts to stand from where she's been sitting. "Nerissa," she asks, "can you hold him?"

"Oh. Sure." But honestly, I don't want to hold her baby. Not yet. He needs to grow on me. She doesn't give me that time and space before little Ruari is suddenly in my arms. He's tiny, and helpless, and without a voice. He's so beautiful and innocent.

But I'm not tiny or helpless. I have a voice.

"Who's my real father, Tatiana?"

Both she and Kendra snap their heads in my direction, wearing similar expressions of genuine confusion—faces contorted, brows creased, mouths tight, eyes hyper-focused on me and still vacant-looking. In any other situation, it'd probably be amusing how much they look alike. How exaggerated their distress.

"I'm sorry, what?" my mother asks.

"William Banks is sterile," I reply.

"What are you... how... exactly what are you talking about?" A little color rises in her cheeks.

"It's simple, Mom. I need to know who my real father is. And oh, yeah, it'd be nice to know why you lied to me." I manage well enough to keep the emotion out of my voice while my stomach rolls over and my breathing speeds up.

Tatiana's face falls into a stone mask, and she suddenly looks so much older. "Kendra, would you please excuse us?"

"Of course." Kendra retrieves Ruari from my arms.

"Wait." I lean over to kiss his soft, red fuzz and breathe in his scent. "He's perfect."

She smiles warmly, then takes her son and leaves.

"Can you please tell me why you're questioning William being your father?" my mother asks.

"Like I said, he's sterile."

"Why on earth would you say that?" Her voice rises now in anger.

"Because I learned Alakier isn't his son. It's a long story, but William couldn't get Anastasia pregnant. She had a love affair with a man named Jaxson. And *he* is Alakier's father. Not William Banks."

"That proves nothing," Tatiana shouts.

"Why so defensive, Mom?"

She paces in front of me, and her nervous demeanor is the nail in this coffin. Finally, she stops and faces me again, her eyes reflecting a mix of shame and resolution. "Nerissa..." She almost whispers it. "I couldn't tell you. It was too dangerous."

"Yet you made it a point to lie to me about it last Season. Why?"

"I had to." She can no longer meet my eyes and stares at the ground instead.

"*Why?*" I yell.

"I... can't. I'm sorry."

"Who is it? Who's my father?"

She shakes her head and presses a hand over her mouth.

"Tell me, damnit!" I scream, tears pouring down my cheeks now. "Don't you think I deserve to know?"

"I can't," she whispers.

I stare at her for a few torturous seconds, fully expecting her to break and crumble and finally speak the truth. But she doesn't. And I'm done. So much for being able to feel—for being able to express emotion. Fuck that.

I turn and storm back into the cavern, my mother yelling behind me, "Don't tell him, Nerissa. Don't tell him he's not your father. He doesn't know. Please!"

I don't stop, don't slow for a second, then plunge into the

water at the tube inlet and swim back through the underwater caves, all the way past the Hub, and into the open ocean.

The swim back to Panacea is a complete blur—somehow even more of a blur than when I'm under the cloak of the *Long-Dark-Haul*. But when I reach the sand at Concordia, my emotions finally catch up. I lay sprawled on the beach like a dying animal; the pain pouring out of me is relentless. When I realize I said goodbye to none of them, I stand, turn toward Albatross, and seriously contemplate going back. When will I be able to hug Kendra, to hold Ruari again, and feel? Will I ever?

But I can't face *her* again. I can't listen to my mother's lies and excuses, can't even fathom her reasons for them. And I won't give her an ounce of satisfaction. She'll think I returned for her. No.

A brisk gust rolls in off the water and reminds me of how cold and numb I am, freezing and sweating at the same time. I wrap my shaking arms around myself and my heart sinks. I left my collection bags, too, before my sister maids could give me the harvest. I need to go back, or I'll be punished.

Maybe I can reason with him. Maybe.

"Don't tell him he's not your father. He doesn't know."

I shake the thoughts from my head and turn toward the building, trudge up to the beach pavilion, and back through the employee entrance. I walk slowly down the hallway, through the locker room, and back to the side door. Part of me wants to stay here, to warm up, and to be alone. I could explore the resort, maybe find an unlocked room and take a bath. And a nap. But I flush my brief fantasy from my mind. It's time to find Gabriel. Time to see whether I was imagining his change of demeanor last night. *Please* let me be right.

I open the door and step out of the building into the sunlight. Without the wind, the day is warm and pleasant. I close my eyes, turn my face to the sun, and take a deep breath. Then another.

Stay focused. Let's do this.

I pull myself to attention and head for my board. Balanced on the controls in its upright position, a small, folded piece of paper sits in wait. I snatch it up and devour the brief message. The handwriting is familiar.

Be at the river Friday at noon where we first met.
Do whatever you must to be there. Everything will be explained.

My heart is galloping, my eyes filling with tears of relief. Looks like I didn't need to go searching. Gabriel found me. I knew it. I just *knew* it. Even through the blaze of William's *Wildfire*, my heart recognized my real Gabriel. And now, even after the awful experience with my mother, I'm so grateful. Because for the first time in a long time, I feel hope.

I tuck the note into my wetsuit, then think again. I read it over, kiss the words, hold it to my heart as though I can absorb its energy, its power. Then I rip it into tiny pieces.

I ride my board back up the road. At the old bridge, I look up the hill, onto the ridge, and smile. Then I sprinkle Gabriel's note into the breeze and watch it scatter.

The fountain in the Bio-Gen lobby is running. Water pours

out of *Alexandria's* mouth in a constant, graceful stream and gently splashes its way into the koi pond. In all honesty, it's mesmerizing. But that water may as well be fire, or sludge, or diarrhea. It's a disgusting display of an equally disgusting human being. She should be represented appropriately.

"It's nice, isn't it?" William startles me from behind, and I jump. "Oh." He chuckles. "You must have been in deep thought."

"Yeah," I say, composing myself, "I was. It's okay."

"You must have missed me," he adds through a huge grin.

I don't know what he's getting at or how to answer him. "I'm sorry?"

He raises his brows and squints, tilting his head ever so slightly. Then he frowns and looks at the windows and back at me. "It's so early. I gave you the entire day. It's hours until sundown.

"Oh, yeah. The water was really rough today." The water, of course, was its typical self—so much so that I don't really remember the swim either way. "I thought it might take me longer, and I didn't want to be late, so I left early."

"I see." I can tell he doesn't believe my lame explanation, but he seems to be in a decent mood, so I get right to it.

"Um, I'm really sorry, but I don't have the harvest."

His face twitches in concern, and he looks at my waist. "Why not?"

"The water was so rough, my family didn't want me to harvest. I ignored them, but when I got to the Wreckleaf fields, I couldn't see anything. They were right, so I turned back. I figured it was better showing up empty-handed than not showing up at all."

He stares down at me. "Why are you lying to me?"

"I'm not." I hold his gaze and try not to give myself away. Breathe, Nerissa.

"I've been out on the water today. The channel is perfectly normal. In fact, it's quite a nice spring day."

"You're right, and that's why I argued with my mom and the rest of them…" I'm talking too fast, too nervously. I force myself to slow down and control my anxiety. "That's why I didn't listen to them and went to the ship graveyard. But you know how it is… I mean, the ocean is so crazy and unpredictable. You just never know what's happening below the surface."

William gently lays his left hand on my shoulder, almost at my neck. "Well, what do you think I should do about this? I punished you the last time you showed up short."

"It wasn't my fault. I… I swear."

His hand slides up to my neck, his thumb resting in the front, fingers wrapped around the back. And now, no matter how I try, I can't control my fear. I close my eyes and let my mouth fall open, sucking in short, ragged breaths. And finally, I just say it.

"I understand. Do what you must. But please… please not the *Wildfire* again."

William's heavy hand relaxes, then pulls away. When I open my eyes, he's leaning in close and smiling. "*Wildfire?*" He laughs.

"Oh, um… the drug you—" I stop myself. "The training tool you used last night."

"*Wildfire*, yes! I like it. See? I knew you'd come up with a great nickname." He steps away from me and seems to search the floor for his next thought. "Well, okay. I suppose I can spare you the *Wildfire* two days in a row." He smiles.

"Thank you," I breathe.

"How are you feeling, by the way? Drug-free and all?" He reaches out to pet my cheek with the back of a hand.

He's a pendulum, swinging at full speed.

"It's been a great day."

"But?" He leans closer again. "You can tell me. You can tell me anything."

It's like he's put me in a trance, and I can't stop myself from being lured into some false sense of care and concern.

"I don't feel very good," I say weakly, and a few disobedient tears glide down my cheeks.

"Aw, it's okay." He gently wipes the tears on my cheek with the same thumb that was at my throat moments ago. "Come here." He wraps his arms around me and pulls me into him. My face presses against his chest, and I hear his heartbeat as he takes in a deep breath, his nose in my hair like he's smelling me. I close my eyes. I hate myself for closing my eyes, but I do it anyway, and feel myself relaxing.

We stay this way for what feels like a long time.

"There's some cleaning you can do in the labs this afternoon," he announces out of nowhere, instantly breaking my trance.

I pull away from him. "Of course." I clear my throat.

"And this time, you'll do it drug-free." He smiles at me again.

A sharp panic overwhelms me. "But I'm, uh, so much more productive under the *Long-Dark-Haul*." I smile when I say the nickname, hoping he'll be amused again.

He looks like he's concentrating very hard, one finger resting lightly against his bottom lip. "Yes, of course. That's what it was designed for. But I think, in all fairness, since you've not delivered my Wreckleaf harvest, you ought to feel something unpleasant. Like the way you've made me feel."

Sucking in a breath, I imagine working in the labs doing whatever it is he'll have me do while riding out this withdrawal. I've never wanted an injection of something more than I do in this moment.

"I'm sorry I made you feel that way, but I promise—"

"No Wreckleaf for me, no relief for you," he says.

I try a different angle. "Why do you even want the Wreck-leaf? You clearly don't need it anymore. Your tanks are a massive success." Maybe flattery will swing him back.

He laughs. "You're right. My tanks are a huge success. But even though our analysis of my homegrown Wreckleaf is barely discernable from the wild-harvested, Gabriel still wants the original. Don't ask me why."

"So I was harvesting for Gabriel?" I'm stunned. And now I want to kick myself for not going back to Albatross.

"Essentially, yes. We still use a bit of it on the test subjects. But like I said, mine is nearly bio-identical."

Nearly does not mean identical. Nothing will ever truly replace Wreckleaf.

"Well, then, if I may suggest, maybe Gabriel should choose my punishment." It's a long shot but worth a try. Gabriel wouldn't let me suffer any longer.

"Splendid idea!" William shouts and proceeds to summon Gabriel to the lobby. But he has to know Gabriel's not on the Rock; he's on Panacea, enjoying his day of freedom.

Only a moment later, Gabriel strolls into the lobby where we stand in wait. My heart swells with the thought that Gabriel went to Panacea for what seems like the sole purpose of leaving the note on my board, then returned early to keep up appearances. Brilliant.

William explains the situation to him, then asks what he'd like to do. My punishment is Gabriel's call. Anything he wants.

"Master Banks, I agree with your choice one hundred percent. To the labs. No more drugs to mask her feelings. It's only fair," Gabriel says.

My eyes grow wide.

"You heard the man." William is giddy. "Go get changed

and report to the labs immediately." He points, as though I've forgotten the way to my room. But before I leave, he adds, "And Nerissa, I kept my promise. You're next."

"I'm next?" My lips tremble with the question.

"You're next to keep your promise, meaning you're next to become a host for a Harvester."

"I never made that promise," I say in challenge, recklessly ignoring any other consequence. I've just been sentenced to the worst consequence of all. William tilts his head and opens his mouth to respond, but I don't give him the chance. "You don't even need the Harvesters, do you? You've successfully reproduced Wreckleaf. You can grow all you want."

He grins and casually shrugs one shoulder. "I probably don't, but I like to keep my options open. It's great fun creating those obedient creatures."

It's hard to wrap my mind around his sickening God complex. "Why do you need me? You've already got two hosts."

"I told you, Nerissa. The Harvesters grow and live fast. I want a constant overlap, and honestly, I think the other hosts are burning out."

I shake my head and clench my fists at the thought of Lillian and Ana being used as hybrid-making factories—of the fact that even William is *concerned* for their well-being. And a new thought pops into my mind. "Why do you even need hosts?" I ask. "Your other monsters weren't created that way. You made them in a lab. In a dish, I'm guessing. My ancestors weren't born to a host, either. So why do you need us for this job?"

William looks at Gabriel, and the most twisted, maniacal smile spreads across his face. As he throws his head back and laughs, Gabriel shoots me a quick glance before laughing with him.

The room spins, and I have to cover my ears. Their laughter

is deafening and frightening. I close my eyes tight and shout, "Why are you laughing?" And it's like I'm traveling back through a black hole, when William was once before overly amused by my question.

"Stupid, stupid hybrid," William bellows. "I don't *need* you Dolhuphemales to be hosts."

I blink back my tears. "Then why do you use us?"

His laughter cuts short, and he looks straight into my eyes, unblinking—unyielding—as he holds me in an intense, painfully uncomfortable stare. Finally, he says, "Because it's easier. And because I can."

I hang my head and flop into an oversized lobby chair as the truth of who he really is comes flooding back over me. I'm angry, exhausted, and completely ashamed, disgusted by the fact that I allowed myself to find even a second of comfort in his embrace.

"So, after your work in the labs, get some sleep tonight. Because tomorrow is your big day," William adds.

I can't help but imagine the implantation process. How my life will forever change. For no good reason.

The folly of rich men is cruel and runs deep.

I lift my head and find Gabriel looking at me. Staring at me. The note. *Be at the river on Friday at noon.* That's in three days. I can't be forced to endure an implantation tomorrow. *Do whatever you must to be there.*

"The first few weeks are really tough. Isn't that what you said?" I ask, trying to sound as steady and resolved as possible.

William still seems amused, the smile never having completely left his face. "I did say that. That's why I recommend a good night's sleep. The process is also quite challenging."

"Do I have to be in that gel? That stuff I saw Lillian in?"

"Not if you don't fight."

"I won't fight. Just give me the *Long-Dark-Haul,* and I won't fight at all."

"Well, that's an interesting idea. I'll think about it. But once you're pregnant, no more of it. That drug is not safe for the fetus."

God forbid we compromise the *fetus.* But he just gave me another idea. I may be grasping at straws, but it's worth a try. I swallow hard and push past my fear and sadness.

"I know I messed up today, and I feel really bad about it. I don't ever want to disappoint you..." I pause, then stand again to pace beside the armchair for effect. "I'll take my punishment. I know it's what I deserve. But you got me thinking. If that drug, the *Long-Dark-Haul,* is bad for the baby, I can't imagine any of the others are safe, either. And my body is full of them. I mean, my blood must be beyond toxic. And that can't be good for the pregnancy and the baby at all."

He looks at me, and I feel his mind working, sorting out my sudden change of mind. I'm praying I've appealed to his sense of righteousness and his constant need to always be in control. I don't know if he's buying any of it.

"Go on," he says. "What do you propose?"

"I'm not even twenty-four hours clean. Give me a few more days—a week, even—to get all the residual toxins out of my system. You said there's been some difficulty with the implants sticking. Why don't we give it the best possible chance?"

"But you just said you want to be dosed at implantation so you don't fight it."

"No. Never mind. I don't need it. I'm strong. Dolhuphe-males are tough, remember? That's what you told Doctor Picker and Doctor Bigelow."

William looks at Gabriel, who holds a stoic, solid expression. "Gabriel, what do you think?"

Gabriel takes a large, deep breath and exhales slowly

through his nose, studying me. "Well, I think she may have a point."

"Yes, that's what I think." William probably only agreed with him to make it seem he'd thought the same before asking for another opinion.

I can hardly breathe as I wait for William's final word.

"I can trust you, right, Nerissa?" he finally asks.

I need him to believe I've suggested this plan because I want to be of service to him, because I *want* to help. I walk slowly toward him and stop just inches away, my face below his, my eyes wide and soft. "Of course you can. I understand my role here. I understand what I'm invested in and what I'm here to protect."

He smiles, caressing my cheek with the back of his hand again. I smile back at him. The pendulum has swung again.

"Okay. You have one week. All the residuals will be out of your system by then. Complete withdrawal won't be easy, nor will the procedure."

"I understand," I say. "But I think it's important."

"Well, I admire your courage. It's quite valiant. Now, get changed and get to the labs." He spins on his heels and walks out of the lobby.

I wait until he's out of sight and exhale my relief. I turn toward Gabriel, happy to have a moment alone with him. But he's turned his back and walks away from me too.

CHAPTER 18

ALEXANDRIA

WHAT IS REAL? WHAT IS AN ILLUSION?

WEDNESDAY, MARCH 12TH

I've been lying awake in my bed since before the sun rose over Panacea, staring out over the water to Albatross, my pillowcase damp with my tears. I haven't slept at all since my session working in the labs until late last night.

Once again, William Banks had the upper hand. As we agreed, I wasn't given more drugs yesterday. My body is still buzzing with a low-level, constant shaking. It was worse last night, but it's hard to know if it's because of the toxins leaving my system or because of the horrors I not only witnessed, but also took part in.

The things I saw and did yesterday made my first visit to the labs in the old building look like child's play. I guess I should have known better, but somewhere inside me, I'd convinced myself that in this new building—in this more advanced, highly evolved, technologically sophisticated structure—things would be different. They'd be more... humane. More civil—easier to look at, to digest, and to be a part of.

217

I've never been more wrong.

And I got to feel all of it on top of my withdrawal—cold sweats, aching all over, a pounding headache, nausea, and those damn shakes. I was forced to wipe up blood, excrement, and body parts. I poured a steaming-hot green liquid—one I'm sure had the new Wreckleaf in it—into the eyes of an imprisoned animal and watched them literally melt in front of me. Only after the thrashing animal stopped screaming did I record my observations. Then I cleaned it up and positioned another test subject in its place for a new concoction.

I was told that the tests were imperative to the development of a new beauty product to be launched in the upcoming Season—a breakthrough in cosmetic advancement.

The tourists will be so happy to have clearer, smoother skin without the worry of the sun damaging their new, chemically-exposed dermal layers. How wonderful for them.

Sometime after the second or third hour, I stopped reacting, stopped crying. I don't remember what I did, but something inside me turned off—a brilliant subconscious coping strategy, I suppose—and I simply did as I was instructed. I went through the motions, unfeeling. The guilt, the shame, the sadness, the fear I felt within myself and my victims just left me. But that changed once I was relieved of my duties and sent back to my room.

Immediately I took off my clothes and threw them in the garbage. Stepping into the shower, the water hit me as though it were washing off my iron shield—one I imagined stained with the blood and lives of my victims. After I scrubbing my entire body until my skin turned red and raw, I crumbled on the shower floor and cried until the water went cold.

I don't remember crawling into bed. But here I am, puffy-eyed and quivering. A torturous murderer. I've killed before, but never like this. Never the innocent.

There's a knock on my door.

"Nerissa, it's Hani. Can I come in?" She enters anyway. "Good morning. It's time to get up and get ready."

Forcing myself to roll over, I lift my head. "Get ready for what?" Please don't let it be more lab time. Please.

"Ms. Bigelow is coming today, and Officer Banks wants everything to be perfect."

She looks like a demented lemon with a black stick up her butt. Alexandria's outfit is ridiculous. Her bright-yellow, pouffed-at-the-waist and tapered-top-and-bottom suit is hideous. And how she doesn't trip and fall on those enormous, shiny black platform shoes is beyond me. Her jet-black tights make her skinny legs look like tiny, dead tree branches. Top it all off with a matching wide-brimmed hat and gloves, and none of us could have missed her coming from a mile away in a midnight downpour.

William has gathered all his officers and employees in the opulent Bio-Gen lobby to welcome Queen Bigelow as she makes her grand entrance with her own entourage. We're lined up on either side of the room, uniformed, and instructed to remain silent and smiling.

Alexandria may as well have arrived on a magical, flying dragon. The exaggerated collective awe and admiration are sickening. I will not smile at this bitch.

"Welcome, Alexandria. Welcome home." William's voice bounces off the walls and fills the space, as if he's just spoken through a microphone with some kind of special reverb effect. He bows slightly and extends his arm toward the lobby and in the direction of her tribute fountain.

She walks forward, her clicking shoes the only sound aside

from the water streaming in the fountain. She slowly removes her matching yellow gloves, one finger at a time, without a word. She rolls her slightly squinted eyes over the enormous space, her head turning this way and that, up and down, taking it all in, evaluating.

Then she stops and draws in a breath. William looks like he's about to faint, or crap his pants, or die. This is without a doubt the most irritatingly amusing moment I've experienced in a long, long time.

"I love it," she finally says.

William lets out an enormous sigh and a nervous chuckle, bending at the waist in relief. "Oh, I'm so glad you're pleased, Alexandria."

"Seriously, William… I absolutely love it. You followed my instructions to the letter. Good work."

William beams and wipes the sleeve of his suit jacket across his forehead. "And the fountain? It turned out nice, didn't it?"

She doesn't need to look again. "Yes. Perfect." She turns on her heels and scans the two rows of Bio-Gen staff. When she finds who she's looking for, she throws her hands up in the air and struts forward. "Ah, Price. There you are," she squeals.

"Hello, Aunt Alexandria. So good to see you," Dr. Bigelow replies. The two engage in an awkward half hug, which is what I'd expect. She never struck me as a hugger. "Welcome. I knew you'd be pleased," he continues. "Officer Banks has done an incredible job of getting the building up and running. I think you're going to be very impressed with the rest."

"Well, if the rest is anything like this, I think you're correct." She smiles, smacking her gloves against her open palm and looking up and down the rows of poised soldiers. "William, brief introductions, please, as I know most everyone. And then let's get the tour…" She stops when her gaze comes to rest on mine. I swallow hard. "Well, lots of familiar faces today."

I stare at her and hold my ground until she returns her attention to William. The two go about introducing their respective investors, scientists, lab techs, and officers. As she said, most already know each other; in those cases, short and friendly banter ensues as they're reacquainted. When the higher-ups are all formally introduced and ready to see the building, William turns, as an apparent afterthought, toward the row containing the rest of us—the employed slaves of Bio-Gen: the cleaning crews, the maintenance people, the front desk and security teams, Gabriel, and me. I wonder why Anastasia, Lillian, and all the little demon Harvesters aren't here. Don't want to display that ugly side of your work, do you? Instead of a person-by-person introduction, we are collectively reduced to, "This is the rest of the employees," with William's lazy wave in our direction. I find his lack of creativity disappointing. At least Alexandria spares us a brief glance and a smile. What a gal.

"Let the tour commence. Please, Alexandria... follow me." William is obviously elated, practically floating in his wing-tipped loafers as he leads the pack into the heart—or should I say the bowels?—of the new and improved Bio-Genesis monstrosity.

Two hours later, after being expected to wait patiently with eager anticipation for their return, Lemon Lady and the rest of the circus come strolling back into the lobby, laughing and smiling, smack-dab in the middle of some amazing story told by the Queen herself. We all reform our line, standing at perfect attention and here to assist—or silently comply, at the very least.

Alexandria looks directly at me.

"Ah, yes, William... this one." She walks very slowly toward me. Her smile is gone, replaced by an expression so brazen, I'm actually curious to hear what she could possibly have to say to me. Her chin is tucked slightly as she peers at me from beneath unevenly raised brows. A crooked grimace suggests she not only knows a secret about me but that she's been waiting to say it for a long, long time.

This one.

She comes to stand directly in front of me. I meet her stare, but I'm still shaking inside, still quaking, still buzzing. I have to remember that my feet are indeed on the floor—and that I am alive.

"Nerissa John." Her eyes flit up and down my face as she takes in every detail, like she's cataloging me for investment purposes.

"You can just call me Nerissa, Alex."

She offers a mocking pout, then laughs; the little pop of her over-stuffed lips when she opens her mouth flicks a tiny bit of spit onto my cheek. I have the ferocious urge to grab her face and kiss her—to lock her lips with mine and suck the life right out of her. *Ms. Bigelow never acquired a taste for Aqua Tonic.* She'd drop in ten seconds, dead as a poisoned rat put out of its misery.

One other employee stands between Gabriel and me, yet I feel the lightest touch on my back as he reaches behind our mutual neighbor and attempts to calm my anger. I'm sure he can feel it even from where he stands. Breathe, Nerissa. *"Breathe, child."* That's what he'd say right now.

She turns and looks at William. "Well, you weren't kidding about this one." She laughs again, then turns back to face me.

"I understand you've been quite an asset to William these past months."

"Did you enjoy your tour, Alexandria?" That alter ego has once again slipped into the driver's seat, and I'm astonished by my own words.

"Well, yes... I did, as a matter of fact." She sounds intrigued by my lack of respect, and it feels as though she's inviting me to challenge her. It must finally be amusing, finally something different than always having her ass kissed. Challenge accepted.

"Did you see everything?"

"I do believe I did. Pretty amazing stuff, don't you think?"

Gabriel pinches my side really hard. I don't flinch. It's just a little pain.

"Well, I suppose so... if you like the idea of being a drug dealer and, oh, let's see... a murderer and a rapist and a liar and—"

"That will be enough!" William yells as he storms toward me.

Alexandria extends her arm to stop him. "It's all right. I'd like to hear what this one has to say."

"My name is Nerissa!"

"Oh, I know exactly who you are. And actually, Ms. John, I owe you my thanks. We all do. All of this"—she spreads her arms wide and looks around the lobby—"wouldn't have been possible if not for you."

William laughs and walks away from us. Even though Gabriel is still probably pinching me, I don't feel it anymore.

"We'd still be dealing with that old, practically obsolete building," Alexandria continues. "It worked for a while, but not enough was happening in there. But this? This is a masterpiece. My opus."

"So you..." I look away from her to address the entire gathering. "All of you know about everything that's happening in this building? The test subjects, the Harvesters, their hosts? The fact that Aqua Tonic is dangerous and addicting and that it's being grossly misrepresented in its tests?"

Alexandria giggles, gazing at me like I'm an ignorant and naïve little child. A tiny, insincere frown folds her mouth. "William can have as many little side projects as he wants, as long as the skincare lines continue to improve, grow, and produce such phenomenal results. As far as the Aqua Tonic is concerned, that is a work of pure genius. Do you have any idea how much money that's going to make us?"

"So it's all about the money? That's all you care about?"

"No. I care about expansion and experience and security. Money makes all those things possible."

"But what about people?" I say, gritting my teeth. "Don't you care about what your expansion and experience will do to *them*?"

She shrugs and pouts, shaking her head. "Sacrifices will always have to be made, won't they?"

I step forward. Alexandria doesn't budge. "Like me and my family?" I ask. "Do you know what you did? You could have *saved* us!"

Apparently, she's had enough and turns away from me. But I'm not done.

"Do you know what *he's* done to us? What he does to me? Do you care even a little? I'm a *prisoner* here!"

"You're an intern," she replies, her back still turned to me. "And a damned lucky one, I might add."

"That's a lie, and you know it," I shout. "I'm being held here against my will!" I look around the room at all their faces. Nobody seems interested in listening. No one bothers to even meet my gaze as I desperately pour my heart out in front of them. I guess money is the bottom line for everyone.

Alexandria walks toward the middle of the lobby and her tribute fountain. She stands with her back to all of us, observing and admiring her *expansion* and *experience* and *security*. William reluctantly follows her.

"What happened to Moriyah?" I yell. "Was she one of those necessary sacrifices, Alex? Where is she?"

William reaches her, and she turns to face him. "Jesus, William. This one is a real pain in the ass."

That's it. That's all I can take. I launch myself across the lobby. Gabriel is immediately at my heels, and Emmanuel MacNamire is close behind, but nothing will stop me. I'm going to kill her. Right here, right now.

I'm just a few feet away, when Gabriel grabs a fistful of my shirt and yanks me back. Alexandria turns around at the same time and sneers at me, her top lip curled up in disgust. Emmanuel MacNamire now has both my arms in his rough grip, pulling them back and up behind me. I can't move.

William walks toward me, and once again, Alexandria stops him with a raised hand. "Who do you think you are?" she says, seething now as she steps up to me.

"I know exactly who I am. *And* who I'm not."

"You're nothing more than a pathetic hybrid," she hisses.

I spit in her face as hard as I can. "You've killed us! You've killed us all, you horrible, evil bitch!"

She jumps away from me, but her poised expression never changes. Once again, William steps forward, and this time, Alexandria says, "Just a moment, William." She wipes her face with one yellow glove, exaggerating the effort of it. When she's satisfied, she once again comes as close as she can to me and locks onto my eyes. I have absolutely no idea what she's thinking, her face as expressionless as humanly possible. "On the contrary, Ms. John. The only thing that's kept you or any of your remaining family alive is this building. And this building exists because of me."

Emmanuel MacNamire has me by one arm, squeezing so tight my fingers tingle. Gabriel has my other arm, and he's kept up well with MacNamire's strong grip.

They're *escorting* me to my room, moving quickly down the corridors behind William as he yells, rants, then mumbles to himself. I no longer understand what he's saying. I don't even care anymore. This may be the end for me.

My two escorts shove me into my quarters, and I practically fall into William—a hot, sweaty, red-faced mess. He brushes me away, so disgusted. He doesn't even want me to touch him. I regain my balance and face him.

"If it were up to me, you'd be put out of your misery. Right now," he barks.

"Go ahead. Do it."

He shakes his head, a pained, insincere smile contradicting itself. He paces a bit, removes his sweat-stained suit jacket, and drapes it over a chair. "I can't." He grits his teeth.

"Why not? Blood loyalty?"

"Because she likes you."

"What are you talking about?" I spit.

"Alexandria. You remind her of herself, and she thinks you've got promise. That is, once you've been broken in."

"I'm nothing like that miserable bitch! How can she even think—no. Don't ever—" And then I laugh. It's all I can do at this point, and to my complete surprise, William's pained expression relaxes, and he laughs with me.

Then William raises his hand, and before I realize what's happening, he delivers a hard slap to my face, backed by the pooling fuel of anger inside him. The force spins me around before I fall to the floor. He's still laughing.

I touch my cheek and lip, the sting so sharp and powerful, it pulsates under my fingers.

William's laughter abruptly halts. "Stand up," he orders.

I find my footing and do as I'm told. Gabriel and Emmanuel watch from the edge of the room. So does Hani, who I didn't even know was here.

William slaps me again—same side, same force, same fury. This time, my vision fills with tiny stars, but I don't fall. Then he wraps his hands around my neck. "How dare you embarrass me like that?" He squeezes, and I do my best not to fight—to just allow him his moment so he can come back to his senses. But I can't breathe. "You made an absolute *fool* out of me. After everything I've done for you!"

He squeezes harder, and my instincts take over. I fight him, trying to release myself—kicking and scratching him, thrashing and heaving. But nothing breaks William's death grip.

"That's enough, sir," Gabriel says, pulling at William. "Sir. Master Banks... you don't want to disappoint Ms. Bigelow. Sir, she can't breathe. You're killing her! Enough!"

Just as the world closes in, he releases me. I collapse to the floor. Hani kneels beside me as I gasp for a life-saving breath, choking and gagging. The room comes back into focus.

"Sir," Gabriel says, his voice returned to its lowered volume, "allow Gabriel to get you comfortable in your own quarters. A drink, perhaps? A shower and a change of clothes before dinner?"

"Shut up."

"Sir? Please... allow me to assist you."

William pushes Gabriel out of the way and steps toward me. I'm sure he's about to kick me, but then he seems to reconsider and turns. He paces the room, running his hands through his gray-tipped hair. A moment later, he stops in his tracks and stares at the ceiling.

Hani helps me to my feet and guides me toward one of the gray, velvet chairs. William turns and looks at me, his indecision discernible, his eyes a mix of sadness and anger. This is a man wrestling with difficult choices—choices, I assume, he never thought he'd have to face. Heed Alexandria Allerton Bigelow's words, give in to his own raging impulses, or tap into his unexpected fondness for the girl he believes is his daughter, his own flesh and blood.

He drops his arms against his sides. "You are one lucky little hybrid. Do you know that?"

Lucky me. I don't say a thing.

Something washes over his face—some decision marked by a subtle softening of the lines around his eyes and mouth. A small, pained sigh escapes him. He walks to the kitchen and disappears. Cabinet doors open and close; so does the refrigerator. There's clanking and a bottle opening and the sound of glass on glass. Then silence. But I hear it. William is drinking. None of us move.

A few moments tick by, and he reappears around the corner. In his left hand is a beautiful crystal champagne flute filled to the very top, the sparkly pink liquid spilling over the edges. And in his right hand, he carries a syringe, also filled to capacity.

He takes a long drink, nearly draining the glass, and walks toward the rest of us. "Gabriel, you want to assist? Fill this up." He extends his arm toward Gabriel, who takes the glass but doesn't move. "What are you waiting for? Now!"

"Sir, what's in the needle?" Gabriel asks calmly.

"Punishment. A big, *hearty* dose of punishment." I can

already hear the alcohol in his voice, his words loose and wavy. "*Wildfire*. You know, I really like that name."

Just the word sends me into a defensive recoil. No, not that. Hit me again or send me to the labs—hell, just kill me. Please don't put that horror into my veins.

"Master Banks, I thought you had decided to clean her out for implantation," Gabriel reminds him, his voice soothing and calm.

"Hm. Why haven't you filled my glass yet?"

Gabriel hands the glass to Hani, who quietly disappears around the corner into the kitchen and returns quickly with another full glass. She hands it to William, who doesn't even look at her. He stares at me once again, like I've seen him look at me so many times—like I'm a suicide victim. One he was never sure he even liked but who he's not sure he doesn't care for, either. He drains the entire glass without a pause. "You know, Nerissa... we really must have dinner and wine together again soon."

"How about tonight?" I offer—a weak but desperate attempt at distraction.

"Oh, ha! Well, maybe, yes. After we take care of business."

"Sir," Gabriel gently interrupts, "we don't want to interfere with the implantation. No injections, sir."

"Well I changed my mind!" William roars and throws his glass sideways. It smashes into a thousand, tiny, glittering pieces across the floor. "And there is no *we*, understand? *I* am in charge here. Only me." He briefly surveys the damage he's created, wipes his mouth with his fingertips, and walks toward me.

"Please don't," I beg. "I'm sorry. I'm sorry I was so disobedient. I swear it won't happen again." I lower my head and press my hands together, touching my fingertips to the space between my eyebrows. "Please... I promise."

He stands directly in front of me, looking down on the quivering, pathetic waste I've become. Then he pulls in a long breath, grabs my hair, and forces me to look at him. A barely perceivable moan escapes him. "Why should I even consider not punishing you this way?"

"Because I am so very sorry. I was completely out of line—"

"And disrespectful."

"Yes," I whisper. "And very disrespectful. And it will never, ever happen again. I swear. Please, please don't."

He releases my hair and stares down at me. "I think you're right. That kind of behavior will never happen again. Because you'll learn your lesson here." He lifts the syringe and examines it closely. "*Wildfire*... a master training tool, indeed."

"Sir." Gabriel steps between us. "Please allow me. If that is to be injected, allow me to do so, sir."

"What? You don't think I can administer a proper injection?" William grabs my arm. "You don't get to have all the fun. It's my turn."

"I insist, sir. Allow me." Before I can register what's happening, Gabriel snatches the needle, shoves it into William's arm, and pushes down on the plunger. The needle is stuck so deep in William's skin that even after Gabriel releases it, the syringe stays imbedded. The full dose floods William's body in an instant. William blinks, trying to process what's happening to him in what looks like slow motion. But the *Wildfire* spreads quickly, leaving no room for rational thought or action.

For a tiny moment, everyone seems frozen, unsure of what to think or how to react. Then the screaming starts. I slam my hands over my ears and watch Gabriel turn and run toward the door. Emmanuel MacNamire follows him. But one slick, seamless move by Hani—reaching innocently to pick up the broken glass—makes Emmanuel nearly trip over her. It's just enough time for Gabriel to exit the room and pull the door closed behind him.

The world around me warps and bends. I can't tell what's real and what I'm imagining, let alone if any of us will survive after this. Above all that, the only thing I really care about as William frantically jumps around the room—on fire from the inside out, his horrific pain and terror fueled by the stuff of inescapable nightmares—is whether I'll ever see Gabriel again.

CHAPTER 19
DADDY

DO WHATEVER IT TAKES...

"I've decided not to wait. After all, there's no time like the present."

"Wait for what?" I ask.

"Implantation," William says. "Your implantation. We will proceed this weekend."

"But I'm not cleaned out yet." As I say that odd statement, I'm suddenly and faintly aware that I've been drugged. The last thing I remember is Hani standing in my living room, watching William.

She just stood there, no emotion on her face, and studied William's suffering through the three distinct stages of the *Wildfire* injection. Gabriel surprised all of us with that. The sight of Hani's silent observation made me turn my attention to William to do the same. I just watched.

A small pang of guilt—or maybe empathy—rose inside me when he fell to the floor, his screams morphing into intermittent shrieks, then sloppy, garbled moans. I knew the burning had changed to lightning strikes and then that uncontrollable, mind-bending seizure state. But none of it was enough to make me try to comfort him, to relieve him of his fear. I didn't have the urge to press a cold, damp towel to his head or hold his hand and tell him he'd be okay. I just watched, like Hani, until Emmanuel came thundering back into the room with two other men.

He yelled something about administering an antidote, and the other two men tended to William. Emmanuel stomped right up to me, grabbed my face, and said, "You're going to pay for this." He was breathing heavily, as though he'd been running, and he spit on me when he spoke.

"I didn't do anything," I said. And then I felt guilty. I didn't want to sound like I was pointing the finger at Gabriel, even though Emmanuel saw the whole thing.

Emmanuel shoved me in a chair and grabbed my hair with both fists. I wasn't sure if he was going to kick me or kiss me. Instead, he slapped me violently across my ear and jaw. As I tried to shake off the pain and disorientation, Emmanuel jabbed a needle in my arm. Panicked, I thought it was my turn for the *Wildfire*. But as I felt the familiar tide wash through me, I knew what it was. Everything went dark. And now, here I am.

William gives a half-hearted chuckle. "No, you most certainly aren't *cleaned out* yet. But you'll be clean enough and drug-free for the procedure, the duration of the pregnancy, and the delivery."

I try to find my bearings. We're sitting at the dining table in my suite. It's dark outside, but the extravagant chandelier overhead lights the table setting with rich, moody ambience. We're here for dinner and, of course, wine.

"What day is it?" I ask, hoping and praying it's not past Friday.

"It's Thursday." His raised eyebrows suggest he's waiting

for me to say something else. When I don't, he picks up a beautiful bottle of wine and pours me a full glass, then drains his in one gulp and refills it. "I'm fine, by the way, in case you were wondering. So... cheers, I suppose." He raises his glass and tilts it toward me, the wine dribbling onto the perfect, white satin table runner.

I pick up my glass with weak fingers and gently touch it to his, our wine splashing and mixing together. "Cheers," I say and take a small sip. "I'm sorry I didn't ask you how you're feeling. I just... I'm a little out of it. I wasn't even sure what day it is." I puff out a tiny laugh and try to sound amused by my lack of awareness.

William takes a long, thoughtful drink and considers me. "Well... that was one hell of a night. Took me all day to recover. Like some pathetic weakling." He finishes his glass of wine. "But damn! That *Wildfire*, as you call it... whew!" He laughs fully, over-exaggerating the humor of it. William doesn't like to be perceived as frail by anyone, including himself.

"There isn't a man alive who could withstand that drug," I say. "And you got a really big dose."

He looks at me, staring hard, his eyes a mix of insecurity and relief that I've let him off the hook for his display of weakness. Little does he know Hani and I just stood there and watched him, taking great satisfaction in his misery and helplessness.

"Massive! That dose was massive—oh..." His self-glorification dissolves into what sounds like... remorse?

"That massive dose was meant for me," I say softly.

"Hm. Indeed it was."

He refills his glass, and I follow his lead in sipping from mine. There's a long, not entirely uncomfortable silence between us as we both drink and settle into our newfound awareness of each other's experience, influenced by William's most potent training tool.

I finally ask the question I've been wondering since last night. "So... where's Gabriel?"

He stares at his wine glass for too long while I wait for an answer I'm not sure I want. "I have no idea," he says. "Mac-Namire went after him but lost him somewhere on the Rock."

"You mean he didn't take a boat across the channel?"

"No." William sighs and takes a drink. "Honestly, if he tried to hide somewhere out here, chances are he's dead. Probably slipped off a cliff. If you stray off the path, this place is pretty hard to navigate after dark."

"Oh."

"He'd be lucky if that was his fate. Because if I ever see him again, so help me..."

"Yeah, I didn't see that coming last night." I try to sound perplexed.

William looks at me as though he's evaluating my statement for its truth—as though he's measuring my loyalty to him.

A quick rap at the door breaks the moment and the strange connection.

"Come in," William says.

Hani enters, pushing what appears to be the very dining cart we used as a makeshift table in my cottage. The sight of it spreads an unwelcome pang of nostalgia inside me for what feels like years ago and, dare I say, simpler times.

Hani catches my gaze for a split second, and in that tiny slice of time, I see her almost maternal protection, unspoken, but so very cherished—like a lush and inviting oasis in the middle of a cold, barren wasteland. In this moment, whether it's ten seconds or even less, I feel loved. And that feels safe.

I smile softly at her and watch her arrange an elegant

dinner in front of us. William moves his arms for her to serve him, and as she places his plate before him, Esmerelda rises in my mind. I'm ashamed of myself for feeling even remotely at ease with this ridiculous setup. I will not allow what happened to Esmerelda to happen to Hani.

But how will I stop him this time? I'm powerless.

Gabriel. Friday at the river at noon. Tomorrow. *Everything will be explained.*

As Hani places my plate in front of me, I say, "William, can we please talk about the weekend? About tomorrow?" Hani slows for a brief second in apparent curiosity, but William doesn't seem to notice.

"Ah, yes... the implantation."

That's not what I was expecting him to say at all. "You said I had a week, remember? A week from Saturday. Tomorrow's only Friday. I was hoping to have the day to myself. You know, one last day... to prepare."

He seems to wrestle with something in his head, his brow creases as he places his napkin in his lap and picks up his knife and fork. "That was before. Things have changed. But you know... let's not discuss this right now. Let's enjoy our dinner."

I glance up at Hani once more. She doesn't meet my gaze this time, but instead unfolds my napkin and places it gently on my lap, resting her warm hand on my thigh for one brief second.

"Okay, you're right. Let's eat and... I don't know... have some fun for a change." I shrug and try to seem nonchalant, popping a perfect green bean into my mouth. "Oh my gosh, this is delicious! Try the beans."

He pulls in a long breath and, as he lets it go, settles himself into his chair with a smile.

An hour and a half later, after an enormous gourmet meal, a decadent chocolate cake topped with brandy-soaked cherries and fluffy white cream, alongside numerous bottles of wine, I'm stuffed and William is drunk. Very drunk. I sipped at my wine all night, and even though I didn't drink much in comparison, I still feel a little swishy. But not enough to ruin my plans.

Throughout dinner, we chatted and reminisced like two old friends. We laughed about some of our earliest encounters together. William practically fell off his chair, roaring with laughter about how daring and brazen I was. *"Like father like daughter,"* he howled.

I gritted my teeth and giggled away as he pored over the story of how he designed and implemented the creation of Walter, his security animal—how few attempts it took to produce "that ugly, terrifying creature." And he bragged about the original Cooperative.

"Did you know I wrote that myself?" he slurred, patting himself on the back.

He confided in me that he was "a little scared" of Alexandria and that he thought she was a ballbuster but a *genius*, and how incredibly thankful he is for her. Her money, he means.

After flippantly recalling his pride in and amusement over the last and most deplorable year and a half of my life, as I came along with him on his knee-slapping ride, laughing and stroking his insatiable ego with self-deprecating agreement and patience, he couldn't have been more pleased with me.

He suddenly got very serious and said, "I want to tell you a story."

Another story. Another tale of self-importance and admiration to endure.

But this story was different. This one was worth listening to. And in an instant, I was sober.

NINETEEN YEARS EARLIER, OFF-SEASON

"If you valued that little hut you called home, you would have done as I asked the first time."

"Sir, I do—I mean, I *did* value my home. It was my *home*. There was no need to burn it down. We could have negotiated."

"Gabriel, I don't negotiate!" William yelled at him. "I hope you understand that at this point."

"Officer Banks, my wife was injured in the fire, sir. She was trying to save our dog. She needs care."

William couldn't fathom how this dirty, old, shaking imbecile thought he gave a damn. "Are you ready to stop whining and do as I asked of you?"

"I am. I'll deliver the letter. I promise."

"Good. If you get it to her within a few days, I'll make sure your wife is taken care of."

"Sir, Gabriel doesn't know if that's possible. I don't know how to find your friend or when she's on the island, and I'm not sure my wife will last a few more days—"

"Gabriel, make it happen. Come on, you helped me once, and you were rewarded. You know how things work."

The simpleton bowed his head, and William found it hilarious. When Gabriel finally held out his hand, William passed him the letter.

"Attaboy. Hey, tell Tatiana I miss her. It's been weeks since our *date night*." William laughed. "Next time, I want to remember it."

FOUR YEARS AGO, AUGUST 6TH

"Sir, we have a report of a hybrid sighting on the island."

"Excuse me? A what?"

"A patron at Wave nightclub reported witnessing an exchange between a male tourist and a woman who claimed to be something other than pure human."

"Wave nightclub? You idiot. They're just drunken tourists. Hybrids like that've been extinct for decades. Come on, everybody knows that."

"Yes, Officer Banks. Sorry to waste your time, sir." The cadet slinked out of his office like a dog with its tail between its legs.

"One moment, Cadet."

The cadet ran back without haste and snapped to attention. "Yes, sir?"

"Let's put the kibosh on this. Do a little follow up for me."

"Sir?"

"Is the patron who reported this still around?"

"Yes, sir. He's still at the office in the resort district."

That was exactly the answer William Banks was hoping for. "Splendid. I'll message Officer MacNamire. I want the two of you to go round up our good samaritan and head over to Wave. See if you can gather up our male tourist and his *hybrid*." William offered a convincing enough smirk. "Bring them out here, if you find them."

"All the way back out to the base, sir? Not to the resort district?"

The pesky, uncooperative cadet was getting on William's nerves. "Uh, yeah. You heard me. Back here. I'm up to my eyeballs in work, so they can come to me. Too bad if it's inconvenient for them. We've got to let them know they can't go around scaring people with stories of dangerous, illegal, and *extinct* hybrids walking around freely. Now get a move on."

"Yes, sir. Right away."

FOUR YEARS AGO, AUGUST 7TH

"Listen, we've been here all night. And I'm tired. I'm sure you are too. And this dank, cold room is no place for someone like you. Just tell me about yourself and your family, and we'll get you back to them." The little Beauty was so gorgeous, so perfect—even with her mouth taped shut—William could barely hold his concentration. But she was scared, shaking in her little fucked-up feet. "I'll take the tape off. No funny stuff this time. You just tell me who you are, why you were in that club, who your mom is, where she is, and all that business. Then we'll get you home."

She nodded, and William slowly pulled the tape off her mouth. The word *delicious* popped into his head. She looked good enough to eat. William wondered if she was his offspring. What a coincidence that would have been.

"Okay, good... What's your name, Beauty?"

"Anastasia. Can I please have some water?"

William snapped his fingers at MacNamire, who watched her like a dog. The dimwit couldn't roll his tongue back in his mouth or pick his bottom lip up off the ground, and he didn't flinch. William snapped again. "MacNamire!"

"Yes. Yes, sir?"

"Get her some water." William turned his attention back to Anastasia. "Now, go on. Tell me who you are. Tell me every-thing. There's nothing to be afraid of. I'm here to help."

FOUR YEARS AGO, AUGUST 8TH

"You will return her to her family and never speak another word of this, William."

William's father spoke to him like he thought he still had any control over what William did. Nonetheless on the base, where William considered himself in charge—his turf. He'd had enough of that, no longer a child his father could order about.

"Did you have any idea about their adaptation? Remarkable! I mean, everyone's heard the lore around Wreckleaf, but my god. Do you understand the potential goldmine we're sitting on?" William shook his father's shoulders in excitement. He wanted his father to finally see things the way he did. But the man was not excited. Or amused.

"They adapted because they were left alone to do so. Yes, it is remarkable. But it is not our place—not our right—to take them out of their world. We are just their guardians. Here to observe and record. That is all."

"Well, I'm tired of being just their silent guardian. And I'm tired of them being the one and only thing you give a damn about. For the record, I did not take them out of their world. They walked into ours. Into *mine.*"

"You knew they did that on occasion. To find mates. How else could they have survived this long? Unless there are other adaptations..." His father's eyes grew wide and wild, his fingertips wiggling in unison. He began pacing the room like a lunatic. "If they somehow evolved to asexually reproduce due to ingesting the sea plant..."

"Yeah, well, that's not the case, and that's not what this

one and her friend were here for," William tried to convince him.

"How do you know that?"

"Because she told us everything. She explained she was just here for practice. For *scouting*. I told you that an hour ago." His father often made him feel crazy, never listening to a damn thing he'd said. The old man had to be going senile.

"Where's the other one? Her friend."

"I already told you that too."

"Tell me again."

William didn't want to tell him about Nerissa. She belonged to him—truly. "The *sister maid,* as she called her, was dancing the last time this one saw her. She doesn't know where she is. My guess is she swam back to Albatross."

"Good, and that's where Anastasia will be returned as well."

William had had enough of him. "I have a better idea."

Officer William Banks told his father about his concept for the Cooperative. He did not get the reaction he was looking for. Instead, his father only laughed at the idea and reminded William they had been given an incredible privilege, that their only job was to pass the sacred torch along. They weren't authorized to remove the Dolhuphemales for another eight to ten decades, if they survived that long. William certainly wouldn't.

His father carried on about how William always wanted to ruin his life's work. William questioned how it could be his life's work if nobody else knew about it and reminded him his boss was retired, knocking on death's door. Besides William, they were the only two people left on the face of the planet who knew for a fact that this breed had survived. They'd let three of them go during the Elimination Program. Nobody knew. Not even the survivors knew they'd been spared. The program made it look like these creatures had just barely escaped with their lives. The great hybrid experiment.

"William, my boy, not all work has to be met with grand recognition."

"And not all grand recognition is wrong. I'm not about to announce to the world that we've confirmed a breed once believed extinct is still alive. Of course not. But we're going to put them to work for us for a change. Payback, if you ask me. I want what only they can give us."

"Absolutely not."

William was done reasoning with this stubborn, feeble-minded, dried-up old fool. "Would you like to meet her? I mean, before we let her go."

His father was intrigued, but wrestled with his sense of responsibility, pitting it against his thirst for privileged knowledge. "Yes, I would. But only briefly, and then she must be released."

"Oh, yes. It'll be brief."

William lead him down a graveled path to a small, red-roofed cottage. Anastasia sat in a chair, tied down and blindfolded, her mouth taped shut again to keep her from doing that singing thing she did to make the men dizzy with lust.

"William, untie this girl immediately."

He did as his father commanded and retrieved a small knife from a drawer under the counter. After he cut the ties at her wrists, he pulled off the blindfold. She looked groggy, but her eyes darted nervously back and forth—an animal looking for a way out.

"This is Anastasia. Ana, this is Dr. Nicholas Banks."

"It's a true honor to meet you, young lady, and I'm so sorry for the trouble. You'll be returned to your family soon. William, please remove that tape from her mouth."

William also followed this order. As soon as the tape was

ripped off in one fast pull, she started pleading with his father. "Help me. You have to help me!"

Nicholas Banks stepped toward the imprisoned girl. "There, there. Don't be scared. You're safe."

William had never seen this side of the man—so tender, so kind. His father had never offered William such niceties.

"He told me he would kill me if I didn't cooperate," the girl moaned.

"No. That's not true—"

"He said I'd never leave, and he'd kill my family if—"

William's father reached out and put his hand on her head, so lightly, like some king anointing his prodigy. He had no idea what was coming. Of course he didn't. And as the knife sliced his neck from ear to ear and his blood sprayed all over Anastasia—and god, how she could scream—Nicholas Banks turned around to face his son. He still had the stupidest look of surprise on his face.

"Anastasia," William beamed as he stared as his father's slit throat, "that was Nicholas Banks. My father."

She stopped screaming. And she never challenged William Banks again.

A week after Anastasia was acquired, the Dolhuphemale breed was forced out of hiding, and the Cooperative was signed.

As William wraps us his long story—having become more and more intoxicated with every sentence—I find myself at the literal edge of my seat. I've chewed my thumbnail down as far as possible, and my face feels wet and swollen. I've drained my wine glass twice in a desperate attempt to numb my rage and sadness without missing a single word.

"Isn't that something, Nerissa?" He rolls his head back. "Hey, fill up my glass. We need to make a toast."

"Why did you tell me all that?" I ask in almost a whisper.

He tries to look at me—tries to focus—but instead just smiles and closes his eyes. "You deserve to know the truth."

"Why now?"

"We're a team now. We're in this together, forever...." He chuckles.

I get up and walk around the table to stand next to him. His head bobs back, and he gently but sloppily puts his hand on my lower back and kind of pats me. I pick up the wine bottle, feeling its weight. I remember the night on the Alvarez's boat, *Easy Money*, and the tequila bottle. The one I smashed over Tommy's head.

Two deep breaths.

I fill his glass and put down the bottle. "Here you are."

He lifts his head with great effort, his eyes rolling back before he regains his focus. I hand him his glass, and he tries unsuccessfully to bring it to his lips.

"You still with me, William?"

"Oh..." He laughs. "I'm drunk."

"Well, yes. I think you might be." I guide his glass to his lips, and he takes a slow, sloppy gulp.

"Thank you very much." He laughs again. "But you know, I always remember everything. Everything, Nerissa."

"Yes, I know. That's why I want to ask you something." I say, helping him sip from his glass again, this time placing my other hand behind his head as it starts to bobble back.

"Ask me anything!" he yells and throws his arms up in the air.

"I've had a lot to drink tonight, too. So much..."

"Yes, we've had a lovely time, haven't we?" He attempts a

smile but can't seem to hold it. His hand finds my lower back for another friendly pat.

"We've had a great time. Actually, this has been the best night I've had in a long time. I'd love to do it again soon."

"Me too!" he yells, once again flinging his arms above his head. "Whadya wanna ask me?"

"A favor."

"Oh! You and yer favors. Okay, okay. What is it?"

I help him with another sip, then make sure he can see me as I also take a sip from his glass. He finds this very amusing and snorts, his head wobbling back and forth.

"I'd like to do this again with you before implantation, and I'd also like one more time off the base alone, without drugs. You know, to kind of get ready to be a mother." I give him a sip. "So let me have tomorrow to myself. Saturday, we'll have dinner and drinks again. I'll rest Sunday. Or work in the labs, if you need. And then let's save implantation for Monday. Sound good?"

"Woah, woah... yer talkin' too fast for me."

"Okay, so tomorrow..."

"No drugs."

"Right. A day to myself, off the base."

"And Saturday... you want to drink?"

I laugh a little. "Yes. Dinner and drinks together on Saturday. Just like tonight. Like a last..." I don't know if I can get this off my lips, but I force out the words. "Like a last daddy-daughter dinner date."

"Oh!" There go his arms again. He rolls his head up and tries his best to look at me. "That is just... so..."

"So that's a yes, then." It's most definitely not a question.

He just hums a long breath.

"William, do I have your word?"

"I always keep my word, Nerissa."

"I know. So… yes? I can have the day to myself drug-free tomorrow. Just like you said? William?"

I seem to have lost him, but then he says, "Call me Daddy."

No.

"Call me Daddy and give me a little kiss, right…" After three attempts, he brings his index finger to his forehead. "Right here."

No.

"Daddy-daughter dinner date. Like you said," he slurs.

"Thank you for a wonderful evening. Thank you, William."

"Do it right… Nerissa. Or no deal."

I could convince myself the wine is what's making me feel like I want to vomit, and that may be. But if I have to do what he's asked me to, I imagine I'll just collapse and die.

The river at noon. *Do whatever it takes to be here.* Gabriel. He'll be there. I know he will.

I close my eyes and concentrate really hard on nothing. There is nothing, this is nothing, he is nothing. I snap my eyes open so I make sure to land in the right spot, lean over, and kiss William Banks on the forehead, his skin slightly oily under my lips.

"Thank you, Daddy. Good night."

I spin around and walk toward my bathroom.

"You're welcome, Nerissa. I loved this."

Before I close the door, I ask, "I have your word, right, Wil—right, Daddy?"

"Yes… yes, you have my word. I love this… I love you…"

I close and lock the door, lift the toilet seat, and throw up.

CHAPTER 20
MERIDIAN

IS THIS REAL?

I locked myself in the bathroom and waited for William to leave my suite. I threw up twice more, rolling over everything he'd said, what he made me say, and all his impossible stories, before falling asleep on the cold tile. I don't know what time it was when I brought myself to bed, but as my eyes open now, it feels like I've only been asleep for ten minutes. It's already past ten in the morning and no one has woken me. I'm either dead, in a drug-induced hallucination, or William has kept his word and I have the day to myself. Drug-free. And if that's the case, I have no idea how he could have possibly remembered anything from last night. I wish I didn't.

All right, shake it off, Doll. It's time to get up and make my way to the river. The clock is ticking. Time for some answers.

I change out of last night's clothes into more casual, comfortable attire, including a swimsuit underneath. I'm not sure I'll have the chance to swim. After all, I don't expect Gabriel to jump in the water with me while we talk. I'll take a

249

quick dip if I get there before noon. Even though the river may still be cold, it could be my last chance... before I become a *mother*.

There are leftovers in the fridge—last night's dinner—and I grab a couple bites. I quickly realize the dining table has been cleared and cleaned, as though our dinner never happened. Hani must have been here, but I don't remember it.

I grab a light jacket, leave my suite, and head toward the elevator. The door glides open, and as I step in and he steps out, William and I practically run into each other. There's a terribly awkward shuffling and shifting as we each apologize and excuse ourselves for not being more aware or seeing each other.

"Going down, I take it?" he asks.

"Yes."

"Please." He extends his arm and gestures for me to step inside. Then he joins me and requests the main floor. We descend in silence. And when we reach the lobby, he steps out and slowly walks by my side. I match his pace.

"Thank you for dinner last night," I say, sincerely meaning what comes next. "And for giving me today."

He stops and regards me for a moment, and now I'm afraid he has no idea what I'm talking about. Like he's completely forgotten what we'd agreed upon. He looks ill, his face pale and slick. His obvious hangover has left him vacant.

"Yes, you are welcome," he finally says. "I've arranged for dinner tomorrow evening as well, just as you requested. It will be even grander. Our last dad—" He doesn't finish his sentence, but I know what he wanted to say.

"Oh, yes," I stammer. "I look forward to it."

"Nerissa, I don't need to worry that you're going to go looking for Gabriel, do I? Because that would not go well for either of you."

Can he see the tiny beads of sweat forming on my upper lip? Can he hear my heart racing? See my hands shaking? "You said he's dead. That he probably fell off a cliff in the dark the other night."

It isn't until this exact moment that I really consider that to be a possibility. Maybe he really is dead. Maybe I'll never see him again. I'll never have any answers or explanations about how he came to be William's loyal servant.

"Yes... I did say that, but there's always the possibility he survived and escaped, however remote. And you didn't answer my question."

"I have absolutely no interest in looking for Gabriel." I steady myself. "You have to remember, he betrayed me. I have nothing to say to him."

"Ah, yes. I suppose he did." He starts walking again, his arms behind his back, strolling along. He laughs, "Now he's betrayed me as well. Another thing we have in common."

Not knowing how to answer, I just nod.

"Why do you suppose Gabriel did that to me? Shot me with the injection that was meant for you?"

"I think Gabriel is a selfish, self-serving old man who's manipulated both of us for his own purposes." I try to sound as bitter and stern as possible. "And he just finally decided he didn't want to play by anybody's rules anymore."

"Hmm... I suppose you could be correct. But I don't know what he thought he could have gained by doing that. He must have realized he'd be executed if he were caught." He stops again and faces me. "It was as if he was protecting you."

"Ha! No, he wasn't. He just snapped. He's old and crazy, and he just lost it."

William returns to strolling down the hall. "Where did you say you're going today?"

Does he really not remember, or is he seeing if I'll lie to

him? "Well, I wanted to go to the river, but I think I've changed my mind. I just want to see my family and hang out on Albatross, you know?" I suddenly don't want him knowing I'm going to the river.

"Well, I suppose you could do both. You have the full day, but be back at sundown, as always. Oh, I almost forgot. This is for you." He offers me a small, aluminum-wrapped package. "It's a breakfast sandwich. Freshly made."

"Thank you, but that's okay. I ate some leftovers."

"Knowing you, you only ate a few bites." Yes, he nailed that. "I insist. You need to keep up your strength for Monday's implantation. I think you'll like it. I had them put Wreckleaf in it."

Just the word falling off his lips makes my mouth water, even if it's not the Wreckleaf from the shipyard. It's been too long since I've had any actual leaf beyond just the supplements I'm given. I take the sandwich. It's warm.

"Thank you, William. That was very thoughtful. I'll see you tonight."

"Sundown," he reminds me.

"Yes, or before." I smile and turn toward the main entrance.

"And Nerissa..." he calls out, and I turn around. "Be careful."

"I will. Thank you."

The channel is rough, but just as William expected, I've mastered the small boat and easily clear the channel in no time at all. After finishing the breakfast sandwich, I feel instantly stronger, more alert, and ready for my day.

Out of the boathouse and up the limestone stairs, I trot up the gravel path at the top of the base and approach the gate.

Nobody even looks at me anymore. I mean, they look, but not as though I'm an intruder—or a prisoner. I'm a permanent fixture now. And unless they have direct orders from William Banks, they leave me alone and don't ask any questions.

The stony guard sees me coming and turns to release the gate. It swings open, and I step out, not saying a word to the mammoth sentry. Our eyes meet briefly as I pass. I wonder if he wishes he were leaving for the day.

As always, my board waits just outside the gate. I hop on and drift quietly down the road. I'm nervous. Will Gabriel be at the river? Is he okay? And if he doesn't show up, what will I do? It will surely mean he's dead, as William suggested. But if he *is* there, like I expect him to be... will he finally hug me? Will he wrap his arms around me, explain everything, tell me it's all going to be okay, and finally be my old Gabriel, no longer under the watchful power of Officer William Banks?

Oh, please, Universe. Please let that be the case.

Before I turn off the road onto my nearly erased footpath, I scan all directions for any unwanted company. I don't want anyone to know I'm here. As far as I can see and hear, I'm completely alone. And it's only eleven forty-two. I've got fifteen minutes to swim.

I park my board in a hidden spot, follow the path the rest of the way on foot, and reach the fallen tree trunk, where I take off my clothes. The forest is fresh and alive. I stand in my swimsuit, breathe in the crisp air, and hold it in my lungs for a long time. Finally letting go, I slip into the river and melt—becoming one with the water. I must forever hold this moment in my memory. This is such a happy place—such an oasis. I'll need to travel back to this exact time and place in the days and weeks to follow.

I am safe. I am complete. I am a creation of the Universe. And I am perfect exactly as I am.

I repeat this mantra to myself over and over, first in my mind, then out loud as I surface and float on my back, eyes closed, and allow myself to fully relax and let go.

The river cradles me in its protective embrace.

"I am safe," I say aloud.

I need or want for nothing in this moment.

"I am complete."

I am made of the same things as the stars, as this water, as the air above and the earth below, and I am meant to be.

"I am a creation of the Universe."

I am as faultlessly as I am intended to be in this moment.

"I am perfect exactly as I am."

"Yes, you are."

My eyes pop open, hoping I didn't imagine what I just heard. He sounds different. My focus sharpens on the canopy above and the songbirds all around who now usher back in the spring. I don't move or make a sound, just float—listening, concentrating, hoping.

"Nerissa..." An almost inaudible whisper floats across the river's surface.

As though I'm moving through thick mud instead of water, I deliberately lift my head and slowly turn my body toward the source of my name. I knew he'd be here. I knew it. I want to burn this moment in my memory forever. I close my eyes and breathe.

I turn toward the small wooden docks at the bank of the river, and when I'm sure I'm facing the right direction, I say, "Gabriel, I knew you'd come." Then I open my eyes with a huge grin.

My smile falters, and I gasp. It's not Gabriel. And it's not real. What I'm seeing isn't real. It can't be.

Closing my eyes, I dunk my face into the water, violently shaking my head when I come back up and reopen my eyes.

But the image hasn't changed. Now, not just through the mud of the riverbed but through wet concrete, I move in slow motion toward the bank. I can't feel my body, though it obeys my command to move forward. The world has gone silent, except for the rush of my heartbeat in my ears.

With agonizing slowness, I step out of the river. Tears blur my vision, and I blink them away, desperate to regain my focus. To see him before he vanishes, as I'm convinced he will. My shaking hands cover my mouth, one over the other, but they can't contain—they can't control or mask—the outright primal cries struggling to escape.

On the freshly sprouted grass, I take the final steps toward the red wooden dock. When I reach it, I fall into him—the only thing my body can do to make me believe this is real. He catches me in one arm, gathers me into his embrace, and I fall apart completely.

"Devin? Are you real? Is this real?"

"Yes. It's me. This is real."

CHAPTER 21
RENDEZVOUS
THIS HAS TO BE A DREAM, DOESN'T IT?

FRIDAY, MARCH 14TH

I cling to him, pulling him as close to me as I possibly can before he dissolves—before I wake up from my dream. Because this has to be a dream, doesn't it? He holds me tight in a desperate and impossible embrace. I can smell him—his sweet, familiar scent. How can this not be real if I can smell him?

I pull just far enough away to look at his face. Devin's beautiful face is somehow both different and exactly as I remember. He's crying. I lightly touch his cheek, and he looks into me like he always could. I lean in to kiss his tears away, his skin warm and soft under my lips. He unlocks his hold on me and takes my face in both his hands before pressing his lips to mine. We melt together, once again. Liquid grace.

His kiss is like medicine or magic—or something entirely different without description. I'm here, but I'm not quite connected to the earth. There's only him, and this is something

I never thought—not in a thousand lifetimes—I would ever feel or think or experience again.

When our lips part and my eyes flutter open, we don't speak. I can't speak as I soak him in, searching for an explanation to this impossible reality. We just look at each other, both of us breathless.

"You are so beautiful, and I missed you so much," he finally says, his fingers gliding down my cheek.

"How... how are you here? I watched you die." My breath catches.

He smiles gently—that perfect, captivating smile. "Well, I promise I'm not dead. What you saw *almost* killed me." He looks down at his left side, and I follow his eyes. I hadn't noticed it, but he's clearly holding his left arm differently—his entire left side. But I can't see why, his long-sleeved shirt hiding the details.

"Does it hurt?" It's all I can think to ask.

"Not anymore. Not really."

"Show me."

He smiles again. "I will. Later. I've got something else more important to show you, and a lot to tell you."

I'm suddenly nervous, my heart in my throat, and then I remember. "Gabriel. I thought I was meeting Gabriel here. Is he? Do you know if he's—"

"Gabriel's fine."

"How do you know?"

"Because I saw him this morning."

My head is spinning. "Oh my god, Devin... the note. To meet here today. You left it?"

"Yes."

"I thought Gabriel left it. And that's how—you're never going to believe everything that's happened. I thought Gabriel hated me and that he was somehow on your stepfather's side. That he was brainwashed or drugged and... so this must mean he's his old self. I knew it. I just couldn't believe..."

Devin strokes my hair, then takes my hand in his. He looks at me so tenderly, with so much love and understanding, patiently waiting for me to calm down. In an instant, his eyes tell me everything.

"You already know, don't you? You know where I've been, what's happened to me. Gabriel told you everything, didn't he?"

He pulls in a long, deep breath and slowly nods, never taking his eyes from mine. "This will be a lot to take in," he says.

My legs fold under me, and now I'm sitting on the weathered red dock. Devin sits in front of me, his hands on my knees, the left one somehow heavier.

Every time I look at him, I have to keep reminding myself that this is actually happening. That he's real, that we're here, together. I lower my head and inhale, trying to clear my thoughts, trying to prepare myself for all he's got to tell me. I concentrate on the songbirds above and breathe. I am safe. I am safe in exactly the right place at the right time.

"Okay," I say. "I'm ready."

"Are you sure?"

"Yes, tell me everything."

"Okay," he says. "Let's get you into some dry clothes first. You're shivering."

Only now do I realize how freezing I am, sitting here in nothing but my wet swimsuit, the spring air curled up around me.

He helps me stand, and we walk along the riverbank back to where I left my clothes. Once I'm dressed and more comfortable, Devin and I sit down on the tree trunk. He reaches into his pocket and produces a bottle of water and a small baggie. "Here. Have some."

I take a long drink while he opens the baggie and pulls out a small bundle of perfect, beautiful, fresh Wreckleaf. I nearly spew the water everywhere. "Where did you get this?"

"From Gabriel. Well... I'll explain." Before I can protest, he puts a single frond into his own mouth, chews, and swallows it.

I somehow know that I don't need to worry about this, that Devin will not experience any ill side effects from the Wreckleaf—like he did that day at his house. I don't know how, but I just do.

"I like your hair," he says, like it's just another day. "It looks good short."

I laugh softly. "Trust me, this isn't short." I eat all the Wreckleaf and drain the bottle of water. He waits patiently.

Finally, when I'm finished, he begins.

"I don't have a very clear memory of that last night... on Black Rock. I remember trying to stop you from leaving. It's pretty fuzzy, but I didn't want you to go out into the channel with that storm."

"I thought you were trying to stop us because you were going to turn us in," I say. "Like prisoners."

He shakes his head. "No. Never."

"You looked so... not yourself. I was so scared and... sad."

"I was completely addicted to AQT. I was out of my mind with it. I wasn't sleeping, wasn't eating. You were one-hundred percent right. And I knew it then. I just didn't know how to stop. I didn't really want to. I didn't want to feel anymore."

"And that's how *he* wanted it. William."

"You're right. William Banks has never given a damn about me."

I work on bringing myself back to that night. I've deliberately tried to erase it from my memory, not wanting to replay that nightmare in my head ever again. But it never really left, and now, as the images take shape behind my eyes, it's like I'm reliving it. But Devin is here, alive.

"How did you survive? I saw you get struck. I watched you fall. You were... gone."

"I really don't remember those first few days, which is probably a good thing," Devin says. "But I remember the pain. A lot of pain, and darkness. And his voice."

"Whose voice?"

"Colton's," he says. "He saved me."

"What?"

"Colton got me off the Rock the same way he got on. Through the cargo tube. The boats were gone."

"No." My eyes grow huge in disbelief.

"That's what I said when he explained everything to me. When I was coherent enough to understand. He mostly carried me. Or dragged me." He smiles and shakes his head, as if he can still hardly believe what he's saying. "The tube was already damaged and hadn't been fixed. They don't usually replace it until right before the next Season opens. Colton said we nearly died trying to make it through. Almost fell into the channel three times, then the falling debris from the explosion slammed into it. It just barely missed us."

"What about your injuries?"

"Colton said he thought I was dying. Honestly, I guess I was. But the only thing he said he could do was to keep moving. He didn't exactly have a plan, but he knew he wanted to get me off the base and let his father think we'd both been killed on Black Rock."

"He does," I say. "He thinks you're both dead." I remember that months-old conversation between William and me.

"Well, Colton's the only reason we're not."

"Where did you go?" I ask. "I mean… where have you been all this time?"

"So, I do remember when Colton got me through the gate and onto his board. He kept telling me I'd be okay and to just hang on. That he was going to take me home and get me all cleaned up, and I remember thinking that was a really bad idea. All I could tell him—at least that I remember—was, 'The cave,' over and over. I don't know what else I said or how he found the place, but the next time I woke up, I was slung over his shoulder. He'd somehow already gotten us both down the cliffside."

"He took you to Gabriel's cave."

"Yeah. And that's where he brought me back from the dead. With everything still inside that cave. All of Gabriel's supplies. All his herbs and medicines, and of course the Wreck-leaf. I'm convinced it was the Wreckleaf that really saved me. I mean, after Colton. And you'll be happy to know I no longer drink AQT."

"The picture…" I drop my gaze and remember the picture Gabriel showed me that night after enduring William's *Wildfire*.

"What picture?" Devin asks.

"Gabriel showed me a picture of you with the horses. He said he found it in his cave, but I don't remember…" The memory is so fuzzy and incomplete. And as I try to pull it back, I snap my gaze back up to Devin's again, realizing he must know about the horses, about Delia and Esmerelda and the fire. "Devin… the horses."

"Colton went to the house to gather a few things. The picture came from my mother's studio. We know Delia's gone… and Esmerelda. My mother knows too. But Goliath and Neptune are safe."

"Are you sure?"

He nods. "And I heard the house burned down."

A small pang of guilt rises in me, but I ignore it. "I had to... to put her to rest. Esmerelda."

"I understand."

"And Leyla? Have you spoken to her?"

Devin takes my hands in his. "Yes, from the very beginning. We had to be very careful, and we couldn't communicate very much. If anyone found out—"

"The very beginning," I said. "You mean since she got off the island? Since you were injured?" My mind is a spinning, tangled mess of images and blurry memories. And Leyla's voice rises above it. *Nerissa, he's alive.* "She was talking about you," I whisper. "She tried to tell me you were still alive. That you were so angry and I was the only one who could stop you from... I thought she was talking about William. But she was talking about you..."

"I wanted to kill him," Devin says, "and she wasn't here to stop me. And then she was cut off completely from being able to reach your family. When she realized you didn't know I was alive, we decided it might be better that way. At least until we could gather everything we needed to bring William down."

"What?"

"We just couldn't risk it. You might not have been able to keep from letting anything slip if you knew. We... we know about the injections. That he's been drugging you every day."

"How?"

"Gabriel told us. When he could. And he really wants to explain everything to you. He tried to lower the doses you were getting. He'd even sneak in at night to feed you Wreckleaf."

I can't believe what I'm hearing right now. Those same fuzzy, confusing images from the last seven months bombard me. Words and stories and what I thought were dreams—or drug-induced imaginings—dance together, and I feel both crazy and clearer than ever. I start to cry. I can't help it. I'm so relieved and so hurt at the same time. Hopeful but betrayed.

As if he can see all this in my eyes, Devin once again wipes away my tears and stares intently at me. "I can't begin to imagine the horrible things you've been through," he says. "Please believe me, I didn't want to leave you as his prisoner. Colton had to physically stop me from trying to get you out. More than once. I wanted to kill William Banks. I still do. But we had to wait while Gabriel gathered evidence, and he swore to me he wouldn't let anything bad to happen to you."

A bitter laugh escapes me. "Yeah, nothing bad happened to me."

He breaks his intense stare and bows his head slowly, squeezing my hand. "Please forgive me. We had to leave you there. We couldn't risk him knowing I was alive. Knowing anything. I'm so sorry. Please, Nerissa... forgive me for leaving you there."

I don't think I can forgive anyone for what's happened to me. But I can't blame Devin, either. "I understand why you did what you did," I tell him. It's the only thing I can offer. He takes a deep, halting breath and nods. "Why now?" I ask. Devin's brows draw together in confusion. "Why are we here? Now?"

He looks up at me again. "Because we believe we finally have enough to end him. Even with Alakier as living proof and her own pile of evidence, my mother was still ignored and discredited. No one believed her. So we had to find another way. Gabriel's been gathering pictures and recordings and copies of documents. Falsified test results. We have real, tangible proof of the horrors at Black Rock. All William Banks' lies and deceit—his purely evil crimes. We have testimonies from a lot of people. People just waiting to tell the authorities the truth about him."

"It doesn't matter," I say softly.

"Of course it does—"

"They don't care, Devin. They already know about everything that happens in that building, and I'm telling you, they don't care."

"What makes you say that?" The concern in his voice is almost alarming, and I hate to have to say this to him.

"Because I've seen it with my own eyes. William's investors and the top officials. They all know. They took a tour. Alexandria Allerton Bigelow herself spelled it all out for me. There's too much money to be made. They couldn't care less what's going on under their noses. It's all about the profits, end of story."

Devin exhales hard and winces, bending toward his left side.

"Are you okay?"

"Yeah, it just still catches me sometimes. The pain."

"Let me see."

He doesn't argue against my request this time but slowly straightens again and pulls his navy-blue cotton shirt up over his head and off completely. He's thinner. A few red scars, like fingers, reach around his torso and shoulders, but it's not nearly as bad as I expected.

"That's not so bad—"

He turns around to show me his left side, and I gasp. From the top of his shoulder blade all the way to his waistband—and probably farther below it—a jagged, six-inch-wide red and purple scar dominates his skin. Just below his ribcage, there's a divot that looks as though somebody scooped out a chunk of his flesh, taut and dull. His left fingers graze the void as he gauges my reaction from over his shoulder.

"I lost a lot of blood here, and if this had been up or down just a few inches, I would have died."

It's only now that I notice his left arm and hand. The skin is a different color, almost opaque, without the usual translucence of normal, healthy skin. And then I see it—a small, blinking light under the surface of his forearm.

"Your arm…"

He lifts his arm in front of his face and turns back to face me. "Right. I've had some upgrades."

"What does that mean?" I ask, staring in disbelief as he slowly twists his arm back and forth, admiring it.

"Most of this arm was left right where I fell that night." It's very matter of fact, the way he says it.

"Oh, my god."

"Yeah, and Anastasia's aim didn't help. It would have been so much easier to stop all the bleeding if she'd made a good, clean cut. Then again, if she'd had better aim, I'd be dead. So, I guess I can thank her for that." He looks at his arm thoughtfully. "Anyway, this hand and arm are mostly new, and now my transmission's perfect. And mostly untraceable."

"How did you…"

He looks at me, frowning a little, as if he can't understand why I'm asking so many questions. Then he seems to realize I'm still in the dark about so much. "Colton and I put things in motion with Gabriel, and when I was strong enough, we left the island."

"You left?"

"Yeah, it was tricky. We couldn't risk being seen. But the zeppelins coming in once a month off-Season don't really carry many people. Just a few locals and mostly supplies. They weren't looking for anyone who shouldn't be there. Made it pretty easy to sneak onboard, and my mother was waiting for us on the mainland."

• • •

DDEVIN and I spend the next half hour talking about the injury that almost killed him. He pores over the details of his recovery, then his operation on the mainland, and his return to Panacea under a false identity.

I fill him in on as many details as I can think to recall. He knows a surprising amount. And as he nods in understanding, I'm filled with such a deep relief for the validation that my instincts about Gabriel were right.

"I still have so many questions," I tell him, "and I need to know what happens now. I don't have much time, Devin. Just a couple more days before he implants me with one of his Harvester clones."

Devin frowns again, this time much darker with worry than before. "Gabriel told us he agreed to let you detox before the implantation. We thought we had a week or two. Closer to when the next zeppelin arrives."

"He changed his mind. That's what he does." I sigh. "It's happening on Monday, and after that, I won't be able to leave."

"I thought I'd have some time with you... I guess we'll just have to change our plans."

"Wait, whose plans? You said you have testimonies from people who want to tell the truth about him. Who is it? You and your mom? Because, no offense, and I'm sure you already know, nobody will care."

"I think it's time to show you." He puts his shirt back on and holds out his hand. "Come on. Let's go for a ride." I take his hand, and he pulls me up and into his arms once again. We stay here for a long, perfect moment. I'm nervous about what he's about to show me, unsure whether I want to see or know.

"It's all going to be okay. I promise," he says, as though he's read my mind. Then he rests his lips on the top of my head before leaning down toward my lips. When he kisses me, it still feels like I'm dreaming. Devin is here. Devin is alive.

We ride up the hill past the Oval, all the way to the Sapodilla tree.

"Too bad they're not quite ripe," Devin says, pointing to the small fruits dotting the branches. "I know somebody who'd love one." He smiles at me.

He doesn't need to say another word. I step onto the footpath at the edge of the brush. Devin gently takes my wrist and stops me. I turn to look at him. His eyes are soft and kind.

"This has been a lot to take in," he says, "and there's more. I just want you to be prepared."

"Well, I'm talking with a dead man right now. How much weirder can it get?" I laugh. But when he doesn't, he's got my attention. "Now you're scaring me a little, Devin."

"There's nothing to be scared of. It just might be a little overwhelming."

"Okay, then. Let's do it."

We begin our trek down the treacherous cliffside, almost completely exposed to the elements. The wind smacks at us hard enough that I briefly lose my footing. I imagine Colton carrying Devin on his back down this path. It was nothing less than an incredibly selfless act of love and pure physical strength. I need to thank him—if I ever see him again.

I concentrate on the uneven ground—sometimes slick and rocky, sometimes spongey and soft.

"Devin, look." I stop and point at the ground, where an enormous paw print is just barely discernible. "What could have made that?"

"A dog, maybe. Come on."

"A dog? Down here? It would be huge. I mean, as huge as..." I can't even say what I'm thinking, my mind tumbling this way and that, trying to imagine exactly who and what are waiting for me. I step past the paw print and look ahead. As I scooch past the enormous gray boulder jutting out onto the path, the familiar scent of Gabriel's fire wafts up into my face. A wave of pure happiness washes over me, and I move faster. I turn another bend and I can see the glow of the fire. People are talking, and there's something else. It's a... baby? I turn briefly to look at Devin. He smiles faintly and nods toward the fire, urging us to keep going.

I round the final turn and step into the warm, well-lit cave before stopping dead in my tracks.

"Well, hello, child. You're finally here." A huge smile spreads across Gabriel's face. The cave falls silent as the rest of the occupants turn to face me. Maybe I fell off the cliff to my death and this is heaven. Or maybe it was before, when I went to the river. I could have drowned and Devin's angel was sent to retrieve me, to bring me here to see all these smiling, beautiful faces before I transition completely out of physical form.

"Hello, my baby," my mother says gently. As she steps to the side and strides past the fire toward me, I see Kendra behind her. She smiles at me, her baby boy bundled in her arms. Behind her, beaming with love and joy, his hand resting lightly at Kendra's waist, is Officer Richard Klein. Lying just behind him, attached to a heavy chain, his loyal companion Walter rests unaffected, gnawing contently on an enormous, meaty bone.

My mother reaches me and envelopes me in a tight embrace.

"Mom? How are you here?"

Devin steps around us, finds Colton, and they fall into a rough, friendly hug, slapping each other on the back. Just as they pull away, Leyla steps up to wrap her arms around each of their necks and pull them close. I blink in disbelief.

"Are you okay?" my mother asks and quickly examines me, but I can't answer her except to briefly meet her gaze and nod.

So much is happening all at once—so many faces, so many voices. But all I see is one, and I can't seem to get to him fast enough. Gabriel and I lock eyes and for the first time ever, I watch tears roll down his cheeks as we step together.

"Gabriel is so, so sorry, dear one." His ancient voice is medicine, my old Gabriel. I throw my arms around his neck and bury my face in his shoulder. "Can you forgive me, child?"

I pull back to look at him. "There's nothing to forgive." I smile and sigh. "I knew it."

"I have much to explain—"

"You don't have to explain anything," I interrupt. "I understand completely. And you're here, now. That's all that matters."

"But I must explain. To you and everyone else here. But in a bit, there are others here to see you. And oh, yes... Hani sends her best."

"Hani?" Before he can answer, I feel a hand on my back and turn around.

"Hello, Ms. John. It's so good to see you."

"Marcus?"

"Yes, the one and only." My old manager laughs and fans himself with his hand, then leans in to quickly kiss each side of my face.

Behind Marcus and a full foot taller stands my Concordia co-worker Taren, even more handsome than I remember. And next to him, in sharp contrast—like a small, timid bird—Moriyah Bigelow waits patiently. I hug them all, in total awe and disbelief, not fully comprehending why or how they're here.

Leyla comes next, and when she wraps her arms around me, I can no longer hold back my own tears. We don't speak.

Neither of us can, nor do we need to. We simply hold each other and cry.

Something slams into my leg. "Nissa!"

"Alakier." I release Leyla and squat down to the boy's level. Alakier squeezes me so hard, we both tumble over in a puddle of happiness and giggles.

"Where's Mommy, Nissa?" The room comes to an abrupt silence.

"Oh, well..." I clear my throat. "She's back on the other island, but she's fine. She's..."

"Let's let Nerissa settle in, okay, Alakier?" Leyla bends over and offers her hand to him. "How about we go sit by the fire for a while and I'll tell you a story?"

He reluctantly agrees, taking her hand and letting her lead him to a cozy seat on the other side of the fire. A helping hand is offered in front of me, and I take it. Colton hoists me up from the floor. I brush off my clothes and stand there awkwardly.

"Thank you for saving him," I finally say. "Thank you for saving his life, Colton."

"He's my brother. He would have done the same."

"You're right," I say. "He would have."

"I'm... I'm sorry for treating you so unkindly."

"There's nothing to apologize for. We've all been through a lot. And it has to be really difficult to..." I pause, considering my words. "To speak against your own father, the man who raised you, this way."

"Well, thanks for letting me off the hook. But nothing excuses how I acted toward you. And I don't have any problem telling the truth about my father. Not anymore. Oh..." he seems to think carefully about his next words. "I guess you and I are, um... also family." He smiles. "My half-sister. There's more blood between us than Devin and me. Weird, huh?"

"Oh. Yeah, I guess so..." But as I say the words, I know

they're not true. I now know William Banks isn't my father. And he can't be Colton's, either. I step back from Colton and address everyone. "I have a lot to tell all of you." I smile and look around at all their faces. "But I guess we all do, don't we?"

"Yes, child, there is much to go over. But first, we are going to settle in, ground ourselves, and share some food and beverage." Gabriel pauses and raises his hand for everyone to wait while he seems to think. "Gabriel has the snacks and drinks to iron out all our stress and kinks. I've got the bubbles to smooth out our troubles. The everyday magic to transform the tragic—oh!" He laughs a deep and hearty laugh. "That is a good one, if I do say so myself."

Gabriel's words and laughter fall over the room like an enchanted cloak, and the mood is instantly lighter, softer, easier. We all indulge in Gabriel's offerings, chatting and hugging and orienting ourselves to this unusual gathering. Kendra and I hold each other in a long embrace and fawn over her baby boy. Soon, everyone settles into a spot around the fire, our bellies full, our thirsts quenched. Alakier has fallen asleep in Leyla's lap, unaffected by the conversation and laughter. Likewise, Walter has spread out on his side and snores away, oblivious to the goings on around him. Somehow, no one seems concerned by Walter's presence. Ruari is still awake but content in Kendra's loving arms, cooing softly.

Devin suddenly stands, clears his throat, and begins. "Thank you all for coming. I know it wasn't easy getting here. This gathering is... unlikely, to say the least. In a lot of ways, it's a miracle that we're all here together. A miracle that many of us are even still alive, myself included. But we're here for a reason. We were brought together for a purpose, held fast by one particular link in the chain. Nerissa."

As everyone's eyes fall upon me, I feel overwhelmed with both love and terror. I have a responsibility to all of them. Their gazes are full of hope, looking to me for some kind of answers, some kind of guidance, even. But I'm no leader. Please don't let me disappoint them.

"Nerissa has been right about everything from the very beginning," Devin continues. "William Banks is a power—and money—hungry monster. And he's got some powerful people on his side willing to look the other way in the name of progress and profits. We've all seen some of the things he's capable of doing, but I don't think any of us know how far he's willing to go."

Devin lowers his head and inhales. Nobody makes a sound.

"Today, we're here to join forces. To share our stories and plan our next move. You'll all have a chance to speak." He looks at me. "And a chance to ask questions. I know there are a lot. But to get started, Gabriel will begin."

Devin sits as Gabriel rises to his feet next to me. "Last Season," he says, "after Nerissa came to this very cave, where we sat at this very fire, she divulged to me the truth of what had been happening behind closed doors on this island and Black Rock. After the dear child relieved herself of the enormous burden she had been carrying with her, things took a turn."

Guilt spreads over me like an illness. Gabriel reaches down for my hand, gently squeezes, and continues.

"It was not long after our meeting, about two weeks before the close of the Season, that I was followed by two of Officer Banks' goons. Somehow, I didn't know they were following me until I was almost at the mouth of this cave. But let me be clear. I do not believe they or anyone knew exactly *what* was discussed or even that Nerissa was here. Even that this cave exists. They were only following orders to watch me, it seemed."

I close my eyes and take a deep breath.

"The two young men seemed fascinated with this cave and my belongings, especially my remedies. They asked many questions, none of which I answered. And they promised each other to come back at the end of the Season to *clean up*. They grew quite physical, and I had no choice but to obey their orders. They forced me to come with them. That if I didn't, they would kill Nerissa, because she was 'putting her nose where it didn't belong.' But halfway up the cliff, one of them turned back for something he wanted from this cave. The other one roughed me up to the point I could barely walk—I assume to keep me from escaping or shoving him over the cliff while we were alone."

My heart aches listening to his story.

"I was turned over to Officer William Banks. Fortunately, my abductors didn't seem to reveal the location of my cave. I think they wanted to keep it for themselves. And they are no longer a threat to our safety here."

"Why?" Moriyah asks, looking around the cave like she feels exposed and surely unsafe.

"Because I killed them," I blurt. "I killed Tommy Alvarez and his friend Bradford... for raping Kendra, and for thinking they killed Gabriel. And for stealing his old shopping cart, his favorite relic."

The only sound is the crackling fire, and all eyes are on me again. What must they think of me now? But this news comes as no surprise to my mother or Kendra—and surely not to Devin or even Gabriel at this point. Yet here I sit, a murderer. And even as ashamed as I feel, I'd do it again in a heartbeat.

"I was taken into the *custody* of Officer Banks," Gabriel continues, "cited for being a traitor and a threat to the Panacea government. Of course, the truth was simply that I was too close to Nerissa and *he* didn't like it. And he wanted something from me."

"He told me you were dead," my mother says quietly, almost to herself.

"Yes, I know," Gabriel replies.

"Wait, *who* told you Gabriel was dead?" I ask my mother. She fidgets in her seat, looking first at Gabriel, then back at me.

"William," she says.

"Directly?"

"Yes," she says flatly. "You knew that."

"You had a lot of *direct* contact with him over the years, didn't you?"

"Yes, I did."

My mother has a way of leaving out details that eventually prove to be of significant importance. As she and I hold each other's gazes, I hope she knows I'll call her out on it. She'll tell me who my real father is, in front of everyone. Today. And then she'll explain herself and her relationship with the man she claimed is my father but isn't.

"I'm sorry for interrupting, Gabriel," I say. "Please continue."

"I will not bore you all with the details, but things were quite difficult at the beginning. He wanted information—about the breed and our relationship. About Wreckleaf. He insisted I help him with his formulations. I wouldn't speak a word. Didn't budge. To be honest, I thought I would indeed die. The abuse and then the neglect was... well," Gabriel pauses, and my heart aches even more for him. "But I suppose I should consider myself lucky."

"Lucky?" I practically yell.

"Yes. I was lucky I was being held on the base in one of the cottages. Had they brought me over to Black Rock, as they had intended, I would have died in the explosion."

"You were meant to be here, Gabriel," Kendra says softly.

"Thank you, dear one. I think so as well. As soon as I caught wind of what had happened, I knew who had caused it." He smiles at me. "And a few days later, I knew they had you. I decided to pretend he'd finally broken me—what he'd been trying to do for weeks. And he ate it up. Felt like a conqueror. He had you right where he wanted you, and with some of my own conditions, he had me right where he wanted, too."

"What conditions?" I ask.

"Oh, simple ones. I agreed to tell him everything I knew and to help him with his testing and formulations if I could simply be unbound in a room to myself. And if I could eat and have the chance to gather some medicinal herbs from the island. I didn't tell him I had Wreckleaf or that I planned to retrieve it. Remember, Tommy and Bradford didn't tell him about my cave."

"So, he let you leave the base?" Marcus asks, his left hand over his heart, his right resting against his cheek.

"He let me go... because he told me he had you." Gabriel looks at me again. "And he'd kill you if I didn't come back. I took the opportunity to shock him by telling him I didn't care if he killed you."

Just hearing Gabriel say those words brings a hard lump to my throat. Even though I know none of his act was real, the uncertainty I felt for so long spreads through me again in a cold wave, and I shiver.

"He reacted just as I'd hoped. Just as I'd expected. He was giddy, telling me how happy he was that I 'finally came to my senses.' I asked him not to tell you I was alive. I said we'd drop that bomb at the perfect moment. He couldn't have been more full of himself. He'd broken me. And he let me leave the base on ego alone, certain his loyal new convert would return as expected. I didn't know what I was going to do. I didn't have any plan. But after I came to this cave the first time, I knew I wasn't alone."

"The picture of the horses…" I say in awe.

"Yes, dear one. I took a big chance showing you that picture, but I wanted to tell you so badly. To relieve you of your pain and fear. But I also feared if I told you Devin was alive, you'd accidentally tell the officer. I'd spent months proving my loyalty to him."

"So you could gather evidence," I say.

"Yes, that, and so he'd allow me to take over your injections. As soon as he did—even before that—Hani and I started to reduce as many of the dosage amounts as we could. You were so intoxicated by it all. So empty." He pauses to calm his breath, visibly shaken by retelling the story.

"Not only that, but Gabriel helped Colton stabilize me and heal my wounds enough to get me off the island," Devin adds.

"Yeah, I thought he was crazy when he insisted on coming to this cave," Colton says. "But honestly, I don't think he would have survived otherwise. But I didn't know what to do with all the remedies and concoctions. Devin pointed out the Wreckleaf, and we started with that on his wounds. And this fire." Colton spreads his fingers out toward the flame and stares into it. "We probably would have both died without this fire. Without this cave."

"Gabriel came back as often as he could, always with something useful in his hands, and taught Colton what to do. They saved my life."

"And when he was strong enough," Leyla adds, her voice thick with emotion, "Colton risked his own safety again and brought my son home to me."

"And then you came back. You all came back." I look around at all of them. "Why?"

"We all exchanged information that last night at the Banks' house, remember?" Moriyah says. "After my aunt got Giovanni's message, she shipped me back home in a hurry. She didn't say anything to me except to mind my own business. I tried talking to my parents, but they just said the same thing. I kept messaging you, all of you, but nobody would respond, and I didn't know what to do. Then Leyla finally contacted me and told me everything she knew. I'm so... sorry. I don't know why my aunt didn't help."

"It's not your fault," I try to convince her, but her eyes are full of shame.

"That's what I told her, Beauty," Marcus adds.

"Marcus," I say, smiling at him. "I can't believe you're here. How did you—"

"Well, our sweet little mouse got in touch." Marcus gestures toward Moriyah.

I contain a tiny laugh. "Why did you contact Marcus, of all people?"

Marcus purses his lips and looks sideways at the ceiling. Not meaning to, I've clearly offended him.

"Mostly, I just needed someone to talk to," Moriyah explains. "Anybody, really. But I already knew Marcus really likes you and he'd want to help if he could."

I raise my eyebrows. "Marcus likes me?"

"Oh, not like that, darling. I assure you." Marcus wobbles his head at me. "That's this one." He points at Taren, who sighs heavily and shifts his gaze along the floor. "But yes, despite what you may think—or what you may remember—I do indeed care for you, Ms. John. And I despise that abrasive beast of a man *and* the way he acted toward you. The way he acted toward me too, for that matter. And I'm fully prepared to speak on your behalf about him and his gross behavior."

"Marcus," I coo, and his cheeks flush lightly. "That is so sweet. Thank you."

"You're welcome, darling."

"And Taren?" I wait for him to meet my eyes. "Thank you so much for coming."

"You're welcome. But I've been here the whole time."

"What?"

He shrugs. "I never left at the end of the Season."

"Um, I'm sorry. I still don't understand."

"Going back to the mainland for the winter—to some crappy job and living with my dad who doesn't really like me around—didn't sound all that great. So, when the custodian job at Concordia opened up, I applied. Marcus put in a good word for me, and they hired me even though I had absolutely no experience."

"You're the off-Season custodian at Concordia?" My eyes widen, and he smiles at my realization.

"Of course, they didn't ask *me* if I wanted the job," Marcus says. "Even though they know I'd be *fantastic* at it." He snaps his fingers above his head.

Taren turns his head to eye Marcus with a raised eyebrow. "You'd be miserable, Marcus. It's winter. There's nothing to do except walk the halls and repair the damage before it gets out of control. Manuel labor, Marcus." Taren stares at him.

"Ew." Marcus exaggerates a shiver. "Yes, I suppose you're right."

"So, how's the job been?" I ask Taren.

"Well, like I said, there's not much to do. But every once in a while... something unexpected pops up."

"I messaged Taren as soon as Ms. Moriyah contacted me," Marcus adds. "Gave him all the details."

"Nerissa, I was a server," Taren says, dipping his head toward me. "I saw firsthand what that energy drink did to people. I'll do whatever I can to help."

"Thank you." I look around the cave. "Thank you, every-one." My eyes settle on Walter. "Um... just curious." I point at the giant animal, now sleeping like a baby. "Why does nobody seem bothered by the enormous hybrid security animal in our presence?"

Everybody just smiles, and now I feel like the joke's on me.

"Remember, dear child, Gabriel is not just a peddler of mind-altering goods but a purveyor and scientific agent of all substances magical, restorative, and remedial," Gabriel declares proudly, gazing upon the sleeping Walter.

"Oh."

"We've been working on Walter's manners," Richard Klein adds. "Gabriel's 'puppy-potion' really helps." He chuckles.

"*Puppy*-potion?'" I can't help but laugh.

Devin was right. This is overwhelming—this outpouring of love, support, and concern. This coming together of purity and good intention. I miss Giovanni; she should be here. I know a part of her is.

"Where have you been keeping him?" I ask Richard, nodding toward Walter. "He's not exactly easy to hide."

"Well, I obviously couldn't take him off the island. Kendra offered her house in the Oval."

"The Oval?" I ask, astonished by this choice. "The locals live there year-round."

"Yeah, it's a little risky. But we've been really careful, gotten our routine down to a science. And now with Gabriel's new potion, nobody will ever know a thing." Richard beams at his beloved animal.

"I still don't..." My head's twirling again now, trying to put together all the pieces that keep popping up out of nowhere. I look at my mother. "How did you all get together? I mean, with our transmissions entirely blocked, how did you plan this?" I gesture to the surrounding cave.

"Oh, we had a very special helper," Kendra says with a grin.

"Who?"

"*Me*! It was me, Nissa," Alakier shouts from his spot on Leyla's lap, startling us all after having looked like he was asleep. "I'm a really good swimmer!"

Devin stands and steps behind me, resting his hands on my shoulders. He knows me. He knows how much this part upsets me.

"You sent Alakier to Albatross? Alone?" My stomach and chest burn with anger and horror, but I try to keep from yelling at them all.

Devin steps around me to sit in front of me on the floor, blocking the light from the dwindling fire with his back. "When I was well enough to fly back to the mainland, Gabriel, Colton, and I made a plan. Colton and I returned two weeks ago with my mother, Alakier, Marcus, and Moriyah. We had no way of contacting Gabriel except to wait for him here at the cave. We waited three days, and then he found us, just like we'd planned before we left."

"You've been here two weeks?" I ask, hanging onto his every word.

Devin nods. "Then we had to figure out how to tell your family we wanted to meet. We stood as lookouts in different places along the shore, night after night, hoping one of them would come to Panacea."

"They can't," I say, suddenly concerned now for my mother, Kendra, and Ruari. "William, he said... well, they're open targets now."

"We figured something like that might have happened. Even when I left you the note to meet at the river today, we still hadn't heard from your family. It wasn't an easy decision, Nerissa, but sending Alakier to Albatross was the only option we had left."

"I did it, Nissa. I did it all by myself," Alakier boasts again, still sounding quite tired.

"I know," I tell him. "You're so brave, Alakier." Even while I say this, I'm staring at Devin, slowly shaking my head. Then I whisper, "He's so little. He could have been killed."

Devin frowns at me, as if the guilt still touches him a little. "But it worked. Tatiana was here just a few hours later, and she brought Alakier safely back with her."

"They filled me in on everything," my mother says. "I went back to let the rest of the breed know what was going on, then Kendra, Ruari, and I headed here late last night."

"And I brought Richard and Walter," Kendra adds.

I look over Devin's shoulder just as Richard leans over to kiss Kendra.

"Okay, okay." I drop my head and rub my temples—my brain feels like it's about to explode. Devin stands and steps away a little, knowing I need some breathing room. "I just need a minute, please." I get up and walk slowly to the mouth of the cave, pausing to look at the beauty before me. The shadows have grown long, and the sun glitters off the deep blue waves in the distance as it slowly descends behind us. I'll have to leave soon to make it back to the base on time. But there's still so much to know.

I take a few deep breaths and try to clear my mind before I turn around and walk back to the fire. Gabriel arranges three new logs in a perfect triangle, and the flames kick back up with an instant, new warmth.

"So... I'm incredibly thankful to see all of you. I'm so moved by you wanting to be here. Wanting to help. But I'm not sure what we can do to stop William Banks. We all know how it went last time... and like I said, his investors and supporters don't care about anything but the bottom line. So, I'm not sure what you're planning, but whatever it is, I don't think it'll make any difference." I hate how cynical I sound. But it's the truth.

"We have the word of an officer this time," Devin says, and I glance at Richard Klein. The man meets my eyes with absolute certainty. "As well as the actual son of Officer Banks. Not *just* his stepson."

I want to stop him and ask Colton if he's absolutely certain William Banks is his father, but I can't. Not yet.

"We have the word of the pavilion manager of the most prestigious resort on the island," Devin continues, "the server and custodian of said resort, the niece of Bio-Gen's biggest investor, and all the rest of us."

I don't have any control over my unconvinced frown.

"They have no reason at all to just make up their stories. They have nothing to gain and everything to lose. People are implicating their superiors. Some of us are implicating our own family members. No, it wouldn't make any sense... unless what we're saying is true. And it is. The rest of the world will believe us this time."

"But even if they do, will it matter?" I ask.

"If I may jump in?" Richard says and steps toward the fire.

I nod, returning to my seat around the flames.

Officer Klein clears his throat and pauses briefly. "I may have been no one in Officer Banks' eyes. He painted me out to be inferior to him in all ways. The truth is, I'm *Specialist* Officer Klein, and I created Walter, as well as Officer Banks' water hybrids and so many others."

"He told me *he* created Walter," I say.

Richard laughs. "Absolutely not. Walter was his idea, and he did help design him, but William Banks isn't a scientist. I am. And I specialize in many areas, including veterinary microbiology and theriogenology, intergeneric and interfamilial hybridization, and animal behavior."

I don't even know what he just said, but I'm soaking it all up as much as I can. We all are.

"I conducted or oversaw all the research and diagnostics at the former labs. I know exactly what William Banks was doing, because I was doing it too. And I regret that very much. But he *was* my superior, and I did have to follow his command."

"So he made you do unspeakable things, then took all the credit for your work," I say.

"Yes. And honestly, I didn't care much. At first. But after Walter was created... well, I grew a little attached to him. We'd created this life and acted as if it were some gross anomaly unworthy of respect or decency."

I know how that feels, and I want to have empathy, despite my growing restlessness. But I don't have much time left. "I'm sorry. But how will this information help us?"

"Thank you," Richard says with a nod. "Like I said, I know firsthand what went on in those labs. The testing and the falsified results. The creatures that have been and undoubtedly still are being created. Illegally, I might add. And I'm very well-connected. My grandfather was also an officer. A high-ranking officer. He's been retired for some time now and lives on the mainland. I don't keep in regular contact with him, but I know he's still very much a part of the FWG family. I chose to stay on the island because of Walter, and my transmission was blocked—just like yours. I couldn't reach out to anyone after the labs were destroyed. I had no way to tell anyone that I was even still alive. A part of me was fine with it. I'd had enough of the life I'd been living. Being here—unknown and left alone—isn't so bad. But now that I know nothing has changed, I want to go back to the mainland and tell my other superiors everything. Officer Banks is very good at making people think he's in charge. He's not. And not everyone will turn a blind eye."

Devin nods. "With all the evidence Gabriel's put together—"

"And all of us willing to speak against him," Colton adds.

"We may finally have a chance to take the bastard down." Leyla finishes their thought and glances first at her son by birth and then at Colton, the older son of her heart.

For the first time in a long time, I feel that pull in my stomach. That pang of excited nerves—of hope—no matter how implausible or faint our chances may be. It feels good. I stand and walk slowly around the fire, cracking my knuckles and chewing my lips, thinking.

"Okay, how?" I ask, speaking to anyone and everyone. "When?"

"You've narrowed down the timeline a little," Devin says, then turns to face everyone else. "Nerissa told me earlier today that William's moved up the implantation to Monday." A collective gasp and mumble of dissent rises in the cave, and Devin turns again to look at me. "We'd planned to contact Officer Klein's superiors on the mainland to arrange a meeting." He lifts his arm. "I've got top-of-the-line transmission, now."

"If they agree to meet with us, it will have to be in person," Officer Klein adds. "But the next zeppelin doesn't leave for two weeks."

"Right," Devin continues, "and if they agree to a meeting, it'll be on their schedule. Then, if everything goes the way we want it to, *if* we have our meeting and convince the authorities to come back with us and shut Bio-Gen down, we'll have to wait until May third to take the next zeppelin back with them. Otherwise, it'll be another three weeks of waiting to come in with the tourists for the Season."

"If..." I say. "What if you can't get a meeting? Or convince them of what's actually happening? What if nobody cares?"

No one has an answer for that. We all look around at each other, at the floor, at the fire. An answer is nowhere to be found.

"So my daughter is going to have to wait," my mother says, her voice icy, "pregnant with one of William Banks' monsters, while you're all on the mainland trying to convince the powers that be to return to Panacea and shut the whole thing down?"

"I'll do my best to convince William we should wait a little longer," I say. "I've done it before. I—"

"Yes, Tatiana," Devin says softly. "That's the best we can come up with."

"No," my mother replies. "Just come back to Albatross and be safe. Or get on the next zeppelin with them—" She stops, knowing I can't, knowing what will become of the rest of our family if I cross William Banks again. She looks up with wide eyes, her mouth open—like she's had an idea.

"Mom?"

"Why don't we *all* just get on the next zeppelin? There's so few of us left. We could stow away. Couldn't we, Devin?"

Devin slowly shakes his head. "That's... how many? Twelve of you and a baby? I really don't think it's possible. You know, to sneak you onboard and hide all of you. I'm sorry."

"I can't leave, Mom," I say. "You know that."

"If we all leave together, there's nobody left for him to hurt," she says, her eyes desperately pleading with me.

"Anastasia and Lillian are still on the Rock," I say softly. "He'll kill them."

She closes her eyes and frowns a little, clearly ashamed she'd forgotten them.

"Look, it's not a perfect plan," Devin says, "but it's all we've got. And it'll work. I know it will."

"It has to," my mother says.

A hush falls over the cave, everyone staring silently at everything but each other.

"You know, there might actually be something I can do. If I really need to," I say quietly. All eyes lift again to focus on me.

"William got really drunk one night and told me a story. And I don't know if anyone would believe me, or if it would even matter, but Anastasia watched William kill his own father right in front of her. If I could convince her to talk, we could tell someone about that, too."

"Oh, my god," Leyla whispers. "He told everyone his father had become senile and walked off one day. Nobody ever found him."

"He killed Nicholas?" my mother asks, and the fact that she used his first name makes me stop.

"Apparently."

"But he was drunk when he told you that story?" Leyla asks. "I mean, the man's head is twisted enough as it is. There's no way to prove he wasn't just too drunk to know the truth from his own fantasies." Leyla shakes her head.

"Unless Anastasia verifies it," I remind her. "I'll have to figure out some way to talk to her. She wouldn't lie to me. She always tells the truth." I look at my mother and wait for her to meet my gaze. "Tatiana," I say, and her name on my lips making her flinch. "I'm ready to know the truth. Who's my real father?"

CHAPTER 22
TATIANA
IT'S THE ONLY WAY...

NINETEEN YEARS EARLIER—OFF-SEASON

"Who are you? What do you want?" Tatiana asked.

"My name is Gabriel. How do you do?" He extended a hand. Reluctantly, she took it. She didn't want to come off as too suspicious. But, why would she? This was an old, local guy on a dark street behind a bar, with no tourists around during off-Season.

"I'm Tatiana. Pleased to meet you. But you really shouldn't sneak up on someone like that."

"Oh, I'm terribly sorry. It's just that I had to speak with you. He'll be pleased to finally know your name."

"He who?"

"I was sent by an admirer to ask if you'd be willing to meet him."

Of course. She should have known one of his cronies in the bar wanted to hook up. Tatiana didn't quite know how to

289

respond. This man seemed harmless, but she had no idea who he was and no reason to trust him.

"Who wants to meet me?" she asked, trying to sound curious instead of concerned.

"His name is Officer William Banks. He's seen you around the island many times and is very interested in getting to know you."

That was hard to believe. Tatiana wasn't often *seen* on Panacea, and that was by choice. "Officer?"

"Yes, he's an Officer of the Panacea Branch of the First World Government. And he asked me to give this to you if I spoke with you tonight." The man handed her a small linen envelope and her caution gave way to intrigue. Tatiana took the envelope. "If you'd please read it now…"

Agreeing to do as he asked, she opened the letter. "Have you read this, Gabriel?"

"Oh, no, ma'am. Gabriel is just a messenger."

"You're friends with this Officer Banks person?"

"No. Like I said… I'm just the messenger."

"Hm… okay." Carefully, she withdrew the note and unfolded it. It was difficult not to react to what she was reading in front of this *messenger*.

Dear Water Doll,

If you are reading this right now, bravo to Gabriel! He will be rewarded greatly for his efforts.

I have wanted to contact you for a very long time. I have observed you whenever possible and wondered what it would be like to meet you and get to know you. Through my own observations, it seems your breed has acquired a very unique skill, and quite frankly, I'd like the opportunity to experience it. I know this adaptation has aided your breed greatly in continuing to reproduce. Just think, from near extinction to thriving. How wonderful for you!

I am alone in my knowledge of your existence, but for two other humans. I'm not interested in exposing you if you agree to cooperate with my request. We can consider our meeting a win for both of us, and I will be happy to know I have contributed to your reproductive efforts. Along with my absolute confidentiality, I expect the same of you. Our meeting will remain between us and, of course, our friend Gabriel, who will honor our privacy without fail. He will fill you in on the details of our meeting.

I so look forward to getting to know you.

Fondly,
William Banks

"Is this some kind of joke?" Tatiana demanded.

"No, I'm afraid it's not. And Officer Banks does not take no for an answer."

"I thought you said you hadn't read this note." Tatiana couldn't help but raise her voice at the stranger.

"I haven't, but he told me what he wants—what he expects."

"Tell him to go to hell."

Gabriel took a deep breath. "Tatiana... please, I mean no disrespect, but this man has great power. If you don't do as he asks, he will make so much trouble for you."

"What kind of trouble?"

"Well, I imagine he'd start with the fact that your kind are supposed to be extinct. Am I correct?"

She didn't answer him. All she could do was stand there, infuriated by this entire situation and terrified by the sudden news that some random human knew who she was—who her entire breed were. That Officer Banks had been watching her and knew exactly how her kind subdued their contributors.

"I don't know you," Gabriel continued, "or your exact situation. Officer Banks hasn't given me details. But I know enough to be certain this man can and will make your life a living hell if you don't cooperate."

"No, you don't know—"

"But..." The man raised a hand to stop her. "He is actually a man of his word and will take care of you if you honor your end of the deal."

"There is no *deal*. I'm not interested in any *deal*."

"Please, dear one. Do yourself and your people a favor. Don't cross this man."

Nothing more than the look on his face—the kindness in his eyes—changed Tatiana's mind. This man came across as a gentle soul, and seemed to be delivering her an emphatically undeniable warning. She didn't know many pure-humans, but something about Gabriel made her certain she could trust him.

Beyond that, wouldn't an Officer come from good stock? He could become a valuable acquisition, especially at this time of year when the selection was always slim.

"All right," she said. "When and where is this meeting supposed to happen?"

Gabriel exhaled a sigh of relief.

TWO DAYS LATER

She arrived at the designated location—a villa set high atop the hillside in the luxury sector—ten minutes early and an hour after sunset. Gabriel waited at the front entrance to greet her.

"Is he here?" Tatiana asked.

"He's been here for hours."

stepping inside, she could hear soft music playing in the room directly down the hall. Following the music, she passed through the entryway and into a large but cozy living space illuminated by dozens of white candles and a glowing fire. Huge windows looked out over the hillside with what must have been an expansive view during the day. The only thing she could see now was the early moonlight shining off the ocean in the distance.

He sat on the perfect white sofa, his legs crossed, one arm stretched out across the back of the sofa while the other rested casually in his lap with a full glass of bubbly pink wine. And he wore the most condescending smile.

"Good evening, Beauty."

"Hello."

He didn't stand, merely patted the sofa beside him. When Tatiana didn't move, it seemed to snap the man out of his little trance, and he sat forward. "Oh, how rude of me." Then he did stand. "I'm William, but you knew that, of course. Please, do come in. Sit down. Make yourself at home."

Reluctantly, she stepped forward.

"Can I offer you a glass of wine, Tatiana?"

"No."

He let out a quiet laugh. "Okay. So, welcome. I hope it wasn't too much trouble getting here."

"No, it was fine. It's always easier after dark, and this place is very private."

"Yes!" William seemed overly excited. "That's what I was going for. Privacy."

"Do you live here?"

"Oh, no. This is just a little place I rent, away from my home. For private matters."

Tatiana didn't have much of a choice but to jump right in. "So, you want me to enchant you?"

He smiled. "Enchant? Is that what you call it? That's brilliant. Yes, I would like to be *enchanted*." He rolled the word around in his mouth like it was a piece of candy.

"Why?"

"Isn't that obvious?" He laughed again.

"You won't remember it," she said. "You understand that, don't you?"

"Yes, I do, but I also understand the end result. I assume that since you were on the island only two days ago looking to do the same thing on your own, it's still the right timing for you."

Was this guy serious? "And you'd like to father a child?" she asked him.

William's face lit up, his smile growing even wider. He was admittedly attractive but ugly at the same time.

"I would like to father a Dolhuphemale."

Hearing him say the word so plainly, like it was some common term, turned her stomach. "How do you know about us?"

William Banks spent the next twenty minutes explaining who he was and how his family had *inherited* the knowledge of Tatiana's breed and its guardianship. Her stomach curdled as he informed her of what she already knew—that not only had his predecessors created her breed, only to destroy them when they were finished, but also how those before him had purposefully and under strict classification allowed a few of her kind to survive without anyone's knowledge. Her breed was to be left alone—to believe they had been lucky to survive. They were only to be observed, for many more generations to come, to see what would happen to them—*scientific research*. Hence, William revealed the beginning of the great Dolhuphemale hybrid experiment.

He clearly couldn't handle the secrecy any longer. It seemed this narcissistic human wanted nothing more than to push his weight around simply because he could. To knowingly father what was believed to be an illegal and extinct creature. Tatiana couldn't imagine a bigger ego stroke for someone like him.

If she cooperated with him, he promised her his confidentiality. After she confirmed she was pregnant with his child, he'd leave her alone, assuring her of the continued protection of her breed—especially of his 'own blood.'

The consequences of not cooperating with him were grim and very simple. "If you refuse me," he said, "I *will* expose your existence to the world. Your breed will be collected, herded like sheep. I will have no ability or desire to protect you from what will surely be unending scientific study and discomfort. Which will most certainly not end well for any of you."

He wanted to know more about Tatiana—much more. How did the breed live? What did they eat? How on Earth did they adapt? And mostly, what had caused the Dolhuphemale saliva to anesthetize their contributors? Intimidated, Tatiana pored over the details of Myrielle and the other last survivors as though she were delivering a history lesson at the arena. She instantly regretted telling him anything. Though he seemed like a man genuinely convicted to his word, William Banks also seemed like the kind of man who could easily change his mind. Instead of divulging more, Tatiana attempted to gather her own information.

"Who are the other two humans who know about us?" she asked him. "The ones you mentioned."

"The first is Nicholas Banks. Officer Nicholas Banks." William cringed as the name rolled off his tongue. "My father." He blew out a disgusted sigh.

"You don't care for your father?" She couldn't help but ask.

William chuckled sarcastically. "My father doesn't care for me."

"Surely that can't be true. He's your father." Tatiana knew she'd struck a nerve.

"Nicholas Banks has singular interest. One singular care in this world. And it's not me, his only son. It's you."

"Me?"

"Your breed. He's obsessed with the lot of you. And that obsession remains at all costs..." He couldn't seem to finish his sentence. And for a quick moment, Tatiana actually felt bad for him. But his face changed from sadness to anger in an instant, his brow creased and nostrils flaring. "Nothing was ever as worthy of his unconditional care and attention as you little hybrid sluts."

Tatiana had to force herself not to stand up and walk out. But being here with him made it clear—just as Gabriel had told her—that William Banks was not a man to anger.

"Who's the other person?" She managed to ask in a soft, curious tone.

"Specialist Officer Reginald Klein."

"Who is he, William?"

But he was finished with her questions.

Before they commenced with the enchantment, William warned her once again, "I am trusting you, Tatiana, to keep your end of our agreement. Should something happen to me here tonight, my associate Officer Emmanuel MacNamire has been instructed in how to proceed with the consequences."

"You said there were only two other people who knew about us."

"Oh, yes. I did say that, didn't I?" He laughed. "Don't worry. My associate only knows the important bullet points. But he's prepared at a moment's notice to take whatever action necessary."

"I understand," she replied. "Are you ready?" She wanted was to get this over with.

William leaned back on the sofa, crossed his arms behind his head, and smiled. "I sure am, Beauty."

FOUR WEEKS AFTER WILLIAM BANKS' ENCHANTMENT

Returning to Panacea to scout for another suitable contributor, Tatiana was approached by the local man Gabriel almost as soon as she made landfall—as though he'd been waiting for her. He looked terrible, like he hadn't slept for days. When he offered her another note, presumably from Officer Banks, he didn't say a word.

She raised a hand and shook her head. "No thanks. Not interested."

"If I don't deliver this to you and watch you read it, I will pay another hefty price."

Tatiana frowned. "What happened to you?"

"Please, just read the note."

Slowly, she took it from him and opened it. Turning it beneath the soft light of the streetlamp at the entrance to the beach, she glanced back up at Gabriel. "You can't just come up to me like this. I don't want anyone to see me."

"I know. I'm sorry. I'll leave you alone as soon as he gets what he wants."

She looked down at the note again and read it.

Dear Tatiana,

Hope you are well. I've missed you, and I can't wait to hear the news of our future child. I want to meet with you again at the villa to celebrate. Once again, Gabriel will provide the details.

I look forward to seeing you.

Fondly,
William

She crumpled the note in one hand and threw it on the ground. "You can tell William Banks to go to hell. I will *not* meet with him again."

"Oh, please, Tatiana..." Gabriel sunk down into the sand, curling his knees into his chest and wrapping his arms around his bent head. "You must—you *have* to. Please."

"My god, what did he do to you?" She couldn't believe anyone would have such a visceral reaction without a large amount of trauma.

Gabriel looked like he didn't want to answer at first, perhaps afraid of speaking against William Banks. But when she asked again, he finally spoke.

"He burned down my house." The man could barely get out the words.

Tatiana sat beside him. "He did *what*? Why?"

"Because I refused to bring you another one of his letters. I said I didn't want to be involved in this any longer, that it wasn't any of my business and I didn't want to bother you again. Just once... that's all it took. He asked me once, I said no, and I thought we were done." Gabriel paused to wipe his face and took a deep breath.

"And then what?"

"And then he burned down my home. My wife tried to save our dog, and she..." His faces contorted as he closed his eyes.

"Did she..."

"No, not yet. But I don't think she'll make it. He said he'd get her the best care once I delivered this note to you and made sure you read it, but I think it's too late."

Tatiana gently laid a hand on the man's back, as he buried his face in his arms and cried. There was nothing she could say that would change his grim reality.

"Tatiana, he is capable of much worse. You must do as he says."

"I'm not pregnant, Gabriel," she said. "William wasn't a successful acquisition."

He lifted his head to stare at her, his face streaked with hot tears. "Then you must try again."

She met with William three more times. He asked her not to enchant him, because he wanted to remember their special time together. Of course, she lied, saying that only through enchantment—a syncing of hormones and such—would she be able to conceive. The man was desperate, determined to father his own Dolhuphemale, so he agreed. Each time Tatiana reported back to him with the news of no pregnancy, he grew increasingly more hostile than the last time. He blamed her for the failed conceptions, and the final time they met, he left her with a welt on the side of her face.

"If you can't give me what I want," he spat, "what use are you? Bring me another maid."

"It's just a matter of time," she told him. "I want to be the one to do this for you. It's just... I still feel a little nervous around you, William. I'm sure that's what's taking this so long." But she knew the truth. The shortcomings were all his. It was William's fault she wasn't yet pregnant. And there was no way Tatiana would ever involve any of her sisters in this.

"Do you know William's father?"

"Dr. Banks?" Gabriel replied. "I know *of* him. Why?"

"I'd like to meet him. Can you help me find him?"

"I don't know if he's even on the island yet, but I'll try to find out. What are you doing, dear one?"

"I'll enchant Nicholas Banks," Tatiana explained. "When I acquire, I'll tell William I'm finally pregnant with his child. Same gene pool, really. The child would still look like William." Even though William had promised to leave her and her breed alone once Tatiana conceived, she knew he'd still want to meet his daughter.

She was satisfied with the opportunity to screw over William Banks. Nicholas Banks sounded like a smart man with morals, and William hated him. Though she'd be unable to actually tell William what she'd done—or anyone, ever—she'd still know the truth. That would be enough. William would have his token hybrid child to puff up his already inflated ego and he'd protect her, "his blood". Tatiana could rest easy knowing her daughter and the rest of her breed would forever remain safe.

"It's the only way," she said to Gabriel.

"It's brilliant," he replied with a thin smile. "I will find Dr. Banks immediately."

Two weeks after what William believed was another enchantment—she finally had the good news to deliver.

"You've done it, William," she said. "I'm pregnant! Due next February."

Predictably so, the man was elated—kind. Just like that, she'd become his Queen.

After his arrival on Panacea for the pre-Season, the enchantment and acquisition of Nicholas Banks was as easy as it possibly could have been. Gabriel located his residence, and Tatiana simply knocked on the man's front door to take care of business.

Once she was pregnant, William kept his word and left her alone—for the most part. There were a couple more notes delivered, mostly just simple inquisitions into how she was feeling. Only one of them really meant anything to her—only one of them she kept, in case she needed to remind William of his promises and his side of their *deal*.

Dear Tatiana,

I hope you are feeling well and that baby of ours isn't causing you too much trouble. I want you to know that I will honor our agreement always. You held up your end of the deal and allowed me to create my own Dolhuphemale offspring.

I am very proud to call her my own, and I will protect her always.

She is my blood. Likewise, I will return to my role as guardian to you and your breed, and I will never again interfere in the natural evolution of your kind. With one exception. I would like to meet my daughter when she is born. That is it, I promise.

I would love to tell my father, just to see his face. But I won't, as you advised.

Thank you, Tatiana. I respect you greatly, and I know you will be an amazing mother to our child.

Fondly,
William Banks

Shortly after Nerissa was born, Tatiana honored William's request and brought her daughter to Panacea one dark night. They went to his villa, finding him there alone. It was a brief, surprisingly tender encounter, and she thought it was the last time she'd ever have to speak with William Banks.

She and Gabriel quickly fell out of contact. After his wife died, he became increasingly recluse, and it seemed William had grown tired of him as well. Not until several years later, when Tatiana took her daughter to Panacea one warm summer day to splash in the river, did a man approach her there. He recognized both her and Nerissa. Frightened, she left without speaking to him further.

After realizing that man had been Gabriel, she went looking for him. Although thrown together by chance, He was the keeper of Tatiana's greatest secret. And if he could keep that secret, he'd surely be able to keep more. Her heart still broke for him.

They struck up their own deal, under the umbrella of a mutual hatred for the kind of power-hungry humans who forever altered both of their lives. Gabriel became her breed's scouting and acquisition assistant in exchange for Wreckleaf. But really, it was his care for Nerissa and how she came into this world that bound them all together.

CHAPTER 23
CHANGE OF PLANS
DO NOT TELL THEM ANYTHING, UNDER ANY CIRCUMSTANCES...

FRIDAY, MARCH 21ST

So the man I was shocked and disgusted to find out was my father actually isn't. Instead, he's my half-brother, and we share the same father—Dr. Nicholas Banks. And this half-brother of mine killed him. A man who sounded decent, a man of some principle and moral, murdered by his own power-hungry son—my despicable, unforgivable brother.

My mother steps toward me, offering a small, aged envelope.

"What's this?" I ask.

"It's the letter. The one William gave me. I brought it with me because I knew we'd be talking about this today—or at least sometime soon. I want you to have it."

"Why? What good can it possibly do now?"

She lowers her head and sighs. "None, I guess. But I just hope it can serve as some kind of symbol. Everything I did... was to protect you, Nerissa. To protect our family."

"I know," I say. "I understand now." She looks back up at me, tears rolling down her cheeks. "You could have told me."

"Can you forgive me?" She doesn't try to defend or explain herself, perhaps for the first time ever. "I should have told you once you were old enough to understand. I should have trusted that you'd be able to handle it. I'm sorry."

"You did what you thought was best. I wish I'd known, but I forgive you, Mom." I lean into her, and she holds me—just holds me. I let her, I let go, and I let myself sink into her. It feels so good.

Then I start laughing.

"What?" she asks.

"I really turned out to be William's dream child, didn't I?"

The twisted levity seems to ease everyone else with us. I'd nearly forgotten about them until soft laughter and a few sighs remind me I'm surrounded by the best people on the planet.

There's something I need to do, something I need to say. I gently break free of my mother's embrace and find Gabriel sitting in front of the fire. He's quiet, but his eyes sparkle with so much emotion and unshed tears, a half smile camouflaging his pain—always the one to keep everyone else comfortable.

I squat in front of him and put my hands on his shoulders. He looks at me with such love, I crumble. Wrapping my arms around him, I cry for the unknown years of pain he's suffered.

"I'm so sorry, Gabriel. Your wife... I didn't know."

"Thank you, child. It's never been something I wanted to relive."

"What was her name?" I feel him stiffen, and I instantly regret asking.

Slowly he softens and takes a deep breath. "Eleanor. Her name was Eleanor."

"It's beautiful." I hold onto him—my lifeline, my tether. And as I do my best to offer him a token of comfort, my gaze travels to the mouth of the cave, where the light is now dim and gray. I stand abruptly.

"What is it, child?" Gabriel asks.

"I've got to go. Now. The sun's setting, and if I'm late, he'll..."

Quick hugs are passed around as I try to absorb a little piece of each of them—something to hang onto while I'm forced to become a mother. The goodbyes are short and sweet —probably better that way. I take one last sip of Gabriel's delicious green drink and another small handful of Wreckleaf, then head to the cave's entrance. Devin stays by my side.

"Nerissa, wait," Officer Klein says. "Please, let Walter and me walk you up the trail to your board. I need to speak with you."

I turn around to look at him. "Okay, but we have to leave now."

Richard Klein and the obedient Walter follow Devin and me to the cave entrance. Gabriel joins us.

Outside, the cold air is a quick reminder that it's not summer yet, and no matter how much I despise my situation, I do look forward to crawling under the covers of my luxurious bed in my ridiculous, opulent suite.

We climb the cliff trail carefully, Walter leading the way. "The name your mother mentioned in her story," Richard says. "The other 'pure-human' to know about your breed from the beginning. Specialist Officer Reginald Klein..." He slows down and turns to look at me.

"That is your grandfather, isn't he, Officer Klein?" Gabriel says from behind me.

I stop. "Oh. Well... that could be—"

"Very beneficial," Richard finishes.

"So he was William Banks' superior?" Devin asks.

"Yes," Richard says. "And Nicholas Banks' as well."

"Did you know his connection?" Devin asks. "To the Dolhuphemales?"

"No. He never talked about it, and I didn't know a thing. I was shocked to hear Tatiana say his name. But like I said, I don't keep in contact with him. Never really did, not even as a child. He was always very reclusive. Likes his privacy."

"But the man honored his obligation to protect the Dolhuphemales' existence," Gabriel says thoughtfully.

"Yes, I suppose he did," Richard agrees.

We reach the top of the footpath and step out of the trees. Our boards wait where we left them. By the looks of it, I've got about twenty minutes until the sun sets.

"All right. I have to go," I tell them.

"I'll ride with you," Devin declares.

"No. What if somebody sees you?"

"Just up until the bridge, then," he says. "I just got you back. I'm not ready to let you go so quickly." He takes my hand in his.

"Gabriel is also not ready to let you go. I'd like to tag along." The man's cheeks flush a little. "If that's okay."

"Of course it is," I assure him. "You can ride with me to the bridge and back with Devin."

"Nerissa," Richard says as we mount our boards, "no matter how distant he and I are, having my grandfather on our side is good. It's very good. Reginald Klein is a powerful man."

"Thank you, Richard. Take care of Kendra and Ruari."

"You know I will," he says. "I promise." A small smile lights up his face. "Take care of yourself, understand?"

"I promise, too. Bye, Walter. Be a good boy." I wave at the beast, and as I do, his ears perk up. Turning his laser focus to something down the dirt road, his nostrils flare and he releases a growl.

"It's okay, Walter. That's a good boy..." After a few more

seconds of Richard easing him, the beast relaxes. "Probably just another small animal or something. His hearing is really, really good."

I laugh. "Mine, too. His must be better. I didn't hear anything."

Walter looks at me, and I know I'm not imagining it when he wags his long, scrappy tail.

"You want me to wait for you?" Richard asks Devin.

"No, man. It's cold out here. Head back down to the fire and tell everyone else about your grandfather. It's good news. We'll be right back."

Nodding, Richard turns Walter around and disappears behind the trees. Devin, Gabriel, and I take off in the opposite direction down the dirt road toward the Oval.

The air has grown cold with the sun's descent, but Gabriel holds me around the waist. But I'm warm, radiating heat and gratitude from the inside as Devin rides beside us. We carefully pass the Oval and onto the deserted open road. On our right, the ocean churns and pulsates in its raw and primitive dance. We arrive at the bridge in no time. Why is it the best moments always go so fast? I don't want to say goodbye. I'm not ready. I know they're not, either.

When we slow to a full stop, I hear something—a rustling or a shuffling of some kind. Assuming it's just the wind stirring the trees and shrubs, the three of us dismount our boards.

Gabriel doesn't speak but wraps his arms around me, standing firm and grounded. Then he sways back and forth, his movements almost imperceptible but enough for me to notice and take comfort in, like he's rocking me.

"I love you, Gabriel," I say, my throat heavy and thick. "Thank you."

"I love you, child. Be strong. Hani will help take care of you, and she'll bring you our messages. As much as she can. But know we are with you. Always."

"I will," I try to reassure him, but the truth is, I'm scared. And he knows it.

We break away, and Devin immediately takes my hand and pulls me toward him. I don't think have fully come to grips with the fact that he's alive, holding me in his arms again. It's like a part of my brain has shut down and I've made a deal with myself to live here in this fantasy.

But it's real. *This* is reality.

"Run. Both of you, now," Gabriel says softly. I feel time slow to a crawl as I watch Gabriel turn and run up the hill into the shrubs, his feet scraping the road and kicking up tiny stones in his wake. I let go of Devin, and he squeezes my shoulders. Pushes me to the side, he steps in front of me. Two men on boards whiz past us after Gabriel. Two more dismount their own boards and stand before us, wielding large weapons pointed directly at us.

"Put your hands above your heads and do not move," says the closest man. He's dressed in an all-black, padded, athletic-looking uniform. His face is hidden behind the mask of a reflective helmet.

We raise our arms high, and I turn my head slowly to look for Gabriel. I only see the two men chasing him, each one twice his size and less than half his age. My body involuntarily turns, and I find myself putting my back to the two men holding us at gunpoint.

"Run," I whisper. "Run, Gabriel. Run, Gabriel!" I yell the last one as loud as I can. One of the men grabs me and shoves me roughly to the ground. Devin lies next to me, his eyes squeezed tight, holding his right knee in both hands. I watch as the large, armed men hit Devin across the back of the head, then stab him with what looks like a large needle. Devin falls still, and I know I'm next. I close my eyes, and I don't have to wait long.

SATURDAY, MARCH 22ND

I'm swimming home to Albatross, and I'm so happy. I'm nearly there. But the ocean, serene and welcoming only seconds ago, suddenly turns violent, the waves as large as houses or buildings filled with evil.

A huge wave hits me, pulling me under. I struggle to know which way is up, which way is out. Another, then another crashes over me. I'm no longer sure where I am. Was I even on my way home? I'm fighting against the incessant waves, choking on the sea, coughing, sputtering.

My eyes open, and another wave pummels me. But I'm not underwater anymore. I can see light.

"Wake up, now!" a familiar voice yells. "If you don't wake the hell up, you can drown in that chair for all I care."

I force myself to come back from wherever I just was. But as I gain focus—as understanding comes back to me—I may have preferred dying within the ocean in my mind.

"Well, it's about time," William says, his voice filled with impatience.

My head throbs, my body aches, and I feel like I've been eating sand. But I try to push all the discomfort aside and assess my situation.

I'm sitting in a small wooden chair in what looks like my old cottage. Orange ropes have been tied around my wrists, chest, and ankles, locking me in place with barely enough room to take a deep breath. I shake my head and flick the water from my face and hair. I'm completely soaked. Emmanuel

MacNamire, standing only feet in front of me, holds a large bucket and smiles.

"Where's Devin?" I demand.

"He'll be here in just a minute," William says, pacing across the tiny space. "Him and Gabriel both."

My heart sinks. Gabriel didn't get away.

Through my lingering grogginess but with as much insincerity and condescension as I can muster, I say, "William, you should sit down. You look like you're going to explode."

And then explode he does. "You told me you weren't going to look for Gabriel. You *promised*," he yells, his face red and the veins bulging on the sides of his neck. "But you lied to me!"

"I didn't promise you anything."

"And my god." He continues pacing, wringing his hands and shaking his head. "That stepson of mine. Well, who knew?" He stops, his face inches from mine. "Did you know, Nerissa? Did you know he was alive? You did, didn't you?" He grabs my chin and squeezes hard. "And you've been playing me this entire time."

"No... I haven't. I didn't... know he was alive." I squeeze the words through my teeth. "I mourned him."

He pushes my face away. "Why should I believe you? Why should I believe anything you say to me ever again?"

A hard knock on the door startles us both. William opens it, and Hani enters first, casting her eyes to the floor after a quick glance at me. Behind her, escorted presumably by the two men who knocked us out and drugged us, comes Devin, hands bound behind him and his mouth taped. He's limping. He looks woozy, lumbering along and unable to hold up his head all the way. His hair bounces in tangled waves over his face. Gabriel enters next, also bound and taped, held roughly by the second of the two men. Gabriel looks at me and holds my gaze with an intensity I've never seen from him before.

The two guards watch William closely, and when he nods, they force Devin and Gabriel to their knees in front of me. All at once, I'm traveling back in time to the night William brought Sarah and Lillian to this very cottage. My breath quickens, and I shift as much as I can—which isn't much—beneath the tightly bound orange ropes keeping me in this chair. William looks at Emmanuel and nods again. Emmanuel puts down the bucket he's been holding and steps behind me. There's a soft flicking sound, then I feel the cold blade at my neck. I wasn't expecting that. I guess I'm naïve.

It captures Devin's attention too. He moans under his bindings, thrashing unsuccessfully against the guard. Gabriel stays calm but alert, and William watches all of it. His eyes dart from me to Devin to Gabriel and back, a tiny smile growing wider and wider.

"What did you think of the *Wildfire*?" William asks, and I'm not sure whom he's addressing. Gabriel's glare turns to settle on the officer. William laughs. "Pretty impressive, isn't it? I figured it was only fair that you got to experience it, too. You know, an eye for an eye." He approaches Gabriel, then steps behind him to relieve the guard, who retreats to stand at the door. "Now, tell me everything you know," William says, looking at me. "I mean you, Nerissa. Tell me everything."

The blade pushes into my neck just enough for me to feel its potential. I don't know what he wants, and I'm not sure how to respond.

"I'm sorry, William," I say. "I'm not sure what you mean."

"You know exactly what I mean. I want you to tell me where you were yesterday, what you talked about, how long you've known my stepson was alive, and how you helped Gabriel escape. Or I'll have my officer kill you."

I swallow hard. "William, I don't... I mean, I have nothing to—"

Devin jerks around under his restraints again, his moans rising.

William turns toward the man holding him and nods. The guard pulls Devin up by the hair and presses a knife to his neck too.

"*No*," I shout. "No, please. Don't hurt him, please." I catch Gabriel's eyes—the intensity never having left his face. He moves his head slowly back and forth, staring at me. He wants me to be quiet, or to cooperate, or he's trying to tell me something. I just don't know what. I suck in a quick breath and shut up.

Gabriel turns his head and looks directly up at William behind him. They stay like that for a long, strange moment. The officer stares at Gabriel like he's some pathetic, sad, worthless disappointment. He's looked at me like that so many times. But there's always also the slightest trace of empathy—or maybe just morbid curiosity. William grabs a corner of the tape covering Gabriel's mouth and pulls hard, ripping it from the man's face in one swift, painful jerk. Gabriel's eyes close briefly, but he doesn't make a sound.

William smiles. "You have something you'd like to say?"

Gabriel takes a slow, deep breath. "Yes, I do." He waits.

"Then get on with it, old man. I haven't got all day."

Gabriel turns to look at me again. "I acted entirely alone. Nerissa had nothing to do with any of my actions, and she was unaware of my plans to escape."

"Ha! I have a hard time believing that, Gabriel," William shouts.

"It's true, sir. Gabriel wanted to be left alone. To be done working for you and done dealing with the hybrids. I just wanted to return to the island and make a new home for myself—live in peace, away from everyone, like I used to many years ago. I do best alone."

William sighs, then spreads his fingers through Gabriel's gray hair and just leaves them there, almost like he's petting him. "And what about my wonderful stepson?" he asks, gritting his teeth in disgust.

"What about him, sir?" Gabriel doesn't flinch under William's odd hold.

"How long have you known he was alive? How long have you been in contact with him? And why didn't you tell me?" He moves his fingers up and down, lacing them deeper into Gabriel's locks.

"I didn't know. The moment your men came upon us was the first time I saw him since last Season. And the first time I saw Nerissa since the night I injected you and fled."

At the mention of the infamous *Wildfire*, William's eyes twitch and he sneers, balling his fist around Gabriel's hair. Gabriel still doesn't move. "Hm... you know, I hate liars. I hate the lot of you."

"I acted alone. They are innocent. They're not lying. Nerissa is not lying," Gabriel says slowly.

William laughs. "There may just be a chance she's telling the truth. But she still needs to be punished, just in case. And I'm sure you've already figured out what her punishment will be."

All the intense steadfastness in Gabriel's eyes—in his entire face—disappears.

"The only truly effective punishment left. The ultimate punishment," William says. He clenches his fist even tighter and pulls Gabriel up off his knees.

Gabriel stares at me. "I love you child. Be brave—" William jerks him backward against his chest, whips a knife from his pocket, flips it open, and slits Gabriel's throat.

Blood pours down Gabriel's body in an unending river, drenching him to his hips as he coughs and sputters. His arms and legs go limp. William maintains his vicelike grip, holding the man up by sheer force of will, staring at me with wild eyes —ensuring I fully witness his power.

I'm in a tunnel, traveling backward out of the room, away from the horror, away from my sanity and my grip on reality, being squeezed, compressed into a tight, tiny ball. As I push back and away, I feel a stinging pain at my own neck. There's a shuffling and a scraping sound, and now I'm on the floor. I hit the back of my head, and the pain brings stars and stinging tears, making the room spin.

"What are you doing, you idiot?" William's voice is muffled and far away.

"I'm sorry, sir. She pushed back, and I tried to grab her. It's just a superficial cut." Emmanuel MacNamire speaks from that same blurry, strangled, distant place.

My eyes flutter uncontrollably, and I watch in flashes as they bend over, lifting the chair to which I'm still bound back into its upright position. I'm dizzy and disoriented, as though I'm looking down a long, glass tube. I try to gather myself back but quickly decide I'd rather not regain any focus as I stare at the scene before me.

Gabriel lies on his side, his hands still bound behind his back, in a lake of his own bright-red blood spreading slowly across the floor as his throat offers up the last of it. His face is placid and peaceful, as though he could just be sleeping, but his eyes are still open, staring at nothing—the light behind them gone forever.

William's pulling off his jacket. He drops it lazily on the floor, half-covering Gabriel's face and head. He instructs the two guards to wait outside, and he and Emmanuel convene at the door to quietly discuss something.

Next to Gabriel, Devin now sits against the wall, also still bound at the wrists with his mouth taped. Gabriel's blood encroaches on his space. He's crying, his head down, not wanting to look. I don't want to look, either—don't want to see any of it. But I can't not see. I'll never be able to un-see—

"Hani, let's get this mess cleaned up," William says, then opens the door to address the guards.

I glance to the left and see Hani, white as chalk, her forehead slick with perspiration, wiping her face and eyes with the back of her sleeve. She smooths down her shirt, inhales deeply, and steps forward. As she passes me on her way to the kitchenette sink, she leans over to pick up some invisible object off the table by my side and whispers, "Do not tell them anything, under *any* circumstances."

William and Emmanuel return to the room with the guards.

They pull Devin up off the floor and rip the tape from his mouth while Emmanuel MacNamire works on releasing me from my chair. He leans in close to my face. "Sorry about your neck, sweetheart." He licks his fingers and wipes them along the cut at my throat.

"What do you think I should do with my stepson, Ms. John?" William asks.

I don't answer. I can't. If I have to watch Devin die in front of me, I'm going to insist they do the same to me. Or I'll do it myself.

"She's gone, sir," Emmanuel says, his voice rich with amusement as he waves his hand in front of my face. But he's right. I'm no longer entirely here. I'm no longer entirely alive. I've lost all desire—and ability—to speak, or cry, or feel. I've entered some void—some dark, vague emptiness. I'm buzzing, clouded by everything and nothing at all.

Emmanuel finishes untying me and pulls me to my feet. I'm like a doll he can pose in any position. Eyeing me up and down, he says, "Death becomes you, Beauty." Then he snorts.

"Leave her alone," Devin says. His voice is weak but clear. We meet each other's eyes and just stay there. Yes, okay... I'll just stay here until it's all over.

William grabs Devin by the wrists and pushes him forward. No, please no. "Devin and Nerissa will return to Black Rock with Officer MacNamire and me," he begins. "The three of you"—he gestures to the two guards and Hani—"will dispose of the body and clean the cottage. I want it spotless. I hate blood." He sticks out his tongue and grimaces.

The body.

I collapse back into my seat.

"Oh, no. No, little Beauty. It's time to go for a ride." Emmanuel snickers as he lifts me from under my arm and points me toward the door.

"Don't worry, Nerissa," William says. "I'm not going to kill Devin. Yet. When and if I do will be entirely up to you. For now, we're going to see how Devin can contribute in the labs. And... we're going to take a look at that fancy new arm of his."

Emmanuel scoffs at my lack of reaction and leads me forward. We step around the blood, but I want to kneel down and soak it all up—or push all of it back into Gabriel and return him to life. One last time, I look down at his face peeking out from under his murderer's carelessly dropped jacket, and as I pull my tortured gaze away, I catch a reflection of myself in the pool of his blood. Whatever I had left of myself breaks completely.

"Hani, when you're finished, come back to the Bio-Gen building. Nerissa and I have a dinner engagement this evening." William's unexpected glee is entirely out of place. "And it seems she may need some help getting ready."

Both Devin and I look at him. Emmanuel laughs at what must be our confused expressions.

"Yes, that's right," William continues. "These types of

commitments must be honored and respected. We are cele-brating tonight, Ms. John. Monday is the big day. Oh! And I almost forgot to tell you. If all goes well, the birth of your first Harvester will be just after the grand re-opening gala before the next Season opens. Perfectly timed to show you off!" He dances beside the door, smiling, seeming to wait for us to do the same. When no one indulges him, he shrugs and steps out into the rainy, gray day. I look back and catch one more glance of Hani, mop in hand. She meets my gaze with a tiny nod, tears rolling down her cheeks.

The boat pulls out into the channel. Devin is tied to one side of the bar, and I'm tied to the opposite side next to Emmanuel, who takes the opportunity to lightly brush his hand across my chest, rest his fingers under my chin, and whisper, "Don't worry, Doll. I didn't make the rope too tight. Not this time. We'll save that for another day, because guess who gets to take over your care? Now that Gabriel's out of the picture, you and I are going to have some fun together."

I stare straight ahead, hearing him but feeling nothing.

"Don't lose all your fight, Beauty. That's half the pleasure, especially now." Emmanuel stands and joins William at the helm.

I look at Devin. He's limp and shivering, but meets my gaze. He knows whatever Emmanuel just said to me wasn't okay.

The strong current pulls the boat diagonally just seconds after we leave the boathouse. William is an accomplished seaman, it seems, and handles the conditions with ease.

A large wave hits us from the stern. The boat tilts and shakes.

"MacNamire, you should strap yourself in," William yells over the crash of the surf. "It's pretty rough."

"I'm fine, sir. Done this a million times, remember?"

Another large wave crashes into us, knocking Emmanuel off his feet and onto the floor, all the way between Devin and me. He tries to laugh off his embarrassment as he stands and wipes the salt from his eyes. Devin's drenched and trying to reposition himself, the last wave having slid him along the bench. He'd be on the floor next to Emmanuel if he weren't tied to the bar.

"Hold on!" William yells. I look up as another massive wave comes at us. I grab the bar, not trusting the weak tie MacNamire made at my wrist. The wave pummels us. When I blink away the water, MacNamire is spinning on the floor of the boat in shin-high water. Devin is stretched along the bench, held fast to the bar just above his head, choking on salt and trying to sit back up.

William stands steady at the helm, steering confidently. But what I see approaching behind us is both terrifying and amazing—a wave, followed closely by another, their size and speed a true testament to the unpredictable power and fury of the channel.

MacNamire finally stands and reaches under the portside bow for the yellow safety strap. He wraps it quickly around his wrist as the first wave hits us. The sea spray mixes with the driving rain and doesn't even clear before the second, larger wave slams into us. It lifts the boat from behind and brings it crashing violently down again. The engine sputters. If it dies, they'll all be doomed.

As the air clears enough to see again and the engine settles, I help Devin back to a relatively comfortable seated position and wipe the salt from his eyes. I look up at William. He meets my gaze for only a second, then his eyes grow huge and wild as he realizes I've moved. He looks around the boat.

"MacNamire!" William yells.

Nobody returns his desperate call.

"MacNamire, where are you?" William steps away from the helm for just a second, and the boat is immediately pulled sideways. He reconsiders and steps back to the helm.

With Devin sitting up again now, I stand and stare at William. The man looks genuinely afraid. He picks up a transponder. "Mayday, mayday." His eyes never leave me. "Mayday. This is Officer William Banks. We're currently in the channel on boat Two, about to make landfall on the Rock. Man overboard. I repeat, man overboard."

CHAPTER 24

FALL BACK INTO PLACE

OLD MEN DIE, YOUNG ONES LIE, TO WAIT
IN HOPE, WE ALWAYS TRY...

SATURDAY, MARCH 22ND

William Banks is a smart man—or a lucky man. Or both. When he saw me standing there in the boat and he picked up that transponder, he knew he was next to go overboard. He was lucky to still have a weapon on him—the same weapon he used to kill Gabriel.

It was the only thing that saved his life.

Moments later, we slammed into the dock. I was knocked off my feet, allowing William to be out of immediate danger. His mayday call also proved helpful. Just as we arrived at the docks, so did four other men, two in dive gear with rescue equipment, ready to risk their own lives in search of Emmanuel MacNamire.

"Don't bother. He's gone," William said as they helped him off the boat.

I know those men must have been relieved. Though they

323

would have attached themselves to their boat with lines, the channel would have eaten them alive.

It wasn't until hours later that the rain stopped and the sky cleared, calming the channel again. Too late for Emmanuel MacNamire.

William is, so far, over an hour late to our *daddy-daughter-dinner-date.* I guess he's not going to honor or respect his commitment after all.

"You must stay awake, Nerissa." Hani flits about the table and rubs my shoulder. "He's coming."

But I can hardly keep my eyes open. And I don't want to.

When Hani arrived at my suite—after I was dragged in by two men, dropped on the floor, and locked inside—she went about doing what she does best. I'd managed to scrape myself up and burrow under my covers—still in my wet clothes—where I cried an unending torrent of pain for an unknown number of hours.

She eased me out of bed and brought me to the bathroom —the only room without video surveillance—where we sat on the floor. She cradled me in her arms, comforting me as she wiped away her own tears too. A long, hot shower eased my muscles and cleared my head. Then she helped me dress and dried my hair. And finally, she spoke.

"I haven't received any kind of message from our mutual party. But I know I will eventually. We must be patient. They're probably reeling from everything too, trying to figure out what's happened and what will need to change. And we all must remember that Officer Banks is listening closely for any loose transmissions. I'm quite sure he doesn't know of anyone else's role, but still, we'd all be smart to stay silent for a while."

"Where's Devin?"

"I don't know," she says. "But I'll find out."

"I don't think I can do this anymore, Hani." My tears return, as I once again dissolve into a blubbering mess.

She holds my head against her chest, stroking my freshly dried hair. "You can, and you must. You have others depending on you, including me."

"He'll just kill us all... one by one... eventually."

"Not if we kill him first—" She clears her throat. "Take him down. You understand what I mean."

Yeah, I understand perfectly.

"Oh, I almost forgot. This was in your pocket. Are you saving it?" She holds out the small, weathered envelope with William Banks' letter inside—the one my mother gave me at Gabriel's cave.

"Did you read it?" I ask.

"Of course not."

"Oh, I'm not accusing you," I say. "I'm just asking. You keep it. Read it when you have the chance. It's pretty interesting."

"And what would you like me to do with it?"

"Whatever you think is best." I try to wipe the contents of the letter from my mind.

Sitting at this elegant table, dressed and primped for William's *celebration* dinner, seems absurd. Hani has once again put out a luxurious spread—everything in its place, sparkling and perfect. But all I can see is the relentless image of the spreading pool of Gabriel's blood with my reflection in it.

Reaching over the table, I pick up a bottle of William's pink wine from a chilling bucket, wrestle the top off, and pour myself a glass. I take a long, thoughtful drink, then refill my own and a second glass.

"Oh, dear. The Officer will not like if his wine is warm when he arrives."

"This one is for you." I hold up the second glass.

Hani looks around the room, into each of the corners, then accepts the glass. "Don't mind if I do, thank you." She takes a sip and puts her fingertips to her mouth. "Oh, my. That's delicious."

"Cheers," I say as unenthusiastically as imaginable.

Hani's eyes dart around the room again. "A toast to your big day. Congratulations." She takes another, longer drink.

I understand she's keeping up appearances in case anyone is watching—which surely someone is—but I don't care about that anymore. I chug down my wine in two long swigs. Just as I'm pouring myself another refill, the double doors to my suite fly open and slam against the walls. That was fast. William storms in, dressed in a neat suit, and marches right up to the table. He slaps the glass out of Hani's hand, and it shatters across the floor. I put my glass to my lips and take a slow, deliberate drink as he stares down at me.

"Change of plans." he says. Bending forward, he sweeps everything from the table onto the floor with one arm. Then he straightens, his nostrils flaring and his mouth in a crooked grimace.

I'm not impressed. "What's the matter, William? Not in the mood for a celebration after all?"

Grabbing my arm, he yanks me up out of my chair. I manage to drink down the last of my wine, then toss the glass onto the floor along with the shattered remains of our abandoned celebration.

"Hani... clean this up!"

"Where are we headed?" I ask as he pulls me out the door and quickly down the hall toward the elevator. When the elevator door slides open, he pushes me inside so hard, I hit the opposite wall.

After a painfully silent, five-minute tromp through the Bio-

Gen building—with William huffing and clenching his teeth so hard I can hear them grinding together—we arrive at the labs. The smell of this place will be forever burned into my memory.

As we come to a halt in front of a white steel door, William finally speaks. "I told you to always remember who's in charge. You seem to have forgotten that. I hope this will remind you. It will be your last chance."

He opens the door, and we enter a bright, sterile white room. In the center, two black chairs face each other. But these aren't ordinary chairs. They look like examination chairs that can tilt back or lift up. And they have heavy canvas straps on each arm and at each ankle.

"Sit down, here." He points to the chair facing the back wall. I do as he says, no fight left in me. He goes about roughly strapping me into the chair. The straps are so tight, I immediately feel my fingers and toes change temperature. I say nothing.

When he's done, he lifts his index finger and says, "Bring him in."

A previously invisible door on the back wall opens. In walks Devin with a drab brown sack over his head—escorted by none other than Dr. Price Bigelow. He can barely walk, the injury to his knee still making him limp. Dr. Bigelow sits him across from me, strapping him in the same way.

"I'm here, Devin," I say, and he lifts his head.

"Nerissa?" he asks, his voice weak.

William pulls the sack off his head. Devin squints and blinks hard against the bright room.

"It's me." I try to smile, try to show him I'm all right. "I love you, Devin."

"I love you, too," he says. His vision seems to finally adjust, and he looks me over.

"Well isn't this just the sweetest thing ever." William

wedges himself between us, and faces me. "This is for MacNamire!" he yells and slaps me with such force, the chair shudders.

"Stop!" Devin shouts. But William ignores him, slapping me again on the other side of my face. "Stop! Hit me," Devin pleads. "Leave her alone."

William whirls around to face him and strikes Devin with a closed fist. "I was planning on it, idiot."

I can't see Devin's face, William blocking my view, but I hear him spit. A large, bloody splotch hits the floor beside us. "Leave him alone."

William laughs, turning so we can both see his face. "Do you know I could kill you both, right here, right now, if I wanted? And you'd have to watch each other die." He reaches out, grabbing each of our throats and squeezing hard.

The pressure is unbearable, and within seconds, my eyes feel like they're bulging out of my face. William looks at me and laughs like a lunatic. Slowly he turns to look at Devin, his laughter morphing into a growl. The pressure intensifies. If I have to die here, at least it's with Devin. And then William can never hurt us again.

"Sir, you need to stop," Dr. Bigelow says. Just when everything starts to go dim, William pulls his hands away. Devin and I both gasp for air, coughing and heaving with burning lungs and aching throats.

As William steps away, Devin and I get a good look at each other. A huge welt has already formed over his split and swollen upper lip, and a blood vessel has popped in his right eye. His neck is purple, the finger marks where William almost squeezed the life out of him paint his skin. I imagine I look very much the same. I catch a glimpse of the underside of Devin's new arm; it's bloody and bruised. He notices me looking.

"I disabled it," he whispers. "Probably permanently."

"You are the most beautiful human being I've ever known, and I'm so thankful you've been a part of my life. A part of me," I say softly, tears falling.

He looks at me with such pain, such love, such regret and gratitude. He can no longer hold back his tears, either. He doesn't even try. Devin never looks away. "I'm so sor—"

"No," I tell him. "Don't you say you're sorry. You haven't done anything wrong."

"He's going to kill us, isn't he?"

I hold his gaze as tenderly as I can. If only I could touch him one last time, wrap my arms around him, bury my face in his chest and smell him.

"No. You're wrong, again." William returns. "I'm not killing anyone. Not today. And you know,"—he turns toward me—"I'd never kill you. I'm loyal to my blood. You know that."

Oh, how I want to scream the truth at him. I wonder if he'd be as loyal to his half-sister as he would to his *child*.

"But that doesn't mean I wouldn't have somebody else do it." Those hateful words tumble out of his mouth in disgust. "So keep that in mind. You, on the other hand." He turns toward Devin. "You are not my blood, and I would have no problem wiping you off this earth. But not today."

"Why not, you sick son of a bitch?" Devin asks.

"Because I have other plans. And you need to watch yourself, boy."

"Why are we here, William?" I ask.

"Remember how I said you needed a reminder that I'm in charge? Well, today is just a taste of what I'm going to do to keep you in line. If you cross me again, things will get progressively worse, until... whoops. Who knows? An accidental death is certainly not impossible." He smiles at Devin.

"Like Gabriel?" I say.

"Yes, exactly like Gabriel." His smile becomes a scowl. "Now, let's get on with it."

He holds up a large needle filled with a familiar, opaque liquid.

"What are you doing?" I demand.

He ignores me. "Devin, let me introduce to you... *Wildfire.*" He gazes at the needle with twisted admiration. "This is my most effective training tool for my Harvesters. They are a very obedient lot. More to come, as we know." He chuckles, then smiles at me. "Nerissa will witness me administer this drug to you and continue to watch from her chair as you experience its full effects."

"No. No, William," I beg. "Don't do this. Give it to me, instead."

He turns toward me. "As much as I'd love to give you a dose as well, I can't. That would compromise your implantation this evening."

"This evening?" My heart falls into my stomach.

"Yes. As soon as you watch your boyfriend familiarize himself with my training tool, he will watch you undergo implantation with a Harvester embryo. Isn't that spectacular?"

"I'm going to kill you, you sick motherfucker," Devin hisses through tightly clenched teeth.

"Oh." William laughs. "I don't think so. But Nerissa, every time you need a reminder of who's in charge, you'll be watching Devin's *training.* And each dose will be progressively stronger. You know, it's still unclear how much *Wildfire* a living being can take. Perhaps Devin will help us determine the limit."

William lifts Devin's sleeve.

Devin looks at me, the fear in his eyes unbearable.

"It's going to hurt, but it won't last forever, and I'm right here." I try to prepare him, try to console him, try to—

William injects the full dose, and as the poison enters Devin's body and his face changes—as the burning begins and the terror spreads—I close my eyes. But I can't close my ears.

Devin screams.

William laughs.

And I cry.

True to William's word and about an hour later, Devin and I are wheeled—still strapped to our black chairs—down the hall into another cold, sterile lab, where Dr. Bigelow and Dr. Picker wait. This one is set up with familiar-looking equipment similar to what they used the day I watched Lillian endure the implantation.

"You said I didn't have to go in that gel box," I remind William.

"Yes, I did say that," he replies. "If you don't fight it."

"I won't fight it. I told you I wouldn't."

"Very well, then. You can get prepped and lie on this table." He gestures to a long metal bed not unlike the one I slept on in my cottage so long ago.

"I'll get the line in for anesthesia," Dr. Bigelow says.

"Oh, Nerissa won't be requiring anesthesia," William says. "Thank you, anyway."

"Officer Banks, with all due respect—"

"I said no thank you," William snaps.

Dr. Bigelow takes a deep breath. "If we are not placing Nerissa in the gel enclosure, I cannot authorize an un-anesthetized procedure. Even inside the gel, it's incredibly uncomfortable. Outside of it, it will be intolerable."

"Well, Dr. Bigelow, that's the thing... I do not need your authorization. You will do as I say."

"Sir, I can't—"

"It's okay," I tell him. "I understand what you're saying. I'll be fine. Let's get on with it."

William laughs. "You see? She's fully prepared. Now, let's do this."

Dr. Bigelow sighs, his shoulders falling. "Yes, sir. Of course. Just let me gather a few things. Nerissa, you can change in that room over there." He points to a door. "And I'll be there in just a few minutes to get you."

"She can just come out when she's changed," William says.

"We keep it cold out here for the surgery. It's best if she stays as warm as possible until we're ready. Much better for the procedure."

"Well, you learn something new every day." William chuckles. "Devin, are you with us, boy? This is going to be good."

"Fuck you."

William laughs. "Same to you."

I enter the small changing room and close the door behind me. A white cotton gown and booties wait neatly inside a metal locker. I slowly remove my clothes, wrap the gown around myself, and slip my feet into the booties. The material is surprisingly soft. I pull it tight around me and fold my arms over my chest. Turning around, I face a mirror. My reflection is not my own. At least, not how I see myself in my mind.

I try to stay calm and not think about what's going to happen only minutes from now. I'm scared. And now I wonder if it would have been better for William to have choked us both to death.

A soft knock at the door makes me jump.

"Nerissa, it's Dr. Bigelow. May I come in?"

I open the door, and the cold lab air rushes in with him.

"I'll be right out," he says, presumably to William as he

enters the changing room. "I just need to make sure she has her gown on properly."

"I think it's on right," I say.

He closes the door, pulls a needle from his lab coat pocket, and speaks quickly. "This is an anesthetic. You will not get through this procedure without it. You'll feel it as soon as I inject it. We'll move quickly to the table so he doesn't suspect anything. But it won't take full effect right away. I can't use that kind of drug, or you won't be able to walk. You'll feel some discomfort at the beginning, but it should subside completely after ten minutes or so. I will proceed slowly. Do you understand?"

"Yes."

"Do not tell him I gave this to you."

"I won't, I promise. Thank you."

Dr. Bigelow quickly wraps a flexible rubber tie around my arm and instructs me to clench my fist. Then he slides the needle directly into a vein. He unwraps the tie and throws it and the needle into the locker before closing the door.

"Ready?"

"Yes. Wait, doctor..."

He pauses. "Yes?"

"Where are Lillian and Anastasia? Are they okay?"

"They're fine," he answers in a bit of a fluster. "They're both taking a rest from hosting for a while. They both... need to take a rest."

He opens the door, and we exit the changing room back into the cold lab. As I walk toward the table with Dr. Bigelow lightly holding my arm, I'm unaware of my feet on the floor. I seem to be floating, and I already feel my senses beginning to dull.

"I think someone's a little nervous," Dr. Bigelow says lightly. "She had her gown on backwards and all twisted up."

He guides me to the metal table, and I lie down. A white plastic cuff is secured around my wrists, and he places my feet awkwardly in two holds on either side of the table—all four limbs contained. As the reality of the situation hits me, I begin to cry. I turn my head to look at Devin. He's sitting limply in his chair, his head hanging low but his eyes still on me. The *Wildfire* was brutal on him. And being strapped to the chair must have been even worse—trapped in a fire, then tied to a lightning rod. I tried my best not to watch, even after William repeatedly smacked me in the head and demanded I open my eyes. He could have kicked me or stabbed me—or lit me on fire. I wasn't going to watch. But of course, I heard it all. Now, Devin will have to endure watching my pain. Hopefully, it won't last long.

"We're ready to proceed, Nerissa. Try to relax, now," Dr. Bigelow says, and Dr. Picker takes his place at the end of the table. "I'll be monitoring your vitals and... Officer Banks, sir. Remember that I will have to put a line in her to administer post-surgical drugs, like antibiotics. Possibly some additional hormones to increase the chances of viability."

"Once the procedure is over," William says.

"Yes. We can wait until the procedure is over."

"And no pain medication," William adds.

There's a brief pause. "Okay."

"Then let's begin."

Dr. Bigelow stands just beside my head. "This is going to hurt," he tells me softly. "Officer Banks, don't be surprised if she passes out from the pain."

THURSDAY, MAY 1ST
FIVE AND A HALF WEEKS LATER

Just like Anastasia told me she experienced—just as my mother had too—William grows increasingly crueler after each failed attempt at pregnancy. With barely a rest between, I've endured three unsuccessful procedures, despite the steady regime of hormones to force my body's readiness. And after those failed attempts came three progressively abusive, consequential *talks* with William. The doctors can't give him a definite explanation, but they suggest it's due to stress. I'm starting to think I'm just one of those women who can't have babies—like Cassidy. Or maybe it's just that my body won't accept something so unnatural. Whatever the reason, William's unpredictable behavior is unbearable.

At the very least, on the third attempt, he abruptly stopped feeling the need to view the procedures, and Dr. Bigelow and Dr. Picker were able to give me proper anesthesia and pain medication. They may be monsters in lab coats, but they're men of science and want to use it accordingly.

The start of first surgery was mind-bendingly painful, even after the drug Dr. Bigelow had administered began to work. I'm not sure if I blacked out because the drug finally took full effect or because the pain was too much to handle.

That was also the last time I saw Devin. Hani has seen him and assures me he's okay. William hasn't used *Wildfire* on him again—at least, not that I'm aware of, because he hasn't made me watch. The last time William was told the implantation was unsuccessful, he threatened me with exactly that. I asked him how torturing Devin and making me watch was going to help get me pregnant faster. He told me he thought it would make me want it more.

For some unexplained reason, I'm being given a small *break*, and I'm scheduled for my next procedure nine days from now. William said I'd better pray it works this time.

Nearly every night, I wake from dreaming about Gabriel. The variations are endless, but one thing is always consistent —the pool of his blood with my reflection in it. This morning, the river of blood ran out of my own body, and along with it came three unborn hybrid fetuses. And when I looked down at their rotting little corpses, not only was my reflection in the pool of blood, but each of their faces was my own. When I jolted awake, Emmanuel MacNamire stood over me, his bloated body half-eaten by sea creatures and stinking of death. As he smiled and licked his lips, his tongue fell out on top of me, turned into a venomous snake, and wrapped around my neck. It took Hani ten minutes to calm me down and convince me I was finally awake.

Hani has received only two messages from our group and sent only one of her own. The messages are incredibly vague, but there's been no stirrings of suspicion. William must believe that he ended any and all alliances when he killed Gabriel and imprisoned Devin. If he ever finds out Hani is involved, he'll kill her. Immediately. And I'll have to watch.

The first message on April 15th from an unknown number— received over three weeks after we were captured—simply read: *"No meeting yet. Will advise."* They must have been going out of their minds with worry, wondering what happened to us. After we left the cave, Gabriel and Devin never returned. It must have been torturous not knowing. But they went ahead with the plan.

Hani deleted the message and waited a full week before sending back a poem: *"Old men die, young ones lie, to wait in hope, we always try."* She said if her transmissions were ever monitored and questioned, she'd explain it as an example of the poetry she'd been working on the last year, and she wanted feedback from her friend. She even created a poetry journal to back up her story.

A few days ago, she received the second message from a different unknown number. It's much longer and to anyone else, it would be completely irrelevant nonsense. It reads:

"Convincing kings and queens to examine their own gold for impurities is a slow and strenuous task not without discord. Three days after the next gray whale beaches, examine they shall. Either way the wind blows, we will ride back to the shore along with the beautiful people."

It seems that after great effort, they have convinced Officer Klein's superiors to conduct a meeting and discuss the evidence they have to present. Unfortunately, the meeting will not take place until after the next zeppelin comes to the island two days from now. So we'll all have to wait. But no matter what happens, they will return to Panacea—with or without backup—on May 24th, along with the first round of tourists.

"That's the night before the Gala," Hani tells me in the bathroom of my suite after we discussed the message, memorized its meaning, and she deleted it.

"Oh, the Gala..." I say. "William will not shut up about that."

"He really wanted you to be pregnant and full-bellied for that one. To show you off."

"I know. We're trying again in nine days. And you know... if I am pregnant, I think I'll slice my stomach open and let the little monster fall out on Alexandria's designer shoes."

She just puts her hand on my cheek and nods. My heart swells with love. Hani doesn't speak much about herself, but I know she cares for me, and I know she loved Gabriel. She was devastated by his murder. I don't know how she managed to clean up a room full of his blood, then come to my suite, set the table, and cook dinner. I never asked, and I never will.

"Hani, if they can't convince anyone to help us, to put a stop to William's plans... what are we going to do?"

"Well, I guess we'll have to stop him ourselves." She smiles, knowing full well we can't do it alone. "Or die trying."

I do my best to keep my mind occupied over the following days. I've been banned from leaving the Bio-Gen building, so I never get a change of scenery or even a swim, and I feel my body deteriorating day by day. I'm forced to consume manufactured Wreckleaf. I used to be able to taste a discernible difference between tank and ocean-made, but I can't any longer. And I hate that I can't.

I think about my family often, wondering how they're getting along, wondering how baby Ruari is doing—growing and discovering—and hoping they're not letting their imaginations run wild when they think of me.

Hani has seen Devin again—in the labs. She didn't want to tell me that's where she saw him, but she couldn't lie to me and thought I'd at least be relieved to know he seemed to be okay.

"What was he doing in the labs? Are they making him work?"

She can barely meet my eyes. "No. They were examining him, I think."

"Examining him?" I yell before I can stop myself. "You mean doing tests? Or experiments, or something?"

"I don't know." She looks down at the floor. "I'm sorry. I guess I shouldn't have told you."

I take a deep, concentrated breath. "No, I'm glad you did. I'm sorry I yelled."

"It's okay, dear one," she says with the kindest eyes, and her term of endearment instantly brings tears to mine.

WEDNESDAY, MAY 7TH

How much different would my life have been, would all our lives have been, if I'd never gone to Panacea with Anastasia that one dreadful night so long ago?

"You cannot rewrite history, child," Gabriel tells me.

"But none of this would be happening."

"You can't know that. Everything is as it should be."

"You're dead, Gabriel. Giovanni is dead... and the others... and it's all my fault."

"Dear one, the Universe is always conspiring in our favor."

I laugh, my dream becoming lucid. "Oh! This is a dream." I look around and notice we're standing on the observation deck, facing the ocean and watching a brilliant, blood-red sunset. The dazzling color spills into the sparkling water and spreads over the horizon.

"Why does that matter?" he asks. "That this is a dream."

"That matters because nobody in their right mind would say such a thing. Nothing has gone in our favor."

"Oh, but it has. Gabriel has served his physical purpose. And my departure was most definitely not your fault. Remember that I will always be with you."

"Like here?"

"Yes."

"This is just a dream, Gabriel. I want you back in real life."

"There is a very fine line between the two veils."

I pause. "I'm scared."

"Yes, I know, child. And it is perfectly fine to feel scared. Embrace your fear. Acknowledge it."

"And then what?"

"And then move on. Take your fear by the hand and allow it to empower you, not hold you back. You are so much bigger than your circumstances. So much bigger than the minor story you tell about yourself." He smiles his sweet, crooked grin, and his eyes crinkle up in joy. "But you must do something very important first. It is imperative."

A soft, metallic click and a door opening behind us makes Gabriel jump onto the stone wall, his back to the horizon. Someone's coming.

"Don't go, Gabriel. Please."

"I am always with you."

A strong wind blows up off the cliff and sends my hair into a frenzy. Gabriel bends down and smooths it back off my face, then leans over and kisses my forehead.

"You said I need to do something first. What is it?" I ask, desperate to keep him here even for one more second.

"Forgive yourself, child," he casually steps backward off the stone wall, falling slowly and fading into the horizon. As I try to absorb the transparent image of his loving face, it vanishes. I'm left staring at the last red streaks of the sun on the water beyond, my face reflecting back at me.

I wake with a small startle. I'm lying on my side in my bed, facing the open window, the soft breeze drifting in and filling the room with the smell of spring. Hani stands directly in front of me, smoothing the hair from my face and smiling. She leans over and kisses my forehead, then wraps me in a soft embrace and whispers quietly in my ear.

"They're coming. The meeting was a success, and help is coming."

CHAPTER 25
INTERCEPTION
THE SHOW MUST GO ON.

I am pregnant. The last implantation was successful. The doctors knew only three days later, and as only cautiously expected, William is a new and, dare I say, improved man. The pendulum has swung hard and wide.

He's been bouncing around the Bio-Gen building like he's high. He checks in on me every hour, asking me if I need anything, smiling and kind-eyed. He even fluffed my pillows one evening before he gently took the underside of my arm and *helped* me to bed. He keeps asking me how I'm feeling, how I'm holding up, and tells me that whatever I need to ease this difficult time, he will have for me instantly.

But I feel fine. The supposed horrible first and furious weeks of the hybrid-Harvester pregnancy have been... fine. The gestation is three times faster than normal, the embryo blossoming into a fetus in no time. And it's supposed to wreak havoc on the host, as it did with Anastasia and Lillian. But I wouldn't even know I'm pregnant if the doctors hadn't told me.

I'm on my way to the labs now. William has insisted that today we listen for a heartbeat—a milestone usually reserved for more than double the length of time I've been pregnant. Dr. Bigelow and Dr. Picker suggested we wait, that it may still be too early, even for these special circumstances. But William isn't having it—he knows his little creature will let itself be heard. Maybe then I'll believe it.

I arrive at the lab door and knock. William opens it only a second later, his excitement spread across his face with a wide, open-mouthed grin, his eyes blinking way too fast.

"Come in, come in.f" He steps aside and I walk past him.

"Hello, Nerissa," Dr. Bigelow says. "How are you feeling?"

"So far, so good. Honest." I'm sure nobody believes me.

Dr. Bigelow looks at Dr. Picker sideways. "Good to hear." He rests his hand lightly on my shoulder. "We moved everything around in the changing room. Let me show you where you can find a gown." He gently nudges me forward and walks me toward the back of the lab. Then he opens the changing room door and flips on the light. "After you."

I step inside. "Thank you. I'm sure I can find what I need."

The door closes behind Dr. Bigelow, and he looks at me.

"What? Is something wrong?" I ask.

"I'm just a little worried that it's too early to hear the fetus' heartbeat, and I'm equally nervous that it won't go over so well with Officer Banks."

"Oh. Well, I never know what to expect from him, so..." I shrug.

"Yes, we know his temper is... well, unpredictable. And he hasn't been entirely reasonable about his expectations. Or, more accurately..." He pauses to apparently think about his next words. "He's been quite aggressive. Quite… abusive with you."

If I'm not mistaken, it sure seems as though Dr. Price Bigelow is concerned for my well-being.

"Well thank you for your—"

"It's just that we can't have him going ballistic in here or anything. Or thinking it's our fault."

Oh, I *am* mistaken. The only person Dr. Bigelow is concerned about is himself. "You're sure I'm pregnant, right? The implant worked and it took?"

"Yes, absolutely. I mean, in a normal pregnancy, this would still be so early, and really, anything could happen. But with this one, at this point… the fetus should be well-established."

"Then I guess we'll just have to keep our fingers crossed that we hear a heartbeat."

"Do you think he'll derail if we don't?"

"Dr. Bigelow, you're asking me about William like he's my husband or something. Or like he's a normal person with a sound and stable mind. He's neither of those, and you know I have no way to predict how he'll behave. Sorry you're so afraid of him. Maybe you should have chosen a different place to work."

Dr. Bigelow hangs his head, turns around, and walks out the door. I quickly find a gown—in the exact spot it was the last time—and step out into the lab. Then I hoist myself onto the exam table. William has pulled a chair as close to the table as possible, his eyes and ears already trained on the large, thin monitor.

"All right, Nerissa," Dr. Picker says. "Are you ready?"

"Yes. Let's get this over with, please."

Dr. Bigelow adjusts a knob on the monitor, and a strange, muffled sound fills the room.

"There! There, I hear a heartbeat!" William shouts, searching the monitor for an image of his tiny beast.

"No, sir. That's Nerissa's heartbeat."

"Oh." William's face falls in disappointment. "It's so fast. I thought it must be…"

Yeah, my heartbeat is so fast because I'm so excited about hearing the manufactured alien taking over my body. Not.

Dr. Picker moves the wand around, searching for the elusive proof William so desperately needs. But there's nothing. Not a sound, not an image.

"Is something wrong, doctors?" William's tone is suddenly thick and heavy. And *scary*.

"I'm sorry, Officer Banks. We expressed our concerns that it's still too early to detect a heartbeat or an image," Dr. Picker says thoughtfully.

William stands abruptly. "She *is* pregnant, isn't she?"

"Yes, of course, sir. Her bloodwork confirmed it. You saw it. And our testing methods are very sensitive and very accurate."

"Well, I know for a fact that because of the Harvester's rapid growth rate," William snaps, "we should be able to see and hear something. Just like we could with the other hosts." I hear that familiar impatience in his voice—the impatience that doesn't have much longer before it dissolves and turns.

"We did not attempt this with the other hosts until they were four to five weeks into their—"

"Dr. Bigelow," Dr. Picker carefully interrupts, "We could try one more thing."

"Excuse me? Doctor?" Price Bigelow looks utterly confused, and if I'm not mistaken, somewhat horrified.

"What are you suggesting?" William butts in.

"We can attempt to inject a micro surgical camera. But it's very risky," Dr. Picker says, and Dr. Bigelow's face goes white.

William stands like a statue. "What kind of risk?"

"Many," Dr. Picker says, "injury to the fetus, bleeding, serious contamination, and of course, spontaneous miscarriage."

William doesn't move, except for his hands, which have found their way to each other and are locked in a twisting, writhing embrace at his own chest. Dr. Bigelow stares at William, seemingly holding his breath, waiting for him to answer.

"Give me statistics," William finally says.

"Oh, you can't be serious!" Dr. Bigelow spews uncontrollably. Absorbing the death stare William shoots him, he quickly adjusts his approach. "Officer, I apologize for my outburst. It's just that attempting to do this is simply brazen irresponsibility. If you can just be patient, sir, you'll see and hear the fetus just weeks from now."

Dr. Bigelow hasn't yet learned that nobody tells William Banks how to act or feel—or what to do. And if I know William like I think I do, he's just been offered a dare—an opportunity to show the world just how bold and godlike he is.

"If Nerissa loses this one, we can implant another." He's made up his mind.

"Sir, please," Dr. Picker says, his voice trembling ever so slightly now. "Please remember, Nerissa endured four procedures before a successful implantation. It may take that many or more for the next."

William is unshaken, and he stares at Dr. Picker with an intensity so deep, Dr. Picker has to drop his eyes before they're seared right out of his skull.

"Dr. Picker, let's try one more time," Dr. Bigelow says. Then he turns his back to us to adjust something at the monitor's controls. Dr. Picker pulls his attention back to the procedure and takes a quick, deep breath. "And... with a little more focus, now."

Dr. Picker readjusts the imaging wand to an uncomfortable angle, and my breath is sucked out of me unexpectedly as Dr. Bigelow swings back around to face us. The seconds tick by painfully and slowly.

Nothing.

William steps toward the table and trains his squinted eyes on the monitor.

Nothing.

I can hardly breathe from the pressure and pain.

Nothing.

"This is a waste of time," William says. "Let's get that camera in her."

"There," Dr. Picker says. And a small, nearly imperceptible, quivering, circular object appears on the monitor. "There's your Harvester."

Dr. Bigelow turns again and presumably amps up the volume. A fast, liquid, swishing sound fills the laboratory.

"And there's the heartbeat," Dr. Bigelow says with a sigh of relief.

William covers his mouth with a hand, his eyes wide and full of awe. He leans closer to the monitor and laughs a soft, muffled laugh. Tears spill down his cheeks.

As quickly as the image and sounds appeared, and before I can even fully accept they're coming from inside me, they disappear. William's hand falls away, and he jolts back into his soldier-like stance.

"What happened? Where'd it go?"

Dr. Bigelow attempts to once again adjust some controls, but to no avail. "I'm sorry, sir. I think that's all we're going to get today. It's a miracle we were able to get anything at all."

"It is a miracle, indeed." William softens and smiles. "You see, gentlemen? We just needed to try a little harder." He laughs, reaching out over where I lie.

Dr. Bigelow shakes William's hand. "Yes, sir. I thought it was too early, but you were right all along."

William laughs. "Of course, I was." He turns to Dr. Picker and shakes his hand as well, then finally looks down at me. "Nerissa, take the day for yourself. Have a bath or a massage. I'll send Hani to arrange whatever you'd like. And I'll see you this evening."

"This evening?" I ask.

"For a celebration dinner, of course."

Of course.

"And we can go over everything that's going to happen at the Gala Grand Re-Opening on Sunday. I'm so thrilled I get to show you off." He gently places a hand on my stomach and looks at it lovingly. I feel sick.

I want to scream at him, to tell him everything going through my mind. So sorry to disappoint you, William, but there won't be a Gala to celebrate your evil. Richard Klein and his superiors will be here tomorrow. The only thing we'll be celebrating is your end. And I'll terminate this monstrosity inside me immediately. I can hardly wait for the relief. To be free. Finally.

"Okay, bye." I say. "See you later." But he doesn't move. I try again. "See you later."

"Yes, you will," he finally says, then turns and walks away. Just before he steps out the door, he spins back to look at me one last time. "Nerissa..."

"Yes?"

"I'm going to be a grandfather." He smiles and winks at me. "Thank you."

I just stare at him, my mind bending in a hundred different directions. "You're... welcome."

• • •

I STARE at myself in the changing room mirror. It's hard to believe I'm pregnant with William's hybrid. I don't look pregnant. I don't feel pregnant. Well, maybe I feel a little pregnant, but not for too much longer.

I've got bigger things to think about right now. Richard Klein will be on Panacea tomorrow with his superiors—with William Banks' superiors—along with the proper authorities. And if everything goes as planned, I'll be reunited with Devin, and my mother, and Kendra and Ruari, and the rest of my family and friends. Tomorrow. I can hang on one more day.

I splash some cool water on my face, pat myself dry, and crack open the door for the cool lab air to wake me up. Before stepping back into the laboratory, I hear angry voices—Dr. Picker and Dr. Bigelow. I turn off the light, open the door a bit wider, and listen.

"That was a really stupid move," Dr. Bigelow says, his voice hushed but highly assertive.

"I didn't think he'd go for that option," Dr. Picker replies in the same hissing tone. "No sane human being would have taken a risk like that."

"Since when did you start thinking Banks is a sane human being?"

"I don't. But that embryo was too small. There's no way he believed it."

"He had no reference point, no scale. And it was so fast. Of course he believed it," Dr. Bigelow insists. "Did you see his face?"

"Maybe. How'd you get the heartbeat?"

"Well, it wasn't the sound of anything inside Nerissa.. It was one of Anastasia's."

I gasp and slam my hand over my mouth. Both doctors stop and turn toward me. I quickly shuffle some things around on the counter, turn the sink on and off again, and cough lightly before I open the door and step back into the lab. I walk slowly, nonchalantly adjusting my sleeves as if there's nothing in my head—as if I'm paying attention to absolutely nothing.

Dr. Bigelow clears his throat and looks sideways at Dr. Picker, who goes about wiping down a small gray countertop.

"All set, Nerissa?"

I look up as though I hardly realized he was there. "Oh, yes. Thank you. I guess I'll be headed back to my room now."

"Would you like an escort?"

"No, I'm fine. But thanks. Bye." I turn toward the door and leave.

I don't remember walking through the Bio-Gen building, before finding myself at the double doors of my suite. I feel like I've time-traveled through some black hole of confusion. And the only thing I *saw* while I walked here were my own thoughts.

I don't think I'm pregnant. The last implantation must have not worked, either, and Dr. Picker and Dr. Bigelow are so afraid of William's reaction, they faked a positive result. The Harvester embryo should have been not only visible but definitely heard with the ultrasound, even faintly. William must have been flipping out at them too, like he has with me after every failed attempt. Of course. They're just trying to make it stop.

That's why I don't feel sick. Sure, I've felt a little queasy since the *positive result*, but it must have been psychosomatic; I thought I was supposed to be feeling awful.

But why they hadn't performed the super-risky procedure and later faked a miscarriage of my fake baby? I guess if they couldn't find an image with their ultra-high-tech camera, William would've been even more suspicious.

Opening my suite doors, I step inside, close them behind me, and laugh. Then I remember the not-so-hidden cameras in every corner of the room. I glide into the bathroom, lock myself inside, and dance erratically to an unheard song with a huge, victorious grin plastered across my face.

I'm not pregnant! I'm not pregnant with a little demon beast I would have had to *take care of* after our rescue tomorrow. Sorry, William. You are most certainly not going to be a grandfather, or an uncle, or whatever. Not now, not ever! God, I hope I get to see his face when he finds out.

I turn on the water and help myself to the longest, most luxurious shower I can remember. The steam is like a cleansing mist of renewal, the smell of the body wash and shampoo transporting me into a colorful, wet garden. Happiness and hope have both been so foreign for so long. They feel decadent and magical—almost like I don't dare acknowledge them, or they'll be swept away to disappear down the drain.

But they won't. I'm safe, now. All I have to do is make it through until tomorrow. The realization of how close to true freedom I am overwhelms me completely. It's dizzying. The joy rises up in me, from my feet to my head—rising and rising.

I double over and vomit on the shower floor.

I wake to the smell of cooking food. After my shower, I climbed into bed. I was in there too long, and the heat and steam and my rollercoaster of emotions from the day had really gotten to me. I just needed to rest for a few minutes. But now, as my eyes flutter open and I get my bearings, I realize the sun's almost gone for the day. I've been here for hours.

With more effort than seems normal, I sit up and swing my legs over the edge of the bed. I'm so, so thirsty.

"Oh, good. You're awake," Hani says from the dining table, where she arranges a vase of lilies. They're so intensely fragrant, I can smell them from here. "We need to get you dressed. He'll be here in ten minutes."

"Oh. I wish you'd woken me up sooner," I complain.

"I tried. Twice. And I had to get this food on. I only just got here twenty minutes ago."

I get out of bed and walk toward the dining area. "Why?"

Hani looks nervous, her eyes flitting about the room as she chews on her lip. "I had a meeting."

"What kind of meeting?"

"Let's go get you dressed." Taking my arm, she quickly leads me toward the bathroom.

Before we there, there's a quick knock on the double doors and William opens them both, letting himself inside. "Good evening, ladies."

Hani lets go of my arm. "Good evening, sir. You're early."

"Well, someone is chatty tonight." He laughs. "And yes, I guess I'm a few minutes early. Forgive me. We have much to celebrate tonight. I couldn't wait to get started. Hani, wine."

Hani obeys his order, and the drinking begins. No doubt it'll turn into a shitshow again tonight. William's on top of the world and ready to celebrate.

"William, let me change my clothes and brush my hair really quick," I say, smoothing down my wrinkled shirt.

He walks toward me, wrapping his arm around my shoulders and pulling me into him. "You are just fine the way you are. Now, sit down. I insist."

"Okay." I let him sit me at the beautifully set table, where he pours me a flute of pink champagne.

"A little wine won't hurt my Harvester at all. Enjoy."

"Don't mind if I do." I drink down half the glass in one large chug.

AFTER MANY GLASSES OF WINE, a course of delicious appetizers, and an unending stream of William's self-worship, he stands and reaches out for me to take his hand. I play along, knowing full well this is the last night of this nonsense. Forever.

He leads me to the wall of windows, where we face the shimmering ocean and Panacea's north shore—already lit up for the opening of the Season.

"Wow. It's really hopping over there," I say. "I almost forgot it's *that time* of year again. Guess I won't be working the beach this Season in my itty-bitty bikini." I laugh. "Nobody wants a pregnant chick rubbing sunscreen all over them."

He chuckles and shrugs. "I think you'd be surprised. But no, you will not be working this Season. We have new attendants in place at Concordia. And we've never been better prepared to indulge our seasonal guests than we are this year... across the entire island."

"What do you mean?"

He turns to me, seemingly disappointed I don't follow him. "The new building... Nerissa, really?"

"I'm sorry...."

"The new facilities here at Bio-Gen have allowed us to churn out an almost unending supply of the beauty products the guests have grown accustomed to. The very things that keep them coming back year after year. And a few new things. Of course, I once again must thank you for that." He laughs and shakes his head at what he believes is serendipity. "Alexandria is in heaven, and even though she puts much more personal attention on the beauty products—she loves her products—than the Aqua Tonic, there is a very healthy supply. And Sunday, at the Gala, she'll announce our approval. She can't tell me everything outright, but she's hinted enough that I know what to expect. It's very exciting, isn't it?"

"They come back for the island," I say, ignoring his rambling and remembering the time I tried to make this exact point with Devin. "Not the stuff."

"Yes, they do come back for the island *and* the products they can only get here."

"Do you like them?" I ask.

"Who? The guests?" William seems surprised by my question, perhaps disappointed that I don't want to fawn over Alexandria's product-lust with him.

"Yes, the guests. The tourists. Do you like them?"

He doesn't answer me right away. He inhales deeply, maybe contemplating my question. "They're our livelihood. They're one of the main reasons this facility was rebuilt. Why we *do* what we do on this island."

"Right, but do you like them?"

"I like what they represent." He nods slowly as he speaks, as if to convince himself of his own answer. "I like what they offer. What they bring to the table, if you will."

"But do you like—"

"No. I do not *like* them. They are pretentious, and entitled, and weak. I mean, there are exceptions, but... no."

"Hmm." I shrug and scoff. "Well, there's that."

"Excuse me, officer, Ms. Nerissa?" Hani's soft voice floats across the room. "Dinner is served."

"I swear that woman has spoken more today than ever."

He has no idea.

"Coming, Hani," I say brightly and release myself from William's hold around my shoulder to return to the table.

"Ms. Nerissa, can you please help me for a moment first?"

"Of course, Hani." I'm definitely surprised by her request. "What do you need?"

"My zipper is stuck."

"Well, let's have a look."

"Oh." She giggles. "Can we please go into the bathroom? It's stuck to my undergarment, and I'm afraid there's a tear." She lowers her head and giggles again.

"Sure. Be right back, William. Don't start without me." I laugh.

"I will wait," he promises with a hand raised in the air.

Hani and I casually enter the bathroom, then she closes and locks the door.

"Okay, let's see where you're stuck," I say, examining her clothes for malfunction.

"There's no zipper issue," Hani whispers.

My brows crinkle up and my wine-infused brain finds it hard to comprehend what she's saying. "What do you need help with, then?"

Hani grabs my hands and squeezes tight. She leans into me very close and puts her face directly in front of mine, only inches away. "There's been an interception," she whispers.

"A what? An inter—"

"Shh... keep your voice down. Whispers only."

"Okay," I whisper back and laugh softly, like we're playing some kind of game and it's my turn. "What's an interception?" I whisper it so lightly, I barely hear myself.

"A transmission interception."

My mind searches for the meaning to this term, and after I let the truth sink slowly into my reality, it consumes me like a tornado—the spiraled vortex holding the translation and turning inward until it slams into my understanding so hard, my knees buckle.

"No."

"Yes. Something arrived for me from another unknown number. I was just about to open it, but it disappeared. Completely."

I consider what that could mean. "Well, maybe it was deleted from the sender. Maybe they changed their minds, or needed to say something different, or..." The air rushes out of me. I know none of those things are true. I know a sender can't delete a message that's already arrived at its destination. But if someone else hacked into a system... well, they could potentially do anything they wanted.

"They're supposed to arrive tomorrow. What should we do?" Hani's whisper comes out thick and shaky.

"I don't know."

At the same time, her CNI pings.

"Display," Hani whispers, and a holographic font fills the wall above the bathtub.

The future is to(morrow)day.

I sigh and laugh at the same time. "See? It's them. They're trying to send us a little joke. To let us know they'll see us tomorrow, and... and the future is bright!" I catch the rise in my voice and reel myself in before I get too loud. "It's okay. They must have just had a little technical hiccup or something."

But even as I say it, I know I'm wrong. Or I'm not being honest with myself. Something caused this message to spontaneously erase, then magically reappear, possibly—or probably—altered, made shorter or longer or edited entirely. And yes, of course it's them. But we're not the first ones to read this message.

"You ladies all right in there?" William yells from the dining room. "Our dinner is getting cold."

I look at Hani. Her fear is palpable, and I quickly try to hug it away. It gives neither of us any relief.

"It's okay, Hani," I whisper. "Everything's going to happen

as planned. They'll be here tomorrow, and we'll be rescued. We'll be free. William will be done. And so will that miserable bitch, Alexandria Allerton Bigelow."

Hani shudders when I say her name.

"That's who I had the..." Hani whispers, her eyes growing wide.

"What? What did you say?" I search her eyes.

"The meeting I had. It was with her. With Ms. Bigelow."

"Nerissa? Hani? Come on, it's time to eat," William yells again. "I'm coming in there if you don't come out now!" We hear his chair scrape across the floor as he rises from his seat, his footsteps getting closer.

I turn, flip the lock, and swing open the door. "We're done, William. Sorry to keep you waiting. That zipper was a real bitch. Let's eat."

The show must go on.

CHAPTER 26
SPINDRIFT

JUST LET HER SPEAK.

Saturday has come and gone. The first tourist-filled zeppelin of the Season arrived, all those aboard presumably happy and relieved to return to their beloved Panacea. But I have to assume that our group, our team, our tribe—our only damn hope—were not onboard. Or if they were, they've been apprehended somehow and disabled from making it to Black Rock. From stopping William and Alexandria. And if they've been captured, they'll all soon be dead—if they're not already.

I've not seen Hani since Friday night. I wanted to know more about her meeting with Alexandria, but we didn't have the opportunity to talk again. In typical William fashion, our celebration dinner went on for hours, and after he was good and drunk, he told Hani to leave. I was once again graced with one of his stories, except this one was like some sort of recited wish list. I tried to change the subject. I even asked him if I could see Devin the next day. After all, William was feeling so excited and indebted to me. Surely he could see his way to a little *reward.* I told him it would definitely help me relax and have a healthier pregnancy if I could just see Devin and make sure he's all right. He ignored my request, and after his third retelling of his plan to have the most powerful, recognized household name in the world, I fell asleep at the table. When I woke up with my hair stuck to a dessert plate, drooling and stiff from the awkward position, William was gone. I helped myself to bed after I threw up my dinner and an unknown amount of wine.

I woke hours later on Saturday morning the same way— purging myself of the food and wine from the night before.

I waited and waited, but Hani never came to my room. I fended entirely for myself. Not that I can't—I've just never had to. I cleared the table from dinner, cleaned the kitchen, made my bed, and got dressed. It somehow felt normal, or familiar, or sane. I pulled one of the living room chairs toward the window and sat for hours, staring out at Panacea and Alba- tross—anticipating the zeppelin's arrival and our rescue.

The hours ticked by, one excruciating moment at a time. I waited alone all day, waited for the doors to swing open and for my mother or Devin to walk in, all smiles and hugs. Or for Hani to finally arrive and tell me *"They're here. It's time."*

But nobody came. And after the bright day turned to night and I was still sitting in that damn chair watching the shore light up in celebration of the opening of the Season, I knew I had to admit defeat. No one was coming. Something bad had happened. I retreated to my bed, curled up, and cried. And even though I'd done nothing more than sit all day, sleep came easily. As I drifted off, I started thinking about how I would end my own life.

As I wake this morning and consider my options, I also consider this; Hani knows something. And now, for whatever reason, she's being kept away from me. Maybe she's locked up or being tortured for information. Maybe she's dead. Whatever's happening, I owe it to her to try to find out. I owe her my life. And if we're never getting out of here, never getting off this Rock, if I'll never see my family or friends again or touch the ocean, if nothing can ever stop William from actually becoming the most powerful and recognized household name in the world... I want to at least know why. What happened to our plan? Where and why did it fall apart? And how, in my final act upon this earth, can I make William Banks suffer the most?

I dress quickly and run to the kitchen to grab a bite to eat. I'm starving, having eaten hardly a thing the day before. I pick at the leftovers in the fridge, fighting off the nausea brought on by all the smells. Maybe the leftovers are already too old. I slam the door shut and get a glass of water instead.

As I'm about to leave, my imagination runs away, and I picture somebody on the other side of the double doors, waiting to grab me. I return to the kitchen and retrieve a small, sharp knife from the drawer.

When I pull open the door, yielding my trusty knife before me, there's no one there. I feel a little stupid, but as I head for the elevator, I slip the little blade into my pocket.

As soon as the elevator door opens on the main level, I hear voices and commotion. I walk down the hall carefully, silently. And when I round the corner to the lobby, my mouth drops open.

An army of workers dart and zip about, having transformed the Bio-Gen lobby into a sparkling showplace. It looks like a nightclub. Or a circus. And it's set up for the party of the century. There are numerous tables, each dedicated to a specific purpose—two for a vast array of appetizers, another for a dessert buffet, others overflowing with beauty care samples, all decorated with massive floral centerpieces. Enormous bars sit at either end of the room, with who I presume is a bartender at each, organizing and prepping for a busy evening. A DJ sets up an impressive, raised table, testing a projected dancefloor in front of it. Behind his setup, spotlights of every color stand in wait. In fact, every corner, every surface has been brought to life with an array of magical lights. Some are small, twinkling fairy lights, others are bold, colorful beams shooting up the walls and making the space appear even larger than it is. My eyes follow an undulating, misty golden light, and at this point, I shouldn't be surprised to see that it lands on the tribute fountain of Alexandria. Another flood of rich golden light falls over the fountain, making it glow.

"Wait until it's dark outside. It'll be even more spectacular."

I spin around and find myself staring at Alexandria Allerton Bigelow. My first instinct is to wrap my hands around her throat and choke her to death. The only thing that stops me is seeing Hani standing only feet behind this horrible woman.

"Hani!" I try to step around Alexandria, but she steps sideways to block me.

"Hani's working. There's no time for idle chitchat," Alexandria says slowly and deliberately.

"Are you okay?" I ask over her shoulder.

"Good morning, Beauty," Hani says robotically. "I'm wonderful. How are you today?"

They've drugged her, or beaten her, or threatened her. Or all of the above.

"Where have you been? I waited for you all day yesterday—"

"This woman is working for me, Nerissa, as she did yesterday. As you will do today. Now."

I laugh in her face. "If you think I'm working for you today, or any other day... if you think William will allow me to do any kind of physical work now that I'm carrying his *precious cargo*—"

She grabs my chin and squeezes hard, leaning close enough to my face that I can tell she's recently eaten onions. "You need to learn to shut your mouth," she spits. "Not everything is about you. And for the record, I don't give two shits about William's Harvesters. I will, however, not put you in any physical stress. Do you think you can handle folding napkins, you spoiled little brat?"

I open my mouth to return my own seething thoughts—to let her know exactly what I think of her and that I vow to do whatever it takes to watch her and William crumble. And then I get a look at Hani.

Standing behind Alexandria, like a small, timid mouse, her head tilted toward the floor, Hani looks up at me and stares into my eyes with an intensity I've never seen there. Then her head moves side to side so subtly, I'm not sure whether I imagined it. She does it again, and then I know without a doubt she's telling me to stop, insisting that I be quiet. The image of Gabriel doing the same thing just before William slit his throat flashes in my mind. I again open my mouth to protest, and Hani mouths the words, *"Please don't."*

"This is *my* night. *My* moment," Alexandria snaps. "And if you do anything, *anything* at all to mess it up, you will be *very sorry*." She squeezes my chin roughly before pushing it out of her hand. I step back and look at the floor, letting her think her authority and her threats have forced me into submissive alignment. But it was Hani. Only Hani. And tonight, when the moment is just right, both Alexandria Allerton Bigelow and the incomparable William Banks will be sorry they ever existed. I don't know how. I don't know what I can possibly do at this point, and I know that whatever it is, I won't be able to get away with it. I will most likely die trying. But there are worse things than death.

I work in the lobby for four hours without coming in contact with Hani, prepping linens and silverware, arranging samples, and being a gopher for Alexandria. I fetch her a coffee, then a croissant with butter and honey, then I retrieve her guestlist and her custom-made *"Welcome to Paradise, Welcome to Panacea"* brochures before spreading them throughout the room. I have to admit, if I were a potential tourist or investor on that massive guestlist, the brochure alone would have me sold. Lies.

"I'm going to release a Panacea lifestyle publication, as well," Alexandria tells me when she sees me studying the brochure. She sounds almost friendly. "It'll be everything Panacea," she says. "Food, resort-wear, and of course, the latest in island-made beauty care."

"And I'm sure you'll shine a light on the island's natural beauty, too, won't you? The things that really keep the tourists coming back. You know, the clean air, the medicinal flora, the water, the local people, the pristine landscape?" I say it with such sarcasm, she actually looks amused.

"Of course. Maybe you'll help me. Be a contributing writer or something." She smiles, the sting in her voice matching my own.

I toss the brochure at her and walk away.

William arrives, all smiles, and tries to wrap his arms around me when he locates me at the sample table. "Hello,

Nerissa. How are you feeling today?" He leans in, and I step back.

"I'm fine." I could lie and say I'm not well, just to get out of working for Alexandria any longer, but I quickly change my mind. I need to stay here, stay focused on my plan. While I fold pretty white napkins, I decide that the only thing I can do is put myself in a position to speak my mind, to tell everyone who I really am and how I got here. I need to say everything I know about what really goes on in this building and how the only real interest is making money at all costs—mostly to the consumer. I'll tell everyone that William Banks' superiors have been informed and *were* on their way, but something happened. I know I've tried to be some kind of whistle-blower to no avail, but there will be a lot of new people here tonight. Maybe someone will listen. Maybe someone will care. The trick will be to make sure I get to say everything before I'm stopped. And I think I know what to do.

I'm finally relieved of my duties and sent back to my room to rest and dress for the Gala. When I step through the doors to my suite, the first thing I see is a handwritten note on the dining table.

"Sandwich in the fridge. Eat. It's going to be a long night. Clothes are hanging in the bathroom. Wear your hair down. He likes it that way."

You've got to be kidding me. I have to assume this is Hani's writing, but it's definitely not Hani. Okay. Let's do this. I run into the kitchen, retrieve a pair of scissors, and return to the bathroom. Where's a comb?

With only thirty minutes before her expansive and impressive list of guests arrive, it's crunch time. I return to the lobby, dressed in a bright yellow, one-sleeved gown that comfortably hugs my body. William's going to have a hard time convincing anyone I'm pregnant. I can't wait to tell him that I'm not.

I glide through the lobby, filled with a mix of nerves and excitement and relief that everything will soon be over. Alexandria was right; the space is absolutely stunning now that it's dark outside and the lights and décor can do their jobs fully. The DJ has filled the room with a moody but upbeat, cool electronic vibe. The bartenders are ready, and throughout the room, beautiful young people dressed in everything from beachwear to evening wear don plates and samples and beverages. Nobody seems to notice me. I guess I blend in perfectly. Until William sees me.

"What did you do?" he asks, like a toddler in a tuxedo who was just reprimanded—sad and angry and defensive.

"Do you like it?" I raise my hand to my newly shorn head.

"*No*, I most certainly do not. Why did you do that again? Tonight of all nights?"

"Oh, I'm sorry you don't like it. I love it. It's very me. And... now the focus can be even more on my pregnancy." I smile. "Plus, now everyone can see I belong to you." I rub the back of my neck where my old FWG brand is clearly visible once again.

William sighs. "All right. There's nothing we can do about it now. Let's get you into your place."

"My place?"

"Yes, Alexandria has a designated place for everyone."

"Of course she does. Where's mine?" I scan the room for some kind of clue as to where the Queen wants me—no doubt out of the way.

William points to a table of drinks—Aqua Tonic and Wreckleaf smoothies, perfectly ironic—and another table of samples with two flawless, tanned, bikini-clad pseudo-sprayers. "Right over there, between the Aqua Tonic and the Panacea Sun Goddesses."

"Ah... I like the silver bikinis. Very rich." I follow William's gesture and take *my place.* Then I spot Alexandria entering the lobby, a small entourage wafting in behind her. She's dressed in an overly sparkly, floor-length, black evening gown. The fabric looks thick and heavy, yet it still somehow doesn't cover enough of her. As she gets closer, her face becomes even more offensive than her dress. Her mile-long, crusty eyelashes surely must be impairing her vision. And those lips—I sure hope she ate already, because she will not be able to navigate her way around even a small morsel of food with those chubs. She looks ridiculous, and apparently, the feeling is mutual; as soon as her hairy eyes land on me, she laughs.

"Hello, Beauty," she manages. "Has William seen you?"

I smile. "Yes. He loves it."

"Doubtful. But suit yourself. Now, do not do anything to ruin my evening. Do you understand?"

"I wouldn't dream of it, Alexandria. I sincerely hope this evening is everything you hoped for and more." I grin.

She tilts her head and raises her eyebrows, looks me up and down, then walks away to praise the Goddesses and everyone else in her path. I run my hands over my dress, smoothing out the angled neckline, and pass over the small knife tucked neatly into place.

"Ms. Bigelow," the DJ's voice fills the lobby, "I've just been informed your guests are arriving." Hani stands at the man's side. She scans the room and finds me. A small smile lifts her mouth, and she quickly turns and disappears.

"Places, everyone. Places!" Alexandria yells from the center of the room.

The front doors open, and a burst of fresh ocean air fills the space. Perhaps the last breath of its kind for me.

Like a parade of well-dressed royalty, the guests are escorted into the building. The reactions are undivided. A universal wave of awe and excitement wash over them as they step into the lobby—into Alexandria's grand, extravagant, and enigmatic alter-world—exclusively designed for them, the world's most elite. I'm sure I'd feel the same way if I were one of them.

The train of guests continues in what seems like an unending stream. I recognize many of the investors and officers who have been here previously—the ones I thought would actually be concerned by the work being done here. Dr. Picker, Dr. Bigelow, and other nameless scientists and lab techs enter, all polished and ready for the evening, and the space slowly fills to capacity. But I'll wait until I'm sure everyone is here. I will wait for the perfect moment. The perfect moment will present itself.

Appetizers and beverages are offered and served, products are demonstrated, samples are passed out, and brochures are handed to everyone who enters. The DJ makes a few quick announcements—pointing out the restrooms, the smoking patio, when and where the tours of the facility will begin, and that the bars are open.

"I've got the creations and libations for your ultimate vacation," the bartender yells into the crowd.

No. He did *not* just imitate—

"I've got the bubbles to ease all your troubles!" the other bartender shouts back from the other side of the room. The guests go crazy with cheers and applause.

I launch out of my place like a rocket toward the closest bartender. "Who told you to say that?" I yell at him.

"Woah…. what's the problem, Beauty?" He sounds genuinely concerned for his well-being. Good.

"You have no right to speak that way. To mimic the way…" My throat feels like it's closing. "The way Gabriel used to talk. The way he used to get people excited to buy a drink from him. Who told you and the other guy to do that?"

"Relax. The big guy over there." He points. "He gave me instructions. Yell at him, not me."

"William?" I ask.

"Who?"

"Officer Banks. He's the one who told you to talk like that?" I nod toward William.

"Yep, that's the guy. Hey, sorry, but I've got a job to do."

My head twirls, my heart pounding in anger and frustration. Marcus' words come racing up from my memory. *"He is a master at what he does. Watch and learn. Let him inspire you, but do not copy."*

"Let him inspire you, but do not copy."

"What?" The bartender is losing his patience with me as he tries to serve three customers their drinks.

"Sorry. Never mind." I start to walk away, then stop and turn back around. "Can I have a glass of champagne, please? Pink, if you have it."

"Sure."

The baffled bartender serves me a crystal glass full of pink, sparkling comfort. I stand at the bar and drink the whole thing, not bothering to return to my proper location. And then I order another.

After my third glass of what must be the most expensive bubbly liquid on the planet, William approaches. "You're out of place," he says quietly.

"Yeah, I needed a drink."

William orders himself a cocktail and sips it at my side.

"You're not going to offer the lady a drink?" I sneer at him.

"You seem to have already had enough," he says, gazing out at the celebration.

I laugh. "Yeah, that's not what you say at our little dinner parties."

He grabs ahold of my hand so no one else can see and squeezes hard. "That's different and totally inappropriate right now."

"You're hurting me. Let go."

"I think it's time to show you off a bit before you're too drunk to stand and look..." He glances at my shorn hair. "Pretty. The guests have all arrived."

Perfect. I'm ready.

William swallows his last sip, puts down his glass, and pulls me from the bar to the DJ. He takes the microphone, and when the song ends, William and I step onto the lit dancefloor.

"Good evening, Beauties and Gentlemen. Welcome to Panacea, Black Rock, and the new and improved Bio-Genesis Wave Technologies facilities. We are so honored and delighted you're here."

The space around us on the dancefloor grows, and the entire room quiets down in an instant. All eyes are on us.

"Alexandria? May I?"

I see her across the room, showing off her fountain. She nods and smiles back at William.

"As you all know," he continues, "we have our dear Alexandria Allerton Bigelow to thank for this evening and for making this dream a reality. Alexandria will speak in just a few moments, but first, I'd like to make a couple announcements and introduce you to someone."

The guests hang on William's every word, doe-eyed

women and puff-chested men, all eager to be a part of this magical evening. This ridiculous, smoke-and-mirrors atrocity. Will they be able to turn a blind eye after I have my turn?

"I hope you're all enjoying the Aqua Tonic and the Wreck-leaf smoothies. For those of you who'd like something stronger, our bartenders can mix you a cocktail with either or both."

"Bravo, Banks," an unknown man yells from the crowd. "It's delicious. A real masterpiece!"

"Oh, thank you." William's cheeks flush, and he nods. "These facilities are now capable of producing perfectly repli-cated Caulerpa Periculosis Abscondita."

The guests look at each other, some puzzled, squinting their eyes and squishing up their mouths, while others nod slyly as knowing smiles light up their faces.

"AKA Wreckleaf. Aqua Tonic's secret ingredient!" A collec-tive laugh fills the air. "We are growing enough biogenetically identical Wreckleaf to continue to supply our AQT demands here and on the mainland. With an approval... well, I don't know. Tonight?" He smiles and shrugs, holding up crossed fingers. Everyone laughs again. "We have enough for that, as well as enough to infuse all the old beauty-care favorites and a few new ones. We've got some incredible products to intro-duce this Season. Please make sure you try the samples."

"William, who is this Beauty by your side?" an immacu-lately dressed and coifed woman directly in front of us asks.

"I'm glad you asked, Bea. And thank you for coming tonight. You look beautiful, as always. This is Nerissa John, and she is a very instrumental part of this facility's success."

"How so?" Bea the Beauty asks.

"Nerissa and her family not only made it possible to obtain Wreckleaf—to introduce Panacea's Seasonal tourists to its incredible medicinal properties—but because of our time spent together last Season, Nerissa became responsible for the rebuild of this facility. And with the continued cooperation of her family and friends providing us with Wreckleaf samples, we perfected our own growing conditions."

His long, rambling, elastic version of the truth has my blood boiling under my skin.

"I heard the original facility was blown up," a young, attractive man in a blue-velvet tuxedo suggests.

"Oh." William chuckles. "Well, there was indeed a fire last Season."

"And an explosion?" the man asks.

"Yes, and an explosion."

The lobby quietly erupts in gasps and whispers.

"But," William adds above the hushed stirrings, "because of that event, this event and this facility are a reality! And I have one more announcement to make."

This is it. The perfect moment is about to reveal itself to me.

"This Beauty, Nerissa John, is my daughter." The crowd's murmurs rise in volume. "And she's pregnant with my grandchild!" William yells it over the now raucous, elated room. Contagious laughter and cheers and congratulations spill everywhere. William is beside himself with glee. He giggles and yells and pants in excitement. He stands in all his own glory, the adoring crowd of the elite clapping in recognition, sharing their salutations of merriment and good fortune. William doesn't even know I'm here. This is for him—for his insatiable ego—and he's absorbing every last drop of it. Too bad I have to ruin the moment for him and make my presence known.

I grab the microphone from his hand with a loud thump. He's so surprised, he simply watches me. His smile quickly fades.

"Hello, everyone. As William said, my name is Nerissa John. But the truth—the part he left out—is that I'm not supposed to exist. My *kind* are not supposed to exist."

Across the lobby, I hear Alexandria choke on her champagne, and before she's done coughing, she's yelling across the crowd. "Get your pet under control, William." She hikes up her gown in both hands and walks quickly toward us.

"Nerissa, give me that microphone at once." William holds out his hand, expecting me to comply. But that's over. Forever.

"No, these people need to know the truth." I stare at him. He looks sincerely betrayed, with a sadness in his eyes that makes my mind flutter in doubt for a few brief seconds.

He lunges at me and tries to take the microphone by force. I step back just in time. Now Alexandria's beside him. I scan the crowd, and all eyes are fixed upon me—everyone looking cautiously curious. William lunges at me again. This time, I pull the knife hidden in my dress and nearly stab him before he stops himself. Time seems to slow, and I'm acutely aware of the absolute silence following the exaggerated collective gasp.

"What exactly do you think you're doing?" Alexandria demands, her face like lava—red and angry. She steps toward me with no fear, as if she doesn't believe—or doesn't even consider—I'd actually use the knife.

"Stay back." I raise the knife toward her, as a warning.

She stops. "What are you going to do?" she says, mocking me with her flippant tone. "Kill me?"

"Not yet," I say as casually as if I'm just running through my daily to-do list. "I have a few things to say first."

William leans cautiously toward me, his face sparkling with sweat, and speaks as quietly as he can. "This is your last chance, Nerissa. If you don't stop this nonsense at once, I'll have Devin brought in here, and we will finally see just how much *Wildfire* a human body can take."

"Oh." I laugh nervously. "I'm sure that'd be a big hit with your guests."

"As a matter of fact, I'm sure it would."

"You will do no such thing, William. No-one will ruin this night for me." Alexandria doesn't seem to have a grasp on what's happening. This little party is over.

"Then Nerissa and I will go to the labs together, and she can watch in privacy." William's eyes are bulging out of his face, and he launches himself at me again. I drop the microphone and swipe the knife in front of me with very little control. It slices across his cheek, only centimeters from his left eye. Both of us freeze. He claps a hand to his face, blood already trickling between his fingers. I stand there, unable to take a deep breath, steadying the knife in both hands.

"Apprehend that girl!" somebody yells.

I see movement in my periphery, but I never take my eyes from William's. When he breaks our eye contact and looks to my side, I already feel someone approaching. Without thinking, I hurl myself at William, stepping behind him to grab his shoulder and press the knife against his throat. I'm considerably shorter than him, and my position is awkward and difficult to hold.

"I would love to slice open your neck and watch you die. Payback for Gabriel and Sarah," I whisper to him. "And your father."

"What's stopping you?" he asks.

"I have a few things to say to everyone first, and I want you to hear it all."

"Enough of this," Alexandria huffs. "You're ruining my evening. My moment. I warned you not to do that."

"You know what you can do with your moment, Alexandria?" I lean toward her slightly. "You miserable, horrible bitch! You can just shove—"

William twists to the left, and before I can stop him, he spins and ducks out of my hold to retreat into the dwindling crowd. I'm left standing alone with Alexandria in the middle of the makeshift dance floor, breathless and exposed, without another visible bargaining chip. There's only one thing left to do. Even though it's a lie.

I flip the knife around and press it against my lower abdomen, then spin frantically, trying to locate William. "I will kill this monstrosity growing inside me, William. I will eliminate your precious *grandchild!*" I turn in circles, looking like some kind of mental patient, I'm sure. The expressions of those left around the dance floor are the same mix of pity and disgust to which I've grown so accustomed. And there's William. But his expression is one of resolution.

"Go ahead," he says. "I'll just make more."

The scream starts deep inside me as a low, faint rumble. It rises higher and higher, and I lose complete control of my vocal chords, letting out a sound that could shatter eardrums, or rip apart buildings, or crumble mountains. My entire being vibrates, and when my impossibly long shriek finally comes to an end, I've made myself dizzy. And I'm out of options.

"Nerissa," a calm, deep voice says behind me. I spin around. "Why don't you let me help you," Dr. Price Bigelow says. "You don't want to hurt the baby."

I start to laugh. "There *is* no baby. You know that. Do you hear that, William?" I spin back around to face him. "There actually is no baby. And no, you won't be making any more. Not inside *me*, anyway. That's right, I'm not pregnant. I never was. Your own doctors didn't want to—"

"You most certainly *are* pregnant," Alexandria says so loudly, I shudder. She walks toward me, unafraid, and before I can raise the knife in defense, Dr. Bigelow steps closer behind me to wrap one arm around my waist. His other hand grabs my wrist and shakes the weapon loose. Alexandria steps directly in front of me, stops, sighs, then slaps my face. "Get ahold of yourself." Then she snaps her fingers above her head. "William, keep her quiet but stay here." Dr. Bigelow releases me and steps away while William follows her orders and stands beside me again. He wraps his arm around me and pins my own arms tightly against my sides—so tight I can barely breathe, let alone speak. In my stunned silence, I concede. I let go. It's over. This is my end.

Apparently satisfied, Alexandria walks away to address her guests. She works the room, approaching them a few at a time, and eases their tension with soft words, a gentle hand on their shoulder, and an apologetic smile and laugh. She then directs a doorman to retrieve those who have fled outside. She speaks directly to the servers and bartenders, as well as those handing out samples. Finally, she returns to the DJ, asks for a micro-phone, and joins William and me back on the dance floor.

"Dear guests, I am so very sorry for that atrocious outburst. I assure you it's over, and you're all completely safe. Nerissa's rant"—she places a hand on the top of my head—"is over, I promise. Please, allow my servers to take care of you, and we can continue on with our lovely evening. The bartenders are ready to take your orders, the dance floor will open momentar-ily, and tours will begin shortly. I would first like to share a few announcements of my own."

The tension in the room falls away immediately. Everyone seems to take a deep breath, returning to their relaxed states. The space around the dance floor shrinks as the guests file back and turn their attention to their hostess. William holds me tight, as we stand here next to the Queen. I feel like a spec-imen on display.

"To new beginnings, Aunt Alexandria," Dr. Bigelow shouts and raises a glass.

She laughs softly. Someone passes a glass of champagne to her and another to William. "Yes, my dear nephew. To new beginnings."

The room fills with the sounds of glasses clinking and people toasting.

"Cheers."

"Here-here!" William adds.

Alexandria nods and smiles.

"Salut."

"Congratulations."

She sips at her drink.

"Speech! Speech!"

The woman swallows hard. "Did someone say speech? Well, don't mind if I do." The crowd laughs. "First, thank you all for being here tonight. This night is more special, more important than I can ever express, and I'm honored to share it with you. As most of you know, I have been coming to Panacea for the Season longer than I can remember. I practically grew up here."

The guests all smile, nodding in understanding and mutual affection.

"As good fortune would have it, along with a lot of hard work, determination, and *vast* intelligence"—she smiles and wiggles her eyebrows, now with every last guest eating out of her hand, the memory of the crazed, knife-wielding girl in the yellow dress already erased—"I have built an incredibly successful commerce on the mainland. An empire, if you will."

Her ego and her stupid face are so repulsive, they turn my stomach.

"Thank god for that," William says and chuckles.

Alexandria turns toward him, looking annoyed at the interruption. "Yes, William. Thank god for that. Because my love for Panacea is bigger than any love I've *ever* had."

I start to laugh, muffled and sloppy under William's stronghold. His arm around my waist pulls me sharply into him, nearly forcing the breath out of me. Alexandria shoots me a death-stare, then continues her obnoxious tale of purity and love.

"I have been placed in the very fortunate position of being able to increasingly contribute to the growth and well-being of Panacea and her sister islands. This building, for example." She spreads her arms and sweeps her long-lashed eyes over the space. "And the incredibly dedicated individuals who helped make this dream a reality."

I feel William stand a little taller as he pulls in a deep breath and smiles.

"You all know my love for luxury skincare. Well, that's something we've been able to not only accomplish but to perfect. Our lines are totally exclusive, completely proprietary—including ingredients available nowhere else on Earth but here—and reserved for the privileged, like yourselves. We have many new products and projects under our new Bio-Gen roof, and I hope you're as excited about them as I am."

Cheers and applause ring out, and Alexandria politely lifts a hand to hush the crowd.

"As my empire expands, so too does my investment and involvement in this island trio. Not only do I want to see it blossom to its fullest potential, but I also want to protect it, scour it of any destructive forces."

Alexandria turns, looking for someone.

"Is it time?" Dr. Bigelow asks.

"Yes. Bring them in, please."

Dr. Bigelow walks quickly from the lobby and speaks into his CNI. I can't hear what he's saying, but dread is seeping into every corner of my being.

William turns to watch Dr. Bigelow as well, then looks

back at Alexandria. Whatever she has up her sleeve, William doesn't seem to know about it, either.

"Will someone please bring a chair up here?" Alexandria asks, and a luxurious, gray velvet chair is immediately placed behind her. "Oh, just put it there." She points to the center of the dance floor, and the chair is placed under a twirling silver light, illuminated and ready to host royalty. She does not sit down. "May I please have another glass of champagne?" And just like the chair, a crystal flute of champagne is magically delivered to her.

I hear a soft ding followed by an elevator door opening, and Alexandria looks up to the back end of the lobby. I follow her gaze and stumble into a dream-world. Please let me be dreaming.

Dr. Bigelow and Dr. Picker round the corner, followed by an armed guard. Behind him, filing in one by one, are Hani, Officer Richard Klein, Kendra holding baby Ruari, Marcus, Taren, my mother, Lillian, Anastasia, Alakier, Moriyah Bigelow, Devin, Colton, Leyla, and at last, two men I don't recognize—presumably Richard Klein's superiors—followed by another armed guard.

William bursts into laughter while I crumble in his grip and break down in tears.

I meet Devin's gaze, and he somehow manages a smile. He looks tired, like he's aged overnight. He's still limping but he doesn't seem injured otherwise, and his arm looks totally healed.

The procession moves toward us, and Alexandria gestures for her guests to part and make room. The doctors and armed guards lead the prisoners to the edge of the dance floor and line them up in a row facing us.

"Nissa!" Alakier yells. I break free of William's hold and

rush toward them. One of the guards blocks me immediately. William continues laughing.

Anastasia lays a hand on Alakier's shoulder, and he seems to remember he's supposed to stay quiet. I choke back my emotion, so I don't upset him more.

"May I have everyone's attention, please?" Alexandria says into the microphone. Hearing her voice again, I run at her, ready to take her down and kill her on the spot. The same guard—three times my size, speed, and strength—stops me again to return me to William, who wraps his arms tightly around me once more.

"Oh, Alexandria," William coos. "This is something special. What a surprise. Where did they all come from? How did you arrange this?" He's positively giddy. "Hello, Leyla Darling. Tatiana. Klein—" He can't get everyone's names out before he laughs so hard, he snorts.

"Like I said," Alexandria continues, "a vitally important part of the work I'm doing here is to not only protect this island trio, but to rid it of any toxic and negative forces. And then to reward those who have played an integral role in maintaining the purity I expect."

The room is silent but for the sound of the tribute fountain bubbling and splashing—and William's soft, endless chuckling.

"We've had some exceptional individuals raise our awareness and help us create a space and mission that will be impactful and important for generations to come. One such individual is indeed Nerissa John."

William stops mid-chuckle, fully expecting Alexandria to have named him.

"As William said earlier, without Ms. John, this new building would not exist. We would not have the ability to fully utilize the prized sea plant, Wreckleaf, and William would have never been able to create his beloved energy elixir, Aqua Tonic."

"Ah, yes, Alexandria. Nerissa deserves all the credit in the world. We had our rocky start." William laughs. "But look at us now. Father and daughter, about to welcome my grandchild into this amazing facility. Ready to take on the world with Aqua Tonic!"

"I'm not pregnant, you idiot!" I yell. "Haven't you figured that out yet?" An unexpected confusion takes over, and I'm not sure I believe myself anymore.

"And why do you think you're not pregnant?" William asks. "We saw the fetus together. We heard its heart beating. Together." He smiles. "This is happening, like it or not. But I'd prefer, of course, that you were happy."

"I heard the doctors talking," I scream at him. "They're so afraid of you, they faked the whole thing! That wasn't my baby's heartbeat. It was a recording of one of Anastasia's!"

His face says it all. His little upside-down smile and curled brows tell me he finds me amusing, and he doesn't even want to bother trying to explain things to me anymore.

"You are pregnant," Alexandria says. "And I assure you, my doctors are not afraid of William."

My head grows heavier by the second, and I feel like I'm going to pass out. Alexandria motions to the two armed guards, and they take their places, one on either side of William and me. I'm surrounded. They're going to make me watch as, one by one, someone kills every person I love. It'll probably be William. I guess Alexandria's *moment* was something entirely different than anyone expected. I hope her guests can stomach a bloodbath while they enjoy their cocktails and free samples.

She glides past me and to the table with the Aqua Tonic and Wreckleaf smoothies. She picks up a bottle of AQT and returns, holding it above her head, turning it back and forth as the light catches and reflects a shimmering blue wave over the floor. My tangled mind transports me immediately into the ship graveyard and the Wreckleaf fields—the closest I'll ever be again to my silent blue. William beams.

"This drink... this elixir... is possibly the most important piece of the story and how we got to where we are at this moment." Alexandria keeps it above her head, staring at it like it's some precious artifact. "And although this is *my* night, *my* party, a night I've dreamt about for so long, we must give the man responsible for this creation his dues. William, please. Sit down." She gestures to the chair at the center of the dance floor, and William releases me with the tiniest push, eager to take his place and earn the respect and admiration of everyone present—to literally have his moment in the spotlight.

He bounces into the chair, looking up at Alexandria like she's about to bestow upon him the keys to some magical kingdom. All around us, Alexandria's privileged guests watch and listen intently, sipping at their cocktails and looking beautiful in their formal attire.

"William has worked very hard on the Aqua Tonic project, among others." Alexandria once again looks at the bottle. "He has been willing to do whatever it takes to make this dream of his come true. And I must commend him for his blind ambition. An approval for this energy elixir—an approval William hopes will come tonight, during our celebration—would mean an untold fortune. It would mean great success and, ultimately, great power." She smiles at William, and he looks like he may cry.

"When I learned about the AQT project last year and what William was willing to do to make it come to life—thanks to my niece Moriyah—I knew I had to get involved." She nods in Moriyah's direction, and everyone follows her gaze. Moriyah looks like she's about to faint. "Because like William Banks," Alexandria continues, "I too will do *whatever* it takes to bring my dreams to fruition. And I am a very patient woman." The intent guests smile and giggle at her last comment. But she doesn't join them in their laughter.

"This building, for example." She waves her arm through the air and around the room. "This facility is state of the art in every way. The only one of its kind, perhaps in the entire world, just like Panacea. The work that can continue here will be unlike anything from which this island trio has ever benefitted. It took a lot to make this happen. A lot. Thank you, William, for following my instructions to a tee."

William looks up at her and smiles nervously, shifting on his throne, surely ready to crap his pants once Alexandria announces his approval for AQT distribution on the mainland.

I look at my mother; her face is steely and resolved. And when she catches my eyes, she takes a long, deep breath, as though she's suggesting I do the same. I want to run to her, to Kendra and Devin and Alakier—to all of them—and wrap my arms around them. absorbing their love in what is surely our last moments alive.

"However, contrary to what some of you believe..." Alexandria continues, and I can hardly stand to listen to her bullshit any longer. Then she turns and looks directly at me. "William Banks and I are two entirely different human beings." She holds my gaze for a few incredibly uncomfortable seconds, then turns and slowly steps toward William.

"It's been my honor to work with you, Alexandria." William speaks quickly and shifts in his chair again, crossing then uncrossing his legs as she comes to stand in front of him. "I'm so glad you're pleased with the building and—"

"I am very happy to announce that this product, Aqua Tonic, the Elixir of Life"—she holds the bottle high above her and William, and he briefly closes his eyes in anticipation—"will never, *ever* be approved for distribution." William's eyes jerk open, and his face goes slack. "Not on the mainland, not on Panacea, not anywhere. Ever."

William looks up at her, his mouth morphing back and forth between a creased frown and a crooked smile, as if he's waiting for her to say, *"Just kidding!"* Instead, Alexandria Allerton Bigelow turns the shimmering bottle of Aqua Tonic upside down and pours it slowly over William's head. She watches the bubbling liquid drizzle over him—soaking his hair and stinging his eyes and ruining his perfect tuxedo—with such content, with such calm. I've never seen anything like it.

Stunned and confused, William wipes at his eyes. He jumps up from the chair, and the two armed guards are at his sides, pushing him back to his seat. The room buzzes with gasps and murmurs—even laughter. I've clamped a hand over my mouth in complete disbelief.

"*What* is the meaning of this?" William yells, blinking away the stinging elixir, attempting again to stand while the guards hold him down in the chair. "Alexandria! What are you doing?"

Alexandria stands there and watches William's confusion, wearing the most peaceful, satisfied smile imaginable. She tosses the empty bottle at him, and it lands in his lap with a thud.

Then she turns back to me and approaches. I freeze, unable to work out what's happening, unsure if she's about to slap me or hug me. Or kill me. She stands directly in front of me, her long lashes and puffed lips only inches from my face. I'm terrified. And absolutely intrigued.

"Thank you for your patience and your stamina," she whispers. "I promise you it was worth it." She takes my hand in hers and leads me toward William. His eyes are swollen and red. He looks up at me with such sadness and fear, I feel sorry for him.

Alexandria quiets the guests, who seem split in their reaction to this turn of events. Some look just as stunned and confused as I feel; others—many others, including the investors and Officers I remembered from their previous visit—look like Alexandria. Relieved, satisfied, content.

"Nerissa..." William reaches toward me. "What's happening?"

I shake my head slowly, look at Alexandria, then back at him. "I don't know," I say quietly. "I'm sorry."

"No!" Alexandria barks. "Do not apologize to him. William did this to himself."

She stares down at him, scolding him with her glare, then returns the microphone to her mouth.

"William Banks was willing to do anything to see that his product got approval. Anything. Including his lies, deceit, and betrayal of his friends, his family, his associates and superiors, and both the locals and the tourists of Panacea. And even me, his number one investor. One whose company he's enjoyed keeping for years." She pauses and stares at him, then paces across the dance floor. "On top of all that, William took part in coercion, bribery, violence, and even murder in pursuit of his goals. All while attempting to illegally create a small army of hybrids to take over the livelihood of others."

"Alexandria, please." William's sweaty forehead shines under the lights, all the color drained from his face entirely. "That is simply not true. You know me. We're business part-ners. We're friends."

"William has a long history of being an abusive liar." She reaches into a hidden pocket on the side of her gown and retrieves a small, creased, aged envelope. She briefly rests the microphone under her arm, unfolds the envelope, and pulls out a yellowed note. As recognition dawns, William's face turns from white to gray.

"Where did you get that?" he grunts through clenched jaws, looking around the room in fear.

"Good question, William. My friend Hani gave it to me once she knew she could trust me." She turns to look at Hani. "I'm sorry I scared you at our first meeting. I hope you're feeling more comfortable now." Hani nods and smiles.

I've never been unsure of reality more than I am at this moment.

"This is ridiculous, Alexandria. Let's please go have a private conversation," William pleads.

"Here is my favorite part of this letter that William wrote to Nerissa's mother, Tatiana, so long ago." Then she reads it aloud:

"'I want you to know that I will honor our agreement always. You held up your end of the deal and allowed me to create my own Dolhuphemale offspring.

I am very proud to call her my own, and I will protect her always. She is my blood. Likewise, I will return to my role as guardian to you and your breed, and I will not interfere in the natural evolution of your kind ever again. With one exception. I would like to meet my daughter when she is born. That is it, I promise.

Fondly,
William Banks

What William never revealed"—Alexandria folds the note in one hand and places it back in her pocket—"is that he, along with his father Nicholas Banks, were entrusted both with the ultra-classified knowledge of the existence of a supposedly extinct, or shall I say eliminated hybrid species, as well as keeping that breed safe and never allowing them to be exposed. Well now, we all know how that went, since William has made no attempt to either hide or protect that secret." She looks at me. "And when William's father, Officer Nicholas Banks, disapproved of his plans to secretly integrate the Dolhuphemale breed back into Panacean society for his own folly and gains, William murdered him. His own father."

The crowd is stunned into silence.

"That is nonsense!" William yells. His booming voice echoes off the walls, and a bead of sweat trickles down his face. He tries again to stand and is quickly pushed back into place.

"Officer Klein?" Alexandria turns toward the lineup, and an elderly gentleman with a brown wooden cane—one of the two I didn't recognize among my family and friends—steps slowly toward Alexandria.

"That's not Richard Klein," William scoffs, as if it makes any difference. "That little bastard is over there, with the rest of the trash."

Alexandria glares at him. "This is Senior Specialist Officer Reginald Klein."

William freezes.

"I guess you didn't recognize me, William. It's been a long time." Reginald Klein's ancient voice trembles as he speaks. He hands Alexandria a small device. She aligns the microphone to it and presses a button. The room fills with a recording of William's voice telling me a story I'll never forget.

"My stupid father reached out and put his hand on her head. So lightly, like some king anointing his prodigy. He had no idea what was coming. Of course he didn't. Even when the knife sliced his neck from ear to ear and his blood sprayed all over Anastasia—and god, could she scream—he turned around and still had the stupidest look of surprise on his face.

'Anastasia,' I said to her. 'That was Nicholas Banks. My father.'

Yes, she stopped screaming then, all right. And she never challenged me again. Ever.

And then, of course, a week after we acquired Anastasia, the Dolhuphemale breed was forced out of hiding, and the Cooperative was signed."

"You killed my friend, William," Reginald says with such sadness. "Shame on you."

William rocks back and forth in his seat, moaning softly and gripping his stomach. I look around the room at the guests, the employees, and then again at Devin. His smile suddenly means something entirely different than it did just a short while ago. He knew—they all did—what Alexandria was planning, and after they arrived on Panacea and understood it all, they were prevented from interfering. She needed her moment. This was her night, planned for almost a year. No one was going to take it from her. I can't say I blame her. I lean forward and take one small step in Devin's direction, but he lifts a finger, gesturing for me to wait.

"Last Season," Alexandria begins again, "after my niece Moriyah informed me of William's despicable corruption and unethical behavior, I took it upon myself to set things straight. There were, of course, things I could not have predicted. But for the most part, my plans have come to fruition. And along with the brave actions and testimonies of these fine people"—she gestures toward my family and friends—"and those who are no longer with us, we have put together irrefutable evidence to convict William Banks for life."

Tears pour from my eyes, and my knees feel weak. Soft laughter and sighs of relief fill the room, along with harsh words thrown at William. I bury my face in my hands, then hug myself, pulling at what's left of my hair; I don't know what to do with myself. I don't know how to take in this absolute moment of justice. I look at Alexandria, and all I can do is cry and smile. And then I remember.

I place my hands on my stomach and ask with my eyes.

"William." Alexandria's voice immediately quiets the chatter and commotion. "Your little side projects. In particular, your Harvesters. That ends here and now. And as a special treat for you, you will witness each of them being put down. Out of their misery." William is shaking, his face covered completely by his hands. "Look at me, William."

He looks up at her, his face streaked with tears—eyes puffy and bloodshot. Defeat has settled over him, his shoulders have fallen, and he's sunken into his chair.

"I have one more thing to tell you, and then Nerissa has something to say." I immediately feel nervous, but I know what I have to do. "The doctors and I watched and stood idly by for too long as you tortured two young Dolhuphemales with implantation. We had no idea the toll it would take, and we are so very regretful." She looks at Anastasia and Lillian. "We refused to put Nerissa through the same abuse, and my doctors did not perform the final steps in any of the implantation attempts. Until the last one. When you became increasingly violent with each failed attempt, we decided to impregnate Nerissa just so you would stop abusing her."

"I told you you were pregnant," William says to me weakly.

"But... I thought..." I can't finish my question, I'm so confused.

"For god's sake, William," Alexandria hisses. "We would have never put one of your little monsters inside this woman. Haven't you done enough to her? Now, Nerissa has something to tell you. Then my guards will take you into custody and we can really get this celebration started!" The crowd cheers, and Alexandria hands me the microphone before going directly to the bar. She accepts a full glass of champagne, turns in my direction, lifts her glass to me, and drinks.

But she never told me who....

The lights are suddenly as bright and hot as I remember them being all night, and I'm left on the dance floor, all eyes upon me, standing in front of William Banks—a man finally defeated and waiting for me to deliver one final bit of information to him. A final blow that will surely unravel him completely. I clear my throat but have trouble finding my voice.

"Tell us, Nerissa!" somebody shouts.

"What is it you have to say?" another disembodied voice yells.

I look at William. He's crumpled in his chair, his arms and legs folded tightly together—an empty shell. He looks back at me, and only when he sneers in obvious disgust do I muster the courage to find my voice.

"You're not my father, William."

He just laughs and waves a lazy hand at me.

"You're not. You're sterile. I'm pretty sure you always have been."

"That is correct!" Alexandria yells from the bar. "We've done paternity tests. Go on, Nerissa."

Her words give me courage. "I am not your daughter. Alakier is not your son, and neither is Colton. You are incapable of fathering a child."

William's laughter continues, but now he's breathing hard through his nose. His chest rises and falls, and his amused expression quickly fades to anger as he squeezes his own face and bares his teeth at me. His eyes sear into mine. "You little brat. How *dare* you? Who the hell do you think you are?"

I blow out a big breath, plant my feet firmly, stand as tall as possible, and meet his intense stare. "I am Dolhuphemale,

Nerissa, daughter of the beloved Matriarch Tatiana and my late father, Nicholas Banks."

He howls with laughter. "Impossible!"

"You're not my father, William. You're my brother."

Almost before I've finished my sentence, William lurches sideways in his chair, retrieves the AQT bottle Alexandria threw in his lap, and cracks it against the floor. Leaping to his feet with the now-broken bottle in his fist, he lunges at me. This time, the guards aren't fast enough. William presses the jagged glass against my neck before anyone can do anything. I hear my mother scream. The guards point their weapons at William as Devin and Richard Klein approach from the side. William holds me from behind, spinning back and forth, doing everything in his power to avoid apprehension as he threatens my life.

"Woah, Officer Banks. Take it easy." Richard Klein raises his hands in an easy, submissive gesture.

"Fuck off, Klein. Everyone, step back, or she dies. Put down those weapons now!"

The guards hesitate, not knowing how serious he is. They look to Alexandria. She nods. They both drop their guns.

"Kick it to me," William instructs the closest guard. The man does as he says, and William quickly leans over and picks it up. He points the weapon directly at the back of my head, still pressing the sharp glass to my neck. He's breathing hard in my ear, and I'm sure I'm about to die.

"William, this will not end well for you," Alexandria yells.

He laughs. "Yeah, it doesn't seem like it will, no matter what happens. So, Nerissa and I are going to take a walk." He walks backwards, spinning and twisting as we go, watching for any sudden, heroic moves from anyone in the crowd. The glass at my neck cuts into my flesh with every jerky movement. "Do not follow us!"

He pulls me to the north elevator and presses the call button. Of course, we're followed by dozens of people—everyone who loves me and anyone who's had enough of William Banks' tyranny. But he's got an unyielding and unfortunate advantage over me. We enter the elevator alone. The door slides closed.

"Observation deck," William says to the operating system and quickly releases the bottle from my neck to swipe his CNI.

"Welcome, Officer Banks" the pleasant voice answers. "One moment to the Observation Deck, please."

Before we step out, William makes another request. "Disable elevator."

He presses a button on the flush silver panel, and the operator's voice says, "Disabling." The door stays open, and we step out into the night.

William pushes me toward the wall, the orange vines having returned with the blossoming of early summer on the islands. I don't have to turn around to know he has the gun pointed at my back. I reach the wall, look out over the beautiful horizon—a million stars overhead—and breathe in the salty air. William steps up beside me.

"What a night we've had," I say.

He doesn't respond right away, and I wonder how much longer he'll let me live.

"Is it really true?" he finally asks, a strange sense of calm having washed over him. "I'm not your father?"

"You're not my father."

"What a night we've had," he agrees.

"Are you going to kill me?" I don't turn to face him, focusing on the horizon.

He laughs softly, sadly, "I should. But no. You know I'd never kill you. You're..."

We stare out at the wild blue ocean in silence. Standing

here with him, at the top of what he mistakenly believed to be his fortress, his castle, his future, in the clear light of the moon and stars, I see him for who he is. For *what* he is—a scared, lonely, loveless child. William's reign is over. And he knows it at his core.

"We're still blood, William."

He doesn't say anything. Instead, he raises the gun to his own head.

A sudden pang of unexpected sympathy for this sad and desperately lonely man floods through me, and I try to push it away. He doesn't deserve it. But I can't erase it entirely.

"You don't have to do that," I say.

"I will not rot away in a prison cell. I will not let somebody else decide my fate. I will choose how this ends." He doesn't look at me. "Why do you care, anyway? I'd think you'd be happy to see me end my life."

"I just thought you might want to consider your options."

"Options? I don't have any. Turns out I never did."

"You've always had a choice."

He turns to look at me and lowers the gun. "Nerissa, I was born into this life—a life I didn't choose—to a man I detested. I did what I had to do to survive. Surely, you can understand."

My heart is pounding. The irony of his statement rings out, palpable in front of us, and tears spill freely down my cheeks. I don't try to hide. He holds my gaze in recognition, and now we're both crying.

"Yes," I finally say. "I can surely understand."

He smiles faintly and looks down, then a noise behind us grabs his attention. The elevator door has closed. Someone will be here soon. "I need to ask you a favor."

I don't answer.

"Please. We don't have long."

"What is it?"

"I'd like to ask for your forgiveness. Before I go."

Not in a million years would I have expected those words to come out of William Banks' mouth. Not now, not ever. And nothing could bring this impossibly bizarre night to a more perfectly odd pinnacle. "Why on Earth should I forgive you?"

"Because I'm sorry. I'm so sorry, Nerissa."

I don't respond. I can't. My silence rattles him.

"Please." He puts his hand on my shoulder. "I beg you. If not for me… I know I don't deserve it… for yourself. To free yourself."

"I've always been free," I say, raising my voice, trying to convince myself, "because I've always had the choice to decide. Not even you could take that from me."

"Here." He shoves the gun at my hands. "You do it. You kill me. I know you want to."

There was a time when I would have gladly taken the weapon from William and put him out of his misery. But that time is in the past.

"No."

He shakes his head, then violently hits himself above his ear with the gun. He does it again, then again. Blood seeps from under his hair and spills down his cheek to his jaw, then onto his tuxedo shirt, mixing in with the blue-green of the disgraced Aqua Tonic.

"Stop!" I yell.

"Please, Nerissa. Will you just forgive me? There's no more time. It's over. Everything is over."

With great effort, I turn my attention inward and focus on the feeling in my feet, then up my legs and through my body. I am here, alive, the energy of worlds coursing through my blood. I am now, and I am safe. I suck in the crisp ocean air, deep and deliberate, and blow it out slowly. I let it ground me even further in the moment. And with the courage of a thousand souls at my back, I look thoughtfully into the eyes of William Banks—my brother, my blood—and with the purest intent, I release us both from our prisons and purgatory.

"I forgive you," I say softly. The weight of the world falls away from me and dissolves into the night like a shooting star.

A giant rush of air comes out of him, along with a sob. But he pulls it back into his throat with a quick gasp. He turns again to face the ocean, raising the gun back to his head. "Thank you." Then he closes his eyes, and the last of his tears fall, reflecting the moonlight off his face.

From behind, a soft, familiar voice clearly speaks just one word.

"Move."

I step far to my left, and William turns to see who spoke. My mother lunges at him, shoving him over the wall with all her strength. The gun fires a white-hot beam as William flips off the edge, somersaulting backward over the vines, down the cliff, to the rocky shore below. To his end.

"I do *not* forgive you," my mother says and turns to me.

Fireworks explode behind my eyes, and a deep, hot, intense pain pulsates in my belly. "Mom?"

She catches me when I fall forward and lowers me to the ground. "It's all right. I've got you. Hold on." She pushes against my lower abdomen, and I look down at her hand, where blood pours out of my seared flesh under the pressure.

Across the deck, a stairway door opens, and someone rushes toward us.

"No! Tatiana, what happened?" Devin drops beside me.

"William's gun went off."

"Where is he?" Devin screams. "I'm going to kill him!"

"He's gone," my mother says.

"It was an accident," I manage to say through the pain. My eyes want to close. I'm so tired. But an urgent need to speak keeps me here. I spend a few seconds focusing on my thoughts, adjusting my position through my pain.

Devin looks at my mother, his eyes full of concern. He gestures to the blood pouring from my belly. "Come on, we need to get you to a medic. Tatiana, do you have any Wreckleaf?"

I look up at my mother. "No, Devin," she tells him. "I don't. And I don't think we should move her. Just let her speak."

I pull in a deep, painful breath. "It's okay. Everything that's happened... it was all supposed to happen.

He chokes back a sob. "I hate him so much for doing this to you."

"I know, but this world needed him, needed my brother, in its own weird way." A small laugh sputters from my mouth, and with it comes the taste of blood. My eyes flutter, and I finish with a whisper. "And I forgive him, in his humanity."

"She's delirious, Tatiana. We need to get her help. Now."

"Devin." My mother's voice is sweet, and loving, and more soothing than I ever remember hearing it, mixing with the song of the ocean and the whisper of the wind and the twinkle of the stars above. "Help is coming. There's nothing left to do but listen."

"Nerissa, I'm so sorry," Devin whispers.

"You have nothing to be sorry for." I struggle to get the words out, but take a small breath and continue. "I was always supposed to exist, just the way I am. To take the journey I took." I reach for his hand and place it on my stomach. "It's your baby, isn't it?"

His body crumples next to me like a ragdoll, and he gently takes my face in his hands. My mother settles on the ground behind me. Her soft, cool fingers are at my forehead. She starts to sing, and I fall back into the feeling of coming home.

"You can let go now, precious one.

It's time to rest.
Your work is done."

A large, warm tear slides down my cheek. Devin leans forward, tilts his head, and catches it in his soft kiss. I close my eyes. From behind and above—from around and inside—my mother's voice fills every space and lulls me into a dark, peaceful sleep.

"You are the Universe, and that will always be.
The Universe is you, and you are free.
You can let go now, precious one.
It's time to rest.
Your work is done."

CHAPTER 27
MY BEAUTIFUL DEATH
I AM FREE...

SUNDAY, MAY 25TH

Death is beautiful. Death is release. Descriptions of the cold, lonely darkness—the sinking, faceless, stony void—it's all wrong.

Death is quiet, peaceful. It's a soft ride over a familiar blue wave. It's a loving, welcoming voice. Death is a brilliant, quick movie of every favorite moment, every enveloping feeling. Love. I like the faces the most. All those faces, all those smiles.

I have lived. And it's been an amazing ride. It isn't how I would have imagined. But here, now, I know I wouldn't change a thing. I am free. Gabriel was right all along. I've always been free, because I always had that choice.

"I'm glad to hear that, child."

"Hi, Gabriel. I'm so happy you're here with me."

"I've always been with you."

Death is reconciliation.

"Gabriel, is it over?"

"This work is done. Some has just begun. And you're okay."

"I know."

"Forgive yourself now, child. It's time to move on."

"I do. I forgive myself."

Death is a liquid, luscious, deep and wild blue. It is the shattered light in a frenetic comfort. The poem in my heart. My ancient, silent blue muse.

"Gabriel?"

"Yes, dear one?"

"Is it *really* over this time?"

"Yes, child. This is the end. Now wake up."

"I don't want to leave you."

"Remember, Gabriel is always with you. Now wake up, child. You got what you came here for."

It's time to rest. Your work is done.

EPILOGUE

SPINDRIFT: NOUN; SEA SPRAY, ESPECIALLY
THE SPRAY BLOWN OFF THE CREST OF A
WAVE DURING A STORM OR A GALE.

MAY, THE FOLLOWING YEAR

"It's beautiful, isn't it?"

"It is. They did a great job. A real tribute."

"Gio would love it." My mother sighs.

"She would." I drop my head onto her shoulder and gaze out at the expansive, beautiful property. Not a detail was left unfinished—not a single expense spared.

I wasn't sure I liked the idea at first—a memorial park on what was the Banks' property. It almost felt sacrilege. Like *he'd* get all the credit somehow. But when I saw the plans, the idea grew on me. I couldn't deny the beautiful irony. The justice of it all. And when *she* suggested I get involved, when I could put the touches on the project that nobody else could, Alexandria Allerton Bigelow's genius became undeniable.

Demolition was the most cathartic. The fire I started all that time ago destroyed a lot of the Banks' mansion, but not all of it. After we retrieved the few items that survived the flames,

I was given the honor of setting it ablaze again. This time, nothing would be left.

As the soft flame rippled over the ground and grew, five years of emotion tumbled out of me—quietly at first. Then the fire engulfed the remainder of the debris, transforming William Banks' evil into nothing more than ash and memory. With the kindest permission, I let myself unleash my sadness and anger with such ferocity, with such totality and abandon, I collapsed to my knees before it was all out of me. Then I sat for hours—watching, feeling, and allowing myself to exist.

Many days and a heavy, cleansing rain later, the embers had burned out completely. The land was cleared, the pool filled, and construction began. As if none of it ever existed, everything was removed—except for the stables. Neptune and Goliath now share their updated home with two other horses previously kept by poor locals on the other side of the island. Now, they'll all live as they should—like royalty, pampered and adored and safe. A place where so much sadness and misery once existed was thoughtfully transformed, magically transcended, into a beautiful sanctuary—a sacred collection of memories and love, welcoming all who wish to sit and reflect in its peace.

My mother and I stare at a low tribute wall made of impenetrable black granite, etched with the names of *all* those who lost their lives over these last years, marking the entrance to the park. Next to that, a detailed map outlines every step along the way, comfortably shaded by an enormous, fruiting sapodilla tree.

We step under a fancifully decorated, arched moon gate covered in beach glass, driftwood, and shells, then round a soft corner. There she is ahead of us at the center of the park—the bronze statue that once stood in the Banks' garden room, the one that became Esmerelda's headstone. The life-sized, leaping dolphin with an enraptured, long-haired Dolhuphemale at its tail. I had mixed emotions about putting her here, but looking at it now, at the center of this park, standing at its heart as a reminder of how we came to be here, nothing could be more perfect. This is exactly where she belongs. To sweeten the deal, a small plaque was created to reassign what this beautiful statue should really represent. It reads:

Emancipation Ignites Power and Fuels Responsibility.
Brought to you in part by
Bio-Genesis Wave Technologies
in partnership with
the Allerton-Bigelow Marine Research and Conservation
Foundation.

The saying on the plaque always reminds me of the ring I was so fortunate to have returned to me. It will never leave my hand again—a reminder of our hard-won independence.

"There you are! We've been waiting so long." Devin appears from behind a soft, swaying stand of prairie grass at one side of the park, shouting and waving his arm above his head.

"Sorry," I say. "I had to look over the tour schedule. The first zeppelin arrives tomorrow, and we're expecting a lot of curious tourists."

"Well, I understand, but we've got dinner plans with Richard and Kendra."

"And Ruari," I add.

"And Ruari, too. But more importantly, I have a present for you, and I can't wait any longer for you to open it." He smiles, and my mother uses that as her cue to take the other little bundled package Devin's holding. "She's sleepy, Tatiana. The fresh air knocked her out."

"This is the only present I ever need, ever again," I say and kiss her cheek as Devin passes our baby to my mother. "I love you, Gabriella."

As luck or maybe fate would have it, the weapon William fired—I choose to assume accidentally, as he was shoved off the observation deck's wall to his death—did not prove fatal. It almost did. The white-hot beam sliced into my lower left abdomen and nicked my large intestine. Had I been any further along in my pregnancy, I would have lost the baby. Had William been even a foot closer, or at a slightly different angle, I would have been gone. And so would she.

Gabriella. My daughter. Our daughter. The most beautiful, unique love of our lives. Not only was I spared becoming a host to one of William's Harvesters, I was given the gift of absolute perfection. The big picture was always behind the scenes, but always at play.

When the time is right, Devin and I will try for a boy. And now we know, with a steady diet of Wreckleaf, that can happen just as naturally as it should. For all of us. The Dolhuphemale breed will not die out and will no longer continue to be strictly female, nor will our identities be secret any longer. We are truly free. As it should be.

"Here. Open it," Devin says and hands me a small, wrapped package.

My mother walks away, singing quietly to the baby, and leaves us alone beside a fragrant, flowering shrub.

I turn the gift over in my hands and pull at the teal satin

ribbon before gently tearing off the plain paper. My voice nearly sticks in my throat with a small gasp, but I find it, delightfully weak and full of emotion.

"*Loving Nerissa; A Journey to our Heart's Truth*. Oh, my god. Did you..." I hold the little book like it's a bird about to fly away, with guarded care, like it doesn't really belong to me, like it never really should.

"Yes, I finally did. I finally listened to you and published my writing."

"But... about me?" I'm humbled and a little embarrassed, feeling like it should only be about him. "I don't know what to say. This is so... I'm so proud of you."

Devin takes my face in his hands and pulls me into that now familiar space and looks at me like only he can. "It's always been about you. Always."

I could have never anticipated the outcome of that last night with William at the Grand Re-opening Gala. I don't think any of us could. Alexandria Allerton Bigelow was in control, and nobody knew to what level except her. From the very first moment her niece Moriyah informed her about the corruption right under her nose, she quietly devised a plan. The long con. And she played it out like a master, always staying true to her own mission, at *all* costs, patient and unyielding. William worked for her, blissfully unaware, building her dream, while she carefully crafted his demise. She got exactly what she wanted, exactly as she envisioned. And she had her coveted moment in the spotlight—one I imagine was incredibly satisfying—as she poured that bottle of Aqua Tonic over William Banks' head and informed him of how things really were.

Her empire continues to expand and thrive with the final

acquisition of the Bio-Gen Research Facility—with Devin, Colton, Specialist Richard Klein, and Doctors Bigelow and Picker at the helm. The labs and center will be used exclusively to protect and grow the well-being of Panacea and her sister islands, just as Alexandria had always intended.

Every last bottle of the old Aqua Tonic was destroyed, along with all of the formulations. Alexandria designed a new and improved version, devoid of the toxic, addictive concentrations of C. Periculosis Abscondita—one that could actually be deemed a health elixir. She renamed it *Pure Beauty*. And of course, the beauty-care products are being churned out in full force, barely able to stay on the shelves. Alexandria saw the wisdom in allowing the tourists to take a limited amount of products home with them at the end of the Season. "These products simply can't be duplicated elsewhere. It's a win-win for everyone," she loves to say.

Alexandria Allerton Bigelow is a force to be reckoned with —the dark horse nobody saw coming. She is spindrift—the spray blown off the crest of a wave during a storm or a gale. She is also the wave. She is the storm. And she is the gale. Perhaps she truly is *our champion, our angel, and fairest Beauty.*

My name is Nerissa John-Navarre. I'm the lone pebble thrown into glassy water... and I was always supposed to exist, after all.

Acknowledgments

Thank you to Matt, Quintin, and Sage—my reason for being and my greatest joys. You are my inspiration and my aspiration. You are all exceptional examples of how to take your own path and never compromise your truth. Thank you to the exceptional team at Bow's Bookshelf. Thank you to my readers. Your unending support and love are the fuel for my creativity.

ABOUT THE AUTHOR

JD Steiner credits her studies at the acclaimed Chicago Writer's Loft for her drive to create new worlds and relatable characters, while crafting her stories into rich, dramatic, and relevant fiction. JD draws her own inspiration from the entrepreneurial spirit and stories of real people. An advocate for artists of all kinds, JD lives and works north of Chicago, Illinois, nurturing and promoting the creative aspirations of all.

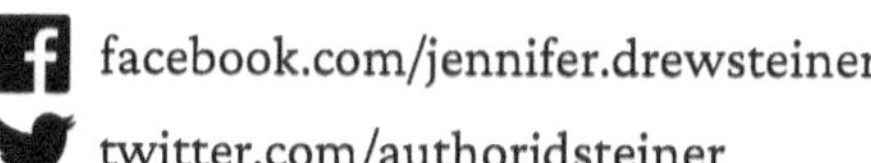
facebook.com/jennifer.drewsteiner

twitter.com/authorjdsteiner

instagram.com/authorartistjdsteiner